THIS LIFE

PART I

CARA DEE

Edited by Silently Correcting Your Grammar, LLC.
Formatted by Eliza Rae Services.
Proofread by M. Hughes.

playlist

"What are the Irish without music?"

The Lonesome Boatman, version by Dropkick Murphys
Crystallize, by Lindsey Stirling
Heart And Soul, by Twin Atlantic
The Opening Act of Spring, by Frank Turner
Drunken Lullabies, by Flogging Molly
Chip, by The Real McKenzies
Resolution, by Matt Corby
When It Comes To Us, by Frances and RITUAL
Feels Like Falling In Love, by The XCERTS
City, by Ciaran McMeeken
Philadelphia, by Parachute
Lions Roar, by Speak Brother
Rock The World, by The Script
An Irish Pub Song, by The Rumjacks
Cooley's Reel, version by Coming Up Threes
Drunken Sailor, version by Barleyjuice
Die A Happy Man, by Thomas Rhett
The Lonesome Boatman, version by The High Kings
Wonderful Tonight, by Eric Clapton
At Last, version by Etta James
You Are The Reason, by Calum Scott

An Angel, version by Declan
Hear You Me, by Jimmy Eat World
The Parting Glass, version by The High Kings

For the entire This Life I playlist, visit Cara's Spotify at:
open.spotify.com/user/caradeewrites. You can also find a direct link
on her website.
www.caradeewrites.com

thank you

To the amazing fandom where it all started for me. To the readers who told me to publish, and to the readers who asked me to listen to Whistler and his princess.

An extra thank you to Lisa, Eliza, Marty, and Katy.

prologue

Finnegan O'Shea

01.12.15
11:23 a.m.

I'd learned three things in prison. Patience, focus, and perseverance. That prison turned us into better criminals was no bullshit declaration, and after spending five years in the can, I was ready to walk out a changed man. I wasn't a kid anymore. The eighteen-year-old who'd been larger than life and conceited as fuck had mellowed out—okay, that was a lie. My thirst for life was still unquenchable, and my loud mouth was a default setting.

My trigger finger wasn't shaky anymore, though. My arrogance was better placed. When I fired, I knew what I was doing. Figuratively. It wasn't like they allowed target practice in prison.

"Finnegan!"

I spotted my aunt in the sea of visitors and made my way to her table. It was good to see her, and I gave her a tight hug.

"Are you ready to come home?" She smiled up at me.

"You have no idea." I sat down and cracked my knuckles, waiting for her to get settled. "You got something for me?"

She huffed. "I'm feeling more like a messenger and less like your family these days."

"I'm sorry." I side-eyed the CO standing a few paces away and risked the no-touching rule after the initial hug. "How's the baby?" I patted her baby bump. "You gotta be due any day now."

"It's cute that you try to care." She grinned wryly, looking a lot like my father in that moment. Other than...well, not like a man. My aunt was a stacked little thing, but the grin and the glint in her eye were Pop. He called her Ginger Snap, sometimes affectionately, sometimes to be a dick. "I do have some news for you."

"Yeah?" I stared expectantly.

"It seems the rumor's true," she replied with a nod. "She had a baby, but it's not a son."

I furrowed my brow, my knee bouncing with impatience. "Then why hide the kid here in the US? A daughter's no threat."

"Finn." She gave me a look.

I gave her one in return. She could tear me a new one when I got out and had time for her feminism. Priorities.

She sighed. "The girl is turning sixteen in a few months. She lives with her father in one of the old mining towns around Gettysburg."

I didn't know what to do with this info. "Biological father?" I cocked a brow.

"Your dad didn't tell me. I'll ask him to keep searching if you want."

I nodded slowly, thinking. "Yeah, thanks." Okay, so this changed shit. There was no hidden son to keep an eye on for the future. There was a teenage girl. No threat, but...maybe leverage if I needed new friends one day.

She would be legal in a couple years.

"How badly did you wanna get out of the city?" I asked my aunt.

She narrowed her eyes at me. "What're you up to, boy?"

I flashed her a grin.

02.02.15
11:02 p.m.

Lights went out shortly after the COs had completed the final head count for the day.

I kept staring at the ceiling, fingers clasped over my stomach.

The guy in the bunk under mine was new, and his nightmares would start soon.

Nightmares are unfinished business, my grandfather used to tell me.

He used to tell me a lot of things.

As my cellmate began stirring restlessly, I released a breath and shifted my hands to under my head. On a particularly bad night, he talked in his sleep. Drugs, wars, drug wars.

"Come here, lad. I'm going to tell you something."

I couldn't have been more than...five or six, maybe. My grandfather picked me up and sat me on his lap after I'd been hiding under his desk in his study. No matter how much I loved my parents, my grandfather had been my world. He spoke, I listened.

"Did you hear the tune I played at the memorial? I want you to learn it. One day, you might have to declare war against someone, and this is how we salute the men who are about to depart from us."

I whistled the familiar, haunting tune to myself, thinking back on how he and his crews had taken care of a problem oozing down from the Jersey gutters. In a few months, he'd shown everyone that Philly had and always would belong to us.

War declarations were on my mind a lot lately.

3

"Learn the song, Finn. The O'Sheas will hear it, and they will come."

02.10.15
4:57pm

"You might wanna cover that up before the folks get here."

I let go of the chin-up bar and hit the floor with a grunt, then looked over my shoulder to see my brother in the doorway.

"Ma's favorite son is out of prison. I don't think some ink is gonna bother her." Wiping my forehead, I reached for a bottle of water by the window.

"Favorite son," Patrick scoffed.

I smirked and chugged from the water.

The Celtic cross and our last name on my back were a statement. I'd had it made in three sessions in as many days as I'd been free.

Once upon a time, finding the next gig that earned me the most money within our syndicate came first, whether I worked in Philly or flew over to Chicago for a few weeks. I'd rediscovered my affiliation since then, and our organization was inevitably going to split into the two original clans that'd been in charge for generations. Our unity worked well at one point, but now the days of the Murrays were numbered. My uncle was a fucking traitor, and it was time the O'Sheas reclaimed the top rank.

"When will they be here?" I asked.

I'd missed our parents, having only seen them once or twice a year while I was away.

Patrick checked his watch. "They should be landing any minute."

I nodded once. The lucky bastards had spent the past five years back in Ireland in an attempt to let the rumors about us fade. I was thrilled they were returning to Philly now. We had a lot to talk about.

4

Three to four years—that was how long I believed it would take for me to execute my plan. My uncle had grown pompous and lazy, and he spent his days in his penthouse in Chicago most of the time. To become a part of his inner circle and eventually take everything from him, I'd have to think long term and be who he wanted me to be. More traditional than I already was, a top earner, someone he could trust...

I had to be a family man.

A man with a family was less likely to make rash decisions and betray his boss because it would put everyone he held dear in danger.

This Irish fuck was gonna find himself a wife.

Speaking of... As the doorbell rang, I knew I was about to find out my chances pertaining to a certain lost daughter. I signed off on the delivery and accepted the envelope, then retreated to my room and locked the door.

I had to find my own place soon.

"Let's see who you are, kid." I sat down in the chair by the window and flipped through the documents Aunt Viv had sent me.

Emilia Porter. Sixteen years old. A photograph fell out from between the pages, and I picked it up. Gangly little girl. Dark hair, hazel eyes. She couldn't be more than twelve or thirteen here. She *did* live with her biological father. And they were poor as shit.

I frowned and scanned the text, wondering why. The girl's mother was well-off.

Poor worked for me, though. It was enough to go on, and I wanted to call my aunt before I hit the shower. Aunt Viv and her husband had just had their fourth child and wanted to move out of the city. I knew exactly where to send them.

02.10.15
6:03pm

My brother's condo was on the fifteenth floor, and as I peered

5

down on the street below, my parents looked like ants getting out of a yellow toy car.

"You think Dad's even gonna wanna take the top rank?" Patrick wondered.

He had to. Patrick and I were too young; he was only a year older than me at twenty-four. Under normal circumstances, even if we turned into golden boys with pretty wives and kids on the way over the next couple of years, the older generation wasn't going to take us seriously until we were well over thirty.

I folded my arms and chewed on my thumbnail, one of the habits I was gonna have to kick in order to be more respectable. "We need him." Somehow, we had to convince Pop.

I'd originally believed Patrick was gonna be the toughest to win over because, unlike me, he didn't stick to our faith or our traditions. Maybe I wasn't excited to get hitched, although it paled in comparison to Patrick's anticipated blunt "Fuck no." Or so I'd thought. He'd shrugged at the marriage bit and only protested a little about us basically inventing personas that our uncle would approve of.

Luckily, Patrick's hatred toward the old shit-in-charge outweighed everything.

"We'll talk more about this after dinner." I turned away from the window and pushed up the sleeves of my button-down. "Ma's gonna be stoked."

He snorted. "No doubt. She's been asking for grandkids since our First Communion."

Almost, anyway.

"Perhaps she'll find our wives at some kid's ceremony," I joked. Hopefully, I'd already found mine.

"Finally," Patrick groaned. "Maybe your humor's making a comeback. You've been stiff as a goddamn stick since you got out. All closed off." He side-eyed me. "I won't be surprised if Mom and Dad don't recognize you."

That made me scowl. I was funny as fuck.

6

chapter

1

TWO YEARS LATER

Emilia Porter

"Y ou guys will never believe what I found out," Franny said in a hushed voice as she sat down at our picnic table.

Looked like our school's biggest gossip had arrived. When we graduated in a couple months, I had no doubt she was going to take things to the next level and out-gossip her mother, who took care of the rest of the rumors that flew around our little town.

"I'm sure you'll enlighten us." Sarah unwrapped her lunch and grimaced, picking out the pickle.

I leaned back against the table and closed my eyes, wanting to soak up as much of the sun as possible. Spring was almost here, and my skin needed a revival.

Franny, unaffected by our lack of interest, did enlighten us. "I was outside Nurse Walsh's when her office phone rang, and guess what? She referred to someone as *Shan*. It can only be one person!"

My forehead creased, and I cracked my eyes open to frown at her over my shoulder. "Even if it is?"

Ever since the school nurse moved here with her husband last year, there'd been a minor buzz about who she might or might not be related to. To be honest, I wasn't sure where the rumors had started. Knowing Franny and her mother, it wouldn't surprise me if they'd cooked them up.

Franny tossed me a look of impatience. "She specifically said 'you may be my big brother, Shan, but you don't boss me around.' Like, jokingly. She was laughing. And then she finished with, 'Okay, I'll see you soon. Don't be late.' Get it? They're probably coming *here*!"

Again, *so*? On the off chance that our school nurse was related to a man who was involved with the SoM, it didn't mean anything to us. Mobsters visited family too, I guessed.

That said, I wouldn't exactly say I *wanted* them here. The Sons of Munster dealt in heinous crimes and ruled the underworlds of both Philadelphia and Chicago.

"I wish you'd take this seriously," Franny said. "What if it's got to do with her list?"

"What list?" I asked as Sarah groaned. "What?" I must've missed something. I adored Franny; we'd grown up together, but she was a pain in the butt I tuned out more often than not.

Sarah shifted in my direction and put down her soggy sandwich. "Fran and I hung out when you worked last weekend, and she told me she's seen a list of names in Mrs. Walsh's office. You and I are on it. And four other girls."

All right, this required more of my attention. I swung my legs over the bench so I faced the table instead. "Just how often do you hang out in Nurse Walsh's office, Franny?" I quirked a brow and stifled my amusement.

Sarah snickered.

Franny did not. "*That's* what you focus on? I'm working on a paper—but that's beside the point!"

"No, that *is* the point," I laughed. "A lot of us are working on papers. I'm interviewing her tomorrow for my paper on women working in healthcare. Maybe that's why I'm on some list."

When my stomach tightened in hunger, I opened my Coke and took a sip. The sugar would have to do until my shift at the diner. I got a free meal there.

"I don't think so." Franny seemed worried. "I have a bad feeling about this."

Jeesh.

I could admit even I got a twinge of a bad feeling on my way home from work that evening. I passed an empty auto shop that didn't appear very empty anymore. The garage was closed, lights off everywhere, but there was a brand-new sign above the storefront that read O'Shea's Auto Repair.

My steps faltered.

This doesn't mean anything.

It was a large chain. They had shops all over Pennsylvania, Jersey, and Virginia.

Pretty much everyone had learned about the O'Shea family some years ago when a bunch of murders had taken place in Philadelphia. We were only a couple hours west of there, so it'd been on the news here for months after the national stations had moved on.

If I wasn't mistaken, it was the eldest son of Shannon O'Shea who ran the garages. Patrick. He was around twenty-six or something. He'd served a year in prison, while his younger brother, Finnegan, had done five years. I didn't remember the charges, only that they'd been acquitted of murder. The youngest son got out...a couple years ago? Something like that. I hadn't heard anything since then.

Shannon had walked. No charges. Maybe people couldn't believe he was involved. He was former military, went to Mass every Sunday, showed up at charity functions with his adoring wife on his arm, and worked as a psychologist specializing in children in foster care.

It'd been fairly quiet about the whole family for a long time, and I hoped it stayed that way. It didn't make sense for any of them to open up shop here. It was a dead town full of drunk working-class people surrounded by forest.

I couldn't fucking wait to get out of here.

"Dinner's ready, Dad!" I called.

I'd borrowed a handful of cookbooks from the library, and hopefully Dad would notice my improvement. God knew he was very aware of my approaching birthday, which meant he'd no longer be obligated to let me live under his roof. College was out of the question; my grades weren't good enough because I had to work most afternoons and weekends. So it would take me a while to save up before I could leave this place. In the meantime, I had to do everything in my power to prove myself useful to have around.

"Smells good." Dad entered the kitchen and immediately grabbed himself a beer.

We'd be better off if he didn't drink and gamble away half his goddamn paycheck every month...

It made me a bit bitter. We could've been doing better, sort of like Franny and her family. Our fathers worked for a company in Gettysburg that drove tourists to the same historical sites day in and day out. Dad didn't have a wife and two kids to look after. He only had me, yet our house was falling apart, food was sometimes scarce, and I bought approximately two items of clothing a year. Going to a salon to get my hair cut was unheard of. At this point, my hair reached my ass because I wasn't awesome with the kitchen shears. Instead, money went to bills and booze.

On that end, I was already useful to him. He needed me to take care of groceries and car insurance, but that didn't mean anything. He wasn't very fond of me.

It was okay, I supposed. I wasn't fond of his drunken ass, either.

"How was your day?" I filled his plate before I took a little for myself.

"Same old." He chewed on a piece of chicken slowly, testing the flavors. "Talked to Chief earlier..." No surprise. His best buddy was a fellow alcoholic, one whose job was to protect our town. Laughable. "You were a kid when this happened, but do you remember the problems they had with organized crime in Philly?"

My head snapped up.

Now what?

"Yes?" I replied cautiously.

He nodded and gathered more sauce on his fork. "I heard from Chief that one of the families involved in that mess is moving here."

Fuck me running, Franny was right. "Why would they?" It didn't make any sense. We lived in the shadow of Gettysburg, had a shit economy, shit school district, shit everything. Our town used to be booming—like, a decade ago. The mine had been open back then, sending many young families our way to start their lives.

Dad shrugged. "Who knows? But I want you to be careful walking home at night from the diner. We can't have you injuring yourself and miss out on work."

Thanks for your concern.

The next morning, I came to a stop as I left the house. Every piece of property on this street was run-down, and the cars were buckets of rust. A black sports car stuck out like a sore thumb.

Shouldering my backpack, I pulled up the hood of my sweater and picked up the pace. The nice weather from yesterday was gone and replaced by a dreary drizzle.

I was going to look like a drowned cat by the time I got to school.

I sidestepped a puddle, my old sneakers already taking in water.

The low purr of an engine caught my attention, and I frowned at the sports car rolling up next to me on the sidewalk, window down.

"Do you need a ride?"

What, without the offer of candy first? I snorted and walked a little faster. "No, thank you." Idiot. His car was one accident short of being a stamp, it was that flat. I couldn't see the owner of the rich, unquestionably masculine voice—couldn't see how big he was —and I had no desire to be ditched in a dumpster somewhere.

Whoever he was, he chuckled. "Can't blame you, Miss Porter. Have a good day at school."

"*Wait.*" I stopped instantly and bent over to see who this fucker was. Evidently, he knew my name. "Who are—um...you?" My words kind of dried up as I got a look at him. The man was lethally handsome. Dark copper-colored hair met fair skin and gunmetal eyes, his striking features complete with a trimmed beard, straight nose, and eyebrows that made him look severe in some way.

The corners of his mouth twisted up somewhat. "Your knight in shining armor?"

"Funny," I replied.

He was new in town. Older. Clearly rich...

Don't say this is Patrick O'Shea.

I couldn't remember the pictures of the sons that'd floated around.

He tapped his long fingers along the wheel absently, thinking. "My name is Finnegan."

Nope, no better. I straightened, shock sending me back a step, and decided it was *really* time for me to haul ass.

I heard his laughter, ignored it, and kept walking. Oh God, oh God, oh God.

The O'Sheas were actually here.

Sarah wasn't in school, which bugged me. Since she wasn't a gossip, she was the one I could tell everything to. That would have to wait now, and the morning classes dragged on for what felt like an eternity while I grew increasingly antsy.

I'd officially been face-to-face with a criminal.

Why the hell did said criminal know my name?

Had my dad done something? Oh God, I hoped he didn't owe the wrong people money.

Nothing ever happened in this town, so this was gonna be big. Rumors were going to fly. People would make assumptions and warn others to stay away, while simultaneously being too curious to practice what they preached.

I tapped my pen against my knee, constantly looking at the clock. Lunch was next, and then I had that interview with Nurse Walsh. Who was related to the crime family hailing from Ireland. Who had a strange list with my name on it.

Maybe I would end up in a dumpster, after all.

I shuddered at the news I remembered from years ago. A trafficking ring had been infiltrated and blown up, a storage facility with cars, diamonds, and money had been seized, and the authorities had made more arrests than I could recall.

The man I met mere hours ago...had he sold human beings? Had he dealt in drugs and blood diamonds? Was he a killer?

It sickened me to consider, and I decided to skip going to the nurse's office after lunch. I didn't wanna be even slightly associated with those people.

Once the bell rang, I gathered my books and headed straight for my locker. I had a Coke and a peanut butter and jelly sandwich waiting for me in there, and I brought them outside where the rain had thankfully stopped.

I grimaced at the wet picnic table and spread out a plastic bag to sit on.

"Emilia!" Franny jogged over. For once, I was happy to see her. While I wasn't comfortable sharing much, I had questions. "Where's Sarah?"

"I don't know. I'm guessing she's sick," I said.

Something dimmed in Franny's eyes, and she sat down across from me. "I wouldn't be too sure. My mom saw Patrick O'Shea outside her house last night."

I froze. Okay, *what* was going *on*?

This couldn't be about Dad borrowing money, at least.

I hesitated to speak, having a feeling I'd regret it, but in the end, I needed to get it off my chest. "The other one—Finnegan O'Shea? He offered me a ride to school this morning. He was parked outside my house."

Franny's eyes widened. "Oh my God, why didn't you tell me? You have to go to the police!"

I made a noise. "And say what? That a guy was parked on public land and offered me a ride?"

"But—" Worry was written all over her, enough so that it gave me a reality check. Christ, I was overreacting to the whole thing. "Oh, I don't know what to say, Emilia. This could be serious. They're murderers."

"Or it could be nothing at all," I responded coolly. Honestly, I needed to take a chill pill. Besides, relying on Franny and her mother did no one any good. So what if they were right on occasion? Ninety percent of the time, they were dead wrong.

The next couple of days were relatively normal, except that Sarah was still not coming to school. When I called her house yesterday, her dad said she was sleeping.

I stopped by after school to drop off some homework, and her mother smiled politely and told me Sarah would be home soon.

"Is she at the doctor's?" I wondered. There was a free clinic in the next town over we went to when we felt really awful. They'd helped me with antibiotics when I had an ear infection.

"No..." Sarah's mother tilted her head, curious. "She's away with that new boyfriend of hers."

Come again?

I would freaking know if Sarah had a boyfriend. We told each other everything—or so I thought. She also wouldn't skip school to be with some guy. She valued school and had better grades than I did. If there was anyone she tried to get away from, it was her father. Definitely not school.

I trailed home confused, for once really bothered I couldn't afford a cell phone. Neither could Sarah. Otherwise, this would've been the perfect time to text her and ask what the hell was going on.

On my way home, I stopped by the grocery store to pick up a couple cans of tomato soup. I had a coupon that was about to expire, and I'd timed it with another coupon I had for bread. Buy one, get one free. I loved seeing that sign. We had scallions, cheese, and a little bit of leftover chicken at home, so we were having soup and grilled cheese for dinner.

There would be enough for Dad to bring for lunch at work tomorrow, too.

That fucking car! Reaching my street, I stopped short at the sight of Finnegan's sports car. Did I worry, or could I get pissed? I didn't want him around. Jaw set and shoulders tense, I steeled myself and aimed for my house. The car seemed empty, which was troubling—

My head whipped to the side as my front door opened. None other than Finnegan O'Shea walked out of the house I'd grown up in, and okay, the anger took a hike. I didn't have the balls to be infuriated with a mobster. Fear trickled in instead, though I tried to hide it.

He spotted me as I reached our mailbox.

"Afternoon, Emilia." He smirked slightly and shrugged into his suit jacket. He wore all black. Black suit that fit him like a glove, black shirt, black shoes. Who'd died?

"It's disturbing that you know my name," I blurted out.

He found that amusing, and he flicked a glance at my house behind him. "It's disturbing that you live in this shithole." He muttered something else under his breath. All I caught was "also disturbing" and "nothing like the picture."

I frowned, not coming any closer. Excuse me, but we couldn't all rape and murder and live in mansions, and what picture? A shudder traveled down my spine.

"Talked to your pop. He's...charming." Finnegan's gunmetal eyes flashed with mirth.

"What do you *want*?" I grated. "Have we done something wrong? We don't have any money."

That caused his eyebrows to lift. "Why the fuck would—" He decided against whatever he was planning on saying. "Never mind. I have a business deal I wanna discuss with you. Are you available for dinner?"

The words coming out of his mouth were so foreign that I just blinked and stared. Business deal with me? Ridiculous. Available for dinner? Also ridiculous!

After having stood still for a moment, Finnegan started walking slowly, casually, toward his car. I wanted there to be a safe distance between us, meaning I mirrored his steps to get closer to the house.

"Not interested," I muttered.

"You don't know what I'm offering."

I couldn't *not* be honest. "I don't associate with criminals, and I don't think you have anything I want."

The bastard laughed and rounded his car, opening the door. At that point, I reached the stoop and was within arm's length of my door.

"I think there's one thing," he told me. Curious how he ignored the remark about his being a criminal. He jerked his chin at the house. "I can get you out of this place." Next, his gaze met mine, and he grew serious. "You'd be set for life and independent."

I rolled my eyes and grabbed the doorknob. "That doesn't sound like a trap at all. Let me guess, you're offering me money to be a drug mule or something equally criminal and dangerous."

He smiled. He actually smiled. "Have dinner with me, Emilia. Just one dinner. What's the worst that could happen?"

"People could see me out with a—"

"Oh, for fuck's sake." His accent changed right then. He sounded Irish almost. The humor was still very much present, and so was a hint of frustration. "Say criminal one more time..." He snorted and shook his head. "This is nothing illegal. But you've made your decision, eh?"

Hell. Fucking. Yes.

I merely glared at him as he grinned and got in his car.

There was something about him that royally pissed me off, and I wasn't sure it was the mobster stuff. I looked at him, and I just wanted to slap him. Was that normal?

I entered the house with a huff, idly curious as to where my fear went, and walked straight to the kitchen to start dinner. "Dad, I'm home."

His gruff reply came from the living room. "No work today?"

Staring at the messy kitchen, wondering how the hell he could destroy a surface so quickly, I felt like I was being sucked deeper inside a black hole. I hated this place, and Finnegan's "offer" buzzed in my skull. Not that I'd ever agree to dinner with a murderer, but it didn't mean he hadn't dangled my ticket out of here right in front of my face. Prick.

"I don't work on Thursdays," I repeated for the millionth time. "What about you? Didn't you work today?" Because as much of a drunk as he was, I couldn't imagine he was able to drink five...six, seven, eight...nine—impressive—nine beers between getting off work and my coming home from school.

"Don't get on me about working, kid," he grumbled. "I slave away every fucking day to provide for you. How about you show some gratitude?"

There was no reasoning with him. After setting the groceries on the table, I pulled my hair up into a messy bun and began picking up after him. There were two takeout containers, making me believe Chief had been here too. Someone had spilled coffee on the floor, and there was a broken glass on the counter. Christ.

Speaking of guests, though... "What did that guy who was here want?" I asked.

"Oh, you saw him. That was Finnegan O'Shea—can you believe that?"

Yeah, I could.

"What did he want?" I asked again.

"That's none of your concern," he replied curtly.

Finnegan O'Shea

"You wanna rob our own warehouse?" Patrick stared at me like I'd grown a second head.

"No, dumbass. I wanna fix the hole in our sinking motherfucking ship. Someone's interfering with my operations, and I think I know who it is." I never should've given the fucker a job. He belonged in Pat's crew, not mine.

Pat got up from the table and grabbed us a couple beers from the fridge. "So a mock-heist?"

I nodded and explained my plan, how we'd move a car to a new garage and from there make it seem like we'd stolen it. If we deliberately made room for error, it was likely they'd swallow the bait and fuck us over somehow. But instead of us risking a police chase, we'd be on rented land handling our own property.

"Third time this week, Finnegan."

I looked up from my pew and nodded with a dip of my chin at Father O'Malley. "Evening, Father."

He smiled and paused at the end of the pew. "May I?"

"Of course." I kept my hands clasped casually in my lap and

glanced around us. Other than an elderly lady kneeling by the altar, we were alone in the church. I couldn't say I expected anything else.

The priest sat down next to me and sighed contentedly. "It's not often a young man like you comes to church on a Friday night. What's your brother up to tonight?"

I smiled faintly and scratched my nose. "Nothing good, I bet."

Father O'Malley tilted his head. "You seem troubled."

I nodded. Truth was, I was rattled and fucking offended. "I've made my mother worry, apparently. And Patrick says there's something wrong with me."

He offered a beat of silence and then suggested a confession might be in order. I wasn't sure it'd do anything good, but I agreed.

With a crew of six, we were well under way to steal a concept car from ourselves. As if stealing it the first time hadn't been enough. Kellan and I got into the alarm system and turned it off, and Patrick shone a flashlight into the garage bay where the beauty waited.

Over the line of communication, I said we had about two minutes to get the car out of here. Eric's voice filtered through, and he let us know the alarm hadn't reached the authorities or the private security company. In reality, I owned the security firm, but Gary didn't know that.

"Let's get this done." I walked over to the old Firebird and touched the hood reverently. This was the shit that got me hard. "She has a buyer, doesn't she?"

Patrick nodded. "Dubai."

Collector, no doubt. Most of the concept cars we were contracted to get our hands on didn't run, either by design or age, and they were sought out due to the limited number of them. There were only three of this particular edition made, so the price tag was impressive.

I slumped down in the confession booth and let out a heavy sigh. When I was a kid, I hated the cramped spaces of these and could never sit still. I'd changed a lot since then.

"Forgive me, Father. It's been..." I squinted in thought. "Two months since my last confession." I made the sign of the cross.

"How have you been doing since then?" he asked. "How's work?"

"Busy," I replied bluntly. "Busy but good." Starting the security firm had been a stroke of genius on my part. I'd gained legal access to technology and knowledge that were invaluable to my, uh, actual work. It helped that I had Eric on board, one of the few men I trusted with my life. Because he'd been screwed over royally too. Whereas I'd only gotten thrown in prison after a year of a bitch trial, Eric had lost his brother and sister-in-law.

He was as motivated as I was.

"And your social life?" Father O'Malley hedged carefully.

My mother made her confession to him every week, so I had no fucking doubt he already knew about my social life. Or lack thereof. It was one of the reasons she worried. And one of the reasons I was offended.

"People say I'm not funny anymore," I said irritably. This was weighing on me a lot lately. "I don't blame them for saying I was... off or whatever before—I mean, when I got out of lockup. It's an adjustment. But to say I'm not funny...?"

"Prison's no dance."

Exactly. I'd been tenser. It'd taken me a while to reset my internal alarm and get used to freedom. Sometimes, I could still wake up and expect a guard to make the morning head count.

I'd missed five years, and they were five important ones. The last of my teenage years and the few first of my twenties—that was when other guys were out late at night and raised all kinds of hell.

Missing out on that wasn't what made me angry, though, and I *was* angry. I was fucking livid. It pissed me off that others around me weren't as focused and determined as I was. A lot of O'Sheas had been taken to the cleaners when everything went down. Lives had been lost, families ruined, and years got wasted in prison.

A handful of guys were in the can to this day, and a couple would never get out.

"Patrick wants me to go out partying with him," I said. "I can't do that. I'll lose my focus."

I'd turned to my faith instead. It kept me on a rigid schedule. I was healthy, I had my goals in sight, and I didn't make mistakes. Sure, I went out for a few beers here and there, but I didn't stumble home at dawn or wake up in the wrong bed.

Unlike my brother and many of our friends, I didn't believe in premarital sex for myself, and an overactive of social life was nothing but a string of distractions. Just look at them. In the two years I'd been out, I was a hell of a lot more successful than most men who hadn't served a fucking day.

"A night off doesn't have to steer you away from your dreams, son," Father O'Malley pointed out patiently. "It's important you give yourself some rest."

I'd rest when Uncle John was six feet under.

"Guys, we have a problem."

At the sound of Gary's voice in my earpiece, I lifted a brow at my brother. Everyone I was with right now could be trusted. I held up a hand, stopping Patrick from speaking. It was my job. If Gary was the one who'd worked against us, someone have mercy on his dead ass.

"That's not what I wanna hear," I replied and adjusted the gadget. "We need you here in—" I checked my watch "—thirty seconds. The vehicle is ready to be transported."

Kellan and Colm were loading the Firebird onto the platform as we spoke.

The connection crackled, and then Gary answered. "I can't get there! I'm being pulled over, man."

Bullshit.

"Traffic cameras say otherwise," Eric informed me in my ear. He'd switched to a private line so Gary couldn't hear him. "He's stopped at the side of the road. There's no one around."

"What do I do, boss?" Gary put up a good front, pretending to be halfway to panic.

"We abort," I snapped and signaled to my brother.

"Cops're here!" Pat shouted, his voice echoing in the garage bay. "Clear a path out back—stat!"

I disconnected the call and lit up a smoke, irritated as fuck. Now I had to deal with Gary too.

"I've found a wife," I mentioned to Father O'Malley. That should earn me some points. The way I saw it, it counted as having a bit of a social life.

"Oh, really." His wry amusement left a lot to be desired in the way priests shouldn't fucking judge. "You've met a nice girl and fallen in love, or...you've found a future bride the way your brother has?"

"Love," I scoffed under my breath. Let's not get crazy. Emilia Porter was...hmm, the jury was still out. Bloody gorgeous, for sure. Almost breathtakingly so. First time I saw her was like a kick in the chest. It'd taken a minute for my heart rate to go back to normal. Hell, I hadn't even known it was her. I'd stopped outside of a random diner and seen her.

Then I'd compared her to the picture and realized it must've been the same girl.

I'd expected to see the same gangly kid in the photo, and that couldn't have been further from reality. She'd matured and filled out, and it was fucking with my head.

But she fit the bill as a future wife.

According to my research, she should be timid and compliant, and that suited me perfectly. She wouldn't get in my face. I'd find a way to get her to agree to a marriage of convenience. In turn, she'd get away from her father, who seemed like a right tool, and I'd look more trustworthy to my uncle. When I worked, she'd stay at home or do whatever the fuck she wanted.

Her lineage might also give me leverage if I had to resort to Plan B.

"I think starting a family will make me happy," I lied. "You know, have someone to come home to."

"Every man needs that," he agreed. "As long as it's for the right reasons." He paused, and I waited for the spiel. "Son, nothing makes me happier than seeing you at Mass every Sunday. You're a strong voice in our community, and even at your age, people look up to you. But it's my duty to guide you and make sure your faith isn't misplaced."

Here we go. "My faith is my strength." It wasn't a lie, technically. "It helps me stay on track."

"Are you describing your love for our Lord or a day planner?"

Cheeky bastard. Shouldn't he be happy? With a few exceptions, I was a good churchgoer, and I respected our traditions.

"Let's just move on to my sins," I said tiredly.

"Bless our family and friends, and these gifts which we're about to receive from your bounty, through Christ our Lord," Pop recited.

"Amen." I tucked into dinner like I hadn't eaten in two weeks, and while Ma and Patrick started talking about his new "girlfriend," I had more important things to discuss. Besides, no one with a brain volunteered to be around when our mother was in quiz-mode.

"Did you talk to John?" I asked quietly.

Pop nodded once. "He knows something. He asked if you were having issues with your orders."

I clenched my hand around a fresh roll and gritted my teeth. "I knew it." The fake heist Patrick and I had set up had been kept secret even within our organization for a reason. Easier to hear canaries that way, and boy, was someone singing.

"The food is already dead, dearie," Ma pointed out to me. *"No*

*need to choke it. Finnegan, you do make me worry. You're always
so angry."*

*I blew out a breath and let go of the roll. The last thing I
needed was an extra dose of her concern, so I placated her with a
smile and assured her I was fine.*

*I avoided my brother's intrusive gaze. It was another thing I
didn't need, his reminders that I'd changed and lost sight of the
happy-go-lucky son of a bitch I used to be. I was still that guy, for
the record. I was just...focused.*

*Everything came down to that. I'd relax once I had
accomplished my goals.*

I listed my sins dutifully. Going against my personal feelings, I
apologized for judging my mother and brother harshly for being
worried about me. They did it out of love, and as reluctant as I was
to admit it, I *wasn't* the man I'd been. I'd grown colder, and I didn't
know how to stop. Not before...well, my uncle was gone.

I didn't mention that last part to the priest.

Then I took a breath, and he allowed me a moment of silence to
gather my thoughts.

For the past two years, coming to church had offered relief,
temporary as it was. It was a Band-Aid atop a wound that probably
needed invasive surgery, but I didn't have time to dig deeper
right now.

I wanted more. I missed the old days when everything was
easier, and I hoped to come back to that. Or find a new way to
better days ahead. Until then, I'd keep coming here instead of going
to clubs and indulging in other vices.

Relaxing further, I reminded myself that everything was going
according to plan. Patrick and I were moving in to our new houses
next week, and our parents would follow shortly after. Perhaps
living the small-town life for a few months would do us good. It was
calmer—or dead—out there where Emilia and Sarah lived, and we
wouldn't be working much.

Additionally, the girls were a challenge, and I enjoyed those a shitload. It would be a welcome distraction to get Emilia to agree to marry me. As meek as she undoubtedly was, no one said yes to an alleged mobster right off the bat.

I'd seen an ounce of spark in her too. I'd have some fun exploring that. A wife with a temper wasn't part of the goal, but it couldn't hurt if the end result was the same. Uncle John would quit doubting me and let me in.

A submissive wife with a streak of defiance. Was that even real? No, I couldn't imagine her tough-girl front was very thick. Sarah sure as hell hadn't put up much of a fight. Money had been enough, and Patrick had already, unbeknownst to Sarah, set a date for their wedding.

Ma didn't know that tidbit yet either.

"Where ya been?"

"I bought a CD and a couple books." I closed the door to my car and buttoned my suit.

Patrick shook his head as I joined him, and we crossed the old shipyard together. "You have Spotify on your phone. No one listens to CDs anymore."

"I do, fuckface." In fact, my little shopping trip had brightened my mood. Father O'Malley had told me about an old man who imported demos by Irish bands, and those were hard to come by in the US. Most of those musicians never went into large-scale distribution.

"I remember when you threw yourself into mosh pits and cranked up Dropkick," Patrick said. "Now it's traditional music or Irish spiritual shit."

I ignored the sarcasm and bitterness in his tone and pulled the CD from my pocket, still in the little plastic bag. "This ticks off three boxes, actually. Irish, classic, and electronica."

He snorted and rolled his eyes.

Fine. He didn't have to be excited. I was looking forward to listening to it.

"How are things going with Sarah?" I asked.

He made a face. "I mean, she's agreed, but she ain't exactly fond of me."

That made sense. I was sending an incentive to Emilia on Monday. I had a feeling it would get her to agree to dinner.

Reaching the warehouse, I followed my brother toward a smaller, closed-off area. His mouth kept running, always about the same thing. I was no fun anymore, et cetera. I was having too good of a day to listen to this again, and why should I take advice from someone who spent his money on booze, gadgets he barely knew how to work, and vacations?

At least there was a method to my madness. More than that, there were good results.

I clapped him on the shoulder and handed him the CD for safekeeping while I worked. "How about we have this conversation when you don't come to me to borrow money?" *That shut him up—and pissed him off—and I left him behind.*

Gary was duct-taped to a chair in the middle of an office nobody had used for years. The vinyl flooring had been torn up in places, revealing concrete underneath. Around Gary's chair, splatters of blood told of Kellan's fun. He stood in the corner, smirking, and I chuckled. He had promised to break Gary's nose.

It did look broken.

I retrieved a tissue from my pocket and extended it to Gary. "You got blood everywhere, mate."

He glared at me and growled something behind the strip of tape that covered his mouth.

"Right. I guess your predicament doesn't make it easy to clean up." *I pocketed the tissue again and rounded the chair.* "Why're we here today, kids?"

Patrick leaned against the wall and folded his arms.

Kellan joined him. "Maybe Gary knows the answer. After all, we're just gullible O'Sheas."

"That's true. What the fuck do we know?" I gripped Gary's hair and yanked his head back, then tore off the tape. Christ— immediately, he started yelling. "Use your indoor voice!" I scolded. "Do you know why you're here, Gary?"

"You got the wrong goddamn guy!" he spat out. "Whatever you think I've done—someone must've framed me."

I frowned and studied his face. "You are Gary Lindsey, aren't you? Low-man for the O'Sheas but secretly sucking Murray dick?" He was getting ready to shout again, so I pushed his jaw closed and slapped the tape across his mouth. Then I heard Kellan's and Patrick's low voices, so I looked over at them. "What're you two doing?"

Kellan was inspecting my new CD. "I'm telling your brother your new taste in music is actually stellar. I've seen some of this shit on YouTube. It's good."

"Thank you," I exclaimed. "That's what I've been trying to tell this fuckwit."

Patrick wouldn't hear a word of what we said, so Kellan decided to prove it. He pulled up one of the songs on his phone, and I instantly relaxed as the room flooded with the sounds of two violins.

How could my brother not appreciate the beauty in this? One violin chased the other until the tables turned. It was the foreplay of music. In the background, an electronic loop of waves increased the tempo, and I closed my eyes to give it all my attention. The notes filled my head.

I was decent at best with a violin, but I could fake it well enough when the violin and bow were made of air. Mimicking the violin that was a bit more aggressive than the other, I kept my eyes closed and let the buildup take me. Through teasing loops and heavy bass drops toward Gary's sentencing.

Brilliant fucking song.

"I'm not gonna admit shit," Patrick said as I played the last notes. "If they play this at a club, I'm outta there."

I took a deep breath and reluctantly returned to the present. Then I saw my furious prize sitting so close, which lifted my spirits again.

Gary. Was. Seething. It made me smile.

"Don't worry, I haven't forgotten you." I patted my pockets, wondering where I'd left my—there. Inner chest pocket. "The question now is how you earn back our trust." His eyes widened at the sight of the knife, but there was hope too. He wanted to redeem himself. "I'm just fucking with you," I laughed. "There are no second chances when you screw me over."

I yanked back his head again and slit his throat.

"Anything else you want to confess, son?" Father O'Malley asked.

Not that I could think of. I pinched my lips together and racked my brain—and my conscience. It was the anger I'd aimed toward my mother and brother that bothered me the most, really. It wasn't healthy. They were my family, and I was beginning to feel guilty.

"I don't think so," I replied slowly. "It's... I don't know. It's more than anger. It's resentment. I'm lying to them when I say everything is fine, but what if I'll never be the bloke they remember? I don't have time to fix anything right now, and I guess arguing with them is easier than admitting that who I used to be might be lost."

Father O'Malley was a patient man. He was also practical, and he suggested baby steps. If I missed who I once was, I could start by admitting it to myself. Then I should set goals to achieve my "personal happiness." Once again, he advised me to rest more and stress less. Lastly, he strongly suggested I stop lying to my family. I could reword myself, he said. I could say I was working on it.

It was good advice, though I had no clue how to follow it. My personal happiness, as he put it, was directly tied to my long-term goal for the syndicate. On the other hand, that did mean I was working on it.

I exhaled, glad I'd come here tonight, and I recited the Act of Contrition, feeling a bit better.

"Keep coming to confession, son," Father O'Malley said. "It's good for you."

I nodded and shifted in my seat. "I will, Father."

"Very well. Go in peace and serve our Lord with love in your heart."

chapter

3

Emilia Porter

"Sarah!" After a weekend of going insane, the sheer relief of seeing her outside the school during lunch was overwhelming, and I jogged over to the picnic tables. She wasn't in class earlier, so I'd resigned myself to another day of not talking to her.

She looked tired and mustered a weak smile when she spotted me, but that wasn't what set off warning bells. Her clothes were brand-new and looked expensive.

In sixth grade, her dad gave her a black eye for forgetting her jacket on the school bus. Money just wasn't something many had in this town. Drunks and abusive losers, sure. Loving parents who weren't depressed and impacted by the economy, no.

"Where have you been?" I asked her, dropping my textbooks on the table. "Do you know how worried I was? And what the hell is this?" I gestured at her new coat. "Did you win the lottery?"

"Okay, slow down, hon." She patted the spot next to her on the bench, and I sat down with a huff.

"I went to your house. Your mom told me you were out with your *boyfriend*."

Sarah winced and looked down. "I wouldn't call him that."

"So, there is someone." I stared at her, noticing more differences. Her blond hair was straighter than usual. Shinier too. What the fuck, were those highlights?

"There is," she admitted, "and I don't want you to judge me before I've told you everything."

That would've been insulting had she not looked genuinely upset. Being upset made people forget things, such as my *not* being Franny. I had no room or reason to judge.

"That's not how you and I roll." I covered her hand with mine. "Tell me."

Releasing a breath, she appeared to gather her thoughts, and she glanced around us to make sure we were alone.

"You've met Finnegan O'Shea, haven't you?"

Not what I expected to come out of her mouth. I stiffened, and my stomach flipped.

"Patrick—his brother—told me," she went on. "That's who I'm seeing. Patrick, I mean."

My forehead creased—wait. Oh, she was kidding. I chuckled and withdrew my hand. "That's funny."

Except, she wasn't laughing. Then suddenly, her words tumbled out in an anxious rush. "There's a lot going on, Em. I want to tell you everything—every little detail—but I can't. What I can say is that the list Franny was talking about—in Nurse Walsh's office? It's real. The bitch has literally scouted the school for girls who might be suitable for her brother's sons." This was going too fast. Nurse Walsh—right. *Hold up.* Suitable for Shannon's sons? "Patrick got my name from that fucking list." She said that with no small amount of bitterness. "He came to my house—"

"*Wait.*" I put my hand on hers again. I didn't want to freak out over nothing. Franny had already made me overreact once. Possibly. Hopefully. Jesus Christ, I really hoped so. I *needed* Sarah to tell me the reason Finnegan had come to my house was...I don't know, a fluke or something. "When you say suitable, you mean...? Because this isn't the fifties, and you make it sound like—"

"They're looking for wives," she answered flatly. "Trust me, there's nothing cute about it. It's all status."

I swallowed the lump of panic, and it went down like a rock. "This isn't the fifties," I repeated. "People don't just go looking for wives."

She averted her gaze briefly. "Money still talks, Emilia." *Shame.* That's what I saw in her eyes, and it filled me with dread. Had she...? No. No way. She wouldn't. "Patrick said he had an offer for me and asked me to dinner."

I closed my eyes as Finnegan's identical proposal flew through my mind.

Proposal—bad choice of word.

"I can finally get away from here," she whispered.

"Oh God, you—" I looked away and hugged myself. Fellow students stood in little groups all over. I hadn't transported to another time or place. This was beginning to feel way too real, yet I refused to consider what this meant for me. "If he forced you, you can go to the police." Even as I said the words, I knew they were bullshit. She'd chosen this. She wore the clothes to prove it.

"I'm thinking about my future," she said. "Please see this from my perspective."

I faced her once more, and I wanted verbal confirmation. "This is actually happening? Some mobster from the newspapers offers you money, and you ride off with him?"

Her silence spoke volumes.

I shook my head and looked up at the gray sky.

Finnegan had told me he could get me away from here too.

"I decided it was the best option for me, yes," she answered.

Great. I didn't know what to say. I wasn't mentally equipped to deal with a scenario like this.

"You're judging me," she said quietly.

"No..." I wasn't. Running a hand through my hair, I tried to make sense of this, but I knew too little. There was no rhyme or reason. "I'm confused and terrified. Finnegan asked me to dinner too, and I turned him down. Does that mean I'm safe?"

"I don't know. Maybe?" She tilted her head. "Is that what you want? Freedom to stay with your dad until you graduate and start working full-time at the diner? Freedom to get kicked out on your ass?"

Too fucking far. I glared at her.

She looked at me even more imploringly and grabbed my hands. "Listen. I can barely stand the guy. Patrick O'Shea is an arrogant prick, but it's not permanent. He gets to look better in front of his boss and climb in the ranks, and—"

"Mafia boss," I stated. "Let's not forget that these people are the scum of the earth. When we were kids, there were documentaries about their family and all the trials. We're not talking about alleged shoplifters. They've done time for murder, grand theft auto, and armed robbery." I paused and gave her hands a squeeze. "I'm not judging you, Sarah. I know the hell you live with. I understand— and relate—every time you say you wanna get the hell out of here. I do too, with every fiber of my being. But if you go along with this, I need you to do it with your eyes open. This isn't a TV show. You'll be smack dab in the middle of a mafia family."

She smiled softly, a little sadly. "My eyes are wide open, Em. I promise. And I still wanna do this. That's how badly I wanna get away."

I couldn't fathom much of anything here. And as shitty as my own dad was, Sarah's hints were enough to know her father was ten times worse. She never wanted to talk about it.

I'd seen bruises on her more times than I could count, though. I wasn't blind.

"It's not a coincidence we're on that list, is it?" I asked.

"No. Nothing is a coincidence—not even that they picked this town." She blew out a breath and brought out a pack of smokes, handing me one. "Money only talks if there's a demand for it."

I understood that. I borrowed her lighter and sparked the cigarette.

"You said it's not permanent," I mentioned.

She nodded and lit up her own smoke. "I have to agree to be married to him for three years."

"What makes you think—"

"Before you go there, he's told me I can pick whatever law firm I want when we sign the papers. Or contract, I guess." *There goes that argument.* But even so, how could she trust Patrick? Mobsters weren't known for being honorable. "It's three years of my life, and then I'm free. Set for life. I can get whatever education I want. I can become a doctor, Emilia."

Three years. My stomach churned with how much I wanted the same possibilities, but at what cost? I could probably give away three years of my life too, though not without knowing the consequences. A lot could happen in that time. She could be framed for a crime she hadn't committed. She could get pregnant. She could end up *dead.*

This fucking hurt. Sarah was already eighteen, so she didn't have any illusions of being protected for another couple weeks. Every day when we walked home from school, we did so knowing there could be purgatory waiting for us. Her father was never gonna stop taking out his anger on her, and my dad was never gonna stop blaming me for my mother's death. We weren't even special. We lived in a town full of cautionary tales and white-trash clichés.

Sarah had found her escape, and she clung to the possibility and promise of it being true.

"When are you gonna sign this contract or whatever?" I muttered.

"After graduation."

I took a puff from the cigarette, hungry, nauseated, scared, and uncertain.

"I take it he's already giving you stuff?" I gestured at her clothes.

She looked down at herself, then nodded. "Jewelry and money too. I'm saving all of it, and he knows why I accept it."

For insurance. Everything worth something could be sold.

"What did your parents say?" I wondered.

She let out a humorless laugh. "Like they give a shit. Mom doesn't approve of him, but then, neither do I. And I think Patrick's given my dad money too. He's on board. He just wants me out as soon as I graduate."

I swallowed hard at that. There was no way I could count on Dad if he was offered money to kick me out. Would Finnegan be so cruel? What was I saying—of course he would. He was a goddamn criminal.

I'd turned Finnegan down, though. Hopefully, he wouldn't bother me anymore.

After school, I went to the library. My shift at the diner didn't start for another hour, and I wanted to dig up as much as I could about the O'Shea family, starting with Finnegan.

He had his own Wikipedia page.

The word "alleged" popped up everywhere, as it tended to do around mobsters. He'd recently turned twenty-five. Born in Philadelphia. Grew up there, as well as in England and Ireland. He had dual citizenship, both as an American and Irishman. His family was from the southwest of Ireland, specifically the province of Munster. While the O'Sheas belonged to a county called Kerry, the Murray family, with which they'd created their crime organization, was from Cork.

Finnegan and Patrick had gone to an all-boys boarding school in the UK before returning to Philly for high school.

Finnegan had graduated from high school early—at sixteen—

then studied one year at some prestigious college in Dublin. Quickly afterward, he'd come home and gotten sucked into everything that happened in Philly at that time.

I read up on the charges and accusations, coming across a link for a man named Ronan O'Shea. He was Finnegan's paternal grandfather, who'd been the head of the Sons of Munster up until some eight to ten years ago. They were iffy on exact dates. He had been assassinated with his closest adviser, Ennis Murray. Then Ennis's son, John Murray, had become the boss, and things had escalated into a full-blown war.

I sat back and took a swig of my water. Talk about trouble in paradise. It appeared the two families who'd created this behemoth of a crime organization didn't get along very well. I'd assumed all the murders taking place were because of a turf war between different organizations. I mean, wasn't that what it usually was? Turf? But no, everyone involved back then had ties to the SoM.

Today, it seemed like the two families were kept separate. Most of the Murrays were in Chicago, while the O'Sheas were in Philly and parts of Jersey.

I was on Ennis's Wiki page when I saw something curious. The patriarchy was strong, with only sons ruling, and almost exclusively the eldest. But in lists upon lists of names that sounded primarily Irish or English, Giovanni stuck out. The link was red, meaning there was no developed page for him. Giovanni couldn't sound more Italian though, and he was listed as Ennis's oldest son. Not the John guy who was boss today—

"Miss Porter?"

I squeaked in shock and quickly exited the Wikipedia page, then looked over my shoulder to find a man in a suit there. He didn't work at my school.

"Yes?" I pushed down my nerves and eyed him. Crisp white button-down, black suit, definitely a holster hiding under his jacket. If he was another O'Shea, I was gonna scream bloody murder.

"I'm Kellan Caldwell," he said and extended a hand. "I'm a federal agent, and I was wondering if we could talk."

My life was officially over. Finnegan O'Shea had asked me to dinner, and now I was on FBI's radar. Oh God.

"C-Can I see some ID?" I shook his hand nervously and stood up.

"Of course." He retrieved it from inside his suit and flashed his badge just like they did in the movies.

Kellan Caldwell.

The photo matched. Short, very dark cropped hair. Stormy blue eyes. Tall as a skyscraper. But, um, question. Wouldn't it be wise to teach kids in school how to tell if an FBI badge was real? I had no idea what they were supposed to look like.

"What can I do for you?" I asked hesitantly.

"I have some questions." He gave me a reassuring smile. "You're not in any trouble, Miss Porter. But it's come to our attention that you've had some form of contact with Finnegan O'Shea—"

"I turned him down!" I blurted out, panic rising. "He asked me out, and I said no. That's it, I swear."

He chuckled and gestured toward a small seating area at the back of the library. "Can we sit down and talk?"

Like I had a choice.

That whole evening, I was useless. My thoughts bounced from one catastrophe to another, from Sarah to Finnegan, from the FBI to my living situation, from Franny's conspiracy theories to the future. Thank goodness Dad was at the bar getting shit-faced. He would've had a fit if he knew I'd missed my shift at the diner because an FBI agent wanted to talk.

He wanted a lot more than to talk, though. The FBI wanted my *help*. My help! As if I could do anything? I was a nobody.

As I wiped down the kitchen counter for the fifth time, I wondered if I could press charges against the FBI for coercing me into this crap. Agent Caldwell had made it sound so easy, and in retrospect, I'd agreed because I'd been half seduced by his words.

"We wouldn't put anyone in danger, Miss Porter. Much less a minor."

"Of course, this is only if Mr. O'Shea contacts you again. It might not happen."

"The Bureau would be eternally grateful. We need good citizens like you who are willing to do what it takes."

I whimpered and slid down to the floor, my breaths coming out choppy. Me...? Willing to do what it takes? I was in way over my head, and I didn't know how I'd ended up here. Everything had snowballed in such a short time.

"We'd appreciate it if you didn't tell anyone about this. The O'Sheas are notorious for planting bugs and recruiting people to be their eyes and ears."

I couldn't even tell my best friend—*whoa.* My head snapped up, and I gasped. Sarah had told me there was a lot going on and that she couldn't tell me everything. She wanted to, but she couldn't. Holy crap, had she been approached by federal agents too? Was that why she'd agreed to go out with Patrick, to gain information for the FBI?

I touched my lips, my brain spinning. If that was what she was doing, I had no words for how brave she was. Could I be that gutsy?

Because I was a minor, Agent Caldwell had informed me I wouldn't be obligated to do anything other than ask a few questions. Hell, not even obligated. It wasn't like I'd be wearing a wire or anything. I'd merely show curiosity about Finnegan's life. I'd do my best to keep him talking, all while there was some device nearby that picked up every word he said.

The agent had gone on to explain how almost impenetrable the SoM were because of how close-to-the-vest they kept their operations. Everyone with valuable knowledge was basically family, so the authorities had to jump at every opportunity that came their way. Sarah and I were a way in, according to them.

I bit my thumbnail and struggled to keep my anxiety at bay. Part of me wanted to cry and hide under my bed. The other part wanted to scream about the unfairness of it all. How the hell did I get here? I was innocent. I was insignificant. My biggest problem was supposed to be whether or not I'd be homeless in nine days when I turned eighteen. Yep, nine. Dad had actually circled the date on the calendar that was stuck to the fridge. Every day that passed, there was a red X.

Was he gonna kick me out? Demand rent? The latter was a given. It was the former I feared.

Agent Caldwell said you'd be compensated...

Ugh. I leaned forward, and my fingers disappeared into my hair. If only I could vent to Sarah.

I was on pins and needles for the next two days. All I managed to accomplish was cutting Sarah some slack. Because I loved her and had known her forever and she was a genuinely good person. If someone was brave enough to "do what it takes," it was her. I had to believe she'd struck some deal with the FBI.

And while she helped the authorities get info on the O'Sheas, she was hoarding the gifts Patrick gave her. I'd do the exact same. Those expensive items would be liquidated for her to use for her future. It made her smart.

I remained fairly useless. I cooked and cleaned on autopilot, but school and work suffered. I couldn't shake the unease of it all.

On Wednesday after school, Franny walked with me to the diner. At this hour of the day, it was filled with lumberjacks getting off work. Since the mine had closed over ten years ago, the people either worked with logging companies or they commuted to Gettysburg to help them out with their steady stream of tourists.

"I'm so gonna flunk on this test tomorrow," Franny moped.

"Me too." Though, that wasn't new.

In the time it took me to go out back and change into my uniform, Franny filled a table with schoolbooks and ordered a big Coke and fries. Then I lost a couple hours serving people their greasy dinners and chitchatting with Franny whenever I had a second to spare.

During my ten-minute break, I slid into Franny's booth with my free meal of the day.

"Can you quiz me?" I stuck a couple fries into my mouth and nodded at her English book. "Maybe I can get a C if I—"

"Shh." She sat rigidly in her seat, head a bit tilted, and she was jotting something down in her notebook. "I'm listening."

To what? Ugh, gossip. Or so I guessed. After all, it was the main reason she sometimes sat here and studied while I worked. The diner and the hair salon were Franny's crack—same with her mother.

I bit into my burger, and now that I knew Franny was listening in on a conversation, I couldn't *not* try to figure out which one. The four guys in flannel behind her didn't look to be having the most exciting conversation. Maybe it was the two women behind me.

My internal alarm sounded at the faintest mention of O'Shea. It *was* the four men seated in the booth behind Franny.

"Nah, we have fifteen men working on the fortified fence alone," one of them said. "This ain't temporary. Big property like that, and with what's going on underground?" He whistled. "They're pumping in too much green for this to be some summer getaway."

"It's so remote," another man mused.

"I reckon that's the point." The oldest guy of them wore a wry smirk. "If anyone wants privacy, it's that family."

I'd say I'd lost my appetite, but I hadn't eaten anything all day, so I continued scarfing down my burger. Maybe I'd reached my limit for how much I could handle. Maybe I'd lose my mind now. Maybe I'd just surrender and laugh at everything that happened.

"They're calling it a compound," Franny whispered. "The main house—where Shannon and his wife will live—will be ready in a couple weeks."

"Okay." I washed down my food with some soda. "Can we change the topic?"

"Ugh, you're just like Sarah. I think she's avoiding me."

Gee, I wondered why.

No one could escape this, however. Not even Sarah. The town was buzzing, and rumors were flying everywhere. Everyone was sickly fascinated by the O'Sheas' imminent arrival, and many actually thought it would benefit the town's economy.

It was dark when I walked home, and I couldn't wait to get in the shower. If I got lucky, Dad would be passed out in his chair.

Then, since when did I get lucky?

A black sports car parked outside my house could answer that question.

Never, bitch.

The anxiety made a swift return, and I had to force my feet to carry me forward. Leftover salt from the winter road treatment crunched under my shoes. Agent Caldwell was in my head. *We need good citizens like you who are willing to do what it takes.* That person wasn't me, that person wasn't me, that person wasn't me.

Finnegan was parked under a flickering streetlamp, and the copper in his brown hair shone when he climbed out of his car. Just like last time, he was dressed in all black, and he rounded the car to lean casually against the passenger's-side window. He was another skyscraper-tall bastard, and I couldn't imagine folding himself into that slip of a speedster could be very comfortable.

"What are you doing here?" Did I sound nervous? Fuck.

"Not even a hello first?" He offered a wolfish smile, and I swallowed hard. "I stopped by to see if you'd changed your mind about dinner."

Double fuck. I licked my lips anxiously and passed my mailbox. I wished he'd go away forever, but I didn't have the balls to put my foot down. And if I couldn't tell him to fuck off, how was I going to, for lack of a better word, spy on him on behalf of the FBI?

I knew where snitches ended up.

"What do you have to lose?" he asked.

"My life?"

He grinned widely, the sight taking me aback. It unnerved me how dangerously handsome he was. So completely masculine and intense. But that grin revealed something else. If I didn't know any better, I'd call it boyish, a word that sounded so wrong for him. No, not boyish, but certainly something younger.

"Isn't it illegal for you to ask me out?" I was growing frustrated. "I'm only seventeen, you know."

He hummed and checked his watch. "For another week, aye." He paused as he pulled out a smoke and lit it up. "Pretty sure the age of consent in Pennsylvania refers to sexual activity, though. Not dates. *And*...I think that age is sixteen."

I gaped at him. A hot flush rose to the surface of my skin, and I had never been so fucking offended by a person's mere presence before. The urge to slap the shit out of him surged back with a vengeance.

He was way too fucking amused, and he leaned forward as if to reveal a secret. "I'm not going to fuck you, Emilia. It's just dinner."

Right at that second, he could consider himself lucky I'd kept at least ten feet between us. Otherwise, I would've rammed my elbow up into his chin, and then he probably would've killed me.

I blew out a heavy breath and reined in the anger. What I wouldn't give to put him in his damn place! Uh—well. I *had* the chance. That place could be prison, if he said anything incriminating that the Feds overheard.

And so I was nervous as hell again.

Could I really do it? Could I be brave like Sarah?

One dinner.

If I had to be honest with myself, I didn't think something would happen after just one date or whatever this would be. Sweet Jesus, a *date*. With Finnegan O'Shea.

A cold breeze blew past, causing me to shudder, and I hugged myself. It prompted Finnegan to give me a once-over before he narrowed his eyes at me. I got it, he wasn't very impressed. No one was.

"One dinner," I heard myself say. Agent Caldwell's card burned a hole in my pocket. Holy shit, I was gonna do this.

It seemed Finnegan was as surprised as I was, though he masked it quickly, and then he smiled. "Are you available tomorrow?"

Weird day to go on a date—a Thursday. Unless he was eager to drag me into a criminal lifestyle, at which he'd fail so miserably.

"Sure." I was off work, at least. "Just—make it public, okay? No backwoods or ditches."

Finnegan let out a carefree laugh that divided my thoughts. For one, he was even more gorgeous when he laughed. For two, I couldn't wait to be the one who got the last laugh.

"You got it, princess. A public dinner." He chuckled and stubbed out his smoke. "I'll pick you up at seven."

"I can't wait." The snark slipped out, and I clenched my jaw. I wasn't a damn princess.

He winked. "Me either."

Arrogant son of a bitch.

chapter

4

Emilia Porter

Throw up once, shame on me. Throw up twice, call in sick.

There was no way I could handle classes the next day. Besides, if I saw Sarah, I would end up spilling my guts to her about everything. How she had been able to keep this secret, I would never understand. I was a nervous wreck, and it got worse when I realized I'd already messed up. Agent Caldwell had requested I tell him where I would meet with Finnegan, in the event he did call again. And he had, and I hadn't asked him where we were going, and now I was gonna die.

"Take a deep breath, Miss Porter." Agent Caldwell comforted me over the phone. "First of all, what you're doing is amazing. You should be proud of yourself. Not many people would be brave enough to go along with this."

Deeeep breath. I drew it in through my nose and closed my eyes. "I'm not brave." I said that while holding my breath, so it sounded like I was choking. Christ. I exhaled heavily. "How can you record information if you don't know where we're going beforehand?"

"You could call him and ask."

"I don't have his number." Shit, shit, this wasn't gonna work!

Agent Caldwell hummed in the background, and I heard the sound of tapping keys. "I'll call you back in a few hours. Is that all right? We'll figure something out."

"Sure." Not that I knew how he could possibly fix this by then, but whatever. "I'll go back to pacing a hole in my floor."

We wrapped up the call, and I did the worst cleaning job in my room ever. For the most part, I moved knickknacks from one place to another. Not that there was much to move. Nothing in my room was of any value, except for the tin box under the floorboards where I kept my meager savings of tips from the diner.

My life up until this point had barely blipped anyone's radar, and when there was nothing to celebrate, whether I could afford it or not, there were very few keepsakes. I had a box under the bed with some childhood stuff. Drawings and craft projects from school. Clothes in the closet from the thrift store. A desk with an old computer that didn't function anymore, other than taking up space. Two pictures on my nightstand. And my rickety bed. This was all I'd leave behind when Finnegan O'Shea made me sleep with the fishes.

Slumping down on the edge of the bed, I wriggled my toes and wondered how I'd look in concrete shoes.

Didn't Capone do that to his enemies?

I'd just changed the sheets in Dad's room and was on my way down the stairs when the phone rang. My heart jumped into my throat, and I hurried down and into the kitchen. The dirty laundry ended up on the table before I grabbed the phone.

"This is Emilia," I answered. Perhaps Agent Caldwell hadn't figured out a way, and we should postpone—

"Good, you're home." Aw, *man*. It was Finnegan. "You'll have a delivery at four. I just wanted to make sure you'd be there."

He sounded businesslike, which of course grated on me. Was this a date or a business transaction? Well, actually, I supposed it was the latter. He had told me about some offer to turn me into a drug mule. Or maybe that last part was my guess.

"How did you get my number?" I asked, annoyed.

Who cares? You have his now.

"Your father gave it to me."

Oh. Oh! I had him on the phone. I should ask for details about the dinner.

"Okay," I said quickly, closing that subject so I could start the next. "Where are we going? I, um, wanna plan my outfit." Like, did I wear my jeans or my other pair of jeans?

There was a pause, and when Finnegan spoke again, humor seeped in. "We're going someplace public. And don't worry about your outfit."

I huffed. "I need more details than that, Finnegan."

He rumbled a curse, the low sound sending a shiver down my spine. "That's the first time you've said my name."

"Oh," I mouthed. Heat spread across my face—in anger, probably. My body was understandably reacting weirdly because my life had turned into Bizarroworld.

Did he like it when I said his name? His entire existence put me on edge, and I didn't know what to make of him. Besides the criminal stuff. He had to have some sort of agenda where I was concerned. He didn't know me well enough to pursue me like one would with a regular bout of attraction. He wanted something else.

"Gettysburg," he said and cleared his throat. "More restaurants there, and it's close. I found an Asian fusion place I thought we'd try."

Asian fusion place. That better give enough clues for Agent Caldwell. In a small town where reenacting a battle was the main attraction, I couldn't imagine there being more than one Asian fusion restaurant. I wasn't there often enough to remember. When

I could borrow a car, I sometimes went to a strip mall outside of the town limits to buy cheaper groceries.

"Okay, sounds good." I nodded even though he couldn't see me, and I stared down at my feet. Concrete shoes, concrete shoes. "I'll be ready at seven."

"Don't forget the delivery at four," he replied. "See you in a few hours, Emilia."

He disconnected the call, and I stared at the phone. Delivery at four. Right. What the crap was gonna get delivered? There were so many options. I had to call Agent Caldwell right away, and maybe he'd have more ideas about what mobsters sent their dates.

A dead fish. A mold to be fitted for concrete shoes. A book of poetry about what happened to snitches.

Or...the rich asshole sent me clothes.

Don't worry about your outfit.

I unpacked the box in the kitchen and peered inside. Underneath a layer of tissue paper was a dark purple dress, a pair of heels, and what looked suspiciously like a jewelry box. Wait, there was more. The silky fabric of the dress had hidden something furry. It was ridiculously soft to the touch, white, and hopefully not real fur. It was a bolero or whatever they called those short jackets.

I took a shaky breath as my stomach fluttered, and the fact that I wanted to smile made me embarrassed. I'd never owned anything this pretty before. Ashamed of my reaction, I grabbed the box and ran upstairs to my room and closed the door. Then I held up the dress in front of the mirror on the back of my door, picturing what it'd look like on me.

It wasn't okay to enjoy this one bit.

The fabric was so thin and silky and smooth and airy. I'd have to wear my push-up bra to do this dress some justice. Putting the hanger over my head, I pinched the dress at my waist and inspected my body. Was this what girls who went to prom felt like? I'd never been.

I returned to the box on the bed and folded the dress carefully.

There was a card too. I turned it over and snorted softly. A personal shopper named Karla wished me a pleasant evening and told me to call her if there were any issues with the outfit.

The heels were deathtraps, silvery with pearl-like beads sewn along the straps. They probably cost a fortune. How much could I get for these on eBay? If I'd had another pair of shoes that went with the dress, I would've saved these to sell later.

Sarah didn't sell everything, judging by the new threads she wore every day now. Couldn't I indulge too?

Finnegan was going to use me for something, or try, much like Patrick used Sarah. Would it make me horrible if I tried to gain something in return?

None of this felt right, and the unease churned as I showered and shaved my legs. The last date I was on was a year ago. Jimmy and I went to the diner, and then we shared a few awkward and way too wet kisses in his car. And as much as I'd disliked my time with him, there hadn't been this guilt. A moral dilemma, that was what this was.

I reemerged from the bathroom with a towel wrapped around me, and I remembered I hadn't even looked inside the other box. I lifted the little lid, and the unease grew tenfold. This wasn't child's play. Finnegan didn't fuck around, did he? It was a bracelet, a really goddamn expensive-looking one. Amethysts were purple, right? Crystal-clear like diamonds, countless little purple stones were embedded in a silver—scratch that—white gold bracelet.

"Ugh." I clutched my stomach and sat down on the bed. This wasn't my life. I couldn't dress up in gorgeous dresses and wear gems without wondering where they came from. Who had Finnegan robbed to pay for this?

I'd suck it up, dammit. Agent Caldwell and his team were counting on me, and I was going to be brave like Sarah and help law enforcement. I had to believe it would help in the long run. I mean, you couldn't take down a crime family like Finnegan's after one dinner. If he asked me out again, I would go. I *would* do what it took in order to bring them down once and for all.

Feeling better about my decision, I dried my hair and twisted the waves into a loose up-do. Then I did my makeup, which consisted of nearly poking my eye out with the mascara, a bit of eyeliner, and a rosy lip balm. I didn't own anything else, and I could thank Franny for the mascara and eyeliner.

Next, I squeezed my boobs into a push-up bra, and they did look all right. "Huh." Perhaps my shitty diet of free burgers at the diner was rewarding me with nicer boobs. I put on the dress, and it was like slipping into a slice of heaven. Fuck it all, I deserved to indulge.

Now I had a little over an hour to learn how to walk in these heels.

Dad stumbled home at twenty minutes to seven when I was putting his dinner in the fridge.

He paused in the doorway to the kitchen and stared blearily at me. "What're you wearing?"

"A dress. Do you want me to leave your plate in the fridge, or should I heat it up?"

He waved a hand and pushed off the doorframe. "M'goin' to bed."

Good talk.

"Okay. Um, I have a date. Just so you know."

He returned to the doorway, his bushy brows furrowing. Christ, he was way past drunk today. Chief must've bought him drinks, 'cause I knew how little was in Dad's wallet.

"Don't you have work?" he slurred.

"Still not on Thursdays."

He grunted. "All right. The boy better pay. Night."

I sighed and scratched my eyebrow, listening to his heavy footfalls up the stairs.

Throwing a glance at the fridge, I counted the days on the calendar that weren't marked in red yet. Six boxes. Six days until I turned eighteen.

Funny, my finals that were coming up in a few weeks didn't bother me in the slightest. Maybe because there was a chance I'd be homeless by then.

At the sound of the doorbell, I became rigid, and my gaze flew to the nearest clock. The fucker was early! Crap, crap, crap. I was gonna lose my nerves—*no*. Balls. I was gonna grow balls. I could do this. Deep breaths. I'd done all I could so far. I'd talked to Agent Caldwell and relayed the information I had, and he'd coached me; he'd suggested questions I could ask Finnegan. I was as ready as I'd ever be.

I released a long breath and closed my eyes. One, two, three, four, five, six, seven, eight, nine, ten. I was brave. I was smart. Or something.

Walking carefully in my deathtraps, I reached the hallway and opened the door, revealing Finnegan in a new suit that, for once, wasn't black. The charcoal suit fit him perfectly and matched his eyes, and the black button-down had been replaced by a white shirt. *Huh.* Dark purple tie. It went with my dress. Was that on purpose?

"You're early," I accused.

He smiled. "And you're still seventeen, so I'm just gonna say you look nice."

I looked down self-consciously and mumbled a thanks. Then I excused myself for one second to grab the furry jacket thing that I'd hung on a chair in the kitchen. With no phone or wallet, there was no purse to worry about. My lip balm was tucked safely into my bra.

I was in way over my head with Finnegan. Crimes aside, he was in another league. I was young and too inexperienced. I was used to boys who gaped at me and said things like, "Um, you're like, um, so pretty." Okay, *used to* was a stretch, but it was true for the few boys I'd dated.

Finnegan wasn't a boy.

He helped me into the jacket, then brushed his long fingers along my new bracelet.

I hauled in a breath and hoped he didn't notice the goose bumps.

"You ready?" he murmured.

I nodded jerkily and took a step back. He wasn't safe. Standing too close to him was out of the question.

I followed him outside and locked up.

Could a mobster also be a gentleman? Because he held the car door for me and everything. My senses were invaded by the scent of rich leather once I sat down, and the seat was weirdly comfy and encompassing.

I was surrounded by luxury for the first time in my life, and it was turning me into a freaking hillbilly because my brain took its sweet-ass time processing everything.

The engine started with a low, rumbling purr, and I swallowed hard and buckled up.

Finnegan fastened his seat belt too.

It sparked a trickle of amusement in me. "I didn't know criminals bothered with seat belts."

He kept his eyes on the road as he drove, and his mouth twitched at the corner. "There's nothing more irritating than executing a perfect killing spree and then going down for traffic violations."

I dropped my jaw and froze in horror.

He took one look at me and chuckled. "That's a joke, Emilia."

Son of a bitch! I wanted to slap him so bad. I sat back with a huff and folded my arms over my chest.

You'll get the last laugh. Remember that.

Stewing in silence, I thought of the questions Agent Caldwell had proposed. I couldn't very well ask Finnegan about his crimes outright; I had warm up to more personal stuff. The agent had also warned me it could take a long time for Finnegan to open up. In short, this date had to look like a regular date, and at best, maybe I could give the Feds minor clues. Such as dates, locations, and their everyday whereabouts. Every little thing was logged to map out their operations.

"Thank you for the outfit." My voice was too clipped, so I tried to unclench and added, "You didn't have to be that generous." That was better.

"My pleasure."

Finnegan went on to say something else, but I couldn't for the life of me hear what he said. My entire body buzzed as he hit the freeway and accelerated. I looked down at my lap, then at the floor. *Holy fuck.* What roaring monstrosity did he drive? The car wasn't noisy, but it *felt*...like we were in a powerful tank. And it was having the strangest effect on me. Something rushed inside me, and I white-knuckled the edges of the seat.

I didn't know squat about horsepower, but I had a feeling this vehicle had lots of them.

"Oh my God," I mouthed. He kept speeding up, passing cars in a blur, and my heart hammered.

Bad day not to wear panties so I could hide the lines. Bad, bad day.

My breathing hitched. Thank fuck the car was dark. My cheeks flushed, my stomach tightened, and I squirmed.

Looking out the window didn't make things any easier. We were going so fast, sending a rush of adrenaline through me.

"Emilia?"

"Huh?" My response came out all breathy, and I had to cough.

He side-eyed me and frowned. "Are you okay?"

"Um, yes." Maybe a bit too okay. "Did you say something earlier?"

53

At this point, Finnegan could go to hell so I could marry his car instead. Sweet baby Jesus.

"Yeah, I asked if you're hungry."

Famished for Aston Martin, it seemed. "Yes." I loosened my grip on the leather and wiped my suddenly clammy hands on my thighs. "So, um..." I leaned sideways to peer at the speedometer. "What did you say about traffic violations?"

He laughed through his nose and slid his hands over the wheel, relaxing. "Five or ten over the limit isn't too much."

"You're right, it's not. The speed limit here is also not ninety."

"Are you sure? I could've sworn—"

"It's freaking seventy, Finnegan!"

He laughed and slowed down a teensy bit. "Not a fan of speed?"

"I didn't say that." I'd never gone this fast before, that was all. Whether or not I was a fan was becoming abundantly clear. My body screamed yes.

"That's why I asked."

"Jesus Christ, man." I scowled at him.

"You're funnier than I expected," he mused.

Oh, really. "What did you expect?"

He hummed, smoothly maneuvering us through the traffic. "Less sass."

I didn't know how to respond to that, so I didn't. Instead, I squirmed some more and blew out a breath. If he asked me out again, I hoped he brought the car. It was his best feature.

chapter
5

Emilia Porter

As we got closer to Gettysburg, he had to slow down further. We got stuck a few times too. That's when he pulled out a pack of smokes and rolled down his window. He extended the pack to me, a silent offering.

"I don't smoke," I lied. Or maybe it was a half lie. I never bought them. Too expensive.

"Sure you do." He sparked up one for himself before extending the pack again, and I narrowed my eyes at him. I'd never smoked in his presence.

"Have you been stalking me?" I asked.

"Only a little."

Ohh, only a *little*. Well, then, everything was okay! Motherfucker. I gritted my teeth and looked away from him. Every time he spoke, it was as if a little bit of the world I once knew was chipped away. A couple weeks ago, my life was predictable and bleak. Now...now I spoke to an FBI agent on a daily basis, I wore clothes that cost more than...I didn't even know, and I was on a date with a mobster who'd stalked me *only a little*.

"So what's this offer you wanted to discuss with me?" I asked impatiently.

He exhaled some smoke and flicked ashes out the window. "I want you to marry me."

I blinked, having not expected him to answer me right away. And I definitely didn't expect him to say *that*...so bluntly.

I had nothin'. My brain went blank. Part of me knew this was a possibility, considering what Sarah was going through with Finnegan's brother, but denial was such a sweet state.

"No comeback, sassafrass?" he murmured. "You disappoint me."

"Bite me." Shit. That just tumbled out of me, I swear.

"Not on the first date," he replied.

I grew increasingly aggravated around this dude, mainly because I couldn't fucking understand anything.

"Why me?" I had to ask, and I loathed the pinch of desperation that seeped into my voice. "Seriously, Finnegan—"

"Jesus," he whispered. "The way you say my name is sexy as fuck."

I was gonna wring his damned neck before the evening was over. I almost screamed, that's how frustrated he made me. One second, I was terrified of him. The next, I contemplated kicking him in the balls. He also caused my body to go on a roller coaster with the way I reacted to him. It pissed me off.

"Answer me," I demanded.

He took a final drag from his cigarette, then threw it out the window. "I will, eventually. Not now."

Grr.

Finnegan didn't talk much as we entered Gettysburg and looked for parking. Perhaps that was how I managed to calm down.

The restaurant wasn't far from the town center and Lincoln

Square, and we walked the last bit. Spring was in the air, and I saw vans everywhere. Was that an FBI van? No? What about this one? Were they even here?

Finnegan had perfect manners for a gangster. He put himself between traffic and me, he opened doors, and he even pulled out my chair for me in the restaurant. It was a lively place with two chefs cooking for everyone to see near the front of the dining room. Finnegan and I were seated in the back, offering more seclusion, and it wasn't as loud here. Paper lanterns filled the ceiling, creating an intimate atmosphere. A *date* atmosphere. And there were Chinese folding screens all over to offer even more privacy. Definitely a place for couples.

I shrugged out of my little jacket.

"May I take your drink order, sir?" the waitress asked.

I opened my menu.

"I'll have a beer," Finnegan replied. "Whatever you have on tap is fine. And my date will have a vodka cranberry."

What the fuck?

"Right away, sir." The waitress scurried off without asking for my ID, and I looked at Finnegan over my menu.

"How do you know I like vodka cranberry?"

He smiled and picked up his own menu. "I know a lot about you."

Yeah, I'd gathered that. "That's not what I asked, asshole."

"I'm beginning to love your temper." He chuckled. "I didn't know you had one, to be honest."

I closed my eyes. *Someone kill me, please.* The guy exhausted me.

"It's called research, Emilia." He switched gears and quit dodging, for once. "I have access to a lot of information. It'd be stupid not to use it."

Meh, still dodging. "Yeah, criminals tend to have all kinds of access," I muttered tiredly.

"This again." He closed his menu and clasped his hands on the

57

table. "Emilia, I've paid for my crimes. Things are different today from how they were years ago. I'm a changed man. I run a successful firm, a *legit* one, and I'm ready to move on. That's where you come in."

For one second, I thought he'd give me a sliver of honesty. It was refreshing that he broached the topic of his past, but it wasn't enough. The last part wasn't even a decent lie.

"You're gonna have to give me more credit than that," I said. "My best friend has just agreed to marry your brother so he can look good for his boss. But unless he's running for president, I don't think image matters that much."

He nodded, conceding. "What I'm saying is that the SoM I'm part of has changed. You've heard of the organization, I assume."

"The whole country has heard of it, Finnegan."

He offered a crooked smile. "And the management still clings to old traditions. In order to gain trust and higher ranks, it's important to our boss that we're settled. It makes us look better if we're family men, so yeah, image matters."

I chewed on my bottom lip, mulling over what he said. I decided he was probably speaking the truth. Otherwise, I didn't see a reason for him to rush into a marriage for the sake of it. He could've been a serial killer and a cannibal, he was still undeniably gorgeous, and I bet he could pick whatever woman he wanted to go home with for the night.

As for the Sons of Munster *changing*... Cute. "If you're trying to convince me that your syndicate is no longer doing illegal crap, try harder."

"You can believe whatever you want, princess," he said, "but like I said, I've paid for my crimes, and I've never been guilty of anything worse than those."

I narrowed my eyes, knowing very well what he'd been guilty of. High-end cars had been involved—and guns. Lots of guns. There'd been separate charges; he'd been acquitted of a few, and then he'd gotten five years for the theft and an arms deal gone wrong.

If this was true, he wasn't a killer or a rapist or trafficker.

If only gangsters could be trusted, huh?

I wasn't going to let Finnegan fool me.

Our drinks arrived, and at the glimpse of a very male set of hands, I looked up to see our new server—and I almost choked. It was Agent Caldwell. *Don't freak out, don't freak out, don't freak out.* If Finnegan noticed anything weird, or worse, suspected anything, I would be as good as dead. No doubt.

"Cheers, mate." Finnegan smirked faintly and took a swig of his beer. "You ready to order, Emilia?"

"Um, yeah. Sure." I took my glass and guzzled it like a pro. *Phew.* More vodka in this than I was used to. "Another drink, please." I coughed and wiped my mouth.

Finnegan's smirk widened. "I love a girl who can handle her liquor."

Who said anything about handling it? Unless he meant handling it poorly, in which case I was the master.

I ordered a bowl of pho and a shrimp skewer, and who knew what Finnegan ordered. My ears were ringing too loudly for me to hear anything else.

Agent Caldwell walked away after collecting our menus, acting like nothing was wrong in the world.

Wait, had the first server been an agent too? How the heck was I supposed to know?

In an attempt to get my shit together, I refocused on Finnegan and circled back to a previous question. "How did you know I liked vodka cranberry?"

The fact that he knew I liked it didn't interest me in the slightest. It was how he'd found out that I wanted to know because it wasn't something I had stamped on my forehead. Nothing short of reading the journal in my nightstand would let him know I'd gotten so drunk on vodka cranberry at a party last year.

Jimmy kept mixing them for me, and I quickly developed a fondness for avoiding my life by sipping pink drinks that night. It'd been glorious until I threw up in the bushes outside my house.

Finnegan sat back and studied me, thinking, and fiddled absently with the edge of his coaster. "Last year, you felt sick and went to the nurse's office. You admitted to her you'd had one too many vodka cranberrys."

I guess that would do the trick, too.

I should've remembered that part.

"And Nurse Walsh is your aunt," I stated.

"She is."

"She also had a list with my name on it."

His brows lifted a fraction. "You know about that?"

Ha! Caught him off guard, for once. "Spill the beans. Why the list?"

"Actually, it's your turn now." He sat forward and rested his forearms on the table. It wasn't until then I noticed he'd taken off his suit jacket and folded up the sleeves of his shirt. Damn. Forearm porn was a thing.

I shook my head, cursing the distraction, and looked him in the eye. "My turn?"

He nodded. "To answer the questions."

"Seems to me you know everything about me already."

"Far from it." He cracked the cutest grins sometimes. "You're an only child, I take it?"

Oh, please. As if he didn't know that yet. "Yes."

"What about your mother?"

I inched back momentarily and kept my cool as Agent Caldwell delivered my drink. "Thank you. She's dead."

Finnegan cocked his head. "Really?"

"Really. She died giving birth to me." My dad liked to remind me.

"That sucks." Finnegan's brows pinched together. "So it's just you and your pop?"

"Pretty much." I lifted a shoulder. "He has two sisters somewhere, but they don't talk."

"Damn. I guess your birthday next week will come with one hell of a party, then."

I grinned and snorted a giggle, instantly irritated that he'd made me react that way. Finnegan, on the other hand, looked triumphant.

"Shut up," I told him.

"You have a beautiful smile."

I stifled a groan, a sigh, and the urge to bang my head against the table, and took a sip of my drink instead. Damn him. Damn him, damn him, damn him.

"The only surprise I'll face on my birthday is whether or not my dad will kick me out," I said.

"He won't do that."

"How do you know?"

He shrugged. "I've paid him not to."

"Motherf—*Finnegan*." I couldn't believe him. He threw these insane curveballs, usually when I was enjoying a brief second of ease. Now everything was a fucking flurry in my head again.

"I'll explain, hon." He lifted his palms, cautioning me. "You know I went to see him. I wanted to feel him out—or your relationship, I guess. He's the one who said you're out on your eighteenth birthday."

It stung to hear that from Finnegan. It was humiliating. I had no family, and here was this stranger... I swallowed and brought my hands to my lap. So it was confirmed. Dad wanted me out.

"Why would you..." Crap. It hurt too much to ask why he'd pay Dad. It made it too real. My father really couldn't stand me, his own daughter. "If I were homeless, I'd probably consider your fucked-up proposal more seriously."

"Even I have limits." He looked genuinely concerned, and that was worse.

Until it hit me. Jesus. He was smart. Tapping into my morals and doing me favors, doing good deeds... "Christ." I blew out a breath and sent the ceiling a glance. Finnegan didn't want to yank me toward him the whole way. He wanted me to come somewhat willingly, and helping me out would what, warm me up to him? "Good tactic," I noted.

"Thanks." He sent me a self-deprecating smirk, though it died pretty quickly. "I'm serious, though. You don't deserve his treatment."

I *couldn't* warm up to this bastard. I refused.

"You actually gave him money." No wonder Dad been going to the bar more this week. He could suddenly afford it.

Finnegan nodded with a dip of his chin. "You can stay with him as long as you want."

It was never a matter of what I wanted.

"Why are you doing this? Why me?" I whispered in a moment of defeat. I felt painfully vulnerable and exposed, and I was ready to skip dinner and go home. "Please give me an honest answer."

He stared at me pensively. There was an entire world and an ocean of answers behind those intense, calculating gray eyes, and he was his own vault. If there were any information he didn't want to slip out, it would remain locked up. He was impossible to read.

I had a feeling he never walked into a place without an escape route. There was always a Plan B for this man. Everything he did and said was for a reason and had a purpose. That was the air he gave off anyway.

"I think my answers are changing." He cleared his throat and frowned to himself. "I won't divulge why I picked you to pursue specifically yet, but after seeing you, talking to you, I have more reasons than ever." He met my gaze again. "I'm interested in getting to know you, Emilia. I can't anticipate your reactions. You're not the predictable girl I expected, so you've got me hooked."

The irony of him telling *me* that. Our food arrived at the perfect time, because I had no answer for him. He seemed genuine, but I'd forever be left wondering and doubting his intentions as well as the level of truth.

Agent Caldwell's temporary presence reminded me of why I was here. I had questions to ask, and I kept forgetting them.

"Enjoy your meal." Agent Caldwell disappeared again.

Apparently, Finnegan wasn't done speaking. "Listen. My original goal was convenience. To find a quiet woman who wouldn't get in my way. It's a dick move, but it's the truth. Then I met you, and you'd rather tell me to fuck off."

I twisted my lips to hide my smile, and I picked a shrimp off the skewer, dipping it in the little bowl of lemon oil. "I wanna slap you so hard."

He chuckled. "And I wanna see you again."

Goddamn him.

chapter 6

Finnegan O'Shea

"Y ou're in a brighter mood, lad."

"How can I not be? You're feeding me pizza." I sucked grease off the edge of my thumb and grabbed another slice. Ian was making me forget the mayhem going on right outside the kitchen—okay, almost. "Motherfucking Christ!" I yelled. "Are youse building the house or tearing it down, mates?"

Only the kitchen was completely ready in my parents' new house, and old Ian, their chef and Pop's best friend, had come out ahead of schedule to plan next month's menu. Which meant I got to sit at the kitchen bar and test the foods he prepared as I tended to some business on my laptop.

My brother and I also got to boss around the construction crew that was assembling this huge spectacle of a house. Ma was going nuts with windows. She wanted light everywhere, and there would be more windows than walls. Not the safest call if you asked me.

Pop had left me in charge of security, thank fuck. Ma wouldn't know our property was ready to face a minor militia, 'cause the electric fence would be well-hidden inside thick hedges. She didn't know the windows were bulletproof either.

65

I wanted to invite Emilia over and pretend I was an old English earl and suggest a "stroll on the grounds." That was the size of our property in the middle of the woods. We had *grounds*.

There was even a pond.

For someone who'd grown up in cramped Philly, I could do worse.

"Are you finished with the pizza?" Ian asked and extended a napkin.

I nodded and wiped my mouth. "What's next?" I opened a new tab on my laptop browser to check my email. "By the way, good luck getting Ma to eat pizza."

She had to watch her figure or some such shit.

"It's not for her," Ian chuckled, making notes in his planner. "Alec and Nessa are coming to visit."

That was news to me. I furrowed my brow at Ian. "Since when?"

The kids were a hoot, and I hadn't seen them in a while. I didn't count music sessions over Skype with Alec.

Uncle John had accomplished three good things in his life, with the help of two mistresses. One, when Liam was born. He was a couple years older than me and was being released from prison in a few months. Two and three, the twins. Alec and Nessa were only twelve, but they were sharp, too smart for their own good, and complete riots.

"Since your uncle's grown paranoid that someone's coming after him," Ian replied. "Now. I was thinking salmon for..." I tuned him out, anger filling me.

I'd been preparing this move for months. In order to get Emilia to agree to my proposal swiftly, I'd need to give her all my attention. No problem. Pop had agreed to keep me in the loop while Patrick and I set work aside to focus on the girls, but now our father was failing to do the one thing he'd promised.

I should've fucking known that Uncle John was becoming paranoid. Hell, I should've known the twins were coming too.

Everything was a puzzle, and I couldn't afford to miss a single piece.

If my uncle was sending Alec and Nessa here, it could be construed as a sign of trust. He was willing to leave his youngest kids with us.

At the same time, his worrying that people were after him meant he was less likely to invite new members into his inner circle of top earners, and that was a position I fucking needed.

I scratched the side of my head and fired off a text to Dad. He had to realize how much was at stake.

"Yo!" Patrick entered the kitchen and kicked sawdust off his shoes. "My house is ready now. I cleaned it myself and everything."

Good for you.

I hadn't had the time yet to get the last shit ready in my house. Unlike our parents' house, ours were smaller and more practical. Ma had insisted every building on the property match, so they'd been constructed with the same oak wood exterior, but we had a normal amount of windows. Two stories, two bedrooms upstairs, living room and kitchen downstairs. No muss, no fuss.

"I might have to send you back to the city," I said.

He frowned and slid onto the stool next to me. "You don't send me anywhere, little brother. I'm the trifecta—beauty, brawn, and brains. I tell you what to do."

Hysterical. He had brawn, I guess. He crunched more hours at the gym while I opted for running ten miles every morning, but beauty and brains? *Bitch. Please.*

"Really." I gave him a dry look and faced him fully. "Tell me what I need to do, then. I'm all ears."

"Well, I might have to send you back to the city," he told me. "You're about to tell me why."

I rolled my eyes and returned my attention to my laptop. "Pop's withholding something from us. Apparently, John is sending the twins here because he thinks someone's coming for him."

Patrick knew very well what that meant for us.

"Pop wouldn't do that on purpose," he said.

"I don't think so either." I reckoned Pop was swamped and needed help. Being the boss had never been in his plans, but he had to step up for this, at least until Patrick and I were old enough to take over. "He's got the practice and his patients—"

"And Ma."

"Definitely her," I muttered.

Ian gave us a break and served two plates of finger food, and I leaned closer to inspect the little morsels. I'd never seen the point of fun-sized dishes. They were like the cockteases of food, or so I guessed. My experience with women was too limited.

Nevertheless, one didn't turn off the porn right before the come shot.

"How did your date go?" Patrick asked.

"Good." I picked up a cracker with some cold cuts and cheese on it and stuck it into my mouth. "I'm trying not to think about her too much."

"Why's that? Fuck, these are good, Ian."

They really were. I loved deli meat. "Man, she's something else," I said around the food. "I thought she'd be fucking timid."

Emilia Porter was the opposite. Wary and easily frightened, sure, but that was understandable. Her quick wit and feistiness, however...? I'd had no clue I'd crave it like an addict. I was already looking forward to our next date, which she'd agreed to reluctantly.

I had her in the palm of my hand, though she took every opportunity to bite my fingers.

It was sexy as hell.

She was sexy. Someone had obviously forced her to grow up too fast. She might be naïve like any soon-to-be eighteen-year-old, but she wasn't dumb.

There was one thing that genuinely confused me, though. "She thinks her mother is dead. I don't get that."

"Weird," Patrick said. "Did her pop make her believe that?"

"I guess so. I'll do some digging." It'd been one of the things I'd hoped to learn more about last night at dinner, the topic of Emilia's mother. I'd been shocked when she'd told me her mom had died giving birth to her.

One way or another, I was going to use this to my advantage.

"I can go back to the city if you need me to," he conceded. "I don't have much to do around here anyway. At least you have the security installations. The garage is up and running, and Sarah can spit venom at me over the phone."

I chuckled. "Trouble in paradise so soon?"

"Mother of Christ." He crammed two snacks into his mouth and stole my soda. "The girl hates me."

That wasn't strange. Emilia wasn't fond of me either.

"You've charmed hundreds of women into spreading their legs for you in the past." I clapped him on the back. "I'm sure you can get this one to say 'I do' without murder in her eyes."

"Hundreds is a bit of an exaggeration."

I shrugged. I didn't keep track.

He tilted his head at me. "You're sticking to your rule about no sex before marriage?"

"Of course." I frowned.

I'd had some "fun" during my brief time at Trinity in Dublin, and it never sat well with me. I'd stopped it before it any clothes came off, and I'd decided that the first time I fucked someone, she'd have my name. I didn't take sex lightly, nor did I understand why so many others did.

"Well, I guess you're a better man than me." He squeezed my shoulder. "Who knows, maybe I'll never get laid again. Sarah's not likely to put out."

"Don't get a mistress," I told him. "I love you, Pat, but I'll chop your fucking dick off if you bring drama into our home."

We'd gotten front row seats to that shitshow on Uncle John's side. His wife wasn't the biological mother to any of their children, and she showed her hatred toward him plenty.

"Dude, I have some morals," he defended.

"Good, dust them off." I pointed farther down the counter. "Get me that box, will you?"

He handed it to me, and I lifted the lid, revealing a new phone. I was sending it to Emilia later; I just had to prepare it a bit first. For one, I wanted it synced with my laptop so I could access her texts and phone history and see what apps she downloaded. For two, I had to install a call distorter so our friends at the NSA or the FBI didn't get any ideas.

"I'm slightly jealous you got Sarah to agree so fast," I admitted.

Patrick snorted. "Unlike you, I wasn't looking for a particular chick. I asked Aunt Viv to point me in the direction of the student who wanted to get away from her parents the most, and she suggested Emilia's friend—suspected the girl was being abused."

I shook my head, sickened by some people who had the balls to call themselves parents. Family was supposed to be sacred.

"It helps that she's hot as fuck," Patrick added.

I smacked him upside the head. "Be nice to her. If she's suffered abuse, be her protector, not her next abuser."

"*Hey.*" He rubbed the spot I'd smacked and scowled. "I haven't pushed her for shit."

"Good. Just make sure you respect her." I held up the phone. "Now, help me spy on my future wife."

———

Emilia was too fucking cute.

She'd received the phone and was currently learning how to use it. Though, rather than calling me up to help her—I'd preinstalled my number for her—she'd turned to Sarah. Now the two were texting while Emilia worked a shift at the shitty diner.

I'd migrated to my own house down the hill. I was supposed to be assembling the entertainment center; instead, my ass was glued to the couch, and I was reading the messages the girls sent to each other on my laptop.

Can you see this thing?

Yes, Em, it's called an emoji lol.

I smiled and took a swig of my beer.

Why is there one that looks like poop?

I chuckled.

Someone rudely interrupted me by knocking on the door and then entering before I could even tell them to fuck off. It was Patrick and Kellan with snacks and a couple six-packs of beer.

"Have you done *anything*?" Patrick stared at the state of my living room.

"I've been busy," I said defensively. Closing my laptop, I left it on the coffee table, something I'd actually assembled earlier. Ma had picked out Indian teak for me, whatever that meant, and the table was now begging for condensation rings and scratches.

"The plastic's still on the couch, mate." Kellan snorted and crossed the living room to reach the kitchen.

"That's 'cause you spill, Agent Caldwell!" I called after him, and he laughed. Then I faced my brother. "The stalking has paid off again. The girls are texting, and Sarah mentioned being in the mood for Chinese."

His forehead creased. "So?"

For fuck's sake. "So take her out, numbskull! Call her and say you want Chinese. Bond or some shit."

"Good idea." He nodded firmly and pulled out his phone.

So did I, 'cause I'd waited long enough. When the phone had been delivered to Emilia, she'd called me—from her landline—to thank me and stubbornly remind me this didn't change anything. Then, nothing. She clearly didn't wanna text with me.

Fucking Sarah, man. I needed Emilia's attention more than she did. Hell, Emilia'd talked to a fake FBI agent more than me. And I didn't want Kellan to relay information about the girl *I* was gonna marry.

I sent her a message.

Any plans for tomorrow?

Ian had advised me to show Emilia a more casual side of me.

I could do that sometime. Probably. I'd lived on such a tight schedule these past two years that I'd forgotten some things. Like how to have fun. Fuck, I needed to see Father O'Malley soon. Since my last confession, I'd admitted more bullshit to myself, and Patrick and our mother were right. I'd gone too far.

I wasn't willing to change a whole lot at the moment, but dammit if Uncle John was gonna rob me of the ability to show people how to have fun.

My phone buzzed with Emilia's response.

Can you see your name in this message? I work nine to three.

I narrowed my eyes. See my name...? Oh. The name she'd given me in her phone. My mouth twisted up. No, I couldn't see the name in the text convo, but I did have access to her contact list. I knew she'd renamed me O'Dickhead.

No, your no doubt offensive and hilarious name for me is hidden from me. I'll meet you at the diner.

There was one unreasonable thorn in my side. Emilia fully believed Kellan was a legit agent, and she checked in with him often. It made complete sense, but it irritated me. Even now, she confirmed her second date with me to Kellan before she texted me a simple "OK."

On the other hand, I was glad I'd gone this route. I would know if Emilia ever learned to trust me, and better yet, grew a sense of loyalty. Part of me wanted there to be a day she lied to Kellan and said there was nothing to report. I might even want that more than a wedding day.

"All right, let's get your house ready, Finn," Kellan said. "I'd rather crash in your guest room than Patrick's. He watches a lot of porn at night, and he ain't quiet."

Patrick puckered his lips.

"Actually, I wanna pay a visit to Emilia's pop first," I said.

I didn't see why I had to give him money to let his daughter live with him. Not when he was lying to her about the whereabouts of her mother.

I could admit it. I was a fan of blackmailing.

I was an early riser these days, so it was rare that anyone woke me up. This morning was one of those occasions, and I threw a pillow over my head to drown out the banging on my door downstairs.

That was the first reminder that I wasn't in my condo in Philly. The second was the smell. Everything smelled of nature out here. Spring was wet, and the rain turned every surface into Little Trees, except the world was the rearview mirror, and there was no new-car scent. It was pine, dirt, and timber.

The banging didn't stop, and I gave up on sleep after a while. Dragging my ass outta bed, I pulled on a pair of sweats and headed down the stairs. The knuckles on my right hand were sore, and I flexed them carefully.

The steps creaked.

My morning wood took a hike by the time I reached the door. Then it was chaos. Chilled air and two twelve-year-olds were suddenly plastered to me, and as stoked as I'd been to see Alec and Nessa again, it was five in the fucking morning.

"Jaysus, kids," I grunted. "What the hell are you doing here?"

They talked a mile a minute, both at the same time, so it was no use to try to listen. Instead, I peered out the door and was surprised to see Pop's car parked outside the main house. We were a couple hours away from the city.

There was usually a reason if someone felt the need to head out in the middle of the night.

"Oi." I halted their rambling, kissed the top of Nessa's head, and gripped Alec's chin. "You. Talk, cub."

Two dimples appeared with his wide grin. "Uncle Shan has meetings in the city and had to drive us out here early." His accent was thicker, far more Irish than mine, and I'd fucking missed it. His green eyes were always a source of happiness. "We'll be staying with you, boss!"

I let out a sleep-laden laugh and ushered them farther inside. Pop could come over if he wanted to talk. I sure as fuck had questions for him.

"Patrick says you're not funny anymore." Nessa stared up at me and scrunched her nose. "Did you lose your funny bone?"

"He's talking shite," I answered. "I'm the funniest fucker on the planet."

"I'll be the judge of that," she decided. "I'm hungry. Can we eat breakfast?"

I checked my—that was a no-go. I hadn't put on my watch yet. The clock on my new entertainment center helped me. "Ian's serving breakfast at the main house in half an hour. Think you can last that long?"

"I'll give it my best." She saluted me.

I smiled as they kicked off their shoes and dove for the couch and the remote control.

It was good to see them again.

chapter

7

Emilia Porter

S aturday was shaping up to be a disaster of a day, and it wasn't noon yet.

Yesterday had been too good to be true, mostly because the wedge that'd been jammed into place between Sarah and me was gone. I'd arrived at school, taken one look at her, and burst into tears. It hadn't been pretty. But now she knew everything—not counting the stuff about the FBI—and it felt so damn good to have someone to talk to again.

She and I weren't exactly on the same page. I hadn't agreed to a proposal, nor was I doing this for money. But then, maybe she wasn't either. I held out hope she'd struck the same deal with the FBI, and because we had to keep that to ourselves, it was easier to say it was the money that made us agree to date them.

Either way, I had someone to vent to, and so did she. After work, I'd met up with her by the picnic tables at school, and we'd bitched and ranted about the O'Shea men. And it'd been *so* cathartic.

Perhaps today was a reminder that my life sucked even before Finnegan rode into town on his Aston Martin horse. I'd woken up

75

to the sound of Dad throwing the coffeemaker at the fridge. Considering he'd been gone when I came home yesterday, I'd assumed he'd sleep away half the day. Instead, he'd acted like he'd been possessed by a demon, so I'd hightailed it out of there.

Only to come here to the diner and find out we were short-staffed.

"Miss?" A man sitting by the counter held up his empty coffee cup.

"I'm sorry, sir. One minute." I rounded the counter first to serve a family their lunch. Rattling off their orders, I set two plates of food on their table. "I'll be right out with the kids' meals."

"I painted!" The youngest boy in the family presented the coloring sheet he'd gone berserk on with crayons.

"You did? That's so cool." I grinned and ruffled his hair, then addressed the parents. "I'll get you some refills too." Then I returned behind the counter, refilled the man's coffee, and waited for Ben to finish the next orders in the kitchen.

I endured another hour of torture before I had to excuse myself. Laura could handle things for two minutes.

I found privacy in the bathroom and splashed cold water on my face and neck, willing my mind to slow down. I actually liked stressful environments, but this was pushing it. There were supposed to be five people working during the usual rushes. Now we were down to three, leaving Ben alone in the kitchen, and Laura and I had to man the register too.

I looked like roadkill. Make that candy-cane roadkill, given my uniform. I could survive the Santa-red leggings and white polo tee, but the stripy apron and hair band crossed the line.

Grabbing a few paper towels, I dabbed them over my neck and forehead. It was time to get back out there and let Laura take two as well.

Two more hours, and then I was further ruining this day by seeing Finnegan.

On my way out, I tucked some loose waves into my ponytail

and—fuck, stopped short at the door in the kitchen. Through the round window, I could see Finnegan sitting at the counter. Wearing a *hoodie*. I didn't know what shook me the most, the casual outfit or that he was way too early.

Something tugged at me, though. Something that wasn't wholly unpleasant. I watched as he flicked his gaze between the daily specials and his surroundings, maybe wondering where I was.

I liked this less polished look on him. His hair wasn't tidy today either. Before, he'd at least made an honest attempt.

I pushed the door open and resigned myself to be mocked for my uniform, and he looked up from the little menu stand.

A smirk tugged at the corners of his mouth, and he gave me a slow once-over.

"You're early—again."

"And you're adorable," he chuckled. "I'm hungry. What's good around here?"

I took the menu from him and placed it by the register. "Nothing on there. The grilled cheese with bacon and tomato is pretty good."

"Sign me up for one of those." He nodded.

I took out my pad from my apron and jotted down the order. "Fries or mac and cheese with that?"

"Mac and cheese? With grilled cheese?"

I pointed my pen at the diner sign behind me. *Welcome to Mac's Diner. Bringing you every meal with the best mac and cheese since 1969.* Mac Hanson, who'd opened the diner, had passed down the business to his son and daughter. He was dead now. Heart attack.

"We'll see if it's the best." Finnegan saw it as a challenge.

I laughed under my breath. "And drink?"

"Coke, thanks."

Tearing off the order, I pinned it on top of the others, then poured him a large Coke with ice.

"Will I get any special treatment?" he asked with a smile.

I shook my head, hating that I found him funny. "I can ask Ben to burn your food if you want."

"Sassafras." He removed the straw and sipped from his soda.

He was about to say something else, but Laura interrupted, joining me behind the counter with a loud sigh.

"I think things are finally calming down. I'll take a quick break if you don't mind."

"No, of course. Go." I surveyed the diner. All booths were full. As were the guests' drinks, and Finnegan shared the counter with two others. The guy who'd been impatient for coffee earlier had left.

I knew if I sat down, someone was going to need me, so I poured a soda for myself and remained standing near Finnegan, who was watching me.

"I know I look like a mess. Stop staring."

"I will if you will."

"I'm not staring at you," I said.

He raised his brows. "You're literally watching me right now."

"But that's just—ugh!" I wanted to whine.

He cracked a smug little grin.

Sexy, cocky, arrogant asshole.

Thank *God* someone needed a refill. I was quick to leave the counter and grab the guest's near-empty glass. "Is there anything else I can get you, ma'am? Everything taste good?"

"Always good, dear." She patted my hand. "Just some iced tea, thank you."

"Coming right up." I ignored Finnegan's amused stare and did my job, though it was impossible to avoid him for long. Laura came back, and since she was never on good terms with the register, she opted to cover the dining area.

I had no choice but to plant myself behind the counter and manage payments and one mobster.

"One twelve with mac," Ben said behind me. It was Finnegan's order, and I accepted it through the serving hatch.

Finnegan's eyes lit up at the sight of his lunch, and it was almost cute. Okay, it was cute as hell, and I hated him for it. When was I gonna understand that it wasn't all right to find the company of convicted felons entertaining? There was a part of me that was beginning to focus solely on Finnegan to see how he'd surprise me next.

Where was the fear? The horror? The repulsion?

"This looks..." Staring at his meal, he quickly unfolded the napkin around his utensils.

"The guy who opened this place died of a heart attack," I blurted out.

Finnegan's eyebrows bunched together, and he wasn't happy anymore. "Why would you hurt me like that? Why?"

Don't laugh, don't laugh, don't laugh.

"Fucking women," he muttered under his breath and tucked into the mac and cheese.

A snicker broke free. I had to distract myself before I lost my mind and downright enjoyed being around him.

At two, the place was dead—and would be for the next couple of hours before the early-bird rush started. I sent Laura home and put in two final orders. I wanted my free meal, and Finnegan wanted dessert. He'd spotted fried Twinkies and ice cream on the dessert menu and couldn't order it fast enough.

"You're different today," I noted.

It was as if he relaxed when the suit came off.

"You have no idea how many times I've heard that lately." He smiled with chagrin and picked at a straw wrapper. "Can we snag a booth? My ass is in agony."

I spluttered a laugh at the image, failing to hide it with a cough, and nodded once. I didn't wanna eat standing up anyway, so we moved to a booth as soon as our orders were ready.

As we sat down, Finnegan and I exchanged a look, and he appeared as confused as I was. It hit me how average this was—yet comforting and familiar. We were two people hanging out in a diner, something kids my age had done for generations. It was just... different. Very different from our date in Gettysburg.

"Did you have any special plans for us today?" I asked.

"I think I just changed them."

So, we were staying at the crappy diner where I worked, and it was okay. It was more than okay. I relaxed in my seat and stuck a couple fries into my mouth, genuinely content for the first time in weeks. I'd feel guilty for it later; right now, I wanted a break.

Finnegan let out an obscene groan when he tasted his dessert. His car had a similar effect on me, and I felt the heat on my face. This time, I didn't hide my amusement. I guess it didn't matter if a guy was a thug or a CEO; there would always be something about men and their food.

"I'm gonna have to ask Ian to make this," he said.

"Ian?" I poked at my two pieces of chicken and tore off the meat with my fork.

"My parents' chef."

Good lord. "You have a personal chef who cooks for you?"

"My folks do." He nodded. "To me, he's more of a therapist. I talk, he listens."

I quirked half a grin. "I think you just described a priest."

"I already have one of those." The words came out muffled, his cheeks puffed out with Twinkie and ice cream. "And trust, he talks as much as he listens."

"You're not religious, are you?" That would be too weird. I assumed he was Catholic due to his heritage, but come on.

"I am." He nodded slowly and frowned slightly. "Is that a problem?"

Jeesh. Where did I begin? "Not for *me*," I clarified. "I guess that's between you and the man upstairs."

"We're on good terms."

"I'm sure," I replied dryly. "God loves a killer."

He grinned around his dessert and pointed his spoon at me. "I've never killed anyone."

So he kept insisting. I wished I could believe him—I honestly did—and I feared I would if he kept this up. Finnegan was incredibly charming, and he knew it. He used it.

"Let's talk about your birthday." He picked up a napkin and wiped his mouth. "Fuck, this was good."

"What about my birthday?" I dragged a piece of chicken through the puddle of barbecue sauce.

"You turn eighteen. We gotta celebrate it. If there's one thing the Irish know, it's how to show people a good time." He pushed his plate to the side, then rested his forearms on the table. "What do you say?"

I scrunched my nose. "Like a party? I'm not fond of many people in this town. I only have a handful I'd call friends." If that.

"Fuck them," he said. "I wanna introduce you to my family. My brother and my cousins, to be more exact. My folks are still busy packing up in Philly."

That put a rock in my stomach. One mafia guy was enough. I'd pee my pants if I had to meet more, and he had a whole family of them.

"I don't want a party," I answered and stared at my food. "You can get me a card if you want. I'll even spell out happy birthday for you—"

"Emilia."

I looked up reluctantly and was met with a soft smile.

"I'm not budging." He leaned forward a bit. "And it's not a party. It's you, me, my brother, Sarah, and my two twelve-year-old cousins." When he put it like *that*... Things changed at the prospect of having Sarah there. And two kids? "We'll eat and drink and listen to some music. Nothing out of the ordinary."

To someone who didn't have any family, it was anything but ordinary.

81

The bastard was pulling me toward him with crap I'd never had, crap I'd dreamed of. Good company, laughter, family, just a plain good time among people you liked. And it was so wrong. I *didn't* like Finnegan, and I wouldn't like his damn family either.

Make it true, make it true.

"I'll think about it," I said.

"Fair enough." He stole a French fry from me. "I'll win you over." *That's what I'm afraid of, idiot.* "You haven't asked a single question about my offer. Are you thinking about that too?"

I thought about it every hour of the day. Especially since yesterday. Once I'd stopped crying my eyes out and Sarah had comforted me, she'd been persistently encouraging. She wanted me to agree to marry Finnegan, because then she wouldn't have to go through this alone. Moreover, she and I could start making plans for our post-O'Shea future.

She had *lists* of things she wanted to do or get once she'd divorced Patrick.

For a moment, her fantasies had swept me away too, except those thoughts hadn't resulted in anything positive. I'd sat there on the picnic bench and indulged, thinking I could be anything I wanted if I had the money. Which had led to the question, what the fuck did I want to be?

I had no dreams that went beyond getting my own place and making ends meet.

"I don't know what to ask," I admitted. "I assume you're offering me money if I agree."

He nodded.

"And I don't want to be married to a mobster," I replied honestly. "I'm not romantic by nature. If you'd been someone else, I probably would've considered it. I hate my life here, and the money is a one-way ticket to freedom. But you're an O'Shea."

He hummed and peered out the window for a moment, thinking. His car was parked right outside. "And you're dead set on believing the rumors about me." He cocked his head, asking for clarification.

"They're not rumors," I said quietly. "You've been to prison."

"Not for *murder*. Christ." His eyes flashed with frustration. "Emilia, you're judging me for what people around me may or may not have done. I would never—" He released a deflating breath and smirked a little sadly. "You know, on my way over, I thought my biggest issue today would be how to pick out questions on the list my cousins helped me make."

I frowned in confusion. "A list?"

He shifted in his seat to reach something from his back pocket. "Nessa thought it was imperative I ask who your favorite movie star is and if he's cute."

He slid the crumpled piece of paper my way, and I picked it up and flattened it against the table. Question upon question, scribbled in a disturbingly flawless cursive writing. From my favorite color and scent, to preferences on music and—oh, geez.

"'What's my favorite cake?'" I quirked a brow.

"I came up with that one."

I tried to hide my smile.

"But it doesn't matter, does it?" He leaned back and withdrew his hands to his lap. "You legit believe you're sitting here with a killer."

I dropped my gaze quickly. My head couldn't handle this. For all I knew, he could be a skilled manipulator. I would *never* know.

"I'm not sure, Finnegan." I was at a loss. A couple weeks ago, I was a hundred percent certain. Now he'd crammed so many questions inside my skull that it physically hurt. It was the danger of getting to know him. He was funny, smart, and we bantered like professionals.

I didn't know what was real. That was the problem. All I had was me, and the more I saw Finnegan, the less I could trust myself.

"Meet my family next week, princess." He inched forward again and, for the first time, covered my hands with his. *Ugh.* Even his use of princess was sounding less and less like snark. It came out like a term of endearment. Combine that with his hands touching mine, and my brain was ready to call it a day. "See for yourself," he murmured. "My folks can't wait to see you when they come out here. My brother and cousins will be the warm-up. We'll sit out back and get a fire started. Watching Patrick burn his fingers is always fun." Damn him for painting these images for me. "You'll love Alec. He'll probably try to impress you with some live music."

My chest *ached.*

"Okay," I whispered.

"Yeah?" He brushed his thumbs over my knuckles.

I suppressed a shiver and managed a small nod. In response, he brought my hands to him and kissed the backs.

The moment left me dazed, and I retreated a bit once he released my hands. One thing was for certain: I'd never met a man like Finnegan O'Shea before. Time would tell if that was good or bad. If knowing *him* would be bad.

"It's a she." I cleared my throat and fidgeted with my napkin.

"Hmm?" He looked to me.

"My favorite movie star," I said. "Tell your cousin it's a kick-ass woman."

He smiled. "All right."

chapter

8

Emilia Porter

Instead of going home after school on Monday, I stayed behind
with Sarah. She'd accepted my invitation for a "get-together"
with the O'Sheas on my birthday, and it worried me. When I was
weak, I needed her to be strong and resolute. The O'Sheas were
bad people; she had to keep reminding me. If she stopped, who
knew what would become of me.

"When does your shift start?" she asked.

We reached the picnic tables, and she extended a cigarette
to me.

"Thanks. In an hour or so." Butt planted on the table and feet
on the bench, I stared at the cigarette between my fingers. What
was once an occasional anxiety relief was turning into a daily thing
because Sarah could afford it.

She kept showing up in new clothes. Patrick had given her a
credit card, and she was putting it to good use.

"Do, um...do you ever feel like you're warming up to Patrick?" I
asked hesitantly.

Sarah gave me a look that said it all. No, she definitely didn't.

"Hon, this is business. Nothing else. You gotta take more advantage of Finnegan. Remember that he's using you."

Why did that sting? She was right. Finnegan *was* using me.

"I bet if you agree to marry him, he'll give you a credit card too," she said.

Was that why'd she'd gone so far as to agree to a marriage proposal? The way I saw it, agreeing to date Patrick would've been enough to help the FBI. Then again, she had to look out for herself too.

As hobo-like as I looked next to Sarah these days, I wasn't sure I wanted a credit card. I guess that made me horrible at taking advantage. He'd given me a nice outfit and a fancy phone. It felt like a lot already. But, as Sarah pointed out, he was using me. The gifts were part of the allure to reel me in.

"You're right." Not that I had any plans to accept a proposal, but I had to chill. I lit up the cigarette and handed back the lighter. "You seem to be looking forward to Wednesday a whole lot, though."

"Nothing wrong with enjoying yourself." She bumped her shoulder with mine. "We deserve it, Em."

Did we? I mean, yeah, we'd been dealt crappy hands, but I couldn't help but wonder at whose expense we'd be enjoying ourselves—oh, for chrissakes. "I'm overthinking this, I think." I ran a hand through my hair and took a puff from the smoke.

"*That* wouldn't surprise me." She laughed softly and hugged me to her.

It sent a waft of her perfume my way, or shampoo. I leaned close and took a whiff. Definitely her hair. "You've changed your hair again." As the sun made a brief appearance, her light hair glinted in golds and faint reds.

"I'm experimenting for the first time in my life," she chuckled. "Patrick took me to dinner in Gettysburg yesterday, and I stopped at the salon." She sighed and smiled. "We can't all be born with natural highlights like you."

86

I snorted. There was nothing special about my hair, with the exception that it was way too long.

Part of me envied Sarah. A big part. She was able to throw herself into this, all while guarding her feelings and keeping her mind focused. She was happier lately.

I bet it helped to get away from her parents. She'd told Patrick there was no way she'd consider living with him until "after we are married," so, for now, she was renting a motel room down the road. He paid.

"Do you mind if I crash with you tonight?" I asked.

"No, of course not. Is there a problem?"

"Dad," I admitted. "He's angrier than usual. If I didn't see empty beer cans everywhere, I would think he was trying to get sober." Yesterday, he'd polished off an entire bottle of bourbon. Then he'd called me a useless bitch, which was always pleasant. He'd been in a fight at some point too. His cheek had some bruising. "He's made it a sport to break our plates."

"The drunks in this town, I swear." She shook her head. "You can stay with me however long you want. I spend most evenings studying and dodging Franny's calls."

I snickered. Our friend had been growing frustrated with me too. At lunch, she'd asked me if it was true that Finnegan spent Saturday afternoon at the diner. I'd lied and said I hadn't seen him.

The envy festered inside me that night and all throughout the following day. One night in a motel room, and I was fighting panic at the thought of returning home. Sarah and I'd had a girls' night where she spoiled me with expensive takeout from Gettysburg and a cute pajama set that'd been too small for her. For one night, everything had been great. For one night, I'd replaced peeling wallpaper and yelling with silly giggles and music.

Sarah and I were in luxury heaven, despite the unkempt state of the motel room. We acknowledged the leaky pipes and squeaky bed with shrugs, because they didn't matter. The motel room wasn't trying to suffocate us.

She had a date with Patrick tonight, though she said she wouldn't be long.

It was long enough for me to indulge in some alone time that couldn't be ruined by Dad. My shower lasted until the hot water ran out. I shaved, plucked my eyebrows, and performed a half-assed manicure and pedicure on myself. Sarah had started a nice collection of lotions and other beauty products.

I put on some shimmering nail polish too, and while I waited for that to dry, I texted Finnegan.

Hi. Are we still on for tomorrow?

I hadn't heard from him all Sunday and Monday. Or today, for that matter. If he canceled, I was gonna get annoyed. I'd switched to a shift at work that tended to give shittier tips in order to have tomorrow off.

His reply popped up.

Of course. I'll pick you up at six. How are you?

I stared at the words, deliberating. There was a flutter in my stomach, and I hoped it wasn't because I was hearing from him. It couldn't be excitement.

I'm fine. Babysitting Sarah's motel room and watching paint dry. What about you?

Check me out, being all nice and witty.

I'd failed, for the most part, to give Agent Caldwell any good information. I had to rectify that, I guessed. So far, I'd been able to tell him roundabout dates for when Finnegan's parents were moving out here. I'd relayed the info on the twelve-year-old cousins named Alec and Nessa and that they were spending time here. And some other insignificant stuff.

That's good to know. Are you spending the night? I don't want the birthday gift to be delivered to the

wrong address. I'm good. Babysitting my cousins and working on the house.

That didn't sound criminal... I sighed and chewed on my lip.

Yes, I'll sleep here. You don't have to give me a gift. The dinner is a gift.

Putting my phone aside, I left the bed to slip back into my new pajamas. The light purple mini shorts came with a matching short-sleeved blouse and had the cutest pearly buttons. The fabric was soft and thin but not very giving, so I could understand why Sarah had given it to me. She was taller than me and maybe a size or two larger. You'd want some wiggle room in these cute threads.

I'd never really felt cute before.

I returned the towels to the bathroom, then brushed my teeth and jammed my hair into a messy bun at the top of my head.

A message from Finnegan was waiting for me, and I squeaked when I read it and noticed it'd been sent twelve minutes ago.

Have a smoke with me. I'll be there in fifteen.

What were the odds of Sarah *not* having told Patrick the room number? A knock on the door answered my question. No time for hysteria, I scrambled off the bed and gave the room a panicked look. My mess wasn't so messy. Schoolbooks thrown on the dresser by the window, a plastic bag with clothes.

Sarah's shit was everywhere, though.

Fuck it. He'd seen the inside of my house. He could handle this too.

I opened the door and nearly swallowed my tongue. Finnegan should be fucking outlawed. It seemed that no matter what he wore, he made it look like sex. It was a fairly warm evening, and he'd arrived without a suit jacket. Just charcoal pants and a white dress shirt with his sleeves rolled up, and I really, really, really liked the look. Top two buttons undone, revealing a hint of chest hair.

Attraction *sucked*.

"Hi. I just saw your text." I shuffled by the door, hiding a bit behind it. Unlike him, I didn't walk straight out of a magazine.

"Jesus, Emilia." He cleared his throat and scrubbed a hand over his mouth. "I told myself to make it through one date—short as it might be—without pissing you off, and then you open the door looking like this."

I glanced down at myself, then up at him, confused.

He chuckled and gestured at the bench outside the window. "Sit with me. And grab a blanket. I'll be right back."

He walked toward his car that was parked outside the room next door, and I went on the hunt for a blanket. Did that mean he liked the pajamas? I didn't know why that would piss me off. It was flattering, if anything.

No blanket came with the motel room, so I had to borrow Sarah's old afghan that she'd brought from home. I borrowed her slippers too.

Finnegan was waiting for me outside, and my gaze got stuck on the pile of wrapped presents on the bench.

"I told you—"

"Sit, dammit." He nodded at the spot next to him. "I wanna be the first to celebrate my birthday girl."

There were so many things wrong with that sentence, yet it felt like the most welcome affectionate gesture. I exhaled shakily, too stunned to deliver a sarcastic comeback, and took a seat on the other side of the pile of gifts.

The first thing Finnegan did was to wrap the afghan around me. "You make it impossible not to objectify you, hon. Let's show less skin, yeah?"

I gigglesnorted. "*Are* you objectifying me?"

"A bit. Now—" he checked his watch "—we have two hours till it's your birthday, and I'm not gonna piss you off even once."

"Tall order." I stifled my smirk. "It's probably safer to stick to just one cigarette. Two hours would push it."

"I was never one to play it safe." He didn't hide his smirk for crap, and he handed me the top box. "I'm saving one gift for tomorrow."

I accepted the little box and pulled at the ribbon. Underneath the lid was a Zippo lighter engraved with the words, "She'll light your shit on fire." I couldn't help it; I laughed.

Finnegan smiled. "It fits you, doesn't it?"

"Maybe." I snickered and tried it out. "So you think I have fire?"

He nodded and pulled out his smokes. "And light." He leaned forward and lit one. Then he handed me the next box, a slightly larger one. "Alec and Nessa helped me shop for you. I'm kinda clueless in that department." I didn't know about that. "I reckon we went to every store in Philly."

"When was this?" I asked, opening the next one. "Oh my God, why?" *Why* would I need a pocket knife? This was engraved too. It said Princess, and it was really freaking sharp.

"Everyone should have a knife." He extended the smoke to me before showing me how the knife worked. It was one of those switchblade things that ejected from a sheath. "This one comes with a strap if you wanna keep it around your ankle."

I took a pull from the cigarette. He was nuts.

It was the first time I'd thought of him as a gun-toting gangster without it making me queasy. There was something wrong with me.

"Thank you, Finnegan."

"We've barely started." He gave me the next one.

It was a necklace, a gorgeous one with a silver chain and a padlock charm.

"It's got a panic button and GPS tracker," he said and turned the locket. Of course, it was an alarm. I was sensing a theme. "You push this, and it'll send a signal to my phone and my security company. This is in case of an absolute emergency. No one will call you or check in. A team will be sent to your location right away."

What the hell did I say? There was no compartment in my head that dealt with these things. It was completely foreign.

The next couple of gifts were similar. Safety and protection. A bracelet with the same panic alarm. A mini-sized canister of pepper spray that fit into a lipstick case. The gifts were...well thought-out and sweet, and the jewelry was beautiful, but there was this ominous background music playing in my head. Why would I need any of this?

I thanked him, though. No one had never gone out of their way to make me feel safe, and although Finnegan was going above and beyond—and then some—it stirred emotions in me. It wasn't anger.

"I guess you want me safe," I joked.

"More than I anticipated." He offered half a smile and touched my cheek. "The other gifts are more fun, I promise."

I shook my head and brushed my fingers over the silvery pocket knife. "These will just take some getting used to. I appreciate them."

"I'll hold you to that," he murmured. "Getting used to them implies we'll be in each other's lives for a while."

I narrowed my eyes at him and managed to kill my amusement. "Don't piss me off."

He grinned. "Wouldn't dream of it. Open the next one."

I did, and the next, and the one after that. He'd given me a birthday outfit—along with another personal shopper's note. A dress, a black one this time, a bit edgier. Black ballet flats, and a matching leather cuff with a beautiful coat-of-arms plate in the middle. Last but not least, an impressive stack of gift cards.

The whole experience was overwhelming. I didn't gush over the dress like I wanted to, but it was so cool. The young kid in me had wanted silly things like pretty clothes, and now I was getting them. Goddamn him. He probably hadn't bought a dress for any other reason than it being a typical chick thing or whatever. Maybe his cousin had told him to get me another dress. I didn't know. Either way, it was special.

The bodice of the dress was almost like a corset and had a lacy edge that bordered the cleavage. It was strapless too. A punk-rock chick would totally wear this.

"Should I be concerned that you seem to know what size I wear?" I asked.

"Nah. My aunt helped me make an educated guess."

I had half a mind to have Nurse Walsh fired. "Finnegan..." I took a breath and reined in the annoyance. "Don't you realize a lot of your so-called research is invading my privacy?"

His brow furrowed. "How else would I find out—"

"You ask! Like a normal person!"

"Then it wouldn't be a surprise," he argued.

I smashed my lips together in a tight line, wondering if he genuinely didn't see the issue of if he was ignoring it. I supposed if you were guilty of armed robbery and stuff like that, stalking and investigating someone was nothing.

Screw it, he wouldn't understand. I should show him instead. And man, was I gonna make it sting.

My gaze flicked quickly to his car, and then I smiled and patted his knee. "You're a nice asshole, I'll give you that."

He was visibly relieved he hadn't pissed me off.

"Thank you for the presents." I stowed away everything neatly in the biggest box. "When did you have time to buy all this?"

"Sunday," he replied. "We were in the city for Mass anyway."

Because who wouldn't drive two hours just to go to church?

"I'm pretty sure there's a Catholic church in Gettysburg."

"That's not the same." He shuddered. "The thing about Father O'Malley is he'll be there for confession *and* drinking you under the table. He holds the record in our parish."

"I guess having so much faith makes you thirsty."

Finnegan let out a loud laugh. "I gotta tell him that one. That's funny."

I looked away to hide my grin, and he lit another cigarette. So far, so good. We hadn't fought yet.

"One more thing," he said, and he left the smoke dangling between his lips as he patted his pockets. "These terms are up for negotiation, but this is what I'm offering if you marry me." He handed me an envelope folded in half. "Don't read it now."

"Because you don't wanna piss me off?" This might've been the last thing I wanted to think about.

"Right on the money."

Fuck that. I wanted to see just how much money a marriage was worth. I opened the envelope and ignored Finnegan's protest. He should've known better. If he didn't want me to read it now, he could've given it later. Or never.

"Maybe I should go—"

I clamped my hand down on his thigh. His *firm* thigh. "Down, dog."

A low growl rumbled from him.

Crossing one of my legs over the other, I smoothed out the paper and scanned the terms first. Like Sarah and Patrick, we'd be married at least three years. Intimacy wasn't required, or expected, but there would be more money involved for me if our marriage resulted in children. My breathing hitched at that. *Children.* There wasn't a snowball's chance in hell I'd bring children into a business deal.

I had to accompany Finnegan to all family events and social gatherings unless I was ill.

"I'd need a lawyer before even going near a contract," I muttered.

"I'd pay for one," he was quick to say. "Anyone you want. You'd pick him."

"Or *her*."

"Or her."

I sighed and continued reading.

I had to travel with Finnegan when he expected it. "Travel?" I questioned.

He inclined his head. "I'm not working at the moment. When I go back, I'm on the road a lot. I want you with me."

Right. I bet owners of security firms went all over the place. Made total sense.

"We're not talking some security convention in Denver, are we?" I tilted my head at him.

His mouth twitched. "More like car shows in Italy and Germany."

The glare was switched on in a heartbeat, and he'd fucking failed at not pissing me off.

"Emilia, I run the security at exhibits sometimes. It's nothing weird—"

"Ha!" I scoffed and shook my head. *Run security.* Sure. I hadn't forgotten his criminal charges and his knack for finding himself in possession of high-end cars that didn't belong to him.

Shit. I had to tell Agent Caldwell about this.

Next on the list was infidelity. If I cheated on Finnegan, the contract would be terminated, and I'd lose the financial rewards. If we had children, I'd surrender the custody of them too. Yikes. The man was passionate about fidelity.

I frowned and read on. "There's not a single word on what would happen if *you* were unfaithful."

He scowled. "Why the fuck would I be unfaithful? That's ridiculous."

I rolled my eyes. "And me being unfaithful isn't? Christ. You suck at writing contracts."

"This isn't a contract. It's a first draft of my terms."

Yeah, whatever.

Then there was money. A lot of it. Aside from being provided for and given access to Finnegan's funds during our marriage, I'd receive a million dollars for each year I was married to him. At the termination of our marriage, I would receive another two million before walking away. And on the day we got married, he would open an account in my name with two-hundred-and-fifty thousand dollars.

These kinds of sums meant nothing to me because I couldn't grasp how much it was.

I remembered being over-the-moon happy once when I won fifty bucks at a fair. Until Dad had taken it from me.

What Finnegan was offering was insane by my standards.

Well, at least I wasn't pissed. I was numb. Almost indifferent.

At the sound of gravel crunching, I looked up and saw a familiar old woman walking across the parking lot with her dog. And that was the world I lived in. I was staying in my friend's motel room because my dad hated me. I worked at a diner, and the woman walking her dog came in after church every Sunday and ordered tea and a lemon square.

I didn't travel around the world, wear fancy clothes, and have millions of dollars.

Finnegan set the boxes on the ground and shifted closer, his hand resting on my back. "Marry me, Emilia. I swear I'll make it worth it for you."

I swallowed uneasily and side-eyed him. "You're crazy," I whispered. I didn't trust my voice.

"First time I heard that all day." He tucked a piece of hair behind my ear. "Marry me."

I smiled ruefully and shook my head. "I can't."

"I'll keep asking."

Hopefully, I'd keep saying no.

chapter

9

Emilia Porter

"Sarah, I need another pep talk!"

"Coming!" She hurried out of the bathroom and met me by the dresser by the window. I'd been minding my own business and attaching the straps to my new too-expensive shoes when a wave of doubt had crashed down on me.

Thankfully, I could count on Sarah.

She was beautiful. She was all midnight blue silk, red lips, and class.

She grasped my shoulders and gave me a firm expression. "They're criminals. They don't deserve your guilt for accepting gifts. They're using us for their mobster shit."

I nodded and breathed deeply.

"You have to assume everything they do comes with an agenda," she went on. "They're smart people, Em. They've been doing this for generations, and that includes arranged marriages."

Another nod from me.

"We're not their new family members." Her voice softened. She knew I struggled with this part. "We're a business tool for their gains. We can't let them manipulate us."

"You're right." And...exhale. "They'll be getting married either way. It doesn't matter to them who the girls are."

"Exactly. You've got this."

I got this.

I don't got this.

"Okay, they're here." I let the curtain fall again, and I checked myself in the mirror for the millionth time. Sarah had told me to keep my hair down today, and she'd done my makeup. It was heavier than what I was used to.

I'd gotten more practice walking in heels, though. It was the little things in life.

"I'll be right out!" Sarah hollered from the bathroom.

There were three quick raps on the door. Before opening it, I took a deep breath and repeated my new mantra for myself. *It's okay to enjoy this, it's business, you're using each other, it's okay.* One day, maybe I'd believe it.

I froze upon opening the door, 'cause it wasn't Finnegan or a man who could possibly be his brother standing there. It was a kid. Less skyscraper-tall and more...my height. He was dressed sharply, and that included a tilted fedora. Then there was a big, dimpled grin.

"You must be Emilia!" Oh, he was Irish. Actually Irish, not way-back Irish like Finnegan. "I'm Alec. It's lovely to meet ye."

He drew a curious smile from me, and I shook his hand. "You're Finnegan's cousin?"

"Aye, love. Where's Sarah? I wanted to escort you to the car." He winked and tipped his fedora.

I gigglesnorted, charmed by his easy manners. "She'll be out in a minute."

"Okay, then." He offered his arm. "I don't mind going twice. Let's go, Tush."

I let out a laugh and grabbed my phone from the dresser, tucking it into the little pocket in my dress. "Do I wanna know what prompted that nickname?"

"Oh, that's the boss. Finn's been talking about it."

Sweet Jesus. Was that actually true? Looking up, I spotted Finnegan and whom I assumed was Patrick. I'd already been informed they'd pick us up in the older brother's Jeep.

They definitely looked related. Same height, same hair color and style, though Patrick was clean-shaven, and his eyes appeared lighter. He carried more bulk than Finnegan too.

Similar clothes, suit pants and dress shirts, matching smirks.

"Alec was eager to meet you." Finnegan met up with us and grabbed my hand, brushing a kiss to my knuckles. I shivered and blamed it on the chill in the air. It didn't help that my dress was both short and strapless. "Cub, you're missing one."

"I'm going back for her now." Alec mimicked Finnegan by kissing the top of my other hand, and I chuckled. He was too cute.

Then it was just Finnegan and me for a moment.

"You're so fucking beautiful." He pressed a kiss to my temple. I blamed another breeze for my goose bumps. Oh boy. "Happy birthday. How does it feel to be eighteen?"

"It feels like any other weekday."

He laughed through his nose and put a hand on my lower back. "Let me introduce you to my brother."

Patrick reminded me of a bull in a china shop. His handshake was crushing, his smile was wide, and his voice carried. Seriously, my *hand*. "Happy birthday, Emilia. Good to finally meet you. Sarah told me she calls you Em. Mind if I do that too?"

Ow, ow, ow. I opened my mouth, to say something or to scream in pain. God, he was killing my hand *dead*.

"Dude," Finnegan said. "She probably reserves that for mates."

"She and I can be mates." Patrick finally let go of my hand, and I cradled it, feeling a bit sorry for myself. "Ain't that right, Em?"

"I *hurt*," I said and sucked in a breath. "Jesus. I feel for Sarah."

Finnegan punched Patrick in the arm. "What's wrong wit'chu? Huh?"

"It's fine." I shook off the pain—and the embarrassment—and averted my gaze when Patrick's contrite expression managed to make *me* feel bad. They were fucking sorcerers, the bunch of them. "It's nice to meet you too, Patrick. Sure, I guess you can call me Em."

He lit right up again.

Alec was back with Sarah, so Patrick forgot about us for the time being.

"Ma dropped him a lot as a baby," Finnegan said. "Possibly on purpose."

I grinned and stared at the ground.

Patrick introducing Sarah to Finnegan was a less dramatic event. Finnegan shook her hand like a normal person and nodded politely. Then we piled into Patrick's Jeep, and Alec called dibs on the middle seat.

"He'll be on better terms with the girls than us before we reach the house," Finnegan muttered, buckling up in the passenger's seat.

"That's 'cause I'm irresistible, boss," Alec quipped.

"And humble," Sarah noted with a smirk.

I chuckled under my breath and fastened the seat belt.

Alec dominated the conversation all the way out of town and during a quick trip along the highway. He spoke rapidly about the evening they'd planned, from dinner, which would be the "first barbecue of the year," to the music he was gonna play if he could convince Finnegan to join. Then when Patrick took the next exit, Alec changed the topic to sleeping arrangements. Apparently, the guesthouses weren't ready, same with the main house, so we'd all shack up in Patrick's and Finnegan's houses.

Sarah and I would see about that. I had every intention of returning to the motel room.

Civilization was left behind when Patrick drove onto a narrow road that went straight into a forest.

It would suck to be murdered here.

They probably wouldn't do that with a kid around, though.

I side-eyed the black trees we blurred past before a small movement caught my eye. It was Finnegan's wolfish smirk in the side-view mirror. It was as if he knew what I was thinking, and he shook his head, amused.

I scowled.

A few minutes later, Patrick slowed down, and a wide gate came into view. He rolled down his window and swiped something.

The gates opened slowly, revealing...*wealth*. Franny had told me it was called a compound. I'd like to change it to their own freaking community. A paved road led up a hill toward a cul-de-sac and what looked like the main house Alec had talked about. It appeared ready to me, but maybe they were doing interior work. It had three floors and looked very modern.

On the right side of the road was the construction site for three cottage-like houses. Alec eagerly informed us those would be the guesthouses. Then to the left was Patrick's house, followed by Finnegan's. Either they had a big family or a lot of guests coming and going.

Finnegan's car was parked on the grass by the half-built cottages.

"The other side of the hill is prettier," Alec mentioned. "It's where Uncle Shan's building Aunt Grace's garden." He scratched his nose. "I wanted to push Ness into the duck pond, but Pat said I couldn't."

The rest of us chuckled, and I processed everything in awe. Or as best as I could in the dark. No wonder they had so many people working on the property. It was huge.

Patrick parked next to Finnegan's Aston, and we got out of the car, my heels instantly sinking down into the grass. Finnegan was quick to steady me, and I sent him a small smile.

"I don't know about you guys, but I'm starving," Patrick announced.

We crossed the private little road and were shown between the brothers' houses. They shared an enclosed backyard, and a barbecue area was waiting for us on Patrick's side. The coziest-looking one I'd ever seen.

It was lowered a couple feet into the ground and lined with four couches and had a fire going in the center. A pergola with thick vines and mosquito netting covered the pit, and I kind of wanted to make it my home. Potted plants and trees made up for the lack of greenery on the ground. There was no grass at all in their backyard, and an empty pool took up most of Finnegan's side.

"This is beautiful." I pinched Finnegan's middle.

He sent me a wink, then continued farther in with everyone but Sarah and me. Perhaps she was a little stunned too.

A young girl appeared from Patrick's house and declared we'd taken *forever* to arrive and that she was gonna die if she didn't eat soon. In turn, Finnegan introduced us to Nessa before leaving us behind entirely. He, Patrick, and Alec were going to get this barbecue started, and we girls were ordered to get comfortable.

I had *no* problem with this. The plush couches had pillows and blankets everywhere, and I was the first one to remove my heels and get cozied up on one of the sofas.

True to Finnegan's word, his cousins were fun kids. Nessa quickly told us she was the one to go to if we wanted dirt on the boys. She also informed us we couldn't have picked better boyfriends, and Sarah and I exchanged a wry look at that. If only Nessa knew how little *choice* had to do with this.

We didn't mind some gossip about Finnegan and Patrick, though, and Nessa shared some stories that were well-known in the family. Such as the time Patrick got high in school and tried to bribe himself free from the principal's office with Monopoly money. Or the time Finnegan was little and lost sight of his mother, then proceeded to yell, "Find my mommy, or I shoot!" all over the store. Apparently, Grace had been right with him the whole time.

"Aunt Grace has a whole book of funny memories," Nessa giggled. "I read it every time I visit."

It was too surreal for me to laugh and get lost in the moment, but I found myself hiding a permanent grin behind my hand.

In the meantime, the guys went in and out of the house with food, snacks, drinks, and whatever else they needed. There was a big grill by the wooden fence, so I assumed they wouldn't be using the fire we had right here.

"You talking smack about us, doll?" Finnegan exited the house carrying an old wash tub, and he walked down the three steps to us. As he set it down by the fire, I saw it was full of ice and bottles of beer and cider.

"It's my job to," Nessa said.

"If you say so," Finnegan chuckled. "Let me know if it gets cold, ladies. We can bring out the heaters."

No, the fire was working wonders, as were the dozens of blankets. "You guys need a hand?" I offered.

"Nope. You sit tight, princess. Help yourselves to the drinks— uh, not you, Ness. There's soda for you in the kitchen."

Nessa was adorably put off.

See, it didn't make sense for Finnegan to call me princess. I was anything but. Nessa, on the other hand, looked like one. She shared the same dark hair and green eyes as her twin brother, and she was rocking a pretty dress and a hair band with a cute bow on it. Wasn't that what princesses wore? Strip me of my new clothes, and you'd find stained hoodies and jeans that were too big.

Finnegan disappeared inside again, and I watched him pause by the entertainment center in Patrick's living room. Alec joined him there, and the two scrolled for a playlist after docking Finnegan's phone.

After a minute, it was clear that they were bickering.

It was too funny to watch. Patrick passed them, smacked them both upside their heads, and ordered them to "just pick something."

"Em." Sarah sat across from me and extended a bottle from the tub. "I think you'll like this."

"Thanks." I read the label, and it was some wild berry cider. Twisting off the cap, I took a tentative sip, only to quickly take another. It was amazing. I had a whole world of alcoholic drinks to discover. This one was sweet like raspberry soda but carried a kick from whatever booze was in there.

My limited experience with parties had introduced me to vodka cranberry, beer, and something I wasn't sure anyone could name. Basically, Jimmy had taken a little bit of everything in his parents' liquor cabinet and thought it'd be a good idea to mix it all together with OJ.

It'd been a terrible idea.

Once Patrick got the grill going, everything was coming along quickly. The music that poured out of the living room was unmistakably Irish, and the wide edge of the fire pit filled with condiments, salads, chips, dips, and buns.

I was eyeing the guacamole quite possessively. Avocados were always so expensive at the store.

"Credit to my brother for this." Finnegan grabbed himself a beer from the tub and sat down next to me. "He almost had my head when I suggested we cater."

Sarah looked over at Patrick curiously. "You cook?"

Patrick flashed a modest smirk, if there was such a thing.

"He manages to hurt himself every fucking time," Finnegan said, "but he does all right."

Alec jogged down to join us and planted his butt next to Nessa, and he had drinks for the two guys. "He cut his finger in the kitchen."

"It didn't fall off," Patrick defended. "That's what matters."

I snickered and took another swig of my cider.

Patrick soon returned inside, and when he came out again, he was carrying a tray. The delicious smell hit me the second he set it down, and I saw everything from baked potatoes and paper cones packed with fries to mac and cheese and something that was fried. Finnegan popped one in his mouth, complained that it was hot as fuck, and said they were mozzarella sticks.

"Things that come straight from the oven are usually hot," Patrick told him.

Finnegan flipped him off and guzzled his beer to cool the burn.

I looked away and stifled my laughter.

Patrick left the pit one last time to grab the rest of the food, which filled another tray table. Ribs, chicken, burgers, hot dogs, corn, and steak made for one happy Emilia.

"Hot damn, Patrick." Sarah lifted her brows at the sight of all food. "This is the sort of stuff you should bring up on dates. Not how much you can bench press."

A laugh escaped at that, and I shook my head. "Honestly?"

"What?" He sat down next to Sarah and flexed his muscles. "My girl's gotta know I'm strong."

Sarah rolled her eyes and sipped her drink.

"He'll get there," Finnegan said, though I wasn't sure he believed it. "Okay, everyone. Barbecues are always fantastic, but today's about Emilia. Before we dig in—a toast to our new adult." He lifted his beer, and the others followed suit. "May you live to be a hundred, with an extra year to repent. *Sláinte, a stóirín.*"

"*Sláinte!*" the other Irish folk hollered.

My face hurt from smiling, and I had the strongest urge to scoot closer to Finnegan. This was the whole fucking problem. He made me want what I shouldn't.

"Thank you." I swallowed hard and maintained my smile, not wanting anyone to know these things shook me up. "This means a lot to me." I couldn't do nothing, so fanned out my blanket over Finnegan's lap and found his hand under the soft fleece.

He gave my hand a squeeze and threaded our fingers, something that made my heart ache. I was so failing. I couldn't fail harder. And there was no way I could tell Sarah I wasn't as strong as she was.

She might think it was okay to enjoy myself, but this went beyond plain enjoyment.

Everyone filled their plates, and when Sarah asked what the Irish words meant, Alec and Patrick were happy to give her an Irish 101, the CliffsNotes version. Patrick admitted he and his brother were far from fluent, though short sayings and phrases had traveled down the generations. In Ireland, people wished each other good health when toasting, and Alec made a joke about *Sláinte* being the most popular word for that reason. 'Cause the Irish and their drinking...

I sat back a bit and tuned out. And Finnegan did too. Maybe he sensed something was off with me. It wouldn't surprise me.

I hadn't heard from my dad today. I'd told him I had a phone now, and I'd left him the number on the fridge. His only comment was we could sell the phone.

"Hey." Finnegan shifted closer and put his arm around me. "You look far too troubled for being a birthday girl."

I mustered a weak grin. "I'm fine."

"You're full of it, that's what you are." He pressed a kiss to my temple. "You know I wanna give you this, right? This life, I mean—I want it to be yours too." He cracked my heart wide open with those words, and I could've kicked him in the shin. "I don't see just the business arrangement."

I glanced up at him, unsure and with a knot in my stomach the size of a mountain. "What do you see?"

He shifted my hair over my shoulder. "What you and I do is private. I understand we wouldn't be marrying for love, but that doesn't make our union any less real. My family would be your family. The relationships you build with the people in my life would be genuine."

I shook my head. "Genuine for how long, three years? That's torture, Finnegan." I couldn't imagine being shoved into a family somewhat against my will, then fall for some of them, like Alec and Nessa, and say goodbye three years later.

Finnegan's mouth twitched, and he looked both miffed and amused. "Those three years are for you. A minimum. I'm a traditional man, so if it were up to me, we'd marry for life."

That made him even stranger than before. I couldn't grasp what he was saying—or how he could say it. No, I wasn't a romantic, but that didn't mean I never wanted to find love. Somehow, he'd be okay with marrying me—spend the rest of his *life* with me...

I shook my head quickly. Christ, what was I thinking? I was here to help the FBI, not indulge in fantasies about getting away from my miserable existence. Ugh, I was one pathetic pity partier. It ended now.

"Let's eat before it goes cold," I said.

chapter

10

Emilia Porter

"That never happened! Now you're just making shit up, kid."
Patrick mock-glared at Alec, who had an awesome poker
face. I'd been prepared to believe his story about Patrick falling into
the lake when going fishing.

"What can I say, I love to make the ladies giggle," Alec replied
with a sly wink.

I laughed and bit into a spicy piece of chicken, and Sarah
requested another story from their childhood.

"Preferably one that's true." Finnegan reached forward to add
more ribs to his plate. "I'm pretty sure I'm gonna burn Ma's scrap-
book next time we're in the city."

"I'll light the match for you," Patrick said.

Nessa and Alec whispered back and forth, maybe deciding
what story to go with, so Finnegan took the opportunity to steal the
spotlight, all while shoveling baked potato soaked in butter and
herbs into his mouth.

"I have a recent memory that still makes me chuckle," he said.
"Pat, you'll appreciate this." He paused and pressed a fist to
his mouth.

"How about you eat slower?" I suggested.

"But it's so fucking good." He stifled a belch and went on. "I was telling Emilia about Father O'Malley." Oh shit, the story was about *me*? "I mentioned to her that he's the kind of priest who will hear us out and then join us in drinking contests."

"I love that old fucker." Patrick wore a fond smile. "Only reason I go to Mass."

Interesting. He wasn't as religious as Finnegan?

"So Emilia went, 'I guess having so much faith makes you thirsty,'" Finnegan finished, cracking up.

Patrick found that funny too, as did Alec and Nessa, and I didn't really see it. It'd just been a witty retort, not some grand joke.

"Your dates seem a hell of a lot more interesting than ours," Sarah noted wryly.

"*Ouch*, woman." Patrick narrowed his eyes at her. "I have a great time seeing you."

Sarah stared at him for a beat, then slid her gaze my way. "Last date, he asked what cup size I wear."

I winced and licked barbecue sauce off my finger. "Classy. But it could've been worse. Finnegan stalks me to answer his own questions about me."

"Hey. It means I care," Finnegan defended.

"Remind me why you're dating them?" Nessa asked.

Sarah and I laughed.

Alec came to the guys' rescue by sharing another story from this elusive book of memories. Each one offered a glimpse into the O'Shea family, and they left me so conflicted. We were all in stitches as Alec told us about when Patrick and Finnegan took classes in music and how they tried to one-up each other by pranking their instructors. I learned Finnegan played something called the tin whistle, which was basically an Irish flute, and rather than being made of wood, it was metal. Important stuff to know, according to Alec and Finnegan.

Finnegan had filled his teacher's whistle with tobacco once and left a lighter with a bow around it as a gift.

"Good God," I spluttered.

"He smelled like a fucking chimney," Finnegan argued.

"And you thought more tobacco would help?" I stared at him incredulously.

"I'm more surprised they have those classes here," Sarah chuckled.

"They probably don't." Finnegan squinted in thought, then shrugged. "This was over a summer. We usually spend those in Ireland."

"We stayed at the boss's house there last year," Alec said. "You'll love it, Tush."

I didn't know how to respond. Would I ever even see another country? I didn't have a passport.

Thankfully, Nessa ran interference and put us back on track. Where Alec and Finnegan had a special connection, Patrick and Nessa shared a similar bond, and they loved to tease each other. She told us about when Patrick learned how to play guitar; he'd rubbed itching powder on the strings of his classmates' instruments.

"You're on thin ice, squirt." Patrick wagged his fork at her.

She batted her lashes.

"Oh! What about the piano incident?" Alec guffawed. "Aunt Grace still gets mad."

Finnegan groaned a laugh and pinched the bridge of his nose.

"What did he do?" Sarah chuckled.

Alec filled us in. "She paid some expensive guy to teach Finn to play, and the boss superglued his own fingers to the keys—"

"And the teacher's," Finnegan added. "I wasn't supposed to get stuck, though."

I snortlaughed, not the prettiest sound, but that was too funny. Jesus, I couldn't imagine growing up in their house. I'd be on pins and needles the whole time. They'd obviously been hellions.

"Your poor mother." I nudged Finnegan's arm with my shoulder. In response, he gave me a smacking, barbecue-glazed kiss on the cheek, and I squeaked and pushed him away. "Gross!" I reached for the stack of napkins.

Sarah raised a brow at me but didn't say anything. She didn't have to. I knew she was wondering if Finnegan and I were closer than I let on, and I didn't know how I'd answer that.

"I'm so full." I blew out a breath and set my plate on one of the empty tables. Something sharp was digging into my hip as I got settled again, and I looked between Finnegan and me. "Something's poking at me."

"That's what she said," Nessa sang, and Alec whistled and waggled his eyebrows.

"You two are bad news," I told them, snickering. Finnegan solved the mystery, revealing his keys and a fob thing. It looked like the gadget Patrick had used to open the front gates. "Do any of these open your patio door? I need to use the bathroom."

"Yeah, sure." He stuffed a half a buttered roll into his mouth and handed me the keys. "Vhish one."

"Chew, swallow, talk," I supplied helpfully.

He grinned, his cheeks all puffed out.

Fuck, he was cute sometimes. I couldn't get past it.

"You know, my bathroom is closer, hon," Patrick offered.

"Nah, it's okay. It's snooping time," I joked.

"Let her stalk me. It's flattering." Finnegan helped me off the couch, and then I headed toward his house.

Finnegan's living room was spacious, though that's not why it felt empty. A sectional divided the space from the kitchen, and aside from that big couch, a table, and an entertainment center, there was nothing else. Maybe he was still decorating since he'd only recently moved in.

Everything smelled brand-new.

The moonlight and a small lamp in the kitchen guided me across the living room, past the stairs, and out into the hallway. There was a guest bath there, and I had to smile at the soap on the counter. There was no way Finnegan had chosen the things that went into his house. I could, however, picture his mother packing him these little star-shaped soap bars. They even matched the dark green towels and the rug on the floor.

After finishing up, I washed my hands and inspected my face in the mirror. If I didn't know any better, I'd say I was happier. There was a glow to me, something I thought was reserved for pregnant women.

Was I happier?

I certainly yearned more.

I left the half bath and glanced around me, intrigued by everything that revolved around Finnegan O'Shea.

I paused, catching sight of the stairs and all the photos that hung there. Too curious for my own good, I flipped a light switch and ascended the first few steps to look at the pictures. Four frames appeared to be missing. The nails were there. I guessed he was still unpacking.

Family was important to Finnegan, that much was becoming clear. And a *lot* seemed to go down in churches. There were pictures from at least seven christenings and three weddings. Nurse Walsh was in a couple of them, with a man I guessed was her husband.

I recognized Shannon O'Shea too, Finnegan's dad. Which would make the woman standing next to him Grace, the brothers' mother.

Shannon was older than Grace, and it was easy to see where Finnegan and Patrick got their looks. Shannon was equally tall, broad-shouldered, and solid.

Part of me felt like I was intruding. Every face had a smile or was in the middle of laughing, except for a few photos of Shannon and Grace. She looked at him with complete adoration, and he was very protective of her judging by how he held her. They were clearly in love, and it made me queasy. Did she know what her husband and sons did? Did she accept it? Was she involved too?

"That one's from their anniversary." Finnegan's voice caused my heart to jump, and I stood stock-still as he joined me, hands in his pockets. "I think it was their twenty-third."

Twenty-three years with a mobster. Plus the years that'd passed since then.

"Was, um, their marriage also arranged beforehand?" I asked hesitantly.

He nodded, gaze on the photo of Shannon spinning Grace on a dance floor surrounded by friends and family. "I missed this one." He quirked a hollow smile and added, "I was in prison."

"Of course you were." I took another step, toward a set of pictures of Finnegan and Patrick when they were younger. "How did your parents meet?"

"They've always known each other. Our families go way back."

Oh... Maybe that meant Grace *was* involved. The Sons of Munster consisted of the O'Sheas and the Murrays, and there'd been a time when the families were close. According to Wikipedia, anyway.

"Does that mean your mom was a Murray?" I wondered.

Finnegan gave me a sideways look and a smirk. "Have you been googling me, princess?"

"Shut up." I pushed halfheartedly at his arm.

He laughed quietly. "Aye, she was a Murray. Pop snatched her up when she was sixteen."

"Cradle robber."

"Ha! I'll have you know he was a perfect gentleman until they were given permission to marry a year later."

Married at seventeen. Patrick was born a year later, Finnegan told me.

There was another photo that drew me in. Finnegan young, no older than six or seven, and he was sitting next to an older man who was teaching him how to hold one of those tin whistles. There was a Christmas tree in the corner.

"Who's that?" I wondered.

114

"My grandfather." He studied the picture with a soft grin. "It was because of him I started playing the whistle. He used to say every generation needed a whistler."

His grandfather...would that be the former boss? Ronan something.

A picture of Finnegan and Grace was a safer topic. Christmas again, years later. He looked to be at least fifteen or sixteen.

"Your mother looks happy." Could one find happiness in a family like theirs?

"She's gonna love you and Sarah," he murmured. "She always wanted daughters."

I haven't said yes.

My throat closed up, preventing me from saying it out loud. Instead, I wondered what it'd be like to have a mom.

"Did they not want more children, or...?" I cleared my throat, my voice coming out raspy.

"I think they did." He looked pensive. "There were complications when she had me."

"Oh. I'm sorry."

He lifted a shoulder, then leaned it against the wall to face me better. "Did you enjoy dinner?"

"More than I should." I smiled and cranked up the playful scorn.

He smiled back. "There's still cake and more drinks."

"Really?"

He nodded and reached out, twisting a lock of my hair between his fingers. "Nessa made you a princess crown with a truckload of glitter. She may have crafted it in Patrick's closet so the glitter would magically rub off on his clothes."

My stomach clenched, and I looked down between us. I hadn't known the girl more than a couple hours. "She's funny. Alec too. I like them."

"I got you the cake. Do you like me too?"

I laughed silently and peered up at him. We were almost the same height with my standing a step higher. In heels.

"Oh, come on." He flashed one of his predatory grins and gently bumped his forehead to mine. "I've made you a little happy, haven't I?"

I bit my lip. "A little." I pinched two fingers to demonstrate.

"I'll take it." His eyes glinted with something devious. "Now, don't bite my head off. You're about to kiss me on the cheek because I've earned it, and it won't piss you off. Deal?"

"For chrissakes, Finnegan." I didn't know if I was complaining or finding him endearing. Perhaps a combination of both.

A girl had to pick her battles though, and this wasn't one of them. I surrendered with a shake of my head and an eye-roll in amusement. Sure, he could get a kiss on the cheek. My hands came to his upper abdomen, and I closed my eyes and leaned in.

What the—that wasn't his cheek. My eyes flew open. Then I froze. Our lips touched softly, and I noticed how his stomach tensed.

Rat bastard!

I screwed my eyes shut and fisted his shirt, torn between anger and, and...*want*.

The air suddenly grew heavy and electric, and I couldn't for the life of me move out of the way. My senses were invaded by his rich scent, and I was overcome by this stupid fucking attraction. He applied the smallest amount of pressure, testing the waters, and his hand ghosted up my arm.

No, no, no, no, this wasn't how it was supposed to go.

I caved when a violent shudder flowed through me. I couldn't help it. He'd been screwing with my head for weeks, and I didn't have any superpowers. I kissed him back tentatively, yet even the faintest action caused the wildest reaction inside me. Lust surged in my veins, and my pulse went through the roof.

Finnegan shuddered too, and he carefully cupped the back of my neck. All I could think about was how amazing it felt, how warm and comforting it was to be in his arms, how rock solid his body was. I betrayed myself and slipped my hands up his chest, and I deepened the kiss.

He sucked in a quick breath. Maybe he'd expected something else. Maybe he'd thought I would get mad. I didn't care at the moment, and he stopped holding back so much. At the first taste of him, I locked my arms around his neck and pressed myself closer.

He made my mind swim with every sensual kiss that grew hotter and hotter. My breathing accelerated, but instead of breaking away and trying to calm down, I became needier for him. He made a ravenous sound, almost like a growl, and it set me on fire. I whimpered and slid my tongue along his, and it still wasn't enough.

"Jesus fuck," he whispered raggedly.

"Don't stop yet—"

"I won't." He spun me and pressed me up against the wall, and that was so, so, so much better. His mouth returned to mine, and we made out like we'd done this for months.

I moaned and shivered as his hands got greedier. They roamed my back, my neck, my arms, and down my sides.

He hummed, stealing another drugging kiss, and teased his fingers along my bare thigh. The skin-on-skin contact sent ripples of desire through me. Tilting my head back, I exposed my neck for his trail of openmouthed kisses, and I wove my fingers into his hair to keep him close. His beard tickled and scratched in the most delicious ways.

"I think you like me, princess."

I couldn't like him. Yet...here I was, clinging to him as if he were the last man on earth and my only way to survive. He proved it again and again. When he stroked my thigh, I hitched it over his hip. When he kissed my neck, I gave him more access. When he sucked lightly on the spot below my ear, I turned liquid.

"Finnegan..." My voice came out thready and full of need.

He groaned and went all in. He gave me a burning kiss and

pushed harder against me. And I felt him...everywhere. I gasped, quickly spiraling out of control. He was hard as a rock and pressing where I shouldn't want him, but that didn't stop a rush of wetness from ruining my panties.

"We should stop." He broke the kiss and panted against my neck. "I don't wanna stop."

I exhaled a breathless laugh, too seduced to make any decisions.

I felt his smile on my skin as the moment slowly ended.

So why did it feel like the beginning?

There actually was cake. A big white one with chocolate decorations and my name on the top. It was my first birthday cake ever, and before anyone did anything stupid, like eat it, I had to take a picture of it with my flashy cell phone.

Nessa really had made me a crown too. Of pink craft paper and multicolored glitter, and it was attached to a diadem. I wore that shit proudly and ignored all warnings going off in my head. It was my birthday. I clung to the moment exactly like I'd clung to Finnegan. The guilt could eat me up tomorrow.

"Make a wish," Finnegan murmured in my ear.

I suppressed the umpteenth shiver and blew out the candles.

I didn't make a wish, for fear I'd wish for the wrong thing. Other than that, I belonged to the O'Sheas for the night.

Patrick and Finnegan introduced Sarah and me to Bailey's and whiskey drinks. After trying one of the latter, I abruptly switched to the former, and I stayed there. Cider and Bailey's. My night was complete. And cake! And I was getting tipsy. Fuck.

Alec became our DJ, and he tried relentlessly to get Finnegan and Patrick to break out the instruments so they could play some live music. Finnegan was the one who didn't seem sold on the idea, so Alec stomped inside to change playlists.

"Are you saying no to bug him or are you shy?" I teased Finnegan.

"I'm definitely not shy." At this point, he was half sprawled across the couch, and I had to look slightly over my shoulder to make eye contact. He was visibly relaxed and content, sipping his whiskey and sneaking little forkfuls of cake from my plate that was next to me.

"But you *are* hiding. Is there something interesting going on back there?"

He chuckled and raised himself up some, only to shift farther behind me and nearly nudge me off the couch. "Come here." He leaned back against the armrest and lifted his arm. I chewed on my lip, glancing over at Sarah, who was talking to Patrick and Nessa.

"Emilia."

I looked back at Finnegan, and he tugged me to him.

"I don't give a flyin' fuck what the others might think."

Not the others. Only Sarah.

Oh, screw it—goddammit, something was poking me again. It was the same freaking keys, only this time, they were in my own pocket. I pulled them out and was about to return them to Finnegan, but something stopped me.

"How mad would you be if I stole your car?" I asked.

He grinned. "You have no idea. Only I drive the Aston."

I smirked and dangled the keys. "I could jump up and run out to steal it right now."

"But you won't." To emphasize his certainty, he threaded his fingers together behind his head. "You wanna stay here with me and get cozy under the blankets."

I wasn't afraid of Finnegan anymore, and what I really wanted was some payback. I wanted to show I had guts. I wanted to catch *him* off guard, for once. And it was now or never, it felt like. I could do it. Finnegan had a blanket twisted around his legs, he wasn't in a very good position to charge, and he was too cocky to think I'd do a crazy thing like steal his car.

I was barefoot and ready to go.

I removed the crown from my head.

There was no way I could resist. Before I even registered it, I'd bolted up and out of the barbecue area, and I was darting between the houses.

"What're you doing, Em?" Sarah called.

"Emilia!" Finnegan shouted.

I ran faster, my heart hammering, and felt the damp grass under my feet.

I reached Finnegan's car. The alarm gave a beep as I turned it off and opened the door.

"Don't you fucking dare, Emilia!"

"Eeep!" I didn't know he'd be so friggin' fast.

He was running toward me when I pushed the start button. Forgoing a seat belt, I hurried to rev the engine, and I swore my heart soared at the sensation. *Holy shit, I'm doing this.* A loud song began blaring out of the speakers. Bagpipes met furious drums and heavy bass. I estimated Finnegan would reach the car in about three seconds, so I carefully stepped on the gas, and the car jerked forward. Okay, okay, it was a sensitive speedster. Got it.

Finnegan looked livid, caught in the headlights.

I laughed madly and eased forward a bit more.

Come at me, Irish boy.

He pointed next to the car. "Get outta the goddamn car." His growl was muffled but no less threatening.

It didn't matter.

He had this coming.

Raising two fingers, I gave him a salute, and then I was driving away from him, up toward the main house. A heavy breath gusted out of me, the adrenaline pumping freely. Both Finnegan and Patrick were visible in the rearview, once again running toward me. *Suckers.* I rounded the cul-de-sac and sped up. I passed them and their shouting and didn't slow down until I reached the gates.

I rolled down the window and pressed the key fob against the reader, and the gates opened.

"Emilia, I swear to fucking Christ!" Finnegan yelled.

"You shouldn't swear!" I shouted back, buckling my seat belt. "Just ask Father O'Malley!"

At that, the unmistakable sound of Patrick's laughter filled the air.

With the gates wide open, I flipped off the boys and floored it. The last thing I heard was Sarah's cheer and Nessa's "Best. Night. Ever!"

I flew down the road with life in my heart and euphoria swirling in my head. My heart kept pounding, completely seduced by the adrenaline rush, and maybe Nessa was right. Maybe this was the best night ever. One thing was sure. I'd never felt like this before. It was fucking wild.

chapter 11

Finnegan O'Shea

"How fast are you gonna marry her, bro?"

I blew out a harsh breath and watched as the taillights of my car became smaller and smaller. The girl was gunning it.

"I'd give her my name tomorrow if I could." I ran a hand through my hair, wondering where the *fuck* Emilia had come from. I was the one who'd barged into her life, yet she'd fucking blindsided me. She was *nothing* like I'd expected.

She infuriated me, made me laugh, turned me on unlike anything else, and did weird shit to my chest. It seized up every time I saw her.

Patrick looked over to where Alec and Nessa were lingering between the houses. Sarah wasn't there. "Youse can get ready for bed, kids. It's late."

Ness wasn't happy. "I wanna see when Em—"

"You heard him, doll," I told her, pulling out my phone. "Is Sarah spending the night?"

"Doubt it," Pat replied dryly. "You think Em's staying?"

"She is if I have any say." I pressed call on her number and put the phone to my ear. "You'll get closer to your girl if you quit acting like a Jersey juicehead. She doesn't care about your gym routine, big brother."

"Yeah, yeah." Patrick lit up a smoke.

Emilia wasn't answering, so I sent a text to my car. She'd see it popping up on the dashboard screen.

Get back here right now.

Christ, she'd actually taken my wheels. I couldn't fucking believe her. Even as the anger continued to surge, I wasn't sure it was directed at her. I was usually spot-on when reading people, except this time.

"Em's good for you," Patrick noted. "You seem more like your old self lately."

I nodded, having realized that too. Being away from work in the city was frustrating the ever-loving fuck outta me, but she was making it easier to pass time. When I was around her, I didn't think about the syndicate or my crew.

"I wanna bring her to the city this weekend," I said.

His brows lifted. "To meet the folks?"

"Yeah. You think it's too soon?"

He shook his head. "Ma will adore her."

I fully believed that too. More than that, I believed it would help sway Emilia. The girl needed family, and I could give her that.

"Patrick." It was Sarah, appearing between the houses with her purse. To be honest, I was having a difficult time reading her too. Fuck, this was gonna put a dent in my ego. I couldn't decide if she'd be good for my brother. "It's getting late, and I think I'd like to leave."

I observed her and lit up my own smoke.

"You don't wanna stay?" Patrick rubbed the back of his neck. "Em will probably be back soon, and you two can share a guest room if you want."

Nah, fuck that. I wanted Emilia a lot closer and a lot more to myself.

"No, thank you." Sarah cleared her throat and hugged herself a bit. It was probably cold in that dress, something my oblivious brother should pay attention to. "I expect Finnegan to drive Em home when she returns. I'll wait up for her."

You might have to wait a while.

I narrowed my eyes and took a slow drag, realizing Sarah could be any girl—one that I ended up with. She wasn't frigid or ungrateful; she was savvy and in it solely for the payout. In that respect, she was smart. Maybe smarter than Emilia. But was it really about brains? Or was it about the fact that Emilia might be awakening a new side of herself?

She stole my fucking car and had attitude. I just needed to dig it up a bit more and see what else was revealed. Unlike Sarah, Emilia had emotions involved, and I craved every ounce of them.

I'd have to keep my eye on Sarah, even though Emilia was the one who thought she was helping the Feds.

Patrick wanted Sarah to stay, that much was clear, but he wasn't gonna push it. He told her he'd get his keys.

Sarah nodded in thanks, and then it was the two of us.

I tilted my head. "You're a calculating one, aren't you?"

Her head snapped up, and she jutted her chin. "Excuse me?"

I cracked a smirk, my mind spinning further. Whereas Emilia had been neglected and made to feel worthless by her son of a bitch father, Sarah had been pushed physically and abused. Emilia was raw, confused, and lost. Sarah was closed off, didn't trust anyone, and felt she only had herself.

I wasn't sure Patrick could break through her shell.

I was more grateful than ever that I *hadn't* ended up with someone like Sarah, but I felt for her. Never being able to rely on anyone else was no way to live.

"Never mind." I checked my phone and exhaled some smoke. No response from my little car thief. "I'll return Emilia to you when she's ready."

"If you hurt a single hair on her head—"

"You'll what?" I smiled. "Sarah, the last thing I wanna do is hurt her."

She snorted derisively. "Words mean absolutely nothing."

"Including your empty threat, then." I nodded at Patrick coming out of the house. "Your ride's here."

She gave me a once-over, the disdain clear, then turned on her heel and aimed for Patrick's car.

I laughed through my nose before jerking my chin at Patrick. "Let me know if you see my car wrapped around a tree." *Shite.* I'd meant it as a joke, but now I couldn't help but worry that Emilia might get hurt. She'd had a few drinks, and I could guarantee she'd never driven anything that could go from zero to sixty in under four seconds. "Motherfucker, I'm too young to get grays," I blurted out irritably. "She's gonna give them to me, mark my words."

Patrick laughed and opened the door to his car. "Calm your tits, Finn. I bet she's just taking it for a spin on the highway."

"That's supposed to make me feel better?" I asked incredulously. "Get the fuck outta here."

He felt the need to laugh harder than before.

———————

Half an hour later, I was about to flip my shit. The only thing that kept me from going out to chase her down was the text my brother had sent me. Emilia and Sarah had been in touch, and Emilia was on her way back.

I said goodnight to the kids and distracted myself by clearing away from the birthday dinner.

The dishes went to Pat's place. The leftover cake and food somehow ended up in my fridge.

My phone buzzed with a message from Kellan, and I flinched. Had Emilia really reported the events from her own birthday?

It shouldn't bother me. I'd lied to her a fuckload, painting myself as a more upstanding guy, and I hadn't told her about her mother.

I made a face and opened the text.

Congrats, ya gobshite. She said the date tonight was canceled.

"Fuck me sideways." I scrubbed a hand over my mouth, pure pleasure coursing through me. Followed by enough guilt to make me wince. At some point, I'd have to come clean to Emilia about Kellan. I loved him like a brother, and he had earned my trust repeatedly. It was only a matter of time before she discovered the truth.

And her mom...? How would I break that to her?

"More like *when*," I muttered to myself, and the answer was *after the wedding*.

At the sound of a car entering the premises, I stalked out of my house, though I could hear it was the Jeep.

"The twins asleep?" Patrick locked up and nodded toward his house.

"They're in bed anyway. You didn't see Emilia, I take it?"

"Afraid not—"

"Hold on." Just as the gates closed, I spotted a set of headlights. "Can you open the gates for me?"

Patrick and I jogged down there, and soon they were sliding open again. Emilia was idling some seventy-five feet away.

"You sure it's her?" he asked.

"Of course I am." Unless someone happened to be driving a car with headlights that close to the ground, it was her.

"Okay. I'm heading inside." He clapped me on the shoulder. "You're strapped in case, yeah?"

"Don't be so paranoid." I gave him a two-finger wave, and then I was walking out the gates.

Blinded by the headlights, I saw very little around me. The forest was pitch black, and the car wasn't more than a shadow behind two lights.

I was strung tight with anticipation. Impatient to make her mine. Pissed she took my fucking car. Proud for the same reason.

I took a final drag from the smoke, then flicked it away, and I was finally close enough to see the silhouette of her behind the wheel. Her hands were gripping it tightly. *Nervous?* Christ, I'd never get her out of my head, would I?

Not a scratch on the car as far as I could see. I brushed a hand along the hood until I was within reach to rap my knuckles on her window.

She lowered it a few inches and swallowed hard, and I rested my forearm on the roof, bending over slightly to get a better look at her expression. And it was a sucker punch right in the gut to see a hint of something feral in her eyes. It mingled with a dose of nerves, and it was sexy as fuck.

My mouth twisted up. "License and registration, please."

Her eyes narrowed briefly. "What if I don't have it with me?"

"Then I'm gonna have to ask you to step out of the car, ma'am."

Her façade broke, and a soft laugh slipped out. "I can't picture you as an officer."

"And I couldn't picture you as a car thief, yet here we are." I took a step back and folded my arms over my chest. "Get your sweet ass out here, princess."

She unbuckled her seat belt with a huff, then opened the door. Without her heels on, she was shorter than short, and she put her hands on her hips and stared up at me with half a scowl.

"I'll have you know I had a perfect reason to *borrow* it," she said stubbornly. "You're not allowed to get pissy."

"I'd love to hear that reason." I felt like a ticking time bomb, every part of me tense.

Had I ever seen something so exquisite? Her long, dark waves teased her hips, the fire was growing in her eyes, and she was just so fucking adorable. Like a feisty kitten, but one that could potentially cause some actual harm.

I was ready to eat her up.

She lost a bit of her bravery when I caged her in, my hands on the roof of the car. Her gaze flickered.

"Go on. I'm listening." I leaned in and grazed my nose along her jaw.

She trembled and flushed. "I-I...I wanted to know what it was like to drive it."

I eased off a bit, and it was my turn to narrow my eyes. I admit, I got irritated. "You could've asked, Emilia."

Just like that, her nervousness was gone. "But then it wouldn't have been a surprise, Finnegan." She pushed at my chest, and I backed off more. "Now I don't have to ask. Now I can tell you that it was un-fucking-believable to drive your car." *Fuck me sideways twice.* She gave me another shove, only to advance on me. "Are you surprised yet?"

More than she'd ever know. At the third shove, I turned the tables and pushed her back up against the car. I dipped down and covered her mouth with mine, swallowing her shock, and gave up on my heart rate. It was determined to skyrocket around this girl.

After the initial surprise that turned her into a stick, she melted into my arms and kissed me back. I cupped her jaw, sliding my tongue into her mouth, and she threw her arms around my neck.

"How fast did you go?" I asked, out of breath. My self-control took a hike, and I got a grasp of the backs of her thighs before hitching her up, wrapping her legs around me. "Tell me." I pressed my cock against her.

She gasped and exhaled a moan. "Ninety-five."

Fuck. Yes.

"That's my girl." I kissed her deeply, coaxing her tongue out with my own. "You'll break one hundred next time."

"Oh God, it was amazing." She started panting, and fuck me if she didn't try to pull me closer. "I felt like I was flying, and—shit," she whimpered as I gave her a slow, hard thrust and sucked on her neck. "The engine...so powerful... It was exhilarating and terrifying—*ungh*, please, Finnegan."

Hearing her talk, all breathy and desperate, turned me into a starved madman. A storm brewed inside me, tightening a knot in my stomach, and my cock almost hurt. *She* was exhilarating to me.

My teeth grazed her delicate skin. "Please, what? Tell me what you want, baby. I'll give it to you."

At her helpless, soft, "I don't know," I got a reality check. I swallowed dryly and hauled in a much-needed breath. As much I wanted to take this further, I didn't want there to be any regrets. For either of us.

"Spend the night with me," I whispered. "Not—not like that. Sleep in my bed. I won't let things go too far."

She shivered in my hold and flicked me an uncertain look. The conflict was written all over her, and I was ready for it to be gone.

Her flushed cheeks and the desire in her eyes lingered, only now she was more nervous than before.

"You can't fight this forever, Emilia." I kissed her again, slower this time. "You feel this, don't you? This, happening between us? It can't be just me."

Her fingers shook, and she played with the hair at the back of my neck. She nodded jerkily and lowered her gaze. "I feel it, but I'm afraid to get played. This could all be part of some elaborate—"

I kissed her to shut her up. "*Everyone* risks that when they meet someone. Fear of getting betrayed and left behind? That's not unique to our situation." I touched her cheek and searched her eyes. My gut told me her guard had never been lowered like this with me, and I *had* to take advantage. I had to get her to say yes. If not to my proposal, then to spend more time with me. "Give me one night—"

"I have school," she said at the same time. I was losing her; the fog was clearing, and I refused to let it happen. If she went home, she'd shake this, whatever it was, and I would go back to being a convicted felon and mobster. She would regret telling a fake agent that her birthday dinner had been canceled.

"Fuck school." I brushed her hair aside and cupped her neck.

"You need a break. Drop everything you hate and let me take care of you."

She covered her face with her hands. "You're horrible, Finnegan."

"I know," I chuckled.

I could taste her surrender. She was almost there.

I was a dick for playing with her emotions, but I'd show her. All she had to do was give me a shot. I'd take care of her. I'd treat her like a fucking queen, because I had a feeling she'd make me look like a king.

"I'm too weak for this," she laughed shakily. The defeat was everywhere. "I'll stay. One night."

She wasn't weak. She just needed to trip before she could come back with a bloody fucking vengeance and show everyone, herself included, what she was made of.

I was the manipulative son of a bitch who was going to make her fall.

"What're you looking at?"

"You." I continued watching her in the mirror as I unbuttoned my shirt, and she fidgeted with a lock of hair, taking in everything. She'd changed into one of my T-shirts, and I had no words for how that made me feel.

There wasn't much to distract herself with in my bedroom. Other than the bed, two nightstands, and a chair, I hadn't done anything with it. My mother had taken over and had the wall where the bed stood painted in dark red, and she'd ordered me to hang pictures there. They still sat in a box in the hallway outside.

Opening the closet that took up the opposite side of the bedroom, I threw my shirt in the laundry basket, and I discreetly removed the gun tucked into my pants.

Emilia stood awkwardly next to the bed.

At her sharp intake of air, I cringed and figured she'd seen it anyway, but that wasn't it. She was staring at my back, or more correctly, the Celtic cross and my last name.

"That's, um, one big tattoo," she mumbled and averted her gaze to the window. "Are you afraid you're gonna forget your name?"

I smiled to myself and shook my head. I never knew what she was gonna say, and I loved it. In a way, she was shaking me back to life.

As I removed my belt, I dug out the birthday gift I'd been saving. Now seemed like the perfect time.

"Be good, or I'll sleep naked." I dropped my pants and picked out a pair of sweats, then pushed off my boxer briefs too.

There was a squeak from Emilia. "Finnegan!"

"Relax. See?" I slipped into the sweats, pocketed the gift, and left the closet, tightening the drawstrings.

"I can't relax. I just saw your naked ass." She was looking anywhere but at me, and even in the low light of the lamp on the left side of the bed, her blush was clear as day. "Abs, hi. I mean, fuck. Christ."

I pressed my lips together to withhold the laughter, and that wasn't easy.

I was counting my blessings for getting her here, so I decided against pushing it and pointing out how flustered she was. Instead, I changed the subject.

"We gotta settle something important. What side of the bed do you sleep on at home?"

She eyed the bed, and her shoulders shook with a silent snicker. "There are no sides to my bed at home. You either sleep in the middle, or you fall off."

"Noted," I chuckled.

She shrugged and tugged down the tee. "I have no preference."

"Good, 'cause the left side is mine." It wasn't, but the left was closer to the door. I got under the covers, and it was impossible not to notice her awkwardness. I didn't take it personally. If my suspicions—and hopes—were correct, this was as new for her as it was for me. "Get in bed, princess."

"Fine." She slipped under the covers and stayed near the edge. "You promise you won't try to have sex with me?"

"I promise." I left the light on and rolled over to face her. It was time to give her some honesty on that topic, and hopefully, it would ease her fears. Of course, I wanted to dig first. "How did you handle sleepovers with past boyfriends?"

"What boyfriends?" She mirrored me to lie on her side, and she tucked her hands under her cheek. In the low light, her hazel eyes glowed with warmth. "In case it wasn't clear, I have no life. I work and go to school. Hobbies such as football and handing out V-cards are for other kids."

The relief to have it confirmed that she hadn't been with anyone hit me harder than I thought it would've.

"Last party I went to was over a year ago," she said with a quirk of her lips. "I've dated a little, but my main man was always the diner. He's a demanding fellow."

Oh, really. So she'd dated.

"Come here." I couldn't make sense of the tightness that had formed around my chest, but I wasn't a fan. Emilia shifting closer eased it a bit, though. "You're with me now," I murmured and met her in the middle. I stole a kiss, as if to remind myself I could and no one else had that privilege.

"Am I?" She ducked her head and fingered the chain around my neck.

I covered her hand with mine. "I'm working on it, anyway."

"Who's this?"

"St. Christopher."

She hummed and got settled on the pillow again. "He watches over travelers or something, right?"

That was a surprise. "You know of him?"

"Not really." She chewed on her lip, thinking. Debating. "My mom was Catholic." *Is. She is.* "All I have left of her is this little book about saints, and I used to read it a lot. There was one prayer to him—St. Christopher—that I memorized."

Wanting to keep her talking, I asked, "Do you remember it?"

She squinted. "Um. I'm not sure..."

"'Dear Saint Christopher, protect me today, in all my travels, along the road's way.'" I recited the beginning for her.

"Oh yeah." She smiled softly. "'Give your warning sign, if danger is near, so that I may stop, while the road—no, wait—while the path is clear. Be at my window, and direct me through...um.'"

"'When the vision blurs, from out of the blue.'"

Recognition sparked, and she finished the prayer without help. Then she snickered to herself. "We just went from talking about sex to a prayer."

"As religion intended it."

She laughed, finally looking more at ease.

I reached out and touched her cheek, just feeling like it. "Speaking of." I cleared my throat and got serious for a moment. "I don't believe in sex before I'm married, so when I say you don't have to worry, I mean it. It's important to me."

She blinked.

I stifled my amusement. This could go one way or the other, and I was used to both of them. She would either laugh or call me a liar. No one ever believed I was serious. No one of my generation, at least.

"You mean..." She furrowed her brow. "I mean... You mean what?"

I snorted under my breath and tugged at a lock of her hair. "I mean that I made a decision at an early age to abstain from girls and distractions like sex." I paused to let her process that. "A chick my brother went to high school with claimed he was the father of her unborn child, and it freaked him out. They had to do a paternity test, and the first one came out inconclusive, so lawyers got involved."

"Oh my God, you're serious," she mumbled, visibly stunned.

"My uncle has three kids," I went on. "My aunt isn't the mother to any of them—"

"Nurse Walsh?"

"No, on my mother's side," I replied. "I work with men who fuck around and have more kids than they can count. They're always surrounded by drama—"

"Finnegan." She scooted even closer and kissed me quickly, her cheeks turning pink. "You don't have to explain yourself."

It was my turn to furrow my brow. She didn't react right. What the fuck was wrong with her?

"You believe me?" I questioned.

She scrunched her nose and lifted a shoulder. "I figure, of all things, this is one you have no reason to lie about. No offense, but in today's society, having never had sex at twenty-five is kinda...well, you know. Lame."

I muffled my laughter into my pillow before remembering I had her here, and I could force her to join me. Yanking her flush to my body, I sank my teeth into her neck and tickled her rib cage.

"No! Fuck you, *no!*" She let out a shriek and smacked my chest hard enough to make me flinch and hiss. "You freaking savage. You *bit* me!"

I groaned out the last laugh and rubbed my chest. "Mental note. She's ticklish as fuck, and it makes her violent."

"And don't you forget it." She puffed out a hard breath and flopped onto her back. "Goddammit, Finnegan. Why can't I hate you anymore? Things were so much easier back then. Ahh...last week, how I miss you." She scrubbed her hands over her face and sighed. "Today has been..." She swallowed, maybe at a loss, and so was I. Maybe on edge too, for fear of what she'd say. Then she tilted her head at me and offered a small smile. "Thank you. Today was amazing."

Thank fuck. More relief, and my chest expanded with it. The way I reacted to her was bewildering at times, to be honest. Correction: how much I reacted. It was one thing to find her irresistibly beautiful, funny, and intriguing. Even our chemistry was a great fortune. But I couldn't afford to lose my head over this girl.

What we had now was perfect, if only she'd agree to marry me already. Actually, if she agreed to be my wife for life rather than three years, it would be perfect. But I'd settle for those three years, and I'd achieve my goal. After which, there would be a lifetime of other goals, not to mention risks. And love would jeopardize that. I'd grow lazy and lose track of my priorities. Just look at my father. While he'd been a top earner for decades, the syndicate wasn't his top priority. He didn't care about advancing.

No, what I wanted from Emilia was companionship. A partnership and loyalty. The passion was a fantastic bonus.

Being away from my crew and Philly was fucking with my head.

"Now you look all..." Emilia reached out and eased a finger over the spot between my brows. "Don't frown. Say something cocky like, 'I knew you'd like it here today, princess.'"

Her impersonation of my voice failed miserably, and I chuckled and grasped her wrist. I found her fingertips and pressed a kiss to them.

"I knew you'd like it here today, princess." I smiled and rolled on top of her, enjoying the surprise in her eyes, and got settled between her legs. "It's not over yet. Remember I said I was saving one gift?"

She opened her mouth, promptly closed it, then opened it again. "If it's in your pants, I'll—"

"You'll what?" I gave her a slow thrust, which was a *bad* fucking thing. I'd only shot myself in the foot. The hitch in Emilia's breath didn't improve my situation, and I felt a ball of lust dropping to my gut. "Tempting." I leaned down and nipped at her bottom lip. "And, technically, the gift *is* in my pants. Check my pockets."

She couldn't hide her blush from me, and I didn't move off of her.

"It's not what you think it is," I said when she located the little jewelry box.

"Okay," she answered warily and held the box. "Because it looks like a box you'd give someone who's said yes to something."

"And you haven't done that." *Yet.* "Open it." For this, I sorta needed my hands, so I reluctantly returned to lie next to her. "Ever heard of a Claddagh ring?"

"No...?" She pushed herself up a bit to inspect it closer, her hair falling forward. "It's so pretty." She touched the old silver carefully, tracing the design of the two hands holding a heart, and the little crown above the heart.

I copied her position and supported myself on my elbow. "There are a lot of traditions and legends about this ring. Some say suitors give them to the women they intend to marry. Some say mothers should give them to their daughters, and there are rules about how to wear it, with the heart pointing in or out. I was never any good with rules."

She smirked a little. "Shocking."

"Right?" I took the ring out of the box. "I'm creating my own rule." I slid the ring onto her left index finger, and thank fuck it fit. It used to belong to my grandmother, and it'd been too small for her in her final...sixty years.

"The heart is pointing in now," Emilia said.

I nodded. "And when you're ready to accept my family as your own, you turn it outward to represent your heart being open to them."

"Finnegan," she whispered.

"I want nothing more than to give you another ring, one that's just for you and me," I murmured. "But this is for family. They'll love you, and I think you'll love them too."

She swallowed hard and nodded with a dip of her chin. Maybe she was choked up and conflicted and didn't know what the fuck to do or say. I couldn't blame her. She blinked when her eyes got glassy.

Without saying anything, she cuddled up against my chest and nudged my arm, silently telling me I should be a good boy and put it around her. I had no problems with that, and before getting settled a last time, I reached behind me to turn off the light.

"Get some sleep, baby." I kissed the top of her head, lingering and breathing her in. She wasn't even moving or saying anything, yet she was doing weird shit to my chest again. It felt...fucking incredible to have her in my arms like this, and I tightened my hold on her.

Stay. Focused.

Fuck.

chapter 12

Emilia Porter

Finnegan scowled at me. "I fucking swear. Why do you keep doing that?"

Because there was nothing cuter than a morning-grumpy Finnegan wearing a scowl, that was why. With sleep-tousled hair, sheet lines on his chest, and his forehead creased in dismay, he tried to shovel leftover birthday cake into his mouth, and I was the jerk who batted away his fork.

Three forkfuls of cake were currently splattered on the patio where we were sharing a lounger next to the empty pool.

Spring was warm this morning.

"You're cute." I poked his nose.

"I'm *hungry*, and you keep wasting my food."

I pointed at the cake. "That's not food. It's dessert." Which was why I was eating heated-up baby back ribs and a baked potato. Like a normal person. "Cake at eight in the morning isn't good for you." I licked barbecue glaze off my upper lip.

"We can have this conversation when you eat oatmeal instead of pig for breakfast." He let out a playful growl and nibbled on my cheek, and I laughed and squirmed on his lap. "We should probably head inside soon. I'm surprised the twin hurricanes haven't woken up yet."

"But it's so nice here." I set our plates on the side table and got comfy. The sun felt amazing, and I was successfully shutting out the real world and all the guilt, dilemmas, and misery that came with it.

He hummed and hugged me to him. "You're cuddly in the morning. I like it."

I didn't answer, content to soak up this moment while I had it. There was no way I could know if I was cuddly, 'cause I'd never done it before.

Part of me knew I was starved for affection. The other part tried to deny that too.

Finnegan had a few more bites of cake and sipped his coffee, and the silence between us was so peaceful. There were birds chirping, for chrissakes. When did I ever pay attention to those?

"Hey. Gimme a kiss."

I can do that. I lifted my head from his shoulder and pecked him softly a few times. I kissed his smile, he kissed mine, and then we sort of eased into a lazy make-out session that made my toes curl.

His hand came up my thigh, raising goose bumps in its wake, and he paused right below my ass. I couldn't stop kissing him. Slow was good. Slow was great. As long as I didn't have to stop. Tasting chocolate, buttercream, and coffee on his tongue, I squirmed around a bit more until I was seated sideways on his lap, and that way I could more easily play with the hair along his neck.

"Marry me," he whispered.

I shivered forcefully, and my mouth stretched into a grin. "No."

"You like that I keep asking, don't you?" He grasped my chin and swept his tongue into my mouth before pecking me twice. "Give me the truth, Emilia."

I buried my face in the crook of his neck. His perfectly trimmed beard tickled my cheek. And at this angle, it did look perfect. Too perfect. I bet he went to a barber. No one could do that on their own.

"Emilia..."

I made a noise of complaint. "Do we have to talk about this now?"

"I wanna know."

I sighed and fidgeted with the quarter-sized St. Christopher medallion around his neck. The gold glinted in the sun.

"It makes me feel special," I confessed. "I know I'm not, but—"

"You are." He wrapped my hair around his fist and gently tugged my head back so he could make me look at him. "I chose you. You're more than a name on a list. You're..." He let out a small laugh and shook his head. "You're way outta my league. You're stronger than you think, you're smart—"

I snorted. "I'm an immature freaking mess."

"Because I overwhelm you." He dipped down and kissed me. "You've lived a sheltered life, you're neglected as shit, and you were forced to act like an adult way too early."

I dropped my gaze, feeling queasy. And way too exposed.

"Last word I'd use for you is immature," he murmured. "Inexperienced in life? Definitely. You *just* turned eighteen. But you're trying. You wanna do what's right—or what people claim is right. And it seems the last person who gets what you want when you do that is you."

I knew what he was saying, and he wasn't exactly wrong. There was a lovely ring on my index finger that whispered of family, a sense of belonging, and having a home. Being safe and protected. Cared for.

It all came down to trust. I couldn't trust Finnegan's word, and therefore, I couldn't trust his promises. Right?

"Have you ever killed someone, Finnegan?"

"Uh...not what I expected you to ask." He chuckled and reached for his smokes.

I left the little nook of comfort and sat up straighter. Because this was important.

He could tell, and his expression became gentler. "No, Emilia. I've never killed anyone." He gave my hand a squeeze. "I know the rumors you've believed about me, and most of them aren't true." He lit his cigarette and inhaled. "The O'Sheas—particularly my generation—have dealt a lot in expensive shit. Cars, art, jewelry. Collectibles. What you've heard...human trafficking? Rape?" He made a face, and his jaw ticked with tension. "All that is sickening to me. I may not have the highest morals, but the crimes I've been charged with don't make me a man without limits. Hell, I fire men who so much as slap their wives around."

An ounce of hatred trickled back inside me, and it was a good feeling. Though, it didn't mean much. He was so convincing that I started believing him.

"Are you still involved with that now?" I asked. "The cars and art, I mean."

He smirked. "Me? Nah."

I narrowed my eyes. That smelled so much of bullshit—and it hit me. Of course, he wasn't going to be completely honest. He didn't trust me, and why would he?

There was a big difference between his denouncing the crimes that made me sick, and what he was doing now, waving off the theft and stuff. He'd taken me seriously at first and answered. Hopefully, truthfully. He wasn't a murderer; he didn't deal with humans as objects. And then now...that cocky smirk when switching to cars and art. It was the word *alleged* all over again. He wasn't someone who'd say anything incriminating, but what if he was trying to be as obvious as he could? What if he was trying to tell me that no, he wasn't the man I'd accused him of. But yes, he did do some shady crap. He wasn't blowing smoke up my ass by claiming he was a saint.

"Ugh." I closed my eyes and rubbed my temples.

Could I live with someone who stole for a living? Sarah's talk about the future and everything we could do in three years made my heart hurt with longing, though not as much as the prospect of discovering what family was about.

It was the reason I'd acted on impulse last night and sent Agent Caldwell a message where I straight-up lied. I *lied* to a federal agent because Nessa had made me a pink paper crown, Patrick had cooked an awesome dinner for us, Alec had told me I was gonna love Finnegan's house in Ireland, and Finnegan... Finnegan was getting under my skin.

Agent Caldwell hadn't responded yet, maybe because we had plans to meet up tomorrow. And that thought drove a wedge of guilt into my chest. It sickened me, almost. I was going to meet up with him, and he wanted dirt on the people who seemed so fucking wonderful.

"Do you ever hurt anyone?" I asked hoarsely. "Physically, emotionally. Do you hurt people? Other than stealing."

"I don't steal, remember?" There was a hint of the same smirk from before. "Are you trying to bargain with yourself?"

No. Yes. Maybe. I don't know!

"Please answer me. I need to know." Or else I'd for sure lose my mind.

Finnegan took pity on me, and he watched me for the longest time. He exhaled some smoke through his nose and rubbed the back of his neck. "Okay. Honesty. Yeah, I sometimes hurt people. If they betray me or pose a direct threat, I have to defend myself and my family, and violence is a language everyone understands."

That was borderline incriminating. Maybe? Or maybe it wasn't, but it was one hell of a confirmation. Again, he wasn't painting himself as a saint. He admitted he hurt people sometimes. If they hurt him.

The only question now was, could I trust him?

If I thought the conversation on Finnegan's patio was uncomfortable, it had nothing on the feeling I got when we pulled up outside my house.

Once upon a time, there'd been a nice backyard with a picket fence and a lawn. These days, I couldn't separate the driveway from the patch that used to be green. The house used to be white. Now it was gray and dirty.

"Remember what I've said, princess."

It would be impossible not to.

"You can leave everything behind whenever you want. School, work, your dad. There's a new life waiting for you. Just give me the word."

I twisted the Claddagh ring around my finger, anxious. "I will. Thank you for everything."

He inclined his head. "My pleasure. I'll pick you up on Saturday."

Unless I changed my mind. He'd asked me to go with him to the city this weekend, and I'd accepted before he told me I'd meet his parents. The whole thing made me nervous.

Maybe if I could convince Sarah to come along with Patrick...

"Okay. Thanks again for everything—and I don't think you're getting this hoodie back." I leaned over to give him a quick kiss, and he wouldn't have it. He grabbed my jaw and deepened the kiss.

Goddamn him.

"I'm a call away." He pressed another firm kiss to my lips and touched my cheek.

I nodded, half dazed. Then I left his car and returned to reality. My stuff was still in Sarah's motel room, so I dug out the spare key from under a cracked pot and entered a house that reeked of stale beer and old food.

I stood there in the hallway, dressed in my birthday outfit and a hoodie of Finnegan's to cover up a bit, and I just stared. The low rumble of Finnegan's car told me he'd driven away. Was Dad—yes, he was passed out in his chair on a day when he should be at work.

It wasn't noon yet. Two photo albums were thrown on the floor next to the ratty chair, as were a couple Styrofoam containers and beer cans.

Bitterness seeped in and took hold of me. I wasn't his fucking daughter. I was here to clean up his mess and cover the bills he couldn't pay, nothing else. I was a tax cut.

Heading up the stairs, I changed into a pair of jeans and a tee. My shower would have to wait until after I was done cleaning this place. A place that disgusted me more every day. *Fuck* Finnegan for showing me what was out there.

I'd saved the big gift box that my first dress had arrived in, and I found myself stuffing it with the few things I cared about. The clothes and jewelry Finnegan had given me, my journal, my mom's book about saints, and his hoodie. The rest of my gifts were with Sarah, and I thought...I mean, maybe...if I saved up a bit, I could stay with her? I had a box under one of the floorboards with tips from the diner I'd stashed away. There were only a couple hundred dollars, but it was a start.

To make sure, I pulled out my phone and sent Sarah a text.

Hi, hon. When I've saved enough to cover half the motel room for a while, mind sharing with me? I can't stand being in this house anymore.

She was still in class, so I didn't expect her response until lunch time.

Last night when I told her I'd be staying over at Finnegan's, she'd told me to be careful.

I guess I'd failed.

Two hours later, Sarah had read my message but hadn't answered. I assumed she was busy with school stuff, so I continued with what was turning into a spring cleaning.

I threw out the pile of clothes that needed mending. I'd lost a handful of fucks to give, and if Dad kept tearing his shirts in bar fights or when he fell asleep with a cigarette and it burned a hole in the fabric, he could fix them himself. And he wasn't going to do that, so out it went.

I put the thrift store on my list. We needed new plates.

"That...that you, Emilia?" Dad's gruff voice came from the living room.

"Yeah. Did you have a party?" I grimaced and threw away something from the fridge that looked alive. "Jesus Christ, Dad. Could you at least put the food that's gone bad in the garbage?"

He grunted, and his chair creaked and protested. Soon, he appeared in the doorway. He looked like death warmed over.

"Don't give me attitude. Hand me a beer."

I stared at him, almost as if seeing him for the first time. I had no memories of happier times, but there were pictures in his bedroom. Pictures of him and my mom. He'd been smiling in each one, and since then...he'd just decayed. His hair had thinned and gone from dark to silver. He had more wrinkles than he should at the age of forty-five. His muscles had disappeared, resulting in skinny arms and legs. Beer had given him an impressive gut.

His eyes were lifeless.

"A real breakfast wouldn't hurt," I said. "I can—"

"Get me a fuckin' beer," he snapped. "You know, I thought you'd left. You haven't been around in a few days. It was nice."

I gnashed my teeth together and handed him a beer. "It really was. No one's sorrier than me to come back."

He let out a hollow chuckle. "Am I supposed to be grateful that at least one of you returned?"

"What—"

"You look too much like her." In a sudden burst of rage, he threw the can against the wall, spraying foam everywhere. "Fuck!"

"Dad!" I jumped back and glared at him. "For chrissakes!"

"Get outta my sight!" he yelled. "I don't want you here, Emilia!"

I slammed up a wall as emotions threatened to spill over, and I stormed out of the kitchen and ran up the stairs.

Dad wasn't done yelling, and I heard him wrecking the kitchen. "You fucking killed her. You killed her, you killed her—my beautiful Elena, why did she have to kill you?"

I slammed the door shut and leaned back against it, willing my heart to stop pounding. I closed my eyes hard and listened. A drawer was pulled out, and silverware clattered against the linoleum floor. I flinched at the breaking of glass and more shouting.

"Don't let it get to you, don't let it get to you," I whispered over and over. "Don't let it get to you, don't let it get to you."

It was nothing I hadn't heard before.

The mayhem quieted after a while, and I slid down to the floor. If the slamming door was any indication, he'd left. Probably to go buy more beer.

Running a hand through my hair, I blew out a breath and did my best to shake the hurt. My phone vibrated in my pocket, providing a welcome break, and I opened the text from Sarah.

We gotta talk. Meet me at the picnic tables when you can.

School wasn't out yet, but maybe she was skipping last period. God knew I was ready to get the fuck out, so I texted her back, saying I was on my way.

Sarah was waiting for me by the tables as I crossed the parking lot next to school.

She extended her pack of cigarettes. "You look like crap."

"You're gorgeous as always." I lit one up and sat down next to her.

"Did something happen?" She tilted her head, concern flashing in her eyes.

"Nothing new." I shrugged and exhaled some smoke. "I killed my mother and all that."

She winced and rubbed my back. "I'm sorry."

I didn't want to think about it. I was sick—so *fucking* sick—of being some pathetic victim. Sick of depending on others. Unfortunately, if I let the frustrations take over, I'd lose my shit and do something reckless. It was better to bury it deep down.

"You wanted to talk," I said.

She nodded. "Sorry I didn't respond to your message, by the way. I had my phone in my locker and didn't read it until I texted back. My notifications are messing with me too. I didn't get the alert."

My brows knitted together. Was there something wrong with my phone too? I thought that little sign that says *read* meant she'd opened the message.

"Anyway," she went on. "I talked to Patrick during lunch, because I'm thinking about accepting his proposal sooner."

"What? I thought you already said yes."

"Yeah, but I mean, like, get out of here sooner. I'm not sure I can wait till graduation."

Anxiety clamped a hand around my throat, and I swallowed dryly. "Why?"

She took a breath, looking ten times more tired. "You did the right thing ditching classes today, 'cause Franny knows. There're rumors flying around about you and me dating the O'Shea brothers."

I clenched my jaw and closed my eyes, silently counting to ten. Was it really just this morning I'd sat in the sunshine and made out with Finnegan? Nausea churned in my stomach, and I was slowly but surely reaching my limit for all kinds of bullshit. Dad, Finnegan, Franny, Agent Caldwell, work, school, my future— everything and everyone could fuck right off. Hell, at this point I was sick of myself and my roller coaster rides too.

"Patrick said I could transfer to Philly or finish whenever I wanted."

Finnegan had mentioned something similar to me.

"I want you with me, Emilia." She hooked her arm through mine and rested her chin on my shoulder. "It's three years."

If I heard that one more time... The anger that brewed within me was unlike anything I'd ever felt. I was fed up. Limit reached. I couldn't take it anymore. My chest felt tight, and a dizzy spell caught me. *Too much, too much, too much.* I had to cut some strings, starting with Agent Caldwell. I wasn't going to lie to him again, but I couldn't help him out either.

I couldn't keep my mouth shut. "Are you helping the FBI or something?" The words gusted out in a rush, and at Sarah's confused expression, I word-vomited. "When all this started, you told me there was a lot going on, and you couldn't tell me. Then you told me about Patrick and the business offer, so it made me wonder what you left out, and I guess—I mean—you accepted his proposal so fast, and...fuck, I don't know."

"Hey. Breathe, hon." Sarah stroked my back soothingly as she processed my rant. "I'm not helping anyone but myself here. I've told you everything—except... It's just the shit with my dad. I don't like to talk about it." She'd made that clear many times. "Listen. What you're feeling now looks like how I felt when I told you that Patrick had offered me that deal. Everything was closing in on me, and I don't remember everything I said word for word." She paused. "What I do remember is the plan to tell you I was dating him. Then I ended up spilling everything, so maybe that's why I said I couldn't tell you all of it...?"

I *wished* that didn't make sense.

So where did that leave me? Sarah was in it to gain her freedom, however unconventional her method was. No agents involved.

"How about we continue this back at the motel room?" she suggested. "We don't wanna be here when the bell rings."

Good point. I stubbed out my forgotten smoke and jumped down from the bench.

Sarah linked her arm with mine again. "We should have a girls' night with pizza and the story of how my best friend stole a mobster's car."

"Heh." No thanks. I had enough on my plate. I didn't need to add the worry of what'd come over me last night when I drove Finnegan's Aston. Even now, I couldn't describe the thirst I'd felt.

I wouldn't say no to pizza, though.

"By the way, about your text," she said. "You're staying with me until I can convince you to take this bizarre journey with me. Don't think about the money. It's not like I'm paying."

I had no fight left, so I just thanked her.

That night, I got everything I didn't know I'd needed. Sarah and I sat across from each other on her bed, and we laughed, cried, vented, and got drunk on a bottle of wine she'd bought through a friend's older sister.

I told Sarah about Agent Caldwell. She merely listened and comforted me. It felt too damn good to get it off my chest, and I breathed a big sigh of relief.

"I can't imagine." She shook her head. "I would've peed myself just from meeting him at the library like that."

"I freaked out a lot." I scrubbed my hands over my face.

When Finnegan texted to check in and see how I was doing, I told him I wanted the night for myself, to which he messaged me again. And again. And again. I didn't answer, so Patrick started blowing up Sarah's phone.

We turned them off.

"I need more wine." She hiccupped and poured the last of the bottle into her glass. "Oh! Have I shown you this?" She handed me a note off of the nightstand.

I squinted at it. *Languages: French, Portuguese. Physical: Self-defense, martial arts—pick one.*

"What's this?" I asked.

"Classes I'm gonna take." She smiled widely. "The way I see it, if Patrick's got all this money to spend, I should spend it on something I can use. And the minute the arrangement is up, I'm going straight to college."

I smiled and squeezed her hand. Self-defense had nothing to do with her childhood dream of becoming a doctor and everything to do with her hating feeling weak and defenseless against her dad.

"You'll be the best doctor, I know it."

She pursed her lips and raised a brow. "And what're you gonna be?"

"Stop it," I groaned.

"Never. You have to do this with me, and not for my sake. I'm terrified of what you'll do if I leave you here."

I frowned and reached for my glass, emptying it in two gulps.

"Don't you *see*, Em? This is our chance! We'll stay strong if we do this as a team. We'll spend the next three years preparing ourselves and building each other up. We can *trust* one another."

Her words cracked something inside me. *We'll build each other up.* And so a new crying fest began for me.

"Oh, Em." Sarah hugged me to her, and I wept a bunch of nonsense about what I wanted—how much I wanted *this*, but it came back to the same old question.

At what cost?

"I understand that, honey," she murmured, wiping my cheeks. "But at what cost are you staying?"

chapter

13

Emilia Porter

I walked through the corridor toward my locker in a daze. I hadn't been in school five minutes yet, and the stares were already getting taxing. I guess I hadn't thought Sarah was serious when she'd said it'd been this bad. A few whispers here and there, sure, but everyone I passed looked at me like I was dating a mobster or something.

"Hey! Emilia."

I looked over my shoulder, cringing inwardly at the sight of Jimmy.

He smirked and walked over to me. His football buddies stayed behind to laugh and talk shit.

"So is it true?" Jimmy asked. "Are you really seeing one of the O'Sheas?"

For fuck's sake. "Yeah, he knocked me up on the first date too," I deadpanned. With a shake of my head, I continued to my locker, beginning to understand why Sarah had opted to ditch today.

A handful of girls were crowding my locker, snickering like little bitches when I asked them to get out of the way. Oh...fucking great. "In bed with the shamrocks" was written on my locker, along with a poorly drawn clover. Very funny.

I took a picture of it with my phone and sent it to both Sarah and Finnegan with the caption, "School's great!"

Today was gonna suck, wasn't it?

I opened my locker and stopped short. A white paper bag waited inside—and a freaking Snapple. Whoever had figured out the combination to my lock wouldn't leave a bag of dog shit and then go, "Hey, she needs something refreshing to drink too." I picked up the bag and peered inside, and it looked like...lunch, I guess? It was a panini sandwich in a clear plastic container. Wait, there was more. A small box revealed three chocolate truffles. Um, it was a box to hold four pieces.

There was a note too, and it changed everything.

Lunch is on me. Something may have happened to one of the chocolates. Sorry about that.
—Finnegan

An involuntary laugh slipped out of me, and I shook my head. I probably didn't wanna know how he'd gotten into my locker. Had he been here right as they opened the school? I got my phone out again to write another message, and there was a response waiting for me.

One of these days, people are gonna fucking learn that a shamrock only has three leaves. Uneducated gobshites.

Right. *That* was the problem, the number of leaves on the clover. I ignored it and sent him a message.

Thank you for lunch. I won't even ask how you broke in.

His reply was instant.

***Consider it my apology for not respecting your
privacy yesterday. Hope your girls' night was fun.***

I was pretty sure breaking in to my locker wasn't the way to
apologize for that particular thing, but I appreciated it nonetheless.

The bell rang, and I grabbed my books before making it to class
where I found more students staring at me.

Great.

By the time lunch rolled around, I was ready to set this whole town
on fire. If I weren't meeting Agent Caldwell in the library in forty
minutes, I would've returned to the motel already.

As always, I skipped going to the cafeteria, and I found an
empty picnic table outside.

"Emilia!" someone hollered. "Are you really pregnant?"

What the fuck, I didn't even know that person. We had one
class together, that was it. It wasn't the biggest school, so everyone
learned each other's names sooner rather than later, though that
was it. This chick—I'd never spoken to her.

"With twins!" I confirmed.

I finished my admittedly delicious lunch quickly, wanting to
get the rest of the day over with. I didn't know what was worse, my
free period coming up and meeting with the agent, or my last
period where Franny was my lab partner. I hadn't seen her
yet today.

I threw away the trash and was about to head back inside when
none other than Nurse Walsh crossed the lot. It was the first time
I'd seen her since meeting Finnegan, and I didn't know if I resented
her or—no, I definitely resented her.

She walked straight toward me, and she looked concerned. *A
bit late for that, lady.* Other than sharing the same coloring of her
brother and nephews, she was a slight woman and soft-spoken.

"Hello, Emilia." She smiled politely and wrapped her open cardigan around herself as a cold breeze passed us.

"I'm not actually pregnant," I said.

She chuckled lightly and eyed the groups of my peers around us. "No, I didn't think so. That's not why I'm here." She paused. "How are you holding up? The rumors don't escape anyone."

"They're only gonna get worse with you talking to me," I pointed out. "Everyone seems to know that the school nurse put Sarah and me on a list, and now we have the O'Shea brothers after us."

Guilt struck her for a quick second, and she cleared her throat. "I'm very sorry for the pain this has caused you, but I see something in you, Emilia. When you told me of your paper about women in healthcare, I knew I was right. I don't want you to be a pretty girl on my nephew's arm. I want you to be a strong asset. You and Sarah are what our family needs."

"That's so not the point," I told her, half in disbelief. "We were shanghaied into this crap. A yes means absolutely nothing if there isn't an option to say no, and that's why Finnegan chose me."

"I understand why you feel that way," she replied with a sad smile. "He wants you for many reasons, though, and I have faith you will see that one day."

There was no reasoning with this woman. Coercion was coercion, whether you used expensive bribes or your fists. The only difference was that I felt like I was partly to blame now. Because I could technically say no, and then what? My ass would be on the street eventually, and I could only hope to get welfare. I would be stuck in this life-sucking town for the rest of my pathetic existence.

"Good talk, Mrs. Walsh," I said tightly. "I gotta go."

Shouldering my backpack, I headed back inside the school and ignored every stare and whisper. When I caught a glimpse of Franny in another corridor, chatting with some people, I took a detour before I ended up in the back of the building where the library was.

I had some time to kill before Agent Caldwell would be here, so I sat down by one of the computers and went online. No new local jobs for anyone who had rent to pay, go figure. One of the many furniture companies in Gettysburg was hiring, but I'd need a car. Maybe carpooling—uh, never mind. Five years' experience minimum.

It wasn't long before my curiosity took over and I googled the SoM instead of looking for jobs. Only this time, I searched for the Murrays.

John Murray was a lawyer? I shouldn't be surprised. They all seemed to be scholars.

I snorted to myself. Gangster scholars.

Shannon had his history in the military, plus a master's in psychology. Finnegan and Patrick had gone to very nice schools, and they'd done well.

Liam Murray.

John Murray's eldest son was twenty-nine years old, presently incarcerated for manslaughter and possession of illegal firearms. Resting my chin in my hand, I leaned forward a bit and scanned the text. Up for parole in August... Went to Oxford...

He'd gone to the same all-boys' boarding school in England as Patrick and Finnegan had.

The links tended to stop at John's and Shannon's immediate families. The wives didn't have their own pages, only the men and their sons. Figures. I moved on to an image search of—

"Miss Porter?"

"Jesus." It wasn't the first time Agent Caldwell had scared the crap out of me. "Don't you make sounds?" I eyed him over my shoulder.

He smiled faintly and nodded toward the back of the library.

I followed him after logging out, and we sat down at a table in the newspaper section. A cheap attempt to make people think they weren't cutting the budget and couldn't afford more books.

"How are things?" he asked politely.

My stomach tightened with nerves. This was it, and I couldn't chicken out now. "Not too good, actually." I fidgeted under his observant stare, and I had to break eye contact. "My life isn't very easy at the moment, and it's giving me anxiety to keep this up." I watched his hands as he clasped them casually on the table, and that was when I noticed a tattoo poking out from under his shirt cuff. So much for him being prim and proper. "I wanna quit," I blurted out. "I can't handle the pressure."

"I see." He furrowed his brow. "Finnegan hasn't threatened you, has he? If he has, we can make arrangements for you." Before I could spit out any word vomit or splutter some nonsense, he pulled out a small notebook from his inner pocket. "This is a safe space." He slid the notebook with a pen across the table.

"No...?" Oh! It dawned on me. In case I couldn't answer out loud, I could write it down. Wow, so cops really did that. Or Feds, whatever. "He hasn't threatened me," I said honestly. "I hope you guys can take them down somehow, but I can't help."

Did I hope they could throw the O'Sheas in prison?

Well. Probably. I mean...*yeah.* Of course. Yeah. Uh-huh.

"I understand." Agent Caldwell nodded slowly, thinking. "I assume you have nothing to report to us, then?"

I chewed on my bottom lip and wondered if what Finnegan had told me on his patio was something the FBI could use. About the implying that he was involved in...stuff. Christ, it wasn't like I had any details. Although...

I cringed as Finnegan's words replayed in my head.

"Okay. Honesty. Yeah, I sometimes hurt people. If they betray me or pose a direct threat, I have to defend myself and my family, and violence is a language everyone understands."

"I'm trying to remember," I fibbed.

"Take your time." Agent Caldwell leaned back in his seat and folded his arms over his chest. There was a ghost of a smile playing on his lips, and it made me nervous. Could he see through me? I sucked at lying.

"They don't share details," I said. "I mean, I can tell you that Finnegan is obsessed with cake and more than a little possessive of his car, but I don't know anything meaningful. Their parents are supposed to arrive 'soon,' and...I don't know. They're vague."

"I understand," Agent Caldwell repeated. "We appreciate your help, Miss Porter. I'd like you to keep my number if you change your mind or remember anything new, but I will respect your wishes. We won't bother you."

He said something else, something about compensation and a check in the mail, but I tuned out. It was a weight being lifted off of my shoulders. One string that'd been cut. One thing less to worry about.

Thank fuck.

Feeling tons lighter after saying goodbye to Agent Caldwell, I walked through the near-empty halls toward the main entrance. Sarah had cruelly texted me a picture of herself in PJs and holding a bag of Chinese takeout, captioning it, "You sure you don't wanna skip last period?"

I wasn't sure.

I *was* sure that I needed a cigarette before facing Franny, however.

One of the stoners in school loaned me a smoke when I exited the building, and I found my usual picnic table empty. As the sun peeked out, I shrugged out of my sweater and bunched it together between my back and the edge of the table. Then I got as comfortable as possible and closed my eyes.

Stay or go?

To be honest, I didn't believe there was any point in sticking around, other than to keep up the pretense. Anyone who gave a fuck had started studying for finals, and I would no doubt fail.

"But at what cost are you staying?"

"But at what cost are you staying?"

I took a deep drag and tried to shake the memory of Sarah asking me that question.

"Emilia!"

"Crap," I muttered. At the sound of Franny's voice, I forced my eyes open and straightened in my seat. I should've hidden out in the bathrooms or the library until class started. At least in there, she would have to whisper.

Franny stalked over, preppy as ever, and put her hands on her hips. "I'm done being ignored, Em. You and Sarah call yourselves my friends, but—"

"I'm not sure anyone who spreads rumors about me is a friend." I cocked my head, curious. "You're right, Sarah and I have avoided you, but I think you know why. If you know something, so does the school."

She clenched her jaw. "I won't be reduced to some gossip. This is serious. You and Sarah are dating mobsters. People deserve to know."

Exhaustion and amusement mingled inside me. "What you're saying is you're performing a public service? Really, Fran?" The brightness of the sun was getting to be too much, so I held up a hand to shield my eyes. "You have no fucking idea the hell I've gone through, and what people deserve to know isn't up to you."

"You don't even deny it?" she asked incredulously. "Do you realize how incredibly—"

"*Hey,*" I snapped, quickly getting heated. I grabbed my backpack and stood up. "Let me dumb it down so you understand. Sarah and I are dealing with this without you because we can't trust you. So I won't confirm or deny *anything*. Got that?"

She glared. "You're so full of it. You haven't even tried to come to me with this."

"And you think spreading rumors about us is gonna change that?" I got in her face, so freaking fed up. "The first thing you do when you ferret out a rumor is shout it from the rooftops. You think we're gonna take that chance?"

She tried to go for patronizing instead, and she smirked cockily. "See, all I hear is that you're willingly dating a murderer."

"Then maybe you should go fuck yourself." My voice turned cold, and I was running out of patience. "Go back to your gossip. We all know it's the only thing you're good at, you fucking vermin."

That one struck her like a slap, and it made her gasp. I didn't stick around for her retort. My day had to be over. I sure as hell felt finished.

"Man, that must've felt great," Sarah said, lowering the volume of whatever she'd been watching in the background. "Good for you, Em. I wanted to tell her off yesterday, but she was surrounded by her little gossipmongers."

I didn't feel much of anything, other than exhausted. Either I was near hysteria or a complete shutdown. I'd take the shutdown over a panic attack any day, but first I had to make it back to the motel. I told Sarah I'd be there soon, and I was totally calling in sick from work today. She promised to heat up some leftovers for me.

I wrapped up the call as my house came into view. *My house. Right.* All my life, I'd been an unwelcome guest, and another hour inside of it would suffocate me. Luckily for me, it would take less than that to pack up what I owned.

I had every intention of hiding out with Sarah for as long as I could, even if it meant sitting on my ass and waiting for the day I became homeless. And at that, I shook my head. I was already homeless.

You can say yes to Finnegan. You know you want to.

Grabbing the doorknob, I paused for a second and took a deep breath. If I concentrated, I could transport myself back to the night

I fell asleep in his arms. Had I ever felt so protected before? And what did that say about me?

I exhaled shakily and opened the door, cringing when I heard the shower running upstairs. Dad was not only home, he was awake. I didn't wanna face him, so I hurried up to my room and pulled out an old duffel from my closet. I put it on the bed and filled it with the stuff from the box that'd come with my dress.

There was some paperwork I should bring too. Couldn't hurt, even though I might come back here at some point. A girl could hope I didn't.

How sad was it that my entire life fit into a duffel bag?

I looked around the room to see if there was anything else I wanted to bring. I guess the picture of my mother, although I wasn't certain of why. Old school papers, no. Report cards, yes. My meager savings from the diner, yes. The rest of my clothes—that fit, anyway. There was one thing I wanted to bring from the living room too—

"Emilia, that you?"

Dammit. I grabbed the duffel and left my room, spotting Dad outside the bathroom. He was buttoning up one of his nicer flannel shirts, which meant he was heading for the bar.

"I'm not staying." I jogged down the stairs.

"Hey, now. Hold up," he replied gruffly. "Where do you think you're goin' with all that?"

"It's my stuff, Dad." Opening the front door, I set the duffel and my schoolbag on the small stoop. "Unless you want the drawings I made when I was four?"

He stood in the doorway to the kitchen, hands on his hips, belly poking out, and stared at me with so much contempt. "You really leavin' for good?"

I nodded, and I hoped with all my heart it was true. Moving into the living room, I located the dusty album on a shelf and clutched it to me.

Dad narrowed his eyes and pointed. "You're not taking that. My Elena made—"

"My mother," I interrupted. "She was my mom, and she started this baby book for *me*." She'd pre-decorated over a dozen pages with moments she'd never experienced, the only thing missing being pictures and dates. A few pages were complete from when she documented her pregnancy. One photo was of her smiling crookedly and holding up a pair of pink baby socks. It was from the day they found out they were having a girl. Lastly, a picture of her belly the day before I was born. The day before she died.

"You ain't taking it," he repeated. With venom filling his eyes, he stalked toward me, and it slammed determination into me. I wasn't gonna let him push me down this time. I was gonna walk out of here with the album Mom had started for me, end of fucking discussion.

I dodged his hand when he tried to take the album, and I hurried out to the hallway, my heart rate spiking.

"You get back here," Dad growled. A second later, a hand clamped down painfully on my shoulder, and I spun around.

"Let go of me." I glared at him and held the baby book tighter. "You do *not* touch me."

He chuckled humorlessly and scrubbed a hand over his mouth. It lowered my guard for half a second, and I instantly regretted it. He came at me with force and seething anger, the sight of him shocking me to immobility. I flinched as he shoved me up against the door, and then the album was slowly leaving my grasp.

No! No, no, no, no, no!

Adrenaline pulsed in my veins. I pushed back with my shoulder and yanked the book back. "Get off of me!" I shouted. "What the fuck are you doing?"

"It doesn't belong to you!" He stopped trying to take the book from me, only for his hands to slip up to my throat. My eyes widened at the sheer rage in his gaze. I'd been intimidated by him for as long as I could remember, but I'd never actually been afraid.

"You don't deserve it!" he yelled. "You don't deserve anything! If it weren't for you—"

"I get it! She'd be alive if it weren't for me!" I gritted my teeth against the hurt and struggled to push him away from me. The album landed on the floor with a thump, and I rammed my fists into his stomach before gripping his wrists. "Ow—let me go—that fucking hurts!"

"You're done stealing from me," he seethed, tightening his grip on my neck. The crushing pain pulsated throughout my chest, getting heavier and heavier. At the same time, panic closed in on me, and I choked when I couldn't force air into my lungs.

Our gazes locked for one excruciating second. I didn't know him. I didn't recognize him. He hated me with every fiber of his being.

"Don't let anyone tell you you're not a murderer," he rasped. "I don't care what he says. You killed my Elena, you little whore."

I screwed my eyes shut, seeing spots. My nails dug into his wrists. Did he even feel it, or was he too far gone?

Dizziness dragged me down into a cold swamp. My lungs burned and squeezed.

This can't be my life, this can't be my life, this can't be my life.

I felt like I left my body. Desperation and instinct took over, and I slammed my forehead against his nose. A sickening crunch resounded in my head, and then my lungs were filling with air. I wheezed and choked, feeling like his hands were still wrapped around my throat.

He wasn't touching me. He'd fallen back against the kitchen doorway and was cupping his nose.

I saw red. Fury lit me up, and I attacked him with fists and feet. "You almost killed me!" I kneed him in the gut, and as he bowled over and groaned, I landed my elbow across his neck. "What kind of vile monster are you? I didn't fucking murder your precious Elena! I was born!" I stomped on his foot, punched him in his temple, and scratched up his neck in my blind fit of rage.

It wasn't until he landed on the floor with a hoarse cry that I stumbled back and saw the damage. Blood was gushing out of his nose. Three streaks of red grazed his neck, and the only position he seemed interested in was the fetal position.

I forced in some air and looked down at my hands. They were shaking, and I couldn't see properly.

At his pained moan, I tried to get my shit together. *Breathe, breathe, breathe.* I picked up the album and fled from the house. The panic was right there, waiting to take me. His hands were gone. Why wasn't it getting easier to breathe?

I managed to slip my arms into the handles of the duffel and use it as a backpack. Then I grabbed my schoolbag and my baby book and walked unsteadily down the driveway.

"Shit." I had to pause when I reached the sidewalk. Time to call someone. Him. Finnegan. He was the only person I knew who could help me. I pressed call on his number and waited, focusing on breathing through the chest pain.

He answered with, "Well, that's new. The princess is calling me."

Only three words existed in my brain. "I'll marry you."

chapter

14

Finnegan O'Shea

"Obsessed with cake," I scoffed. "And you know she stole my car, right? That doesn't make me possessive of it."

Kellan laughed and threw himself on my couch with a bowl of chips. "Take that up with someone else. Not my jurisdiction."

I grabbed a beer in the kitchen and joined him. The only good thing about not working at the moment was we could catch the football games from Europe on TV. Fucking time zones.

Patrick walked into my house with Alec and Nessa, informing us Pop would be here any minute.

"I don't wanna go home, boss." Alec planted himself next to me, looking uncharacteristically sour.

"You'll be back in no time, cub." I ruffled his hair.

I'd expected their stay to be longer, truth be told. When a territory was deemed unsafe, it wasn't unheard of for the men to send their women and children on vacations that went on for weeks, if not months. Cleanup could take time.

According to Pop, it was mostly Uncle John's paranoia this time. He'd sent the twins away to upgrade their security around the house, and now that was done.

167

All it'd accomplished for me was doubts. Did Uncle John trust us more and that was why he'd sent Alec and Nessa here, or was he up to something and wanted to make it *look* like he trusted us?

Additionally, without the twins around, my boredom was gonna kill me. We'd already repainted Ma's "art studio" in all kinds of neon colors to see her reaction, and it would only get worse from there.

I'd also spend too much time thinking about Emilia. Kellan's latest update on her wasn't as satisfying as I'd thought. Maybe because she hadn't stopped reporting to him based on a newfound loyalty to me, but because she was overwhelmed by everything. She'd legit told him she still hoped the Feds caught us.

"We gonna take bets or what?" Patrick grabbed a handful of chips and shoved them into his mouth.

"Why? We root for the same team," I said.

Kellan cleared his throat. "Actually, uh, I'm a Liverpool fan these days."

I pointed to the door. "Get the fuck out. This is a United house. Your treason isn't welcome here."

The twins snickered while Patrick exclaimed, "That's what I'm fuckin' saying."

"Treason," Kellan snorted.

Un-fucking-believable. You thought you knew a guy... I hauled out my wallet. "Two hundred on United."

"Oh! Can we play too?" Alec looked hopeful.

"No. I've heard you in church," I told him. "When you learn how to repent, you can sin."

The rest of us placed our bets, and the game started.

"That's not how religion works, Finn," Ness pointed out.

"Shh. Watch the game, doll." I took a swig of my beer.

Pop joined us twenty minutes in. Life in Philly must've been hectic, 'cause we usually went to the same barber. He hadn't been in a while, I could tell. His suit was nowhere to be seen either, and the lines around his eyes seemed more prominent.

He asked Kellan if he had any history with mental health issues upon hearing he was a Liverpool fan.

"That's my dad." I clapped him on the shoulder. "Beer?"

"Just one. I'm driving. Cheers, son."

One meant three, of course. I got up and filled a cooler with bottles and ice packs so I didn't have to go twice.

At halftime, we had a bit more time to talk.

"What's this I hear about Kellan pretending to be a Fed around Emilia?" Pop asked.

I shot Patrick a glare.

He smirked and shrugged.

"I'm being careful," I said. "It doesn't matter. She called it off with him today."

Pop eyed Kellan. "Does she suspect anything?"

Kellan shook his head. "Nah. I'm a decent actor." More like we all had experience with the FBI, though I was sure he'd broken protocol once or twice.

"Oh right, you used to do porn," Patrick mentioned.

I laughed.

"The fuck I have," Kellan spluttered. "Dick."

"Is that—" Nessa was cut off by Alec, who whispered in her ear. Judging by her furious blush, her brother had told her way too much.

"All right, enough of that, lads." Pop coughed into his fist to hide his laugh. "And, Finn, don't tell your mother about the Feds. She already feels bad for the girls."

"Noted." I nodded with a dip of my chin and sat forward a bit. Next, I sent the twins a pointed look. "Youse didn't hear any of this."

Nessa shook her head, and Alec pretended to zip his mouth and throw away the key. They were pros. Sometimes I wondered how many secrets they kept.

"Furthermore, your mother and I didn't send you to Aberdeen Grange for you to return speaking slang," Pop told me.

Jesus fucking Christ. "Is Ma not putting out?"

"Aw, man." Pat grimaced. "That's my mom."

I furrowed my brow. "I came out of the same v—"

"Oi! That's enough." Pop gave me a hard stare, only to deflate with a heavy sigh and pinch the bridge of his nose. "How bored are you, son?"

"There's no word in the English language, slang or otherwise, to describe it," I replied.

He shook his head. "What happened to testing the small-town life?"

"I did that. The results aren't looking very promising." I was honest. I knew I'd said this might be good for me. But sometimes I was wrong. "I'll be here until Emilia says yes, and then we're gone."

"Ma will be disappointed," Patrick mused.

I lifted a shoulder. It was our parents who fantasized about country life. Their house here would be their primary home. While I'd be happy to visit on occasion for some downtime, or when I worked with Pop, I couldn't imagine actually living here. If I had, I wouldn't have settled for a small house like this one. Right now, my condo in the city was calling my name.

"When are you guys moving out here?" I asked Pop. They'd gone back and forth between dates a lot.

"Next week," he replied firmly. "I still have a few patients in the city. I'll commute a couple times a week, but everything else is ready."

That was good. The less time he spent with his damn patients, the more time he could commit to making plans for the Maserati event in Italy this fall.

"Game's starting." Kellan nodded at the flat screen.

I returned my attention to the TV but remembered something. "Pop, did you pick up the things I asked you?"

"Aye, they're in the car."

Okay, good. I finished my beer and—my fucking phone rang.

Christ, I just wanted to enjoy the game. *Forget what I said.* It was Emilia, and that was a first. And definitely welcome. Leaving the couch to get some privacy, I stepped out onto the patio and answered her call.

"Well, that's new. The princess is calling me."

One day, I'd have to tell her why I called her princess.

Her breathing was strained. "I'll marry you."

I grew rigid, instantly alert. She'd spoken the words I'd wanted to hear for weeks, but her irregular breathing put me on edge. "Baby, what's wrong?"

"I... My chest hurts. Can—can you pick me up?"

I was already heading inside, and if she sounded any more panicky, I was gonna kill someone. "I'm on my way. Where are you? What happened?" I'd gotten the attention of pretty much everyone, and I nodded at the door to my brother.

"I thought he was gonna kill me," Emilia whimpered. "I punched him, Finnegan."

"Get to the cars, Pat." I detoured quickly and ran up the stairs to get my piece. "Keep talking to me, princess. Are you safe now? Who tried to hurt you?" My gun was in the nightstand, and I tucked it into my jeans at the base of my spine.

"My dad." She was cracking, and my fucking heart broke for her. At the same time, I was relieved it wasn't someone else. Someone with affiliation. "I'm safe, I think. I'm on the sidewalk."

"I want you to walk up the road," I said, hurrying downstairs again. "Can you do that for me? I'll be there in ten minutes." I let out a whistle, and Kellan looked up. I covered the mouthpiece. "You can't be here when I get back."

He understood.

"It's a twenty-minute d-drive, Finnegan." Bloody hell, even freaking out and struggling to breathe, she wanted to correct me. I couldn't wait to marry this little broad.

"You're right, I'll see you in five," I said. Without telling the others what was going on, I left the house after stealing Pop's car keys off the hallway table. "Stay on the line with me, Emilia. I need you to breathe."

I threw the keys to Pop's Jag to Pat. It would take him to town a hell of a lot quicker than dragging on in his Jeep. "Drive to Emilia's," I told him, getting into my own car.

"Why does it hurt?" Emilia groaned between gasps. "I swear his hands are-are still around my n-neck."

"Motherfucker," I spat. As soon as the gates opened, I floored it and connected the call to Bluetooth so I didn't have to hold my phone. White-hot rage flooded me at the thought of her being hurt.

It's probably your fucking fault.

I clenched my jaw.

Jonathan Porter was a dead man. If there was one thing more important than money to him, it was that Emilia didn't learn the truth about her mother. He'd pitched a fit when we visited him, saying I was going back on my word, but one fist to his eye had silenced him. As soon as I'd mentioned I knew Elena was alive and well—living with her husband in Italy—Jonathan had been more docile than a newborn kitten. He agreed; I didn't have to give him money. He would let his daughter stay as long as she needed.

Now he'd put his hands on her.

I hit the highway and accelerated, reminding Emilia to count her breaths. In through her nose, out through her mouth. Slow, deep breaths.

Patrick was in my rearview, and between the two of us, we raked in an impressive number of honks from the vehicles we passed.

I didn't slow down until our exit was next.

Heads turned as we entered the town, reminding me of the call I'd gotten from Aunt Viv today. Not to mention the text from Emilia. Everyone was speculating about us, and the only ones suffering were Emilia and Sarah.

My breath hitched uncomfortably the second I reached Emilia's street. She was sitting on the sidewalk, surrounded by a couple bags. Face buried in her hands. Her hair was tangled and had escaped her ponytail for the most part.

I pulled over and disconnected the call, and then I was by her side. "Emilia. Sweetheart, I'm here." I noticed she had a photo album in her lap, and she was clutching her phone close to her face. "Emilia?" It was as if she was gone. At least she was breathing better, so I picked her up and rounded the car. "I've got you." I pressed a kiss to the side of her head before lowering her into the passenger's seat.

"What if I killed him?" she whispered.

I frowned, then quickly ignored the notion and combed back some of her hair.

"He hasn't been violent before," she croaked. Tears fell down her cheeks, and before I could catch them, she buried her face in her—scratch that, my hoodie. The one she'd borrowed from me the other day. "This smells like you."

"Yeah?" I mustered half a smile and glanced around me. A couple neighbors were being too curious, standing in their windows. Patrick was collecting Emilia's things off the ground. "I'm gonna go check on your pop," I told her quietly. "I'll be back, okay? Patrick's here too."

"Hurry." She started crying harder, and it physically hurt to tear myself away.

I gnashed my teeth together and cleared my throat into my fist.

Patrick joined me by my side.

"I'll be right back. Don't leave her side."

"Of course."

My hands were tied. With neighbors wondering what was going on, I couldn't do anything to Jonathan right now. Even so, I had to survey the damage, and I jogged up their driveway and opened the door.

I stopped short. There was no way Emilia had inflicted actual hurt, was there? She was way too sweet. Yet, there were bloodstains on the floor. I traced the red into the kitchen where the spots were more like smeared streaks.

And there was Jonathan. He'd dragged himself in there and was slumped on the floor by the sink, holding a rag to his nose.

"Sweet Jesus," I muttered. "I'm marrying a fighter."

Emilia had defended herself *well*. Pride swelled up in my chest. I didn't even have to reach for the gun hidden under my Henley. She'd rendered him useless.

Jonathan glared weakly at me. "Go'way."

"In a bit." I moved closer and squatted down in front of him. "Check you out, mate. She turned you into roadkill."

She'd scratched up his neck, done *something* to cause his eye to look swollen, ripped his shirt, and turned his nose into a bloody faucet.

"She tried to kill me," he rasped. "Just like she killed her mothe—"

"Dude. You forget that I know the truth."

He whimpered, his head lolling back against the cupboard. "My Elena's dead."

I shook my head at him. "You are one sorry sack of shit, Jonathan."

A burst of anger ignited him. "She tried to kill me!"

I didn't even flinch. "She didn't, but I tell you what. If you so much as breathe a word about this to anyone, I'll finish the job." There was no *if* about it. "Are we clear?"

Sooner rather than later, Jonathan was gonna find himself with a bullet in his head.

"I get it," he gritted out.

"Good boy." I rose to a stand and pushed up my sleeves. "I'll check in on you soon, Jonathan."

"I won't talk!"

"That's good. I'll still come by to visit." I turned to leave. "After all, we'll be family soon."

"I'll get Pop." Patrick ran ahead toward my house while I helped Emilia out of the car.

Fuck, she was gone again. I carried her across the road, and as I reached my house, Pop opened the door with a worried expression. That made two of us, only I was getting increasingly close to freaking the fuck out.

"She's in and out of it," I said impatiently. "Her breathing's fine, but one second she's telling me what happened, and the next she's crying and panicking until she shuts down."

"Lay her down on the couch, please." Pop went into doctor mode and asked what'd happened. I told him everything I knew, mentioning Jonathan and the state I'd found him in. Before I knew it, more words were spilling out of me. About Aunt Viv and the shit the girls went through at school, what their peers were saying about them on social media.

"I'm not sure they know about that part, though," I said. "Neither of them has accounts on Facebook and that, what's it called, Twitter?"

Patrick nodded.

In the meantime, Pop was examining her on the couch. He checked her breathing, felt her pulse and her forehead, and started removing her hoodie.

"All right. Pat, go out to my car and get my bag," Pop told him. "I trust that you know your way around it since you just fucking stole it."

I pinched my lips together, too worried to laugh, but the smirk was hard to contain.

"Seriously." Patrick shot me a scowl before running out of the house.

"Do you really have a doctor's bag?" I sat down by Emilia's feet and lifted them onto my lap.

Pop shook his head. "Not my field, but I do carry samples of antidepressants and sedatives." He gently pulled the hoodie over Emilia's head and dropped it next to him. "It sounds to me like she's had too much to deal with today. Stop fidgeting."

"I'm trying," I growled. "Can you fix her? I need her to be okay now."

His mouth twitched, and he checked her pulse again. "She'll be fine, boy. The mind is an extraordinary thing with a remarkable defense system. It knows when a person can't handle any more stress. She's likely had a big panic attack, and now her mind is forcing her to recover." He frowned, which obviously made me even more tense, and he pulled down the neckline of her long-sleeved tee.

I inhaled sharply at the sight of the blotchy marks. "He—fuck. That sick son of a bitch. I'll fucking kill him. I'll cut him to pieces—"

"*Finnegan.*" Pop gave me a look.

I pressed a fist to my mouth and forced myself to memorize every mark Jonathan had given her. I could clearly see the dark prints of his fingers. He'd been goddamn rough on her for the bruises to be forming already.

Pop took a breath, not looking entirely calm himself. "When she spoke earlier, was she hoarse? How was her voice?"

I nodded. "Raspy."

"Could she move her head? Was she complaining of pain?"

"She said she felt like he was still choking her." Holy fuck, Jonathan's days were numbered. "She could move okay, though."

"That's good." He carefully felt around her neck. "We'll take her to a physician if she doesn't feel better soon. I don't think she's injured her larynx, or trachea for that matter, but better safe than sorry. She's probably only sore. I'll have Ian make her something later."

"I need whiskey," I said.

"You and me both," he muttered. "I trust that this Jonathan Porter won't be breathing much longer."

"I'll find him a nice resting place."

"Good." He nodded and stood up, and Pat returned a couple seconds later. "Here we go." He opened his briefcase and retrieved a handful of sample packets. "These are all low dosage. You can give her one when she wakes up—if she starts panicking."

I checked the packets, recognizing Xanax and Ativan. "Thanks. Which one's for me?"

He chuckled and gave my shoulder a squeeze. "I reckon a shot of whiskey will take care of things." He faced my brother. "Are the twins packed and ready to go?"

"I don't know. I'll check." Patrick walked out again.

I blew out a breath and ran a hand through my hair.

"She's a lovely one." Pop smiled faintly. "I'm looking forward to meeting her under better circumstances."

"You should've seen what she did to her pop." Now that the worst was over, I could smile about it. "She broke his nose."

"Attagirl." He smirked and nodded. "I'll go talk to Ian before we go. You should get her comfortable. She might be disoriented when she comes to."

"I will. Thanks for the help, Dad."

"Anytime."

Emilia woke up a couple hours later, and though she didn't panic, she did get upset. I gave her the Xanax and made her drink some water, and then she was asleep again.

I barely left my room. I went downstairs once to get something to eat and thank Patrick for coming with me today. Other than that, I stayed in bed with my laptop and set one of my credit cards on fire. After what Emilia had been through, my top priority was to keep her safe and happy.

Texting with my mother and aunt, I learned quite a bit about what women liked having around the house, such as shower products that weren't for men, foods and drinks they liked, and clothes.

I browsed one section in an online clothing store before calling it quits and transferring money to Karla's account instead. She was a personal shopper my brother, father, and I went to whenever a woman in the family had a birthday or whatever. She'd already helped me with Emilia twice.

Most of all, Aunt Viv had told me, it was important that Emilia got to decide for herself.

I kinda forgot about that, but it was only because the girl was asleep, and I wanted the shit shipped here stat.

It was impossible to forget that Emilia told me earlier she'd marry me. I didn't trust those words because of the circumstances; that said, I did want her to stay here. She could do whatever she wanted with the guest room if she wanted privacy, as long as she didn't go back to Sarah and that run-down motel.

Hell, not even Sarah should stay there. When I talked to Patrick earlier, he had just filled Sarah in on the situation, and she was understandably upset. Yet when he'd offered to come get her, she'd declined.

"Finnegan..." Emilia's whisper stirred the silence, and she sat up abruptly. "Oh God."

"I'm here. How're you feeling?" I set aside my laptop and felt her forehead. She was a little clammy. The girl needed a haircut. As beautiful as the long waves were, she could get lost in them.

"Dirty." She grimaced. "Can I borrow your shower?"

"Of course." I left the bed and rounded it to help her. "Uh, how's your throat? Are you sore?" I wanted to know if I should call a doctor. I wasn't about to risk anything with her.

She took my hand and let me help her out of bed. "A little sore, maybe. Not as bad as before."

That was a relief.

She asked for privacy once I'd guided her to the bathroom, and

I told her I'd be back with some clothes. She'd wobbled some, so I didn't wanna be away from her more than necessary.

A pair of boxer shorts and one of my tees would have to suffice tonight. Patrick had left Emilia's bags in the living room, and I had no desire to sift through them.

I gave the bathroom door a knock when she'd flushed the toilet. She opened it and let me in.

"Are you in a hurry?" My forehead creased as I looked her over. She seemed anxious to get in the shower.

"I feel gross." She yanked her shirt over her head, and I did a double take before averting my gaze. *Jesus Christ.* I wasn't sure what'd caught my attention the most, the marks around her neck or her breasts in a simple white bra. "Um, you showed me your ass last time." Was she justifying her quick stripping...?

"I'm not complaining." I side-eyed her. "I'm worried because Bambi can walk steadier than you."

She giggled sleepily, a gorgeous sound that filled me with more relief.

"I can get you a lawn chair to sit in—in the shower, I mean," I said. "I don't want you to trip."

She shook her head and unbuttoned her jeans. My concern wasn't exactly wiped out when she had to support herself on the counter. "I'm fine. There's no way a chair would fit in there anyway."

"You're dizzy," I argued. Leaving the boxers and tee next to the sink, I walked over to the shower. "Let me run you a bath instead. Then you don't have to stand up."

"Finnegan." She put a hand on my lower back as I turned on the water.

I straightened and sighed, only to cough. Now she was in just her panties and bra. Fucking perfect.

This time, however, the marks won. I clenched my jaw and carefully touched her shoulder. "I want him to suffer."

She turned toward the mirror, and I couldn't read her expression. She inspected the darkening bruises the same way I'd study a painting.

Unless I was stealing it, I had no interest in art.

"I punched him," she whispered.

"You did more than that." I came to a stand behind her and shifted her hair to the side. "I haven't been that proud in a long time, princess."

"Really?" She looked skeptical, yet her mouth quirked up slightly.

"Really." I pressed a kiss to her temple and kept watching her in the mirror. "Imagine the damage you could do with some training. No motherfucker would dare put a hand on you."

Her eyes flashed with something, and whatever it was, it pierced through the film of emptiness. "I wanna be strong."

"Stronger," I corrected, gathering her hair in my hands. "You're already strong, Emilia."

"Stronger," she whispered to herself. Then she nodded slowly and made eye contact in the mirror. "I meant it, you know. I'll marry you."

I took a deep breath. My hands fell to my sides. She'd been through too much today to make that decision. Even I had limits. As far as I knew, she was still affected by the anxiety pill. But *fuck* if I didn't wanna seal the deal right this second.

"Ask me again." She turned around and peered up at me. "Ask me, Finnegan, and promise to take me away from here. Tell me I never have to see my dad again. Swear to me I'm free from this hellhole."

She was killing me.

"If you regret this when your head is clear..."

"My head *is* clear," she insisted. "If today has proven anything, it's how fucking done I am. I don't want that to be my life."

I'd made my argument. I didn't have the willpower to give another or dig my heels into the sand. Placing my hands on the counter on each side of her, I dipped down and kissed her.

"Be my wife." I cupped her cheek and rested my forehead against hers. "I'll take you away from here. You never have to see him again. I'll help you get stronger." When she closed her eyes, I dropped two kisses over her eyelids. "Marry me, and I'll give you a better life."

She let out a trembling breath. "Okay. Yes."

"Yeah?" My stomach flipped.

"Yes." She opened her eyes, and the hazel in them shone brighter. "I'm sure. I'll be your wife."

I kissed her again, deeper this time, and my ticker pounded in my rib cage. My hands went to her hips, and I stroked her soft skin, earning myself a shiver from her. In turn, she pressed herself closer to me, and I picked her up and sat her on the counter.

"I have a ring." I grazed my teeth along her bottom lip before sweeping inside for a heady taste. Kissing her was becoming an addiction, same with feeling her, being close to her, *holding* her.

"You do?"

I nodded and cradled her face in my hands. "You take your bath. I'll get the ring and some food."

"Okay." Her smile was atypically shy, and her cheeks were perfectly flushed.

"So fucking beautiful." I gave her another smooch. "Be careful in the tub, okay?"

"I will."

chapter 15

Finnegan O'Shea

"Oh my God, no. Holy crap, this is something else. I've never worn anything so extravagant. Fuck, I can't. Finnegan, I'll lose it—oh wow, it's *heavy*. I love it so much, but I'm legit afraid of it. Or afraid of myself. What if I drop it? It's so *cute*."

I chuckled at her frenetic rant and got comfortable in the corner of the couch.

"Seriously." She crawled up into my lap, mesmerized by the ring on her finger. So was I, but for another reason. It filled me with possessiveness to see it there. It looked right. Perfect, even. "This is scary."

I took her hand and kissed the top of it. "In a good way, I hope."

"As long as I don't lose it."

"The diamond's insured. Don't worry about it."

I'd grown antsy waiting for her to finish her bath, so I'd taken a shower to pass the time. Then I'd gotten the soup and fresh rolls that Ian had prepared in the main house before spending a solid twenty minutes pacing and clearing the couch of her shit. So it was possible I'd gotten the ring on her finger the minute she'd reemerged from the bathroom wearing my boxer shorts, a tee big enough to drown in, and her hair in a damp, untidy bun at the top of her head.

She'd never looked more adorable and naturally beautiful.

"You should eat." I kissed her forehead and patted her stomach. "I can hear it snarling, you know."

She grinned self-consciously. "I'll eat when I can stop staring at this." She stuck her ring in my face, and I laughed. "What's this cut called? Emerald?"

"Cushion." I made a decent art thief, but I knew a whole lot more about jewelry. And I'd wanted something special and rare for Emilia. I'd had help from two designers to find the perfect gems. In the end, I'd chosen a pale blue cushion-cut diamond surrounded by tiny stones in a diamond-encrusted platinum band. If I had any say, it would never leave Emilia's finger.

She bit her lip and lifted a brow. "Did you steal this?"

I coughed around a laugh and squeezed her to me. "No, you little shite, I didn't steal it."

"I had to ask!"

Down to chuckles, I lifted her off of me so she could get some damn food into her stomach. If my suspicion was correct, she hadn't eaten since lunch in school.

"Crap!" She shot right up and stared at me in alarm, and that was how easily my heart jumped up into my throat. "I was supposed to work today!"

Jesus Christ, she couldn't scare me like that. "Sit the fuck down, woman." I took a calming breath. "You don't work there any longer. All that is over and done with. Work, school, you name it."

She sat down, processing, and it was as if she couldn't grasp what I was saying.

"We'll get the paperwork sorted next week," I promised her. "This late into the semester, I reckon summer school or holding off a few months would be best, but I can make some calls if you wanna graduate this May."

"I don't care right now," she whispered. "I'm really quitting all of it?"

"All of it," I confirmed. "It's done." Scooting forward, I opened the containers from Ian and was glad it still seemed warm. "Remember I wanted to take you to Philly this weekend?"

She nodded hesitantly.

"What would you say about staying there?" I asked. I handed her a container of broccoli cheddar soup and a spoon. "We can ease into it if you want. Stay here sometimes and in the city sometimes." I'd be more than okay with that. With my folks moving out here soon, I needed to see Pop often enough for when we discussed Italy. As long as I had more access to Philly than I had right now, I'd be golden.

"And you have a place in the city too...?"

I nodded. "I have a condo in the same building as Patrick in downtown Philly."

She ate a couple spoonfuls of soup, her gaze never really leaving mine. "What you're saying is we could be living in the city within a few days."

She was too cute. "Yes, Emilia. Within twenty-four hours, technically."

"Let's do that."

She sure as fuck wanted to get away from here. And no one could blame her.

"Consider it done." I kissed her cheek before tucking into my meal. It'd been hours since I ate, so I was gonna fill up on bread. A bowl of soup didn't cut it. I was a growing boy. "Will you be ready to sit down with lawyers anytime soon?"

She knew what I was talking about, and she was less hesitant now. "Yes. I'm ready."

Maybe a little too ready. After everything she'd been through, I'd have to make sure she didn't overwhelm herself in her excitement to get away from her old life.

"I take it we're getting married soon?" Emilia questioned.

There was no way to beat around the bush with this. The sooner, the better. "Uh, yeah. However soon you and my mother can put together a wedding." I'd have to speak to Father O'Malley. They took Pre-Cana classes seriously in our church, and I was going to renegotiate those a bit. No way I'd sit through months of premarital counseling.

"Don't look so constipated, Finnegan. I know what I'm getting myself into."

I choked around a mouthful of soup and reached for a napkin. Oh, how I fucking doubted she knew what she was getting herself into, but fair enough. I could be more direct if she wanted.

"It's gonna be a big wedding," I admitted. "I guess I don't want you to change your mind."

"And go back to what I fought myself out of today?" She shook her head. "I'd rather kill myself. You have a big family, and you surround yourself with lowlifes. I'm counting on a packed church."

"Lowlifes," I muttered and bit into a roll. "That's harsh, princess."

"Cry about it." She smirked. "#MobstersArePeopleToo."

I let out a laugh, wondering if life could ever get dull with her by my side. "You're the one marrying a man you call a mobster. What does that say about you?"

"Oh, there's no hope for me." She was being lighthearted about it, so I went with it. I didn't correct her. "Okay, so you said your mom and I are gonna plan this thing. Does that mean you don't care about the hows and wheres?"

"My wedding won't be a snooze-fest, so I'll be in charge of the music. The where is already taken care of. I'll talk to our priest on Sunday."

She cocked her head. "Are we going to church?"

"If you don't mind."

"No, that's okay." She dished up some more soup and dipped her bread in the spoon. What a weird technique. "Sarah helped me download a couple games on my phone. I can feed my fishies or crush candy."

My mouth twitched in amusement. "You're not religious one bit, are you?"

"I'm really not. If I were, I'd have to say God is a narcissistic dick."

"Don't hold back," I chuckled.

"What about you?" She eyed me curiously. "Do you believe in all of it? The sins, the Commandments, the—"

"No." It made me happy that she asked questions rather than dismissed it. "The men who wrote the Bible are just that, men. They have no more credibility than any man today who claims to speak for God."

"Hmm. Okay. So who decides what's right and wrong?"

"The law, mostly, in terms of what gets you behind bars," I replied, a smirk tugging at my lips. "And sometimes I'm wrong."

She grinned. "You don't say."

I laughed through my nose and tried to phrase it better. My faith was, after all, important to me, and I wanted her to get it. "Look. You'll find enough contradictions in the Bible to make anyone lose their mind. Luckily, God gave us the ability to choose our path."

Father O'Malley told us the law was for society to follow. Faith and the scriptures were matters of the heart.

"So you chose neither of those."

"I fucking swear," I chuckled. "I'll give you that one, but I'm gonna try to make you understand sometime."

"I don't outright reject religion, Finnegan." She smiled. "Faith can be both a burden and a strength, but no, I don't get how a man who breaks the law for a living can be religious."

I narrowed my eyes. "Allegedly breaks the law."

"*Right.*" She gigglesnorted.

"You seem...different." I wasn't complaining—far from it—though it did raise some questions.

Ever since she woke up, she'd been affectionate, in a good mood, and open to discussing a future in which she shared her life with my family and me. Sure, that future would be only three years on paper. For now. Somehow, I'd get her to change her mind. Still, she'd been so repulsed by the notion before.

Now she was cuddled up in my lap. We bickered about the Netflix selection and fought for the last Rolo. I got the last chocolate; she got to pick the movie.

"I'm gonna ride this relief for as long as I can." She yawned and played with the drawstrings of my sweatpants. "Just the thought of never going back makes me wanna jump up and down."

I gave her a squeeze and pressed a kiss to her shoulder. "I'll keep you safe and happy."

She tilted her head back and smiled sleepily. "I believe you."

Every time we were this close, I swore I'd never seen anyone so beautiful. It was crazy. She literally had the ability to make my breath hitch, and it didn't bode well for me. I had to keep my head clear.

I stroked her cheek and kissed her. "You should get some sleep." It was already the middle of the night, and unlike me, she'd been on her feet all day and gone through hell.

"Can we stay here? It's cozy."

"Sure." I reserved the right to move her off of me when my thighs couldn't handle her pert ass anymore.

We watched most of the movie that'd already started, then dozed on and off for a few hours. Every time I woke up, we were in a new position, though we stayed tangled together.

I winced. My neck was at an uncomfortable angle, and Emilia was lying on top of me.

The TV had been shut off at some point.

With a grunt, I positioned her next to me instead, regretting that we hadn't slept upstairs.

In the low, predawn light, Emilia's face was cast in shadows and blues. Her skin was free of blemishes and lines, and she looked peaceful. Her eyelashes almost touched her cheeks. She had the softest fucking skin... Why could I never keep my hands off of her? Even now, as she slept, I had to touch her. I traced the shape of her cute nose with a finger, causing her to twitch.

"Jerk," she whispered.

I grinned sleepily and nuzzled her jaw. "I didn't mean to wake you."

The corners of her kissable mouth twisted up, and she slipped a leg between mine. "Then don't stick your fingers in my face." She opened her eyes slowly and blinked a couple times. "Hi."

"Hey." I adjusted the shitty pillow we shared. "Next time we sleep down here, we'll prepare better." We could've at least brought down the duvet.

"I'm perfectly comfortable."

"Because you're not six foot three, you midget. You fit under this pathetic excuse for a blanket. My feet are freezing."

Her eyes sparked with amusement. "You're cranky in the morning."

I scowled. I wasn't cranky. That was the last word I'd use to describe me.

Emilia took the opportunity to get on top of me again, and I could admit I made a noise of complaint. My back ached, and the discomfort had robbed me of my morning wood. If she was going to sit on me like that, I preferred to be hard.

"I never thanked you for coming to get me yesterday." She splayed her hands on my chest as I stretched out as much as I could.

"You don't have to thank me for that." I stroked her thighs absently, enjoying my view. "Have I told you how stunning you are?"

She grinned and ducked her head. "You have. You've given me a lot of compliments."

"Each of them true," I murmured.

"Maybe..." She leaned down and kissed me softly. "You made me stutter the first time I saw you."

I remembered. I figured it was because she'd recognized me.

"I think I hated you a little extra because you're so handsome." She made me shiver with that one, or maybe it was her tongue teasing mine. "Hot," she whispered, "sexy..."

Well, fuck me. She seduced me like a pro, making me crave her. Needing more of her, I slipped my hands underneath her boxer shorts, not stopping until I finally got to feel her delectable little ass. Skin-on-skin, I caressed and grabbed at her ass cheeks as we made out like teenagers.

Funny how she made me forget the soreness in my back.

She *moved*. It was on purpose. I groaned into the kiss when she shifted over my hardening cock, and I had to growl a warning.

She couldn't realize just how sexually repressed I was.

"Careful, princess."

She broke the kiss and sat up, and I tried to collect my breath.

She watched me with mischief in her eyes until the playfulness faded and morphed into something heavier. Grasping the bottom of her tee, she pulled it over her head and dropped it...somewhere. I had no goddamn clue where, 'cause fuck me twice.

"Jesus fuck." I sat up and gripped her waist. "You know you're not obligated to do anything, right?"

"I know." She cupped my cheek and kissed me, visibly nervous but turned on. I could feel her. She shimmied her hips over me, and I watched goose bumps appear on her arms.

I shuddered and extended the invisible leash. Up until the day I married her, I only had one limit. She might have others, so she'd have to run this show before—oh, fuck it. There was no way I could surrender control. I kissed her slowly, tasting her, and stroked the soft skin under her breasts.

Emilia lifted my T-shirt next, and I broke the kiss long enough to take it off. Then I was back, hungrier than ever, and I let instinct take over. I cupped the undersides of her breasts, ghosting my fingers over her nipples, and they tightened under my touch. Her breathing hitched. Our kiss grew wilder, and I had to remind myself to breathe.

"Finnegan..." Her breathless plea shot straight to my cock.

I groaned and buried my face against her neck as she squirmed on my lap, and I couldn't take it. I flipped her over onto her back, ignoring her squeak, and pushed my cock against her pussy. The pressure built up. The air felt thick.

Pinching one nipple carefully, I closed my mouth over the other and sucked. Emilia gasped and arched her back, so I took it as a good sign. I flicked my tongue over the peak, then around it, and I was pretty sure this was more for me than her. I'd seen her cleavage in nice dresses, I'd seen her nipples teasing the fabric of my tees, and I'd thought about having her under me like this more times than I could count.

She moaned every time I went harder, sending ripples of desire through me.

I needed more.

"I want you to touch yourself," I murmured huskily. At her half-dazed, half-confused expression, I grabbed her jaw and kissed her hard. She just looked too delicious when she was turned on. "Slip a hand down your panties and touch yourself the way you do when no one's around."

She flushed in embarrassment, unconvinced. "You'd watch?"

I nodded slowly and looked down between us. Everything about her called to me. From her cute feet and toned legs, to the curves of her hips, stomach, and tits. Then her beautiful face... She was Italian grace and fire, and she didn't even know it.

"Every second of it."

She shuddered violently and gave a small nod. "Okay. If you do it too."

She was a goddamn dream. I kissed her once more, then sat back on my heels between her legs. There was no modesty in my

DNA, so I pushed down my boxer briefs unceremoniously and skimmed my fingers alongside the back of my cock.

"Holy fuck." Her breathing became unsteady, and she scooted farther up to use the armrest as a pillow. "Or I can just watch you?"

I let out a breathy laugh and shook my head. "No dice."

The discomfort didn't leave her, yet she didn't hesitate anymore. She squirmed her way out of her panties, and I had to stifle a groan at the sight of her glistening pussy. My cock throbbed, and I swiped my thumb over the slit to spread the pre-come.

"Use your left hand." I barely recognized my own voice. Maybe a part of me was in disbelief that this was even happening. "I wanna see your ring when you get yourself off."

I wanted to fucking come on it.

I inhaled deeply, filling my lungs with the smell of sex.

Emilia broke eye contact and slid a hand down her body, her middle finger disappearing between the smooth lips. The rock on her finger glinted with each little movement, and I fisted my cock and stroked it unhurriedly.

"Will you let me fuck you one day?" I couldn't not touch her. My free hand went to the inside of her thigh, and it was just as silky as I'd hoped. "Taste you?"

"Yes," she whispered. "Oh God." She trembled when I brushed my fingers along the soft crease where her thigh ended. Two of her fingers dipped farther down, then up and around her clit.

"You're out of this world, princess." I stroked myself a little faster, unable to look away from her. It was the headiest moment I'd experienced so far, and it made me all the more impatient to give her my name.

She exhaled a moan and rolled her hips. "I'm—it's not easy with my left. Can I—"

"Let me help." Something inside me snapped, and I was back to hovering over her. "Use my fingers." Our lips touched, and she gulped. Hell, some nerves tightened my gut too, but I had to do this. I had to touch her. "Rub them all over you."

"Fuck." She reached up and kissed the ever-loving shit outta me, and she did exactly what I'd said. She guided my hand to her wetness, and I moaned into the kiss. Fucking hell, she was so slick, soft, hot, and tempting.

"Emilia," I whispered, out of breath. "Look at me."

Her eyes flashed open. The lust surged between us, and she held my gaze as I dragged my middle finger slowly between her lips. I eased my thumb in between too, near the top, and drew a circle around her clit.

"Like that," she said, sucking in a sharp breath. "More."

It didn't take long before she released my wrist. Her eyes fluttered closed, and her chest heaved with every intake of air. My name fell from her lips, and I knew it would never get old.

"Christ, look at you..." I eye-fucked her and teased every inch of her pussy. Pushing my luck, I circled her opening to see if she'd be okay with it. Judging by her gasp, I hoped so. "Imagine when this is my cock, baby." I entered her carefully, sliding through the slick tightness. "Jesus," I breathed out. Flicking my gaze from my own cock to her pussy, feeling how small she was, there was one obvious question that I was gonna ignore for now. For both our sakes.

"More," she begged. "Your fingers feel so amazing."

"I'm trying to hold back here." I chuckled darkly. "I wouldn't test my control if I were you. You're tempting as it is."

"I wanna test it a little bit." She nipped at my bottom lip. In response, my chest rumbled with a low growl, and I pushed in a second finger. "Oh my *God*, Finnegan."

"Touch me." I spoke through clenched teeth. "Wrap your pretty little fingers around my cock and get me off."

The subservient look in her eyes might as well have been a shot of Viagra straight into my veins. Her hand drifted to my thigh, and I inched up a little so she could come between us. *Fuck, there it is.* I groaned against her neck as her fingers tried to reach around me.

She touched me gingerly. "How do I make you feel good—"

"You can't do it wrong." I shifted away from her neck before I sank my teeth into a wrong place. The last thing I wanted was to remind her of her bruises. "A little harder than that—just like that. Fuck."

I fingered her deeper and applied more pressure on her clit. The urgency spread within me like an unstoppable force, and all the pent-up need that'd been bottled inside me was ready to shatter me.

I only paused once to adjust her grip. "When I say stop, you gotta stop."

"Why?"

"Because I'm gonna come." I kissed her softly and cupped her pussy. "Right here. I have to. I wanna see you soaked in me. Your clit, these lips, your tight little—"

Her gasp cut me off, and she tensed up. Her hand disappeared from my cock, and before I could tell her to touch me again, I realized she was close. Redoubling my efforts, I rubbed her clit in hard little circles and finger-fucked her in sensual strokes.

"You're right there, aren't you?" I rested my forehead against hers, and she cried out a *yes* that rocked me. "Let me see you come, princess." Her scent carried enough sweetness to make my mouth water. "I won't be able to stop myself from pushing my cock through those delicious juices."

Emilia came with a silent scream. Her nails were digging into my arms, her face and chest were flushed, and her skin was almost as damp as mine. She'd stopped breathing. My own breaths got heavier and heavier, and I withdrew from her the moment she was coming down from her high.

I fisted my cock and stroked myself quickly. My brain became foggy. All I saw and felt was her. My cock shone with her arousal, and I didn't wanna fucking leave this spot. Her heat drew me closer to my own orgasm, and right before I got there, Emilia's lips were on my shoulder. Her feet snaked around my calves. Her hands roamed my back, until one of them slipped between us.

I sucked in a breath as she spread her pussy lips. Left hand. *My* ring on her finger.

A drawn-out groan left me, and I slid my cock along the length of her pussy, rubbing the head of me against her clit. Then the pleasure pulled me under. Hot ropes of come shot out of my cock, landing across her sensitive skin. My eyes nearly rolled back at the sensations.

Emilia replaced my hand with hers, intensifying everything. I watched through hooded eyes while she drew another couple releases from me, one staining her hand and engagement ring. The fine hairs along my neck rose. A few final drops trickled down my shaft, and I was left drained and ready to collapse.

I had to lock my elbows into place so I didn't land on her. I wasn't sure she could handle two hundred pounds of dead Irishman.

"Fuck..." The word escaped me in a shallow exhale.

Emilia squirmed under me, and it took me a beat to realize she was trying to make room for me. I was happy to help with that, and soon, I was only half on top of her. Fucking exhausted. My head perfectly comfortable on her chest.

"Let's not move for a few hours," I whispered.

She laughed softly. "Your beard tickles."

I rubbed my chin on her breast and smiled lazily.

I wasn't kidding about not moving for a few hours, but I was ready to break up with the couch, and we were both a mess. With every muscle in me protesting, I dragged myself off the couch and helped her up.

"Shower, then no moving." Naked. In bed.

"Are you a cuddle monster?" she giggled.

Apparently, I was.

chapter 16

Emilia Porter

Don't let this end, don't let this end, don't let this end.

For some eighteen hours, I'd been completely swept away by Finnegan, and I needed it to stay that way. My heart was light around him. I didn't worry as much, and it was so easy to shut everything else out.

Not the smartest strategy, perhaps, but didn't I deserve this?

In time, I was going to have to deal with everything Finnegan represented, what kind of man he was and what he did, so I made it my mission to make this last for as long as I could.

There was no cake on the patio that morning. Instead, he wanted me to get to know his regular morning routine. Wearing a navy-blue hoodie from Trinity College in Dublin and matching sweat pants, he admitted he missed the city life and his old routines. And he hoped to share them with me. So far, it included healthy stuff. I sat on the kitchen counter as he jammed a bunch of fresh fruit and berries into a blender and explained he liked to start his mornings with a run. Then breakfast.

"I mean, you'll do your own thing," he said. "I don't have any expectations that go beyond, you know, having a normal relationship. My way of trapping you might've been unconventional—"

"Trapping me," I chuckled.

He grinned and shrugged, adding ice cubes to the fruit mix. "My point is, our home won't be run in some old-fashioned way. I even do my own dishes."

I laughed and stole a leftover blueberry from the container. "How modern of you."

"Right?" He closed the distance and rested his hands on the counter, and he kissed me quickly. "That said, I hope you come with me."

"Come with you where?"

"On my morning run." He nipped at my bottom lip when I pouted. Running was torture! "You said you wanted to get stronger, Emilia. This is how."

I thought back to the classes Sarah had put on her list. It would probably do me good to write a similar one so I didn't forget my priorities. I'd never had ambitions before, and that had to change. Evidently, I suddenly had a future.

"Okay," I whispered. "I'll go with you."

I was gonna get stronger, dammit.

"Fuckin' A." Finnegan grinned and rubbed his hands together, returning to the blender. "We head out in ten. Do you have anything to wear for now? We'll get you new shit in the city."

"You are way too excited for this." I jumped down from the counter and huffed. "I'll dig out my old sneakers." Hopefully, my yoga pants still fit.

I should've known Finnegan didn't get his sculpted body from eating cake.

"Four more laps, princess. You've got this." He ran past me—again—on his millionth lap around their property.

For the record, their property was freaking huge. If the front wasn't big enough, the open grounds behind the main house were gonna kill me. That space alone was easily a few football fields big. There was an unfinished pool area, patio, orchard, an enormous lawn, and at the very end, a duck pond and small forest. All of it was surrounded by a ten-foot-tall hedge with a fence buried inside it, according to Finnegan.

Music was pouring out of his house, which I couldn't hear when I reached the end of their property.

I huffed and puffed, and that rat bastard was somehow always near when I wanted to pause and catch my breath.

I continued running. Or, let's be fair. I jogged. Finnegan was running. He made it look too easy.

The next time he passed me, he even smacked my butt.

"I'll kick your ass, Irish boy!" I yelled, panting.

"Might wanna catch me first!" he hollered.

I gnashed my teeth together and went a little faster. Who needed to breathe anyway. My clothes stuck to my body, and I felt generally gross.

Three laps later, I was ready to throw in the towel. Finnegan was outside his house doing push-ups, and I just... I snapped, okay? I stalked over to him and sat down on his back, causing him to collapse on the grass.

"*Oomph.*"

"Not so fit now, are you?" I folded my arms over my heaving chest and peered down at him.

He growled, and then the fucker got a better grip, hands planted on the grass, tendons straining in his arms. I yelped and almost fell off of him, and he made me hate him just a bit when he completed his set.

"You were saying?" he panted and rolled over, effectively brushing me off of him in the process. He was smug as hell, but fuck, he was incredibly sexy. He'd shed his hoodie, and his tee was drenched in sweat that made his muscles glisten.

My mouth went dry.

I lifted his T-shirt and eyed his abs. "Um, can we go inside and have actual fun?"

He chuckled breathlessly and sat up. And he gave me another glimpse of his abs when he used the bottom of his shirt to wipe his forehead. "We're not done yet." He cuffed me playfully on the chin. "I wanna test your strength."

"Wanna wrestle?" I waggled my eyebrows.

He grinned and took himself a big kiss. "You have no idea how much you've brightened my life, princess." Telling me things like that...*no bueno.* I *felt* things. He was stirring up emotions in me. "Let's table that idea for later. I'm definitely interested." He stood up and extended a hand. "First, something else." He retrieved his water bottle too, and I guzzled like a champ.

As another song began blaring out of Finnegan's house, he ushered me toward Patrick's place. The side of it, more correctly. It was an empty house wall, aside from some contraption. A wood beam stuck up from the grass, and it had a bar attached to it. The other end of the bar was secured to the house wall. I wasn't entirely new to gym equipment. This was used for chin-ups.

It was high, high, high up.

"Chin-ups," I said with a nod. "I don't do those."

"You will soon," he murmured in my ear and squeezed my butt. He'd clearly developed a fondness for it. "Do you know how to do them?"

"No," I lied. "You'll have to show me. You should probably lose the tee."

Meanwhile, I was developing a huge crush on making Finnegan laugh.

"Are you objectifying me?" he asked.

"Like whoa."

He humored me, thank goodness. He tore off his shirt and...*hnngh.* Definition everywhere. Standing underneath the bar, he jumped up with a grunt and grabbed it, immediately heaving himself higher to start a set of chin-ups. I just stared. Finnegan was solid. Not slim, not bulky. With some meat on his bones and those muscles that rippled when he worked out, he was one perfect sandwich. I mean combo.

His filthy sounds weren't helping. I clenched my thighs together, and he finished the last two chin-ups with sexy growls.

"Whew." I cleared my throat.

He smirked and crooked a finger at me. *Come, princess.*

"Don't mind if I do," I mumbled under my breath. "I'll never reach that thing."

"I'll help you." He positioned me with my back to his chest and gripped my waist. "Maybe lose the tee first?"

Smug bastard. Oh, fine. I was wearing a sports bra underneath. If Patrick waltzed out of his house and wondered what the ruckus was, I wouldn't look totally indecent. I dropped my shirt on the ground and earned myself a couple seconds of eye-fucking from Finnegan.

"Ready?" His voice came out huskier.

"Not one bit." I looked up and squinted, and as he lifted me off the ground, I raised my arms. "Crap!" Merely hanging from the bar wasn't a walk in the cake. I mean park. Okay, I was hungry. Maybe *I* was obsessed with cake. "You can't leave me here, Finnegan!"

His laugh was carefree and booming. "I'm not leaving you." He'd stepped in front of me, though. He could see me making an ass of myself. He'd watch me fall. "Try to pull yourself up. And quit flappin' your feet. You'll just lose your grip."

I groaned through a whine and scowled up at the bar. How cool would it be if I blew his mind by completing at least one chin-up? Taking a deep breath, I closed my eyes, and I *heaved*... With all my strength. My arms trembled and grew hotter and hotter. Had the sun set them on fire?

"Ugh!" I almost tumbled to the ground as I straightened my arms again. "How...how..." Fuck. I couldn't breathe. "How close did I get?"

Finnegan cleared his throat. "Oh...four, five inches?"

"What!" I squeaked. "That's so lame!"

"Now we know where you're at, though." He stepped forward and slid his hands up my hips and waist. "You should be outlawed, baby." He grazed his lips down my nonexistent abs, only to move up again. With his tongue. He licked a hot trail up my stomach, and I let out a noise that sounded like *hhuungh*.

"Finnegan." I gasped, torn between panic and overwhelming arousal. Panic because I was slipping, slipping, slipping. "Eeep!" I wrapped my legs around his chest. A second later, I lost my grip.

Then I was sliding down his body until I was lowered to the grass and covered by one turned-on Finnegan O'Shea. All the air left my lungs as he pressed his thick cock against me and kissed me like a starving man.

My brain short-circuited from all the sensations. The grass tickled me, his sensual touches and kisses melted me, the excitement set off shiver after shiver, and I needed, needed, needed.

Finnegan made me feel normal. Like I didn't come from nothing and had even less to offer. His presence was immense and intense, and when he aimed all his attention at me, I didn't stand a chance.

I tore away when black spots filled my vision and my lungs demanded air. Finnegan continued. He left openmouthed kisses along my neck and collarbone. Our position flooded me with memories from early this morning and what we'd done. From his gentle touches whenever he was near my stupid marks, to his dirty words in my ear and his fingers buried inside me.

"Finnegan," I moaned.

He hummed, pinching my nipple through my bra, and returned to my mouth. "I can't keep my hands off of you."

"Good." I sucked in a breath and swiveled my hips as he thrust against me. "Fuck, that feels..." *Perfect.*

Before things to could get too wild, he slowed the kiss down. With his forehead resting to mine, we caught our breaths and enjoyed the moment. The arousal simmered below the surface, but something else stole my focus when I opened my eyes.

In the bright light of the sun, the dark copper in his hair was almost more prominent than the chestnut brown. I traced his beard with my fingers, across his lips, up along his nose... His eyes were out of this world, and they weren't solely gunmetal at all. There were flecks of green in there. Like the darkest forest.

I stopped breathing and noticed he was watching me just as intensely. It was as if he was trying to figure something out.

"I thought I knew exactly what I was signing up for with you," he murmured. "I've never been happier to be wrong."

I released a shaky breath and splayed my fingers on his chest. His heart was drumming fast.

"You're stuck with me now." I mustered half a smile. There was a voice at the back of my mind, sounding suspiciously like Sarah. She warned me to keep my feelings in check.

"For life, if I have any say."

He couldn't mean that. Not truly.

He tilted his head for a beat, then sighed and faced me again. "We're about to have company."

"Who?" I lifted my head off the ground and looked toward the gates. "Oh my God, is that your parents?"

"No," he chuckled. "It's Patrick."

"Oh." I relaxed again. "I thought he was in his house." Which reminded me... "Um, where's Alec and Nessa?"

"Probably back in Chicago by now. Pop picked them up yesterday, which you wouldn't remember 'cause you were out cold."

I flicked my gaze between his eyes, my brow furrowing. "He was *here*? When I was here?"

"Aye, he checked your pulse and shit. I was worried sick, you know."

I could process Finnegan's worry much, much later. I couldn't freaking believe Shannon O'Shea had given me some checkup, and I didn't know it.

"Well, that's embarrassing," I muttered, my head landing on the grass with a thump. Christ, more like humiliating. "I looked like a train wreck."

Finnegan smirked faintly. "It's cute that your biggest worry is your appearance. A few weeks ago, you would've said something else."

"I don't think you should remind me of that," I said pointedly. Farther away, the gates were opening.

"Good advice." He nodded once before helping me up.

I wasn't ready for our bubble to burst, but I didn't have much of a choice. Patrick exited his car, and Sarah was there too. He must've gone to pick her up.

"I'll fix breakfast." Finnegan kissed the side of my head, then left, probably to give me a moment alone with Sarah. Which I wasn't sure I wanted. She was the voice of reason, and she'd have no issue delivering a reality check.

Patrick offered a two-fingered wave on the way to his house. "How you doin', hon?"

"Better, thanks," I replied. "Thank you for being there yesterday."

"Of course." He winked and disappeared with Finnegan.

As Sarah made her way over to me, I picked up our discarded tees and Finnegan's water bottle. In an attempt to hide some of my bruises, I put my shirt back on. Ugh, sticky. I couldn't wait to shower.

"Hi." I put a smile on my face so she wouldn't see any of my worries.

She didn't respond at all. When she reached me, she just threw her arms around me and held me tightly.

Emotions surged up without my damn permission, and I hugged her back. "I'm okay, Sarah. I promise."

"You have to agree to Finnegan's proposal, Em," she croaked. "You can't stay in town anymore. I could kill your dad—"

"Hey. Honey." I halted her before she could really get going, and I ended the hug to show her my ring.

Her jaw dropped at the sight of it. "Holy fucking shit!" At my laugh, she made a noise and grabbed my hand. "Oh my God, it's gorgeous. How can it both be adorable and flashy?"

"I know. That's what I said." The baby blue of the diamond at the center made it lovely. Then the small diamonds all around the big one—and the ring—cranked up the extravagance.

She beamed at me. "You said yes."

I nodded, unable to speak for some reason. She looked so relieved.

Would she still be relieved if she knew how close Finnegan and I had become?

My fierce best friend was all about strategy and putting herself first for once.

I was getting lost navigating through all these feelings.

"You have no idea how happy this makes me," she said, her eyes welling up. "Tell me everything. Christ—" She was back to inspecting the ring. "This sure makes the other one look cheap."

Okay, that irked me. The Claddagh ring that used to belong to Finnegan's grandmother meant a lot to me. Where the engagement ring allowed me to indulge in feeling like a freaking...well, princess, the delicate silver ring on my index finger carried a deeper meaning.

"Tell me how it happened," she repeated. "And what're the plans? Are we good to finally fuck off from this town?"

She had no idea.

chapter 17

Emilia Porter

A few hours later, I had a ridiculous number of butterflies in my stomach. The morning had passed in a blur that was kind of hard to digest. In a good way, but...almost in a *too good to be true* way.

Sarah had made one comment that'd been difficult to address. She'd seen Finnegan lying on top of me in the grass, and she'd studied me closely when I somewhat bluntly admitted we had good chemistry. And I owned it, right there in front of her. I believed it as I said the words. It was okay for me to enjoy this. Sarah's words, after all. It didn't change anything because I knew what kind of contract I was going to sign very soon. It *was* business. Only, it wouldn't stop me—us—from enjoying each other. Finnegan and I happened to get along, and we were obviously drawn to each other.

I didn't mention to Sarah just how drawn we were. The important thing was, Sarah had agreed with me, and she was glad I could find happiness in this for the moment. *As long as the end goal was the same.* In three years, she and I would walk away.

I ignored the feeling that'd come over me at that 'cause, frankly, I wasn't ready to deal with it.

After that little conversation, Sarah had jumped in, headfirst. The four of us had eaten breakfast together on the patio, and she'd said if Finnegan and I were gonna spend more time in the city, she wanted to do the same. We were two girls who'd waited for this for so long. Hell, I hadn't even thought this day would come. Now, I was in the car with Finnegan, and we were officially on our way to Philadelphia.

Patrick was staying behind with Sarah to help her pack up her stuff and check out of the motel, and then they'd meet us for dinner in the city tonight. *Tonight!* It was unbelievable. Within the hour, I would walk into Finnegan's condo, and it would become my home too.

"When was the last time you were in Philly?" he asked.

"When I was fourteen," I answered right away. Because I remembered it so clearly. Our class had gone to DC and Philadelphia on a school trip. It'd been an awesome weekend.

"But it's only a couple hours away."

I lifted a shoulder and looked out the window. The forests were gone, replaced by fields and suburbs. "I haven't traveled much." Twice was the most accurate answer, aside from a handful of visits to Philadelphia. When I was twelve, Dad took me to Destin in Florida because my grandmother had lived there. She'd died, and Dad had hoped to make a buck off of her belongings.

He hadn't.

Finnegan grabbed my hand and kissed it. "We'll get you a few passports and make up for lost time."

I looked at him strangely. "A few passports?"

He cleared his throat and let out a chuckle. "I guess we like to fly under the radar in my family. It's good to have a few names you can use."

And so it began.

I folded my arms over my chest and stared out the window. Finnegan didn't strike me as a guy who misspoke. He was going to drop little bombshells like this one until they either stopped fazing me or they became too much. I couldn't even begin to grasp the fraud that was part of a crime organization. Fake travel documents, fake signatures, fake promises.

I knew this, though. It was the price to pay. I'd gain my freedom at the end, but the cost was steep. Only a week ago, I'd thought I could help the FBI do their job. How wrong had I been? If Finnegan was going to give me these anecdotes of insignificant crimes—in the grand scheme of things—I'd be sitting on a wealth of information before I knew it. And I wouldn't have the balls to risk getting caught, so he bought a lot more than three years from me. He was buying my loyalty.

"It's for our safety, Emilia."

Sure, whatever. "How does it even work?" I asked. "Your face was once plastered across the news." Granted, I hadn't seen any recent photos of anyone in the SoM. Finnegan and Patrick had grown up enough in ten years. Still, Shannon...? All the others from the older generation? "Anyone over thirty remembers everything that went down in Philly."

"Do you remember?" he asked curiously.

"Not much. Names and charges, I guess. There were like, eighteen murders."

He nodded slowly, switching lanes. "Well, first of all, no one expects to see a specific well-known person when it happens. People might know of me, but I'm a stranger to anyone who doesn't expect to see me. Second of all, my face isn't all that known. If anything, it's my name." Hence the fake passports, I assumed. And the beard...? Maybe. Patrick was clean-shaven, then and now. "Lastly, if I fly outta Philly, I might use my real passport on the first leg of the trip. Right now, it's perfectly safe. We're not under investigation—"

"How would you know?"

He smirked and checked the rearview. "We have friends."

Oh God.

Friends in law enforcement. Fuck. What if they knew Agent

Caldwell? Or Agent Caldwell knew someone who was on Finnegan's payroll? Fuck, fuck, fuck. Yeah, no more talking to the authorities for me. I'd stay quiet. Would Finnegan hurt me? It was difficult to comprehend, but he wasn't the only one in the Sons. I'd be surrounded by people who'd taken lives.

"You won't involve me in your work, will you?" I asked, uncomfortable.

"Fuck no." He side-eyed me with a frown. "Emilia, I realize it's hard for you to trust me. That's why I'm opening up a little. There will always be secrets I have to keep from you, but I'll prove my loyalty. In time, you'll see that you can have faith in me."

Maybe. Probably. He was a freaking sorcerer, after all. He'd gotten me this far, despite what I said in the beginning.

How deep could the rabbit hole be?

Finnegan's home provided a false sense of security. It drew me in and made me gasp, and it was...just so much better than I'd imagined. It was homey, *cozy*, and didn't broadcast its lavishness—other than the downtown location. The walls were all white, except for the one with three huge windows, which was red brick. And I could see the entire place from the entryway. It was a one-and-a-half story condo, with the bedroom located above a...what I could only describe as a musician's nook. There was a baby grand, two guitars on the wall, and a cushy reading chair.

Only the kitchen was separated from the rest of the place, with the dining area set up outside of it.

"Welcome home," Finnegan murmured in my ear.

I remained standing there and smiled behind my hand while he dropped his keys and the mail on the round kitchen table. One floorboard creaked where he stood.

"The grand tour isn't so grand." He flashed a smile and pointed behind me. "One bathroom there, another up in the bedroom.

Kitchen." He nodded down the narrow kitchen. "Living room." Another nod toward the corner where the ceiling was high. A large couch with a chest-high bookcase behind it divided the area, and the flat screen was preposterously big. "And my horribly underused piano corner," he finished. "If you wanna redecorate, be my guest, but the acoustics are best there for—"

"I'm not gonna change a thing," I said. I didn't know I had any preferences until I saw his—our...?—place. It was complete, from the biggest furniture to the smallest accents. Blankets and cushions in rich colors, candles, and pictures. "Did you do this on your own?"

"I was unusually demanding when I bought this place." He glanced around him. "But my mother did most of the work." He faced me again. "I'll show you Pat's place later. You won't believe we're in the same building."

I could actually imagine that, because the lobby downstairs was fancy. They'd covered up the old with gloss and marble.

"I'm trying to picture you guys running to your neighbors to borrow sugar."

He chuckled and returned to checking his mail. "He doesn't have any neighbors. The top floor is his. I have one across the hall. Mrs. Cardigan—which isn't her real name, but you'll never see her without a cardigan she's knitted herself."

"That's sweet." I smiled.

"So are you." He came over to me and grasped my shoulders. "Question. Think you can hang out alone for an hour or two? I have to run over to Pop's office and talk to him for a bit, and then I gotta pick up some shit I was supposed to have shipped to the compound."

Damn, they really did call it the compound.

"Um, yeah. Sure." I could snoop around and see what Finnegan filled his bookcase with.

"Perfect." He kissed me on the forehead and crossed the room to the metal stairwell that led upstairs. He jogged up the stairs and removed his belt. "I'll be home with a late lunch and clothes for you, Miss Porter."

"Clothes?" I looked up at him as he yanked his shirt over his head and threw it over the railing.

"Karla's hooked you up with a new wardrobe." He disappeared from view, making me wonder how big the bedroom up there really was. The space underneath the floor wasn't that huge. "And let me know what you want for dinner. I'll make reservations—what the fresh hell." There was a hint of an echo to his voice that told me he was in the bathroom. "Heads up. My mother's been here. She's replaced my shaving cream with something that sparkles."

I snickered to myself and finally remembered my feet weren't stuck to the floor. If this was going to be my home, I might as well create my own everyday routines. Finnegan already had a full life here, and I didn't wanna get left behind.

"There's a gift basket for you." Finnegan reemerged, dressed in a suit. On the way down the stairs, he fixed his tie. "Why does soap for women look like cake?"

"Because life's not confusing as it is." I wandered into the kitchen and took in everything. All appliances were stainless steel, and if it weren't for the bouquet of colorful tulips in the window, the kitchen could not be more bachelor-like.

Classical music started playing, and it sounded like it was coming from everywhere. It was how I noticed the speakers mounted in the corners of the ceiling. There were two in the kitchen, and I spotted another one as soon as I returned to the living room.

"That's the ring for my landline. Only my immediate family has the number." Finnegan paused near the entryway. There was a side table with a phone—or it had to be—yet it looked more like one of those docking stations for cell phones. Finnegan sent me a wry smile and held a finger in front of his mouth, then pressed a button. "You've been texting me all morning, Ma. I told you I'd call when we made it home."

"And you didn't call, did you?" Shit, it was Grace O'Shea. His mom. I'd heard her voice once before, not that I recalled it clearly. She'd testified in a case about Finnegan's cousin. "Is Emilia there with you?"

I quirked a brow.

"She's in the bath," he lied. "Let the girl get settled in for one day before you attack, eh? We'll see you and Pop at Mass tomorrow."

Amusement filled me, mostly because his accent changed just a bit. Maybe it was 'cause she sounded a little more Irish than he normally did. Though, none of them had distinguishable accents compared to Alec and Nessa.

"I can *hear* you smirking, boy," Grace said. "You've been talking about this girl of yours for weeks now." *Oh, really.* "You'll have to excuse me if I'm a wee bit excited to meet the one who managed to steal your attention."

Finnegan could not look away from me fast enough. This was *fun.*

He cleared his throat and started scribbling a note on the side table. "Right. I think you can hold out one more day. Gotta go, Ma." He ended the call with another press of a button, and whatever he was jotting down must've been important. "So it's possible that my mother doesn't know the extent of our arrangement. She thinks we're doing what Pop did."

"Which was?" This didn't make much sense. His parents had an arranged marriage too.

"She doesn't know money's involved—or that there's an expiration date."

Those were two giant fucking details.

"*Finnegan.*"

He tore off the note and handed it to me. "Numbers you might need."

I eyed it briefly, seeing Alec's name among ten others. Whatever. "Dude. Focus. How the hell does she think I agreed to marry you so fast?"

He sighed and smiled ruefully. "She thinks Pat and I can do no wrong. Seriously. She can be sharp as a tack, but where we're concerned, any woman's lucky to have us. So she knows the marriages are arranged, but she believes the promise of better lives and being with us is enough."

"Basically, she doesn't think women have morals?" I folded my arms over my chest. "Or standards?"

He snorted and looped an arm around my neck, then planted a loud kiss to my forehead. "You say the sweetest things. You remind me of Aunt Viv. She's always raging about women and silly feminism and shit."

Oh, he did not say that.

I pushed him away and plastered a saccharine smile on my face. "Have a lovely day at work, honey. I'm gonna go shower off the dirty thoughts I have about women's rights."

"Hey, what was that?" He narrowed his eyes at me. "I have nothing against women's rights."

"That's generous of you."

I was fucking with him—for the most part. Even the guys who saw us as equals needed occasional reminders that they didn't *let* us do anything. We took it. Finnegan seemed like the type of man who wanted to help. He wasn't messing around; he wanted me to get stronger and be able to stand my ground. At the same time, feminism wasn't *silly*.

"We'll turn this into a heated debate later," he told me.

"Can't wait." We exchanged a long look, and I admitted it was nice to see he wasn't entirely certain of where we stood at the moment. In the end, he tried to kiss it better. Literally. He held me to him and kissed me deeply before walking out.

This was going to get interesting.

In a way, the honeymoon was over before we'd even gotten

married. It was time to get to know the man Finnegan was in his everyday life.

Finnegan was well-read. In his bookcase, I found endless volumes about culture, history, and music. Memoirs by politicians and other leaders. Textbooks about engineering, technology, and physics. Not a single work of fiction. And the books weren't here for show. I flipped open a book about mining in India, of all things, and several pages were dog-eared or highlighted.

Why did he need a book about the history of canvases? Was this a joke? I opened it, and it was chapter after chapter about quality, fabric, and popularity based on origin and era. It was...art, I guessed? *Hold the fucking phone.* It was research. It was freaking research. I scanned the next page and the next and the next. He'd been learning how to detect fake paintings depending on what canvas had been used.

I put the book back.

The FBI should check out this place.

The books made more sense now. Christ, there were four books dedicated solely to the technology behind lock mechanisms for wall safes.

"Well, you're marrying a mobster," I mumbled to myself.

I stiffened when someone rang the doorbell. Finnegan hadn't told me if I could—oh, for crying out loud. Maybe it was Mrs. Cardigan. Whoever it was had been approved in the lobby downstairs.

In the entryway, I peered through the peephole and swiftly took a step back. That *had* to be Grace O'Shea. But I wasn't meeting her until tomorrow! I inched forward again and sucked in a breath. It was her; it was the dark-haired woman from the pictures in Finnegan's house.

Compared to her, I looked like trash. Just great. My jeans and top probably cost less than her nail polish.

I unlocked the door and opened it carefully.

She smiled widely, all red lipstick and perfect teeth. "You must be Emilia." She whooshed past me with a briefcase that she set down on the kitchen table. Then she shrugged out of her thin trench coat, revealing more perfection. She looked like a CEO, except for the unmistakable warmth that radiated from her.

She hugged me before I'd snapped out of my daze, and she spoke a mile a minute. There was an apology for intruding, but she "simply couldn't wait." Next, she revealed that the guy downstairs, Olivier, was married to the guy who did Grace's hair, and that was how she kept close tabs on the "boys."

"I knew Finn had left before his car was out of the garage." She winked, only to hug me again. Holy overwhelming shit. "You are just lovely, Emilia. I've been waiting to meet you."

"Um, hi." I forced a smile and tried to shake the nerves.

She tittered a laugh and click-click-clicked her way to the kitchen. "You're adorable, dearie. Now, I won't take up much of your time, but there are a few things we have to discuss." She returned with a bottle of water and told me to sit.

I sat.

She took a seat across from me and opened her briefcase. "Your friend Sarah is arriving later today, yes?"

"Um, yeah. I mean, yes, ma'am."

"Oh, none of that." She waved that off, the smile never leaving her face. She produced a stack of papers. "Tomorrow at church, I ask that you go through our introduction as if it's the first time we're meeting. It's easier for me to help the women who join our family if I don't have the men hanging over me."

I released a breath and managed to nod. This woman was a hurricane. "Understood." I didn't understand a thing.

"Good. Here we go." She slid me a few papers that'd been stapled together at the top corner. "There is no perfect advice to give you. Every situation requires a different tactic, but in general, I find it best to let others underestimate me. As much as it grates on me, no one suspects the dumb wife of having an agenda." She tapped a perfectly manicured nail on the papers. "That's the contract Finnegan's lawyers have drawn up for your marriage. If he's told you that I don't know about the money—"

"He has," I spluttered.

She nodded once. "I'm not surprised. Did he give you a list of law firms too?"

I shook my head. "He mentioned it—he said he could help me pick my representation."

She rolled her eyes. "That boy, I swear. Patrick is worse in a way, but Finnegan can be conniving. He's a meticulous planner like his father."

I laughed shakily, wondering if I'd gone insane.

Grace clasped her hands on the table and watched me patiently. "I love my family, Emilia. If what Finnegan's told me about you is true, I think you'll fit right in." She paused. "I also think—and hope very much—that my boy's finally met the woman who can become his match. You're probably not there yet because, God bless him, he's not the most honorable of men, and he's had years and years of sharpening his skills. But if you learn to play his game and grow into a force he can't manipulate, you will have a strong and happy marriage." She lifted a brow at me. "One that will last far longer than three years and give me many grand-children."

My mouth popped open, and I looked away.

"Either way, I'm here for you," she said. "To ensure my sons' happiness, a mother sometimes has to go to war against them. I've watched them grow up, and I know how quickly they get bored and restless. And this has nothing to do with what's in their hearts. Finnegan can be completely in love with you, but if he gets bored, he turns into a right tool. He needs to be challenged. Not only for his amusement, but for how it makes him a better man."

Finally, something that made sense. Finnegan hadn't made it a secret that he liked my attitude.

However, love had nothing to do with this.

"We're not marrying each other for love," I told her.

Her mouth twisted. There was a pinch of smugness. "Of course not. It's why you'll stay married, though. It's too soon for me to get a grasp on your feelings, but my son is a lost cause. He just doesn't know it yet."

I suppressed a sigh. "Let me guess, a mother knows."

She tapped the side of her nose.

Sure, whatever. There was no logic behind that. Our so-called relationship was less than a few weeks old. A lot could happen. Hell, a lot already had happened. I was changing. He was revealing himself. Who the fuck knew where we'd end up. One second, I wanted to turn them all in to the police. The next, I was breaking every speed limit to get an adrenaline rush from Finnegan's Aston Martin.

It was safest to change the topic. "What about this?" I held up the contract.

"Ah. I want you to read it. And when Finnegan requests that you sit down with your lawyers to sign it, you need to have a counterproposal." She dug up a business card from her briefcase. "I've taken the liberty of hiring your counsel. She breaks balls for a living and has faced our family lawyers before. She won't let Finnegan get the upper hand."

I accepted the card. *Meredith Campbell of Smith, Campbell & Stern.*

Would Finnegan actually screw me over in the contract? That thought made me queasy. Not knowing who I could trust was going to make me question everything.

"He would manipulate me," I said quietly. "Right?"

Sympathy shone in her blue eyes. "This isn't easy for you, I understand that. The short answer is yes."

Ouch. "And the long answer?"

She smiled a little at that. "Look where you are, dearie. This is his doing. He's somehow convinced you to leave your old life behind and join this one. He's charming and understands how people function. He knows the right buttons to push. But, are you suffering? Or has he managed to trick you into a life where you might actually find happiness?" Her bluntness hurt as much as I needed to hear it. If I was going to grow up, I had to have the truth. "He has no interest in robbing you of the money he's promised. He's going to put *all* his effort into making you stay." She gave me a pointed look. "That's where you need to play hardball. Do not give in to him, Emilia. I want nothing more than for your marriage to be lifelong, but not everything can happen on his terms."

I processed what she'd said and nodded slowly. If it made sense to me, did that mean I could trust *her*?

"Your family is a lot to deal with," I said with a stiff smile.

She laughed softly. "This is only the beginning. We're a bunch of liars, but we love fiercely, and we're loyal to a fault. Well." She made a face. "Patrick is a work in progress on that last bit. My talk with Sarah will sound a little different."

I was a bundle of confusion, and part of me wanted to scream. This talk had helped me, though. Now I knew there was a game to play. I just had to figure out the rules.

"Give Meredith a call and set up a meeting." Grace closed her briefcase. "Don't use your credit card. Tell her to put it on my account. And bring that fantasy of Finnegan's with you." She nodded at the contract. "Oh, and one more thing. Deny, deny, deny. When my son asks to know who's been helping you, lack of evidence means innocence. America taught us that."

I spluttered a laugh and nodded. "Thank you, Grace, I will."

So, secrecy was part of being an O'Shea. Noted. I was gonna learn.

"My pleasure. Next time we see each other, we'll make a lunch date to discuss the wedding."

"Okay."

I followed her out, and she put on her coat again.

"How do I know who to trust?" I blurted out.

The sympathy made a swift return, and she adjusted her collar. "Let it take time. I didn't fully trust Shan for at least four or five years. The only thing I know for sure is that Finnegan *will* prove himself worthy of you. He very much takes after Shan, and they both wear their hearts on their sleeves. It's the one thing they can't lie about—or hold secret. When my boy realizes he loves you, you'll know it."

I stared at my feet, having hoped for another answer. The idea that Finnegan would fall for me felt farfetched, whereas I fully believed he'd try to play me in a room with lawyers around.

"I'll earn your trust too, dearie." She patted my arm, her smile widening at the sight of my rings. "Did he tell you he asked for my opinion on the engagement ring?"

I shook my head.

"That's how I know." She winked. "Unless it's about decorating his home, he hasn't asked for my opinion on anything personal since he was a child. But there's something about you. He's going the extra mile."

Goodness, she had to leave now. I couldn't take another sorcerer.

"I'll suspend my disbelief," I chuckled.

She grinned and picked up her briefcase. "Fair enough. I'll see you at church tomorrow—for the first time."

"First time," I echoed with a nod.

Then it was just me, and I slumped back against the door and let out a heavy breath.

So that was Grace O'Shea.

chapter 18

Emilia Porter

"Emilia, I'm home!"

Well, that was good. After twisting the towel atop of my head, I exited the bathroom and let out a cloud of steam. I shivered at the cold and secured the towel around me.

Grace didn't fuck around with gift baskets from beauty stores. I'd never been so clean, scrubbed, and smooth in my life, I was sure of it. She'd given me everything from lotions and creams to scrubs and salts, from face masks and cleansers to razors and wax strips, from shampoos and conditioners to sponges and special makeup towels. I didn't even know that was a thing.

Reaching the railing, I peered down at where Finnegan was checking soccer stats on the TV.

"Hi, short stuff."

He looked up at me and smiled. "Who you callin' short, ya midget?"

I chuckled. "Did you say something about clothes before?"

"Aye, that's right." He kicked into gear, and my eyes grew large. Right there in the entryway, I counted five—no, six—six white gift boxes, similar to the one I'd gotten my first dress in.

Finnegan stacked them all on top of each other and carried them up the stairs. "I haven't cleared the walk-in yet. I'll do that tomorrow."

"Wow, this is...a lot." I shuffled by the foot of the bed as he set the boxes down.

He hummed, lifting a bunch of the lids as if he was on a mission. "There should be a—there." He unfolded something from silk wrapping. A wallet. He handed it to me. "I saw your gift cards in an old toiletry bag, and I know for a fact that you put your license in your bra sometimes."

I grinned and brushed a hand over the wallet. Black leather with some plaid pattern. "Thank you."

"And this." He retrieved an opened envelope from his pants pocket. "I'll order you the others once you're an O'Shea."

It was a credit card in my name. "I've never had one."

"That would make you one unique American." He walked closer, and his smile was half hesitant. "Did I fuck up earlier?"

I stifled my laugh—mostly. A snicker broke free. "Only a little."

"Then I bought flowers for a reason." He sat down on the side of the bed and tugged me with him so I ended up sideways on his lap. "Tell me what I did wrong."

He seemed sincere, so I didn't mess with him.

"I don't think feminism is silly," I admitted.

"Neither do I, princess," he chuckled. "I like getting a rise out of people. I don't see you as inferior or anything like that. But you gotta admit, you women take it too far sometimes."

I smashed my lips together and counted to ten. It would do me no good to nitpick, and if he chose to focus on a small group of loud screamers, I would simply have to show him. First, though, I wanted to be more comfortable with who I was. Right now, I was nothing but a small-town nobody. I had nothing to my name, and the man I wanted to argue with was my sole provider. Yeah, I wasn't gonna go there.

"Try drowning out the noise and focus on the core issues." I smoothed out the slight frown between his brows. "Do you have any women in the SoM?"

"Of course not." He seriously thought that was a joke. "It's called the Sons of Munster. I'd have a heart attack if you were around that shit."

"Ah. So, it's your issue. Not the women's." I popped a kiss to his cheek and left his lap. "Well, I definitely don't want to put your fragile heart at risk."

"Oh, the fuck you say?" His eyebrows went way up there.

I let out a laugh and started digging through the boxes, and I had the strangest urge to message Grace about this. Which would've been dumb, maybe. Too soon. I didn't yet know the kind of relationship I'd have with her—or if she appreciated gossip like that.

"So did you get lunch?" I asked, holding up a pair of skinny jeans. How on earth did this Karla woman get my size perfect? She'd never met me.

"Yeah, and this conversation isn't over," he said. "Nothing about me is fragile."

Especially not your ego, dear.

That night, Finnegan and I went to dinner with Patrick and Sarah at an Italian restaurant near their building. *Our* building.

Sarah showed up in a new dress, and she was sporting one massive rock on her finger. While Finnegan congratulated Patrick, Sarah leaned in and whispered, "He let me pick it out myself, so I went with the most expensive one on the display," which sort of crushed my excitement. I kept forgetting she was in it to win all of it. And I bet she'd get a lot for that big diamond. It was surrounded by little emeralds, not that I was sure she noticed. She went on and on about the carats and whatnot of the main event.

After we'd placed our orders and received our drinks, Finnegan draped his arm along the back of my chair and kissed my temple. "Is she even warming up to him?"

I should've known he'd been observing Sarah. He observed everything.

"I don't know," I replied softly.

My answer deepened his frown, though he didn't say anything else on the matter.

I wondered what Grace would think of Sarah. She'd probably say Sarah and Patrick were mere days away from falling head over heels in love.

When dinner arrived, so did a new topic. Sports. Both brothers were obsessed with soccer, which they religiously called "real football." They followed hockey and some American football as well—they were hardcore Eagles fans—and I genuinely didn't give a crap.

The thing that stuck out the most tonight was how people came over to say hey to Finnegan and Patrick. It happened the first time right after we'd ordered our drinks; a man stopped at our table to shake the guys' hands.

For sitting so far into the back of the restaurant, everyone sure had a way of running into us.

"Patrick, my boy!" An older gentleman came over with a much younger lady on his arm. "Those were some good bets, eh? Your pop's lucky to have ya."

Patrick chuckled and shook the man's hand. "I told you to trust me, didn't I?"

"Aye, I'll be back next week." He shifted his grin to Finnegan. "Good news travels quick, Finn. Congratulations on your upcoming nuptials." That *was* quick. People knew about us? "Will we be having little Finnegans running around here soon?"

It was Finnegan's turn to shake the man's hand—with a smile less sincere than Patrick's. "God willing. Thank you, Jim. I'll see you and your wife at Mass tomorrow, I take it? Or are you bringing this side piece?"

Holy shit.

Patrick's grin died. Sarah dropped her jaw. I dropped my fork, and it clanked against my plate.

Finnegan looked like he didn't have a care in the world.

"I told you not to bring me here," the woman hissed before stalking away.

I braced myself for Jim's anger, but it didn't come. He cleared his throat, visibly uncomfortable, and confirmed he'd, of course, be there tomorrow with his family. Then he wished us a nice evening and left.

I... How... What just happened?

Patrick was annoyed. "Seriously, Finn."

"Yeah, fucking seriously," Finnegan responded, and now he was irritated too. "This is a family place. We bring our wives and children here. It's goddamn disrespectful."

"Here I was, thinking Em had removed the stick up your ass," Patrick chuckled humorlessly.

It wasn't the first time I'd heard that. It *was* the first time I got a glimpse of how rigidly traditional Finnegan might be. I assumed Jim was involved with the SoM, and given his reaction to Finnegan, maybe he had, um, a lower rank? Shit, I didn't know how this worked. I'd seen documentaries on TV about cocaine and mistresses everywhere.

"Guys," I said quietly, because another man was walking over.

"Can a man eat his dinner in peace?" Finnegan muttered.

Then it was a new round of polite greetings and handshakes, and thank goodness the man wasn't here with a woman. Or, at least, not a mistress.

Was that something I'd have to worry about with Finnegan? Considering his...status, being as inexperienced as I was in certain ways, it felt unlikely right now. And later... Ouch, I didn't want to go down that road. It shouldn't hurt me to think of either, and it did. It actually hurt.

Who could forget the infidelity clause in his contract?

Shaking that off for now, I tuned in to the current conversation instead, and it was a much lighter one. Music. I could handle music. This guy, Mick, owned a bar down the street, and he was offering his place for a party to celebrate our engagements. And he was telling Finnegan it'd been so long since he played live.

"He was a little know-it-all growin' up," Mick told us. "He'd run up on stage and tell the musicians what they were doin' wrong."

I giggled and put my hand on Finnegan's leg under the table. He was quick to thread our fingers together, and second by second, the tension was leaving his shoulders. He even added to the conversation, thanking Mick for the offer, and said they'd think about it.

After Mick left, I didn't want anything to get awkward, so I brought up the music again.

"It's not the first time I've heard about you playing." I'd heard it from Alec first, who hadn't been able to convince Finnegan to play at my birthday dinner. "Now I really wanna hear you."

"You can probably find his tin whistle a mile up his asshole," Patrick said.

Not. Helping.

"What can I find a mile up yours?" I wondered. "One of Sarah's spiked Louboutins?"

While Finnegan hugged me to him and smiled into my hair, Patrick could not look more incredulous. And offended.

Sarah was laughing her ass off.

Patrick and Sarah were going to check out a club after dinner, so we went our separate ways. Finnegan, who was usually so energetic and ready for anything, was tired and not in the best mood. My only problem was these new boots. Ankle boots with a heel, how were those a thing?

"I'll get us a cab." Finnegan stepped closer to the curb, and I tugged him back.

"It's four blocks." I nodded up the street. "Let's walk."

"All right."

He was quiet. He was *brooding*.

It was a nice evening. We were surrounded by skyscrapers and heavy traffic, though the noise was easy to tune out.

I slipped my hand into his, and that earned me half a smile. He brought our hands to his lips and kissed my fingers.

"So...how was your first day back in Philly?" I asked carefully.

He sighed and looked straight ahead. "I guess I wasn't prepared. Rookie mistake."

"Wanna talk about it?"

He shook his head, almost out of reflex because he stopped himself and directed a frown at the ground. I figured he was going to say no, but then he spoke.

"Actually, can I vent for a moment?"

"Of course." I squeezed his hand, secretly thrilled, and I wasn't sure why.

"When I got out of the can, it took exactly three days for my family to start saying I was different. And they were right. I used to walk around with the biggest chip on my shoulder, and I was the comic relief that made everyone lose their shit."

We took the opportunity to cross the street when the light turned green, and I stayed quiet while he lit up a cigarette.

"I got my priorities straight when I was in prison," he continued. "I want more than a crew and the gigs we had." Jeez, he made it sound like he was in a band. "For that to happen, I gotta focus and aim higher. I gotta show the older guys that I can be trusted with bigger jobs. But everywhere I go, I run into these two-bit fuckwits who can't spell loyalty, and they're the ones I gotta impress."

"That guy...Jim?"

He nodded. "He works with my pop sometimes, but he has his own crew."

"Does everyone have, um, a crew?" I didn't speak mafia.

Another nod from Finnegan. "Think of a pyramid. You have

the boss at the top. That's my uncle. He's got his own crew, and their only job is to...uh, oversee, I guess you can say. Everyone has side gigs, but whatever. And the crew I run is down here." He showed with his hand, leaving room for another level of crews before reaching the top. "Before I can reach my uncle's inner circle, I have to be recommended by two higher-ups and join their line."

"I understand."

"The problem is my age," he told me. "Because when me and my boys head out for a job, we make a hell of a lot more money than most crews in my father's generation."

"Doing all legal things, I bet."

"Of course," he replied with a faint smirk. "So it's not what I do, 'cause I'm already a top earner. It's because I'm only twenty-five. And it's irritating as *fuck* to basically work for a generation that drilled all our traditions and rules into my skull, but they won't fucking abide by them themselves."

I looped my arm with his instead and hugged his bicep. He wasn't looking for what I thought, and that was good. I wouldn't know what to say. I could listen, though. And ask.

"Can I ask what rules they're not following?"

He grimaced and took a drag from his smoke. "Maybe not rules. It doesn't go against any law to fuck around and have second families on the side, but this isn't some Italian *borgata*. Real family actually matters to us—or it's supposed to—and you're loyal to family." He exhaled some smoke, frustrated. "Everything's gone to shit since my grandfather was boss. We respected family, and we were men of our word."

He was showing me a whole new side of him, one I instantly knew I could get ridiculously attached to. I wanted family to be sacred.

"I think I got sidetracked," he said pensively.

"Sorry—"

"No, it's..." He chuckled and kissed the side of my head. "It's not you. It's my fucked-up brain. Bottom line, it pisses me off to suck up to men who don't deserve my respect, and I realize now that it's what Philly brings outta me. It makes me miss the days when doing my own thing was enough."

"You can't go back to that?" I mean...it wasn't like Finnegan was hurting for money. That couldn't be the reason he felt the need to climb the ranks.

"No," he answered quietly. "It'll be worth it in the end. Our syndicate has to change, and no one else seems to be willing to do the job, which is another thing I don't get. Fuckers." He took a last drag, then flicked away the cigarette. "Today was a wake-up call. As bored as I was in your shitty town, I was more myself. Patrick isn't lying when he says you're the reason I was less uptight out there."

I let out an uncertain laugh. It couldn't be true. "I don't think I have that much power."

"I wouldn't be so sure," he murmured. "If Philly's gonna try to suck the life out of me, I'm gonna need you here to make it all better."

"On one condition." I smiled up at him. "You gotta play for me."

He cracked a grin and hugged me to him. "Deal."

"Finnegan? Can you come here and see if my dress is conservative enough?" I inched back from the bathroom mirror and tucked away my mascara. I'd never really dressed for church before, so I was more than a little nervous. Plus, I'd be meeting all these people I'd once sworn never to associate with...

In order to cover up the marks around my neck, my only option was this black, knitted, ubersoft turtleneck dress. It seemed modest enough, ending right above my knees, and it had three-quarter sleeves. The concern was it fit like second skin.

"Jesus fucking Christ, princess. You're a vision."

I whipped around and saw Finnegan in the doorway, and I smiled and blushed at his predatory once-over.

"There's nothing conservative about you." He walked closer slowly, adjusting his cuff links. "In fact, you're one indecent little liberal."

I laughed at his punniness. "I think the preferred term is filthy."

"You're that too." He lifted my chin and kissed me softly. "You look perfect. *We* look perfect." He positioned us so we were side by side in front of the mirror. "Check us out. Philly's next power couple."

Christ, he didn't set the bar high at all, did he? While he slipped a hand down to feel up my butt, I adjusted his tie.

"Are you turning into an ass man?"

"No. You're turning me into an ass man. I swear it calls to me."

I'd noticed. We'd made out like starved lunatics last night, and there was always a hand on my ass. Not that I was complaining. I was pretty damn fond of his ass too. I even bit it, which he'd taken as consent to bite me back.

Speaking of ass talk, it was time to go to church.

The church Finnegan's family attended was on the outskirts of the city center, and from the minute we parked, it was easy to see the Irish-American community was strong here. The square across the street was lined with Irish pubs and storefronts with Celtic designs.

The sun was shining, and he put on a pair of shades as we walked hand in hand toward the big church.

I supposed I should put my gift cards to use soon. As good as Karla was at picking out clothes for me, I wanted to do that myself. Starting with sunglasses and heels that didn't crush my feet.

Finnegan shook hands with more people than I could count, and he introduced me as his fiancée to each one.

"My parents are over there," he murmured in my ear, nodding toward the entrance. "You ready to face my mother?"

Little did he know. "I'm ready."

I wasn't nervous one bit to see Grace—again—but Shannon, on the other hand? Yikes. He looked so distinguished. Finnegan took after him a *lot*. Down to the dark copper hair, solid frames, trimmed beards, and suits. Only a few differences stuck out. Where Finnegan wore cocky smirks, Shannon had a tangible air of kindness to him. Silver glinted at his temples; it would be a decade or two before that happened to Finnegan. Same with the laugh lines around Shannon's eyes and mouth. I wasn't gonna lie, Shannon O'Shea was almost as lethally handsome as his son.

"You look alike," I whispered as we approached.

"So I've heard." He flashed me one of his smirks, and then we reached his parents. The two men who'd been talking to Shannon quickly excused themselves.

Grace's eyes lit up.

"Guys, I want you to meet Emilia Porter. I finally got her to say yes."

"You say that as if you had to work a long time for it," I accused. Plastering my most charming smile on my face, I faced Shannon and Grace.

"I did," Finnegan insisted with a chuckle. "Emilia, Shannon and Grace O'Shea."

"It's certainly felt like forever waiting to meet you, dearie." Grace embraced me in a fierce hug. "Oh, poo. I hoped you'd have a purse," she whispered. "I have a phone for you later. Assume my boy's keeping track of your messages and calls."

Fucking seriously?

I was passed from one hug to another while I snapped out my dumbfounded state. Shannon welcomed me to the family and said his son was lucky to have found me.

Welcome to the family, Em. Your fiancé might be tapping your phone, and you're gonna have his children, "God willing."

We'd see about that.

"Where's your brother?" Grace asked Finnegan.

"On his way," he replied. "He texted earlier and said he was hungover."

Did that include Sarah? I hoped she was coming too.

"Why am I not surprised?" Grace shook her head. "You know what, he can find a seat in the back. We should head in."

Finnegan and I followed Grace and Shannon, and as soon as we entered the church, the atmosphere was entirely different. That was when it hit me that I had no idea what I was doing, and I knew Catholics had a truckload of rituals.

I was surrounded by believers. I guesstimated three hundred of them would fill the pews, and most—if not all—became more somber like a flip of a switch. Many of them made the sign of the cross, one of whom I was marrying soon.

"I don't know what I'm doing," I whispered to Finnegan.

"That's okay," he whispered back. "Just follow my lead." He nodded at the third row as we got closer to it. Shannon was there, taking his seat. "You can sit down with my pop. I reckon genuflection isn't for you."

I looked up at him and blinked. "Genuwhat?"

His eyes flashed with amusement. "Have a seat, princess."

Fine.

I left one Irish mobster and sat down next to another. In the meantime, Finnegan and Grace walked up to the altar with several others.

"Are you Catholic, dear?" Shannon wondered.

I nodded, then promptly shook my head. I wasn't anything, really. "I was baptized in a Catholic church," I replied quietly. "My mom was Catholic. But...Dad's a Lutheran, though he only worships Jim Beam. We never went to church." I was pretty sure Dad had only had me baptized to honor Mom or something.

Shannon chuckled under his breath. "That's a horrible bourbon."

I grinned to myself and glanced over at the altar. Finnegan had taken a knee briefly and crossed himself once more, and now he was standing up again. Grace stayed on one knee, appearing to be in prayer. Finnegan returned to us, and I refrained from saying anything. There were evidently dozens of sides to Finnegan, and this was just another one I'd have to get to know. As much as I didn't understand religion, I found myself wanting to understand *him*. Every side intrigued me.

He took a seat and linked our fingers together on his leg. With his free hand, he rustled with something, and I blinked in bewilderment when he revealed a bag of candy.

"Butterscotch?" he offered.

What the fuck—who the fuck was this guy? Oh, *honestly*. Big, bad, tough mobster who kneeled at altars and ate Werther's Originals before Mass: the jokes wrote themselves.

"Is now really the time to eat old-people candy?" I whispered.

He frowned. "My mouth gets dry in churches."

Shannon reached across me and took two candies. "Cheers, son."

This family couldn't be normal in any sense of the word.

While we waited for everyone to get settled, I people watched and noticed more than a few who were curious about us. Or me. Were they all friends or acquaintances of the O'Sheas? That couldn't be. Otherwise, we might as well just pass out wedding invitations on flyers after a service, or whatever Catholics called it. Or maybe do a "while we're all here, let's get hitched" kind of wedding.

I tugged on Finnegan's pinkie. "Is this where we'll get married?"

He inclined his head. "I'm going to speak with Father O'Malley after the homily today. Have you heard of Pre-Cana classes?"

"Um, yeah. Premarital counseling or something."

"They're as horrible as Jim Beam," Shannon muttered.

For chrissakes, I was going to warm up to him way too fast if he kept making wisecracks like that.

Finnegan squeezed my hand. "There's no way we're going through six months of that shite, but I might have to throw you under the bus a bit. You're a lost little atheist, and he's going to have concerns. If I'm not mistaken, you didn't even have your First Communion. So if he requests sessions with you, I'll agree."

How supportive of my husband-to-be! Taken aback by what he'd said, I stared at him for a beat before turning to Shannon.

"Your son is as horrible as Jim Beam too," I told him.

Shannon coughed a laugh, loud enough for him to earn a couple glares from people around us. "Oh, Finn, she'll fit right in."

chapter
19

Finnegan O'Shea

I grinned and brushed my thumb over Emilia's text.
Invitations were sent today. Cake tasting when you get home, FINN. xx

Our recent name dispute was one she couldn't win. I loved the way she said my name, so no, she wasn't going to start calling me Finn like most people did.

"You're whipped already, little brother." Patrick folded his arms over his chest and stared out the window of my office. "Can you focus?"

"Can you?" I drawled. "You're the one who's late to sit-downs and party more than you work." The last two weeks, he'd been short when handing over his cut to the higher-ups, so I'd had to cover for him.

It was great that he and Sarah and found *one* thing to bond over, but it couldn't affect his work. Other than running in and out of clubs together, the only thing Sarah liked about my brother was his money, which he wouldn't have much left of if this continued.

235

"I'm working when I go out," he replied irritably. "You know that."

I inclined my head and leaned back in my desk chair. Whereas I kept my business afloat down by the docks and had my office here, Patrick rarely visited his garages, and he met with associates at four in the morning when everyone was three sheets to the wind. And it'd worked until his fiancée came along and spent eight grand a month on clothes and jewelry.

It was as hard to like Sarah as it was to resent her. She was looking out for herself, and she was taking what Pat was offering. What he needed to do was set a damn limit tomorrow when we were signing the contracts with the girls. Then maybe, just maybe, make an effort to connect with Sarah.

"No one's forcing you to get shit-faced," I said. "But back to focus. There is one obvious solution to your problem. You gotta quit renting property. Buy the lot in Newark—"

"I can't front the dough," he stated.

I widened my arms, incredulous. "And what the fuck am I, shit under your shoe? You've never had any problems asking for a loan before."

He groaned and pinched the bridge of his nose. "I'm sick of borrowing money from you, Finn. For fuck's sake, I'm starting to feel like a guest in my own home."

That wasn't my problem. I kept telling him to set limits and stop buying cheap affection—which wasn't even affectionate—but he wouldn't listen. He wasn't willing to do the legwork to go anywhere. And guess what, that's how you got stuck. For as long as he kept a draining credit card wedged between himself and Sarah, everyone would suffer.

The only issue with working toward a good relationship was that you risked falling in love with it.

I'd fucked myself over good and proper somewhere between waking up next to Emilia every morning and watching her pick out the flowers for our wedding.

I wasn't ready to admit I was in love with *her* yet...though, what we shared? What we were creating together...? I needed it more than air. The few times I came home and she wasn't there, I felt like I'd been punched in the gut.

"I need a business with a bigger profit," Pat said. "How much do you make here?" He nodded toward the door. "Can you launder enough?"

I lifted a shoulder, unwilling to discuss the details. I'd hired five new guys recently, and we were installing home security systems left and right all over Pennsylvania and Jersey. To be honest, I didn't launder much, 'cause I had something better. I had the blue-prints and the keys to the wealthy along the entire Main Line. There were no failing security systems. They simply didn't know there were sometimes people who came and went with valuables from time to time. Especially when someone had just moved or was in the process of it.

Things went missing.

"Come *on*, Finn." Patrick walked over, frustration and helpless-ness boiling over, and sat down in the chair across from me. "We can't all have perfect lives, mate. I'm trying here."

I chuckled, getting pissed. These motherfuckers loved to call me uptight and make digs about my life, yet they came crawling for help sooner or later.

"Remember our first LA Auto Show?" I asked.

He was confused by the change of topic but nodded once. "Good times."

"Good times? It was way more than that, bro. Christ." I reached for my smokes and lit one up. "You were innovating back then. We had one order, *one* window of opportunity according to the old-timers, and how many cars did we score that week?"

Our grandfather had been boss back then, and he'd told us to attend the only private event they deemed safe enough to steal at. Then Patrick had put his genius to use and found a paper trail of transactions, exhibits, and storages.

After calling in six more guys from the East Coast, we'd literally created our own crew during one of the best gigs of my life.

He'd earned the respect of Ronan that weekend.

"Nine," Patrick answered and hung his head. "I hear you."

It made my fingers itch to think about it. Next auto season couldn't come fast enough.

"Has Uncle John given you any orders for this fall?" he asked.

I nodded. These days, Patrick and I ran separate crews, and we only worked together for bigger affairs. Like LA, Miami, anything in Italy, Detroit, and a few others. If it weren't for our weddings taking place soon, we would've teamed up with Pop's crew and hit Monterey this summer. Just being there for the auctions was like sex. Or almost, as I was discovering.

"Not to me directly, though," I amended. "His pompous ass wouldn't call a crew boss on our level."

"I'm sick of that fucker," he grunted.

I inhaled from my smoke and didn't answer. If he were so fucking sick of our uncle, he would've worked harder toward the goal. Our pop had the same issue. He hated Uncle John these days, yet he allowed the motherless prick to rule.

Ma was...torn. Plenty of hatred, but this was her older brother. Who'd murdered their father...and her husband's father. And the reason she couldn't pick a side was because we didn't have "evidence" that Uncle John had done it.

I called bullshit, and I didn't look forward to seeing him at the wedding. We'd act like family who loved each other then.

"If you get your act together," I told Patrick, "I'll see about uniting our crews." I needed a couple new guys anyway. Business was good, and I'd just lost Kellan temporarily because he couldn't show his face here with Emilia around. Now he was working personal security for Alec and Nessa in Chicago. A job Kellan loathed, though it gave me a quicker heads-up when something was going down.

"We did make a lot of money together," Patrick pointed out.

"For a few months outta the year. You know that's not enough." Auto shows were generally held in the fall and winter. "Now, should I get you that loan or not?"

He sighed heavily and waved a hand. "Hit me with it."

"That's the spirit." With that out of the way, I could move on to my problem. "About tomorrow. Did Sarah go with any of the lawyers you recommended?"

He furrowed his brow and shook his head. "No, she found one herself. Why?"

"That's what I feared." I put out my smoke in an old coffee mug. "Emilia picked her own representation too, and I wonder if someone's helping them."

I'd ransacked Emilia's phone, and I hadn't found squat. She texted with Sarah the most, which was understandable. They attended meetings with Father O'Malley, went shopping, and planned the weddings together. Emilia had also struck up a friendship with Alec. He'd texted her last week, claiming she'd had his number for too long without using it. They'd been texting silly things to each other ever since, something I found weirdly sweet. Other than that... A handful of texts from an old classmate named Franny, who'd urged Emilia to talk to the police. In response, Emilia had asked how she'd gotten her number, and it'd led to her blocking Franny.

Approximately a million messages from my mother as well, though they were all wedding-related or her asking the next time they could meet up for lunch.

Our parents had officially moved out to the compound, or so they claimed. They were in the city often. Pop blamed it on patients and sit-downs. Ma's excuses were the weddings and that she had to decorate their new "city flat."

I pinched my lips together, frustrated I couldn't figure it out. Had Emilia made friends I didn't know about? We hadn't introduced them to more family yet. Unless Ma had...

"Brenda," I said as the name popped into my head. "You think she could've helped the girls?"

Brenda was our cousin and Aunt Viv's eldest daughter. She was our age, the only one of Viv and Thomas's kids who was local, and she wasn't fond of Pat and me.

"I hope not." Patrick made a face. "I wouldn't worry too much, though. I check Sarah's credit card activity, and she hasn't paid any retainers."

All the more reason to be concerned. Unless Emilia and Sarah showed up alone tomorrow, *someone* was footing the bill. Additionally, I hadn't come this far by underestimating people, and both girls had their moments.

I hated being blindsided.

Is that Emilia?

Coming from the garage, I stepped out of the elevator to get the mail in the lobby, and I could've sworn I just heard her soft laugh. It was my favorite sound of hers. Possibly... The sound she made when she came was a strong competitor.

I followed the giggles and stopped short when the front desk came into view. Not only was it Emilia, but she was clad in a skimpy cotton top, pajama shorts, and another one of those disgusting face masks. The chick already had perfect skin; why she put that on her face was beyond me.

Today's mask was stark blue and likely promised eternal youth.

"Oi. Giggle Smurf." I passed the wall of mailboxes and aimed for Emilia.

She met my gaze with a grin and leaned against the desk where she'd apparently gotten chummy with whatshisface, Oliver something. As was becoming my new normal, my chest constricted before expanding at the sight of my girl.

"Hi!" she said. "I'm running errands."

240

"As you do in pajamas." I chuckled and dropped a kiss to her hair, which...smelled incredibly fucking good. Better than usual. *Damn.* "You did something here."

"*Yes.*" She straightened, and her smile grew larger. She donned the worst Southern accent and said, "I got mah hair did." The girl drew a laugh from me that echoed off the marbled walls. "Olivier's husband did it. He cut, like, six or seven inches, layered it, and then he gave me highlights." With her hair in its usual untidy bun at the top of her head, it was difficult to see its new length. As for highlights...okay, yeah, maybe...? I thought she'd had them before. "Anyway," she went on, "Gavin asked me to pass along a love note—"

"It's not a love note," Olivier argued. I was quickly losing interest in this part. "It's an apology for shrinking my favorite shirt."

"Whatever, dude. All he did was talk about you during my appointment," Emilia told him. "He's so precious."

I checked my watch. Emilia had started cooking these past few weeks, and I was starving. For claiming she was only half decent at it, she'd quickly gotten me hooked on her food. Furthermore, cake tasting topped standing around for this shit.

"I think the hubby's impatient," Olivier stage-whispered.

I smiled politely.

Emilia snorted. "It's past five. He's approaching hangry mode." She wasn't wrong.

"Lastly," she said, "I came down here to get the mail, and you have a delivery I can't sign for."

"All right." I stepped closer to the desk, and *Olivier* jumped into action to get me a relatively small box. From Chicago. Interesting. I signed for it.

Probably sensing my mood, Emilia wrapped up their chitchat, and we headed for the elevators.

I was gonna have to work on my patience at some point. I did often come home grumpy as fuck, and her face being covered in paste so I couldn't kiss her silly wasn't improving the situation.

On the way up, I began opening the box from Chicago. "So I

know you don't really wanna be near your old neck of the woods, but would you mind spending the weekend at the house?"

"Need a break?" she guessed. I nodded once. "No, of course. We can do that. We'll be there next Thursday anyway."

"Oh?" I dug through some packing material and found an envelope. I recognized Aunt Anne's elegant handwriting, so this must be the engagement present from her and Uncle John.

"Grace, Sarah, and I finished planning the engagement party slash bachelor and bachelorette parties," Emilia explained. "If we do it out there, we'll have more space to be separated without driving back and forth to meet up again."

That was a good idea, actually. We were already pushing it with two weddings, two packed churches, the first one a little over a month away. Friends and family had to show up, and associates didn't dare decline. So to save everyone time, we'd decided to do it up big for one weekend, including our stag nights. I'd stayed out of it, assuming we'd celebrate in the city, but this was good.

"When's the engagement party?" I asked, scanning my aunt's note. I smirked a little. The felicitations were sweet, and the gifts were a way of showing how loaded they were. *Blah.* Now I'd have to come up with a new wedding gift for Emilia.

"Friday," Emilia replied. "Bachelor and bachelorette shenanigans on Saturday, and you can't get too drunk during the day."

I lifted a brow at her, and the elevator stopped. "Uh, why?"

"Because Grace rented us that pub for the night. The one your friend Mick owns?" That was here in the city. "A car service will take us back to Philly after dinner, and then we'll have a wild pub night together." She finished with a proud grin, and fuck me, maybe I did love her. No—fuck. Too soon. Not according to my plan. God-fucking-dammit. "We're talking all the stout you can drink, live music, dancing, and a pub quiz."

That sounded fantastic to me. I couldn't picture a better stag night, and I knew the activities Pop was planning for us during the day wouldn't exactly blow our minds. Pat and I were betting on golf or whiskey tasting.

"My mother would never plan a pub night," I said, ushering her out of the elevator. "Did you do this?"

"Yes, I did. Pat me on the head."

I chuckled and patted her on the head. "You rock, baby." As we entered our place, I handed her the box. "By the way, Uncle John sends his best, and he's giving you a car."

I shrugged out of my suit jacket and loosened my tie. Behind me, Emilia was spluttering something. I was more focused on the two cake boxes on the kitchen table. Fuckin' A. My day was already looking better.

"Oh my God... Finnegan! Listen to this, '...and we can't wait to welcome you into our family with open arms, Emilia. Until then, please enjoy our gift to you.' And there's a key in here!"

I knew that. I'd just read the note. My uncle and his wife were giving her the latest Porsche Cayenne.

"I can't accept this. This is *mental*." She gave me a nearly horrified look. "That's too much money."

She was too fucking cute. Emilia and Sarah were like sisters, yet they couldn't be more different where money was concerned. Emilia didn't shy away from everyday purchases anymore, though she gave herself the biggest guilt trips if something was over a few hundred bucks. And it was stupid, 'cause she mostly bought shit for us. Not a whole lot was for herself, aside from some clothes and beauty treatments.

It was a good thing my parents were paying for the wedding. Ma was making a conscious effort never to show Emilia any price tags.

"You can and you will," I told her. "What do you wanna do for dinner?"

"I, uh..." She was flustered about the car. "I'm sorry, I had a full day. Can we order in? Christ, how do I thank someone for a friggin' luxury car?"

"We'll send them thank-you notes, I reckon..." I aimed for the kitchen where we had our takeout menus.

"Wait, what's this about a charter jet?" She held up the note.

"The engagement gift for both of us," I replied. "They'll charter a plane for us when we go on our honeymoon."

"Mental!" she repeated.

It wasn't, really. She understandably thought it involved a ton of cash. In reality, John would call in a few favors. He had his hands in a lot of pockets in Chicago, and he was part owner in a company that rented out private jets. Given how paranoid my uncle was, it was his preferred way to travel.

"Right. You wanna do pizza?"

"Sure. Sorry I didn't make any—"

"Shut your mouth. You're not obligated to cook for me, princess. I'm just spoiled." Most of all, I wanted that paste off her face and then some couch time. I was wound up tight and had a short fuse. "How long's that face mask gonna be in my way?"

She joined me in the kitchen and puckered her lips. Great, she gave me a small peck. "Five more minutes. Why don't you go shower, and I'll order us more than one pie." At least she'd learned from the night she'd gotten us only one.

No one fucking shared a pizza.

The hot shower that was supposed to reenergize me only made me sleepy. I wrapped a towel around my hips and left the bathroom, and I yawned as I entered our closet. After I grabbed a pair of sweats, the bed looked too inviting. I slumped down on the foot of it, and a beat later, I fell back against the mattress. *Now we're talking.* My stomach growled in hunger, and if the pizza didn't arrive soon, I'd start with dessert.

"You out, hon?" Emilia called.

"Yeah." I scrubbed my hands over my face and yawned again. My eyes refused to stay open.

The quietest thuds of her bare feet let me know she was climbing the stairs.

"Long day?" she asked softly.

"Yeah, I guess." Not longer than usual, just...not the same either. I was difficult that way. It was almost impossible to find a balance. Either I was stressed out and irritable, or I was bored and restless. "When will the pizza be here?"

"Hmm, should be about ten minutes now." The bed dipped with her knees landing on the mattress, and she placed a kiss on my stomach. "Want me to make you feel better?"

God yes.

"You *never* have to ask," I chuckled tiredly. My blood started pumping immediately, and I released a long breath as she ghosted more kisses along my abs. Farther down... She loosened the towel around me. "Fuck..." I kept my eyes closed and breathed deeply while she stroked my thighs, slowly inching toward my cock.

Having these past few weeks to explore each other most nights had awakened something in me. I thirsted for her. I could kiss her for hours and roll around in bed with her until—*holy fuck.*

"Emilia." I almost choked on my tongue, and my eyes couldn't fly open fast enough. Lifting my head, I stared at her in disbelief. Her soft, perfect lips wrapped around the head of my cock was *new.* I groaned and let my head fall back again, and I fisted my hair. Her tongue swirled around me. She took me deeper as I quickly grew hard. "God*damn...*"

I had to see. No matter how much I wanted to just let go and focus on feeling this, I had to watch. My mouth went dry. Part of me couldn't believe it. I thought we'd shared a silent agreement on not going further until the wedding.

"Jesus Christ." I shuddered. Fully hard and throbbing, sinking in and out of her wet mouth... She was a bloody sin, one I'd never even try to resist. She'd closed her eyes, and she was using her hand expertly to play with what she couldn't fit in her mouth, though that didn't stop her from trying to take more. I hit the back of her throat and felt my balls drawing up. "I won't last long, princess," I warned, already short of breath. "Fuck, that feels—unbelievable. Incredible. Oh, *fuck*."

She hummed and went faster. She cupped my balls the way she'd learned I liked it, and her grip at the base of my cock tightened.

"Perfect," I whispered. "So perfect." Needing to touch her, I stroked her cheek, brushed my thumb at the corner of her mouth, and threaded my fingers through her hair. "That's it. Keep sucking me." I tensed up, my chest heaving. I wasn't fucking ready to blow it yet. I needed more time. It was so warm, wet, and tight. She sucked me *hard*. "Too good," I groaned. "I'm gonna come—back off now or—" I hauled in a breath, and she shook her head minutely, with my cock in her mouth, then took me as deep as she could.

It was sensory overload. Everything coiled up inside of me right before I exploded and released. Spurts of come flooded her mouth. She gagged, and shit, sorry, but that *felt* amazing. Motherfucking hell, she didn't move away either. She sucked my cock until she'd milked me dry.

I melted into the mattress and panted as if I'd just come back from a morning run. Shivers ran through me continuously, and I couldn't lift my head to check in on her as she darted into the bathroom.

"Baby?" I whispered raggedly.

"Phew!" She reemerged quickly and blushed furiously. "Good for a first time, right? I'll practice on the swallowing."

I coughed around a laugh and waved her to me. "Get over here."

Once she was in my arms, I curled around her and used her as my body pillow. "You don't have to practice a goddamn thing. Where the fuck did that come from?"

She shrugged a little and kissed my chin. "I've been thinking about it a lot, and I wanted to try it."

There wasn't a chance in hell she'd thought about it as much as I had. That was what morning showers were for. Or when we got each other off with hands and fingers and slipping and sliding together. I shuddered again and held her tighter.

"You've made me one lucky bastard, Emilia Porter."

She laughed softly and stupidly squirmed out of my hold. "Keep that in mind at the meeting tomorrow."

"Hey, where're you going?" I grunted. "This means I can finally get my mouth on your pussy. That's how it goes."

A few minutes ago, she was sucking my cock, yet my talking about eating her out made her flush a new level of scarlet.

"Another time," she insisted. "Pizza will be here soon."

I let out a *hmph* and watched her disappear down the stairs.

Keep that in mind at the meeting tomorrow.

Oh, I would.

I needed more than three years. No one could deny what a perfect match we made. Not even Emilia.

"I guess you still don't feel like telling me who your lawyer is?" I hollered.

She laughed.

I joined her downstairs when the smell of melted cheese, garlic, oregano, and pepperoni invaded my senses.

She set the pies on the coffee table along with a beer for me and a glass of juice for herself. If she was in a Netflix mood, I was game. Another thing I'd gotten attached to, movie marathons with Emilia. We had similar tastes.

Tightening the drawstrings, I took my seat and waited for her.

"I found out something interesting today," she said from the kitchen.

"Yeah?" I took a swig of my beer and turned on the TV.

"Yeah. You made yourself sound almost modest when you told me about this place and how your brother had an entire floor to himself." She returned with napkins and two coasters. "What you forgot to mention was the small detail that you own the whole building."

I hadn't forgotten to mention it, technically. "It's listed as an asset in the file my lawyer sent you, so... If anything, you haven't paid attention to me."

"I swear, Finn."

"Finnegan," I barked.

"Fi-nn," she sang. "Why did you buy the building? And don't give me a spiel about it being a good investment. According to my lawyer, you're not making a profit here."

Fuck, she was sexy when she talked like that.

"You've been looking into me?" It made my crotch tingle. "It's not some big secret. I didn't like how lax things were around here before I moved in. I used to stay with Patrick upstairs, and people could come and go as they pleased. So when I decided to get my own place..." I lifted a shoulder. "Now there's a manned reception desk all hours of the day, upgraded security in the garage, and an empty condo on the seventh floor acts as a panic room."

She pursed her lips, studying me. The girl was getting smarter, more naturally suspicious.

"That's why you're not making any profit?" she asked dubiously.

"For the most part," I lied. Look, I lived in a world where a lot of favors were exchanged. Some of the residents hadn't paid for their places. It was a way to grease someone's pocket without losing any money. What I gained was control and a shitload of favors to cash in. "Can we eat now? And for future reference, I prefer we're naked when you interrogate me."

She snorted.

chapter

20

Finnegan O'Shea

"They're late." Patrick's patience was worse than mine, and he started pacing by the windows. The law firm that represented us had boardrooms with some of the best views that Philly had to offer. For instance, if I threw my brother out a window, he'd fall for quite a while before landing with a splat. That would've been a great view.

"You can't open these windows, can you?" I asked my lawyer's assistant.

She gave me a look of confusion. "Um, no, sir."

Figures.

"It's strategy," Frank replied mildly. "A cheap one, at that." Seated in the middle on our side of the table, he was doing a last read-through of the contract. Probably just to pass time.

"They're not supposed to have found a lawyer good enough to even spell strategy," Patrick argued. He walked back to the table and sat down on the other side of Frank. "Finn, was Emilia acting weird this morning?"

"No." And that was weird. She didn't make much fuss anymore about our morning runs. For the first few minutes in the park, she could even keep up with me these days. Then we had breakfast together when we returned before we got ready for the day.

"Would you like me to call in Maxine and Brett, sir?" the assistant asked.

Frank scowled. "Toots, do I look like someone who needs to resort to intimidation tactics with seat fillers?"

"Of course not, sir," she rushed to say.

I stifled my smirk and leaned back, swiveling absently in my chair. Pinching my bottom lip, I checked the clock for the tenth time in as many minutes.

A phone beeped, and the assistant glanced at her phone. "They're here. According to Mark, their representation is from Smith, Campbell & Stern."

Motherfucker.

I narrowed my eyes, then exchanged a look with Pat.

"Well, it ain't Brenda helping Emilia and Sarah..." He spoke my mind and groaned.

I kept my face composed, but inwardly, I was reeling. Somehow, our mother was helping them, and she'd done it without our knowledge. Not a single text message had set off any warning bells, which meant they'd been prepared from the get-go to keep this from us.

More than that, it meant Emilia was consciously careful about what she said on her phone.

I'd have to up my game.

Soon enough, three women walked in, all dressed to kill. Emilia wore one of those ass-hugging pencil skirts, mile-high heels, and a new blouse under her snug suit jacket. Sarah had gone for a pantsuit with too much cleavage.

Meredith...my mother's lawyer and friend. Oh Christ, this was gonna turn into a bloody gender war. She was known for representing and defending women, and men were easily fooled by her nerdy glasses and lipstick-stained teeth.

I met Emilia's blank expression, and my mouth twitched.

Well played, princess. Well fucking played.

"Ms. Campbell," Frank said and stood up. "I should've known." He waited until the women were seated before speaking again. "Let's keep this civil, shall we? We want this to stay informal and private."

"Of course, Frank," Meredith answered, immediately tossing formalities out the non-openable window.

Frank's assistant jumped up from her chair farther away and served us coffee and opened a box of pastries.

I had my eyes set on a jelly donut, which I wouldn't touch until the victory was mine. Nothing said loser like jelly on my shirt in the middle of a contract negotiation.

"No reason to beat around the bush," Meredith started. "Several clauses in both contracts are severely angled in the favor of Patrick and Finnegan. So let's take them one by one."

Frank waved a hand. "Whenever you're ready."

Oh, she was ready. With stacks of papers lined up in front of her, Meredith began ticking them off. First, it was Sarah and Patrick's contract, where most of their issues appeared to be about money.

My brother had pulled his head out of his ass and demanded the clause to be amended with a spending limit. Sarah didn't like that. In the end, she conceded to a monthly cap of four grand, but Patrick had to agree to a renegotiation in eighteen months.

I didn't call that a win. He'd wanted the limit to be half that, with room for more if he cleared whatever purchase in question.

According to Meredith, that was preposterous and would make Sarah feel "inferior."

"Section four," she went on. "In both contracts, these look the same, and it's the topic of children. In paragraph two, it clearly states that children are not obligatory, yet two paragraphs down, you request to agree not to use birth control—in the event that parties start intimate relations. Pardon my language, but what gives, guys?"

I leaned into Frank and spoke for only him to hear. "I need this one. No birth control or contraception for Emilia."

When I sat back again, she was narrowing her eyes at me.

I winked.

She rolled her eyes.

"Well, you know what they say about abstinence, Ms. Campbell," Frank said flatly. "If your clients don't wish to get pregnant, they can refrain from having sex."

"Oh, I will," Sarah replied with a sugary smile.

"Finnegan, you can't be serious," Emilia blurted out. "You're honestly ready to become a parent as long as you can have it your way?"

This didn't ruffle me for shit, and I inclined my head. "Children are a blessing. I hope to have many with you."

I wasn't lying either. Everything had changed for me. The fact that it would tie her to me for decades to come was a big bonus.

Emilia looked away, her discomfort written all over, and whispered to Meredith.

Meredith nodded. "My client wishes to proceed to the duration of the marriage. It's unacceptable to claim they're only obligated to stay married for three years, then do everything to ensure the union results in children. Furthermore, Emilia and Sarah would have to give up custody if they want to walk free, a notion that's nothing short of barbaric. So we're here to renegotiate those terms, and we propose twelve months instead of the original three years."

"Outta the goddamn question." I got heated quickly, sickened by the thought of only having her for a year. "What the fuck are you doing, Emilia? We're good together—"

"This has nothing to do with feelings," Emilia answered abruptly. "You gotta understand that I have to protect myself, Finnegan. No matter how good we are together, neither of us can predict the future, and given what you *do*...I need something better if you ever want me to trust you. This is my life we're talking about."

I gnashed my teeth and refrained from commenting as Frank cautioned me to stay quiet. But motherfucker, she would get an earful when we got home. She needed to get it through her skull that we were perfect for each other.

"Gentlemen?" Meredith waited for our verdict.

Frank cleared his throat. "Apologies, I was waiting for a serious counterproposal. What you're asking is laughable."

"I want ten years," I heard myself saying, never looking away from Emilia. "Minimum."

"Now, *that's* laughable," Meredith drawled.

"I can agree to five," Emilia said, "on the condition that I go on birth control, and we share custody *if* we have kids and end up divorced."

I shook my head, refusing to go there. "We're not getting divorced, princess." I couldn't bear the thought. Shit, it legit hurt to think about her walking away from me. "That goes against everything I believe in."

"You have to be reasonable!" she exclaimed. "Think about *me*, Finnegan. I would sign away my whole life—"

"So would I!" I yelled.

"And one of us lies for a fucking living!" she yelled back.

"Not this again," I groaned. I was gonna implode with anger if she didn't let that go soon.

"While we're on the subject, Frank," Meredith said conversationally, "are Finnegan and Patrick tapping my clients' phones? You understand that it's in our best interest to figure out how trustworthy the men they're marrying are. You see, we found some suspicious activity on Finnegan's laptop, and it appears he's synced—"

"Fuck my life." My elbows landed on the table, and I dropped my forehead into my palms. "She went through my laptop—fucking great."

"What's yours is mine and all that," Emilia said lightly.

I chuckled darkly and lifted my gaze. "You don't wanna go down this road with me, Emilia."

"I think this calls for a break," Frank said. The look he gave me told me to calm the fuck down. "We'll reconvene in twenty minutes."

My glare followed Emilia as she walked out with the other two, and right as she slipped out the glass doors, I saw her take a big breath and put a hand on her chest.

That little action robbed me of most of my anger.

She was putting on a façade.

"I remember now why you two are my most difficult clients." Frank rose to his feet and lit up a cigar. Then he told his assistant to take a hike. He dealt with Patrick first. "You're not saying much."

Patrick offered a dry look. "My opinion on whether the fiancée I'm never gonna fuck can or can't have birth control isn't very strong."

I snorted, tired, and stood up too.

"She's told me it's okay if I get a girlfriend on the side," he finished.

That didn't sit well with me.

"And you didn't mention this to me, why?" Frank got pissy. "If you and Sarah decide on having separate lives outside of your marriage, it needs to go into the contract. Lest you want her to shake you down when you go out and fuck everything that moves."

"He's not going to do that," I said firmly.

"Why? She's cool with it," Patrick stated.

"Because I'm done with that in our family!" I shouted. "Get your lazy ass up and make the best of your marriage instead, Pat! I'm sick and fucking tired of cleaning up messes because some'a youse act like whiny cunts. If you can't even make your wife happy, how the fuck are you gonna keep a work crew satisfied? Huh? Christ! What happened to loyalty in our syndicate? What happened to being faithful?" I drew in a breath and tried to calm down, and it wasn't goddamn easy. "You're my brother, and I love you, but I won't have you dragging me down. If you wanna get to the top, start working. My patience has run out."

"Good advice," Frank cut in, and I dismissed Patrick's glare. "On that note, you need to give Emilia more, Finn. You may have this grand vision of what your future with Miss Porter might look like, but as long as she doesn't see it, pace yourself. Don't get angry because she's not on the same page. Get to the bottom of why instead and fix it. Right now, digging your heels into the sand will get you nowhere."

Fuck him for using one of my favorite sayings against me.

Resting my ass on the edge of the table, I crossed my feet at the ankles and pinched the bridge of my nose.

He was right, though I didn't know where to surrender control. I *couldn't* agree to fewer years with her.

"Emilia's offer wasn't bad, bro," Patrick said quietly. "Five years, no tricking her into getting knocked up, and shared custody if you split."

Tricking her...

My head snapped up.

Birth control failed all the time.

How hard could it be to make sure she was pregnant before those five years were up? Kids changed things. I couldn't see Emilia walking away freely if a child was involved.

"Pop's gotta have someone in his pocket who can get me placebos," I said.

"Yeah, probably." Pat nodded.

"For the love of all things holy." Frank threw a skyward look and took a puff from his cigar. "You boys realize that while you don't show an ounce of remorse for deceiving your girls, your mother is going to tell them everything she knows."

I did realize that, but how much could Ma really know?

More than we'd expected, that was for sure. This was different, though. So she'd given them the name of her lawyer and possibly warned them we could be sneaks. It was fucking endearing if anything.

"They didn't get everything right, for the record," I pointed out. "I never tapped Emilia's phone. We're on the same plan. Her phone's in my name, so I synced the devices. People do that every day."

"That's great, Finn," Frank responded, nodding. "Want me to make a case for you based on semantics? You think that will earn you the girl's trust?"

"No one appreciates a smartass," I snapped.

Frank ignored me, continuing by saying he'd have his team amend the contracts so they could be signed before the day was over. And I had to agree to Emilia's terms. Five years instead of three, birth control, and shared custody.

He was going to make changes in Patrick's contract too, though, at my insistence, there would be no clause for agreed-upon extra-marital activities. Over my dead body.

"This day did *not* go as planned." I slumped back down in my chair and guzzled my coffee, wishing it were a bit more Irish. "She wasn't supposed to find out about the syncing. I only did it to get to know her better. I mean, come on, she hated me!"

Frank hummed and took his seat again. "I wonder why."

Cheers.

"This'll blow over, bro," Patrick assured me. "Count your blessings instead. Whole other shitshow if she found out about Kellan."

I grunted and poured some cream into my coffee. "I gotta tell her at some point. And *again*, I did it to even the score. She needed an incentive to go out with me, and I was at a disadvantage. Having him as the agent pushed her toward me."

"I have a feeling it's a good thing I don't know what you're talking about," Frank said.

Our twenty minutes were up, yet the women took another seven before returning to the boardroom. Whatever façade Emilia had struggled to keep intact had been mended. She looked twice as determined and fierce if that was possible. Her eyes were sparking with attitude and fire.

I could play nice, I was pretty sure.

"Did you have a pleasant break, ladies?" Frank asked.

"Not the word I'd use, but sure." Meredith stacked a few files together, then clasped her hands together on the table. "Can we reach an agreement?"

"Absolutely." Frank inclined his head. "Finnegan agrees to five years—"

"Three," Emilia interrupted.

I frowned. "Princess, you just—"

"Shut the fuck up," she responded calmly.

Meredith faced me with a flat expression. "Three years, free access to birth control of Emilia's choosing, and shared custody in the highly unlikely event that your marriage results in children." She paused. "Additionally, the contract in its entirety will be nullified should any party do something perfidious such as tamper with any type of contraception."

I froze, my coffee cup in midair. This wasn't happening. I could hear a pin drop—possibly. My pulse was quickly going through the roof, so maybe that rushing sound would drown out the pin. Or a brick. *Fuck me.* Slowly setting down the cup, I scooted out my chair and took a deep breath. Then I checked under the table and felt my whole world collapse around me.

"Holy shit," Patrick whispered.

He'd seen the bug, no doubt. Placed directly underneath Meredith's spot.

Those conniving little...*bitches.*

I started laughing. It was either that, or I'd shoot Meredith where she sat, and I would lose Emilia forever. So I gave up. A bizarre surge of emotions turned me into a madman, and I leaned forward and rested my cheek on the table.

Frank stared at me over the rim of his glasses. "Do you declare defeat?"

I nodded against the cool tabletop.

I got played today. I got knocked down. I'd underestimated Emilia, something I'd sworn never to do. And now she knew...fuck, too much. She knew about Kellan.

There would be no jelly donut for me today.

Legalities meant fuck-all when dealing with us, and they'd taken a page from our book.

"They played dirty," I muttered.

"Do you think this is funny, Finnegan?" Emilia asked.

No. It wasn't funny at all. I dragged myself up and managed to smirk, even as my eyes burned and my vision blurred. "Do I look amused?"

I was another level of crazy. It was a hard blow, and she'd aimed straight at my heart. Unfortunately, I had it coming, and now I knew what I was up against. The love of my fucking life.

I blinked back the emotions fast and got my act together. On the inside, I'd be a mess for a while. I had to rethink everything. By some stroke of luck, she was still agreeing to three years, which bought me time. My priorities changed before my very eyes, threatening my goals, threatening what I'd worked for.

I guess that was the moment Emilia became everything.

As if on cue, guilt seeped into my veins, slithering through me like liquid lead.

chapter

21

Emilia Porter

While Finnegan stopped in the lobby to get our mail, I continued upstairs with only one plan. Pack a bag and get away for a couple days. It was Grace's advice, and I was going to take it.

Shame I couldn't escape the clusterfuck that was my brain.

One second, I was shaking with anger. Another, I wanted to bawl my eyes out. I managed to jump between apathy, hurt, understanding, something...*thrilling* I couldn't identify, and embarrassment too.

I'd never been so humiliated in my life.

I felt so fucking stupid every time I thought of the times I'd met up with Agent Caldwell.

I cringed and stalked up the stairs to the bedroom I'd come to call *ours*. Was any of this mine? Or was I just a pawn in Finnegan's games?

Locating a small roll-aboard suitcase at the back of the closet, I started shoving clothes inside it.

Finnegan walked through the door when I was moving on to some stuff in the bathroom.

He wisely stayed downstairs. He was waiting for me to explode.

"Your car's here," he said.

"All right." I wasn't going to use that today, though. I'd already snatched up the spare key to his Aston, and I deserved a treat.

I'd asked Sarah to tag along, but she wanted to stay behind, and I wasn't in the mood to convince her. Frankly, there was a lot I wasn't in the mood for anymore where she was concerned.

No, what I needed was Grace. I'd head out to the compound and spend some time with the one O'Shea who hadn't fucked me over. If she'd lied to me—and it wouldn't surprise me if she had— she'd made up for it by genuinely being there for me. Unlike her youngest son, she wasn't sugarcoating shit. She didn't share details about anything that could get anyone into trouble with the law, but she straight-up told me what I needed to know.

"Can we talk about this?" Finnegan asked tiredly. "I know I messed up."

"What's there to talk about?" I zipped up the luggage and set it by the stairs. "You read all my messages behind my back, you lied, you manipulated me, you hired—" I stiffened and screwed my eyes shut.

"The Bureau would be eternally grateful. We need good citizens like you who are willing to do what it takes."

I covered my mouth with my hands as a sob got stuck in my throat.

"We'd appreciate it if you didn't tell anyone about this. The O'Sheas are notorious for planting bugs and recruiting people to be their eyes and ears."

It'd all been an act. Had they laughed behind my back at how gullible I was?

I refused to let Finnegan see me break down, so I took a long breath and bottled up my emotions. I would save it for the drive.

"Emilia, please tell me what to do. There's gotta be a way to fix it." He came up the stairs and stopped short halfway up when he saw the luggage. "Where the fuck do you think you're going?" His hands balled into fists.

"Away. I need to think."

"No, you need to tell me how I can *fix* this," he gritted. "Running away won't solve any problems."

"Finnegan, I'm two seconds away from pushing you down the stairs." Rage bubbled right below the surface, and I was ready to unleash it if he didn't watch it. "As far as I'm concerned, there's nothing to fix. You'll get your three years. We sure as shit won't have any children, and then we get divorced. End of discussion."

He clenched his jaw and averted his gaze, though not before I got a glimpse of something. I'd seen it for a fraction of a second in that boardroom too. He'd looked...crestfallen. Stricken. His eyes had glistened, the one thing he couldn't cover with his grins. In that quick moment, he'd been ripped open and exposed.

The kick in the head? It'd hurt to see him that way. A shot at him was a shot at me, and it told me how screwed I was.

"Where're you going?" He cleared his throat and scrubbed a hand over his mouth.

"Your parents'. Meredith will send me the contract, and I'll have it delivered to Frank's office tomorrow."

He nodded with a dip of his chin and let me pass him on the stairs—except, he wrapped his fingers around my wrist.

"I'm sorry, Emilia."

I side-eyed him, quickly wrenching free and continuing down the stairs. I couldn't handle that anguished look. Seeing him in pain messed with me, and it made Grace appear like a freaking ghost in my head. She'd once told me Finnegan wore his heart on his sleeve.

Then I thought about my first date with Finnegan and how Agent—*Kellan*—had appeared as our waiter. Finnegan hadn't given the slightest indication that they knew each other. They'd fooled me well.

"One thing." Because I had to hear it from him. "Was it funny?" I asked, and I couldn't stop my eyes from welling up. "I mean, I assume Kellan gave you reports every time I spoke to him. Did you get together over a few beers and talk about all the crap I fell for?"

"Fuck no, princess." He seemed sickened that I'd think that, but for all I knew, it was another act. "Jesus—no, you—fuck!" He spun around and drove a fist into the metal railing of the stairs, causing the whole structure to rattle. I jumped back, and my heart hammered. "Believe whatever you want, except that." He spoke through the hurt that punch must've given him. "Not that, Emilia. I would *never* turn you into some joke."

I was already shaking my head and aiming for the door. This was why Grace had advised me to come out to them for a bit. Finnegan was too good with his words, and I couldn't be sucked right back in.

"Please don't come out to the house this weekend," I said, grabbing my purse. "I'll call you next week."

To my horror, Grace wasn't at the compound when I arrived. She texted and said she'd be home in an hour.

Shan and Ian were practicing putting on the lawn in front of Finnegan's and Patrick's houses, and a construction crew was working on the three guesthouses. They were almost done.

I must've been a sight. Eyes bloodshot and tumbling out of the car with a trail of tissues, I scrambled to find my sunglasses to hide a part of my personal disaster.

"That's my kind of daughter-in-law," Shan noted to Ian. "She won't hesitate to steal my boy's car."

Ian chuckled and returned his putter to the golf bag.

"Maybe he let me borrow it." My voice was still hoarse from all the crying I'd accomplished on my way here.

Shan walked toward me with a sympathetic smile. "Or he

messaged me because he was worried that you left in a death machine while upset."

Oh. Well, whatever. I'd turned off my phone before even leaving the city because of Finnegan's incessant calling.

"How're you doing, hon?" He gave me a hug. "I heard what happened at the negotiation."

"Yeah," I muttered. "Good times." It'd been Grace's idea to bring a "bug" to use if we got the chance, and the woman was rarely wrong, it seemed. "I hope it's okay I stay here for a few days."

"Of course. This is your home too—here, let me get that for you." He got my luggage out of the car, and I picked up the tissues that'd spilled out from the driver's seat. "Did you talk to Grace?"

I nodded and sniffled. "She said she'd be here in an hour."

He followed me across the way, and I dug out the keys to the house. Shan mentioned they'd had the pool filled recently, and they would give me privacy for as long as I wanted.

"We hope you'll come up for dinner, though."

I came to an abrupt stop in the hallway. "Um." Why were the walls in the living room suddenly pink?

Shan let out a sigh and ran a hand through his hair. "That wife of mine... She makes me feel old." That was silly. He wasn't even fifty. "I fear you're the casualty of war here. The boys painted Grace's studio in some hideous colors before we moved out here, and this is her retaliation."

A laugh bubbled up, the first one all day.

"I'm glad I came here." I smiled ruefully and ignored the tug at my chest. I hadn't spent a single night out of Finnegan's arms since I'd left my past behind, and I wasn't sure how this was gonna go. Part of me missed him already. Yet...fuck, he'd really hurt me.

When did summer begin, technically? Was there a specific month?

The sun was warm on my face, the water in the pool was

perfect, graduation season was in full swing, and the trees were the greenest green.

The best way to drown out the drilling and hammering from the guesthouses was to float around in the pool all day, my ears submerged and the water tickling the corners of my eyes.

It had to be summer.

With one month to go before my late-June wedding to a mobster...

Deep breaths.

I'd stayed calm today so far. The weirdest thing had brought me close to tears this morning; waking up and realizing I wasn't going to church with Finnegan. But I'd managed to hold back my emotions, and I had declined the offer to tag along with Grace and Shan. Even when they lived out here, they made it to Mass every Sunday in the city.

Was Finnegan there now? Was he feeling better? Worse?

I wasn't gonna cry today, damn it all. Three days of it had been enough. Three days of sobfests, venting to Grace, reading romance novels, running, and floating around in my new yellow bikini.

Ian was a cool guy. He and Shan had served together in the military, and they were sort of halves of each other. A yin and yang. Shan had once been the rebellious youngster Ian had taken under his wing, and then when Ian was wounded in battle, Shan stepped up, and their roles were reversed.

I was up at the main house for a sandwich Ian had made me when Grace and Shan got back from the city.

"How much you wanna bet they've brought a message to pass along from Finn?" Ian pointed his bottle of Coke out the window as the mister and missus got out of the car.

"I wouldn't bet against it, that's for sure." I smirked wryly and took another bite of my sandwich. "I've thought about turning on my phone, but I change my mind every time."

"Oh boy." He chuckled, his battle-worn face crinkling. "It's gonna blow up on ya, doll."

Probably.

I'd been careful using it since the day Grace warned me Finnegan was probably keeping tabs on me. I hadn't even been that shocked when I'd snooped on his laptop and figured out how he kept those aforementioned tabs. If he could stalk me, he could check my messages.

Grace had given me a type of phone they called burners. They were cheaper, meant to be thrown away, and had to be topped up with cash. That was where I kept most of my conversations these days.

Shan and Grace walked in, dressed sharply and stylishly in their best Sunday outfits. A far cry from my flimsy cotton dress I'd pulled on over my bikini.

"Hiya, churchgoers." I hopped down from the stool to bring my plate to the dishwasher. Ian kept telling me it was his job, and I didn't accept it. For the record, Shan didn't either.

"Hello, dearie. How are you feeling?" Grace joined me and draped an arm around my shoulders. "You've gotten some nice color."

"Thanks. I'm doing better, I think. What about you?" I leaned back against the counter.

Grace had been unaware of Kellan's role in this whole mess, so she and Shan had argued quite a bit too.

"Eh, I land on my feet." She brought out an envelope from her purse, and I sighed inwardly. "From my son. Let him grovel, Emilia."

Was it so smart I read the note, then? He was a smooth talker.

Shan had taken my previous seat next to Ian, and he rested his elbows on the kitchen island. "If it makes you feel any better, he didn't look well this morning."

"It *doesn't*." That was the problem! My heart hurt and my voice quivered. "I can't stop thinking about the look in his eyes."

"Ah, young love." Ian smiled.

Love.

What if I was falling for Finnegan? I supposed a crush made sense. Love was terrifying. Love threw logic out the window. Logic that said I should get the hell out in three years. Good lord, this was the guy who'd...done what he'd done.

"I've taken the liberty of helping you with one of your problems," Grace said. "Kellan's flying in tomorrow with the twins. It'll do you good to confront that boy. Fucking hellions, the lot of them."

Wow, that was a lot packed into so few words. It would be fun to see Alec and Nessa again. Seeing Kellan, however? I couldn't shake the humiliation.

I stared at the envelope, my name written in Finnegan's flawless handwriting.

"I think I'll return to the pool," I mumbled.

The part about me not crying today became a huge, fat fail when I read Finnegan's letter approximately two minutes later, and I spent the rest of the day in bed.

Emilia,

The first time I saw you, I was parked outside the diner. You were working an evening shift, and you were dead on your feet. Of all the places in the world to celebrate a young girl's birthday, a family was right there, during your shift, with their two kids. You and a coworker brought out a cake and sang for her, and no matter how tired you were, you lit up for that girl. She stood up in the booth and put her princess crown on your head, and you gave her the biggest smile. You humored her, were a complete goof with her, and you made her feel special.

It knocked the air out of my lungs, which has never really happened before. I was in a bad mood that night. I'd gotten lost in this shitty town where I was supposed to find my future wife. I had an address, an old photo, and a name. And as I sat there in the parking lot feeling sorry for myself, I looked at the picture. Then at you. Back at the picture. There was the weirdest tightness over my chest, because you were so fucking beautiful.

It was you I was there to find, and now I'm terrified of losing you.

I'll do anything to earn your forgiveness.

Yours,

Finnegan

Grace left early the next morning for wedding-related errands in the city. She'd be back for dinner with two twins and one asshole. After reading Finnegan's letter about a hundred times, I decided I didn't want to be alone today, so I sought out Shan and Ian, finding them behind the main house.

Shan was reading a medical journal by the pool, and Ian was... doing yoga? In Grace's orchard.

"It helps with his PTSD." Shan's comment and amused look snapped me out of my frozen state, and I climbed the steps to their terrace. "Morning, hon."

"Hi. Am I interrupting?"

"Not at all. Have a seat." He patted the lounger next to his. "I like to sit here until the sun takes over around noon. My Irish skin can't take the heat."

I grinned and sat down cross-legged next to him. "How's small-town life treating you?"

"It's fucking fantastic." He placed his magazine upside down on his lap and leaned back, clasping his fingers across his stomach. "Do you miss the city?"

I pursed my lips, unsure. "A little, maybe." Most of all, I missed Finnegan. "When I don't think how close we are to my useless town, I love it here. It's peaceful."

"Indeed, it is." He watched me pensively. "May I ask a personal question?"

My stomach fluttered with nerves, and I nodded hesitantly. "Shoot."

He smiled faintly and gestured toward my left hand. "When did you turn the heart outward?"

I dropped my gaze and twisted the Claddagh ring on my fore-finger. "Did, um, Finnegan tell you about his special rule?"

"I'm creating my own rule," Finnegan slid the ring onto my index finger and brushed his thumb over the lovely design.

"The heart is pointing in now," I said.

He nodded once. "And when you're ready to accept my family as your own, you turn it outward to represent your heart being open to them."

Shannon's voice shook me out of the memory. "He did. I found it sweet."

It was much more than sweet. The two hands cradled the heart almost protectively, and the little crown atop the heart gave it an almost regal feel. It was the power of love and family—for me, anyway.

"I turned it the day Grace and I picked up the wedding invita-tions," I admitted. "We were looking at templates for the menu at the reception, and I got to see our names. Finnegan and Emilia O'Shea. It was...overwhelming, I guess you can say."

Grace had gotten emotional and said we were family now.

"In a good way?" Shan wondered.

I nodded. I couldn't deny that any longer.

"I'm glad," he murmured. "But does this mean you accept the family for what it is? For what we are?"

Aw, *man*. "Shan..."

He laughed through his nose and fished out a pack of cigarettes from his pocket. "I know, I ask the worst questions." He extended the pack to me, and what the hell, I took one and thanked him.

"I don't suppose I can't close my eyes and pretend it's not there." I borrowed his lighter and inhaled from my first smoke in weeks.

"What's not there?" he countered with a smirk.

He was gonna make me say it.

"The fact that you're criminals." I stuck out my tongue at him.

He let out a carefree laugh, looking a lot like Finnegan.

"I've decided you're all sorcerers," I told him. "I used to be pee-my-pants terrified of Finnegan. Now I'm..." I was at a loss. So much had happened. In a short period of time, Finnegan and his family had become important. More than I could admit.

"Now you're here." The corners of his eyes crinkled. "And in my humble opinion, I hope you're here to stay. You've had a profound impact on Finn, and it's just the beginning."

"Sorcerers," I whispered and took a drag.

He smirked. "Much like him, you resort to sass to avoid the heavy talk."

I groaned, torn between laughter and exasperation. "*Fine.* Look. Grace told me you're all a bunch of liars, and I guess I'm coming to terms with that. I understand why Finnegan doesn't tell me much about his work, 'cause...well, it could put him behind bars, and let's face it, my track record isn't the best there. I already spilled the beans to one fake Fed."

It hit me what I was saying—and what it meant. I wasn't trustworthy either. My morals were a shit-ton higher, but to him, to the people he loved and protected, I was not to be trusted yet.

"It would be weird if you hadn't, dear," he said. "Our family isn't for everyone, and Grace is right. We learned to lie before we could speak."

I giggled. "How does that work?"

"I don't know, but it sounded good, eh?" he chuckled.

It grew silent between us, and I could sense he wasn't going to push the issue again. He'd gotten his point across: if I could accept them as my family, couldn't I accept Finnegan as more than a husband on paper too?

The answer was, I didn't know. Even worse was that I couldn't trust myself, because my heart said one thing, and my head said another. And when two parts of me existed on polar opposites, something was wrong.

"What do you trust when words become meaningless?" I asked.

"Hm. Good question." He nodded slowly, thinking. "It would be easy to say actions, but there will be occasions where you don't see them. In time, you'll grow to trust his intentions and feelings. He's very much devoted to you already, Emilia."

I didn't doubt the devotion, not after hearing him tearing Patrick a new one in the boardroom. No, if there was one thing I could trust, it was Finnegan's loyalty, and that meant more than I could describe.

There'd been a fleeting thought that day, a sense of *that's my man*, when I'd overheard him speaking—and yelling—without a filter to his brother. Unfortunately, it'd been pushed down by the crushing hurt because he was a rat bastard too.

"And then all is fair in love and war, right?" I quirked a brow at Shan.

"There we go. Just don't mistake love for war. He's not battling against you. He's got some questionable methods to ensure he's *with* you."

Questionable methods. *I'll say.*

"Do you have those questionable methods too?" I wondered.

He laughed. "Oh, you have no idea, Emilia."

Fucking great.

I took a couple puffs from the cigarette, then stubbed it out in the ashtray on the pool deck.

"Don't forget the perks, though," he pointed out. "You can adopt your own methods to answer your questions."

Well, there was a scarily exciting idea.

It was what Grace had said. You had to play the game by their rules, and more often than not, there were no rules.

"Hey, excuse me, sir?" The voice came from the corner of the house, and I saw one of the construction workers. "This was dropped off at the gate."

Shan accepted the package. "Cheers, I appreciate it."

"No worries. We're stepping out for lunch. We'll be back at one."

"Sounds good." Shan inclined his head and extended the box to me. "It's for you."

Me? Oh, of course. Finnegan never half-assed anything. He was on a mission now. Opening the box, I spotted a note first, and in just a few sentences, he made me ache.

Emilia,

> *Your pillow doesn't smell like you anymore. I'm not finding your hairs in the shower. You and your attitude aren't there to greet me when I get home. My coffee doesn't taste as good as yours. (What's the coffee/cream ratio?) I miss your voice, that smile of yours, and pretty much everything else that's become a reminder how my life obviously sucked before you. I just plain miss you, princess. Please talk to me.*

> *Yours,*
> *Finnegan*

I swallowed hard and read a line at the bottom, the words written in a language I didn't recognize. Was that Irish?

"What, um—" I had to clear my throat. "What does this mean? The part at the bottom." I showed Shan the note.

He quickly scanned the note before landing on the sentence in question, and something in his expression softened.

"That sweet cock-up. He's got his tail between his legs, all right." He smiled ruefully and sat back. "I'm not going to tell you what it says. And, word of advice, you shouldn't google it until you're ready to know the answer."

That wasn't helpful at all. Who said I wasn't ready?

Remembering there was something buried in bubble wrap in the box, I picked it up and unfolded it carefully. Oh God. I didn't know whether to laugh or cry. That *bastard*. He'd bought us a cake topper, a groom physically dragging the bride along by her veil. I had to cover my mouth, and my eyes welled up rapidly.

chapter 22

Emilia Porter

When Grace pulled up in her SUV and I saw Kellan stepping out of the vehicle, I gripped my knife tighter and stalked over to the kitchen window in the main house. Helping Ian chop vegetables had given me the perfect tool to adopt a few of my own *questionable methods.*

"That motherless *shit*," I seethed.

Grace had no doubt warned him. While Alec and Nessa jumped out of the car in a great mood, Kellan was rubbing the back of his neck and looking around himself.

Since the truth had come out, I'd learned his name wasn't even Caldwell. It was Kellan Ford, and he was dead meat.

"I love him as if he were my own," Grace had told me, "and I'd tan his hide as if he were my own too."

"I think I'll take that, hon." Ian came up behind me and loosened my hold on the knife. "Now, go get him."

"I can't." I mentally rooted my feet into place. "I wouldn't be able to control myself, and the kids shouldn't see that."

Ian chuckled warmly. "Alec competes in martial arts, and Nessa's favorite pastime is target practice."

I needed something like that. I'd grown accustomed to running once a day, but it wasn't enough. Maybe I could get two preteens to help me.

By now, Grace was almost at the house. Alec and Nessa were lugging their bags to Patrick's house. The construction crew was packing up for the day, and Kellan was waiting for something. He stood by the cars and smoked a cigarette, and it sucked how small of a wardrobe change it took to make him look every bit a Son. His fake, typical government-type suit had been replaced by tailored suit pants, a dark blue dress shirt, friggin' suspenders, and forearms covered in ink.

I hoped he didn't want kids.

Stalking out of the house, I passed Grace first, who offered a knowing smirk and a, "Have fun, dearie."

Too late to do anything about the fact that I was barefoot. I could inflict some damage anyway.

"Tush! Yer second husband is here!" Alec popped his head out the door of Patrick's house.

"Not now, kid." I narrowed my eyes at Kellan as he spotted me.

He showed his palms in caution and stubbed out his smoke. "Emilia, before you go to town on me, know that I was only doing my job."

"And I'm here to give you the reward for being the employee of the month, you son of a bitch." Blind rage exploded within me, and I took off in a sprint. It sent a rush of adrenaline through me.

"No need to bring my mother into this," he replied, frowning. Piece of garbage treated this like it was a joke. "Hey, let's talk about —okay, you're really not slowing down."

I flew into him a second later and went apeshit. It was my only strategy. Kellan tumbled to the ground with a painful grunt, and I toppled over him all while slapping the ever-loving crap out of him.

"How could you!" I shouted.

"I was—*goddammit*, Emilia—I was following orders!" He

flinched and jerked, doing his best to dodge my punches, but he wasn't fighting back.

"Yay, get him!" Nessa had evidently joined us. I didn't see anyone but Kellan and the memories of me trusting him, me putting my faith and hope in him. He'd been one of the good guys.

"Aim for the throat, Tush!" Alec hollered.

"Whose side are you on, you feckless little brats?" Kellan growled.

"Hers!"

Heaving a breath, I planted my knee on his crotch and slammed my palm up his chin.

"Ouch, motherf—" Another growl left him, and he shoved me off of him to cup his crotch. "My fucking balls," he groaned. "I fink I bit my tongue."

"I fink you should say you're sorry!" I yelled.

"Okay, that's enough!" He put a swift ending to my thrashing and rolled on top of me. A small rock was digging into my spine, and I squirmed and shrieked like a freaking banshee. "Sweet Jesus, I'mma be deaf after this. Knock it off!" With a tight grab on my jaw, he leaned down, our chests heaving with rapid, shallow breaths, and he glared at me. "I'm sorry I hurt you, Emilia. I would do it again because it's my job, and that's how it is. But I'm sorry. I'm really fucking sorry. Now, if I let go of you, are you gonna hit me again?"

"Try me," I snarled.

He grinned, out of breath, and a bit of blood trickled down from a cut in his lip. "Welcome to the family, dollface." He pissed me off further by giving me a loud kiss on my forehead, then moving away fast as hell.

I managed to kick him in the shin as he stood up. "What the fuck is *wrong* with you?"

"Depends who you're asking." He grimaced in pain and leaned down to rub his leg. "That one hurt."

"Eat a bag of dicks." I threw an arm over my face and swallowed dryly. My heart was still racing, yet the adrenaline was leaving me.

"Not the best insult to throw at someone who's queer," he chuckled.

"Just great." I scrubbed my hands over my face and took a deep breath.

Kellan was smiling down at me and extending a hand. "Friends?"

This fucking family, I swear.

"Are you nervous about getting hitched, love? I'd be shittin' bricks if I were you."

Alec's vocabulary and accent never failed to make me chuckle. Every *my* and *you* became *me* and *ye*, and *love* was *luv*.

"You're twelve," I pointed out. "If you were getting married, it would be a felony."

"Aye, 'cause I'm supposed to wait until you ditch the boss for me." He gave me a wink.

I shook my head in amusement and threw some popcorn at him.

When dinner was over up at the main house, I had been ready to retreat and be alone. Alec didn't let me, and he insisted on keeping me company for a movie or two. We were still on the first one, and I couldn't say I was paying attention.

My resistance had crumbled. I just wanted Finnegan here.

There were bursts of anger whenever I thought of Kellan's "job," but missing Finnegan put me down more.

There was no hope for me.

"Who're you texting?" I asked. "Girlfriend?"

"Nah. Girls are weird. I'm talking to Finn."

It didn't help that I was reminded of him every two minutes.

My phone lay dead on the coffee table.

"What's he doing?" I asked carefully. Was I ready to read the messages Finnegan had sent?

"Not much," Alec said. "He's watching telenovelas and yelling *ay, dios mio* and *cabron* to the couple having bad sex next door."

I laughed behind my hand, only to get confused because there was no couple living next door. There was a Mrs. Cardigan, a sweet old lady who supplied Finnegan with his damn butterscotch candies.

"The tosser's miserable, Tush." Alec placed the phone to his ear, and it hit me that he was calling Finnegan. Shit, shit, shit. How did I look—oh, for chrissakes. He couldn't see me. "Oi, boss. How bored are ye?" He chuckled at something, then turned it on speaker.

"...finished maybe...two boxes of Twinkies?"

I put a hand over my heart. Hearing his voice was painful.

Alec smirked. "Boss...?"

"Fine, three," Finnegan bitched. In the background, I heard a bang. "I fucking swear. Hold on, cub. *Estoy embarazada! Eres el padre! Mentiras, cabron!*"

To muffle my laughter, I shoved a pillow against my face. Oh my God, where *was* he? The walls at home weren't even thin.

Finnegan groaned. "I can't take this much longer. Life sucks without her." He kicked something, judging by the sound of it.

And I was done. I was punishing both of us for something I was too weak to resist anyway.

"I'm more concerned about what you just yelled, Finn," Alec snickered. "Are you learning Spanish or just parroting it?"

"Sometimes you don't need to know the meaning to deliver a strong message," Finnegan replied. "Bad shit went down after Teresa said it, and for the record, she didn't fall. She was pushed." He paused. "I think she's pregnant."

With a shake of my head and tears of both laughter and heartache threatening to spill over, I left the couch to get dressed. I had my foot on the first step when I remembered something.

"Alec," I whispered. "Ask where he is."

At the same time, Finnegan spoke up again, much more somber now. "How's Emilia doing?"

Alec eyed me, deliberating. "Gotta go, boss."

"What the hell?" I threw up my hands. "I have to know where he is if I'm gonna go see him."

"He's at the motel, so let's go!"

"Wait, what? He's *here*?" I was in disbelief, and maybe that was dumb. Of *course* he was here. He was here. Less than twenty minutes away. "I'm getting dressed. And I adore you, Alec, but you're not coming with me."

That stopped him in his tracks, and he looked positively devastated. "But...I wanted to see the reunion, Tush."

A reunion that would no doubt turn R-rated pretty quickly. No thanks.

Five minutes later, I was driving out of the gates in Finnegan's Aston. My stomach was a butterfly-y mess, and I probably looked like a fool. It'd started out so well, with the thought, "Hey, look your best when you tell him he's forgiven." I'd put on nicer underwear, a pair of tight jeans he liked because of my butt, and I'd donned some of the jewelry he'd given me. Then I'd accidentally taken his deodorant, effectively dousing me in the scent of Finnegan. My patience had run out faster than I'd run out the door.

Nothing said class like nice jewelry and a hoodie.

I sped up on the stretch of nothingness that took me from the O'Shea property to the highway, feeling the engine's power under me.

It was time to accept. Time to adapt to the new playbook. Maybe, if I worked hard, I could change the game with time. For now, I was going to be different because *they* were different. The

278

O'Sheas weren't normal. They weren't normal, regular, boring people, and—

Whoa. Boring?

I shook my head quickly, bewildered.

Where did *that* come from?

Nearing the end of the road, I squinted at something that reflected in the headlights. "What the...?" There were two cars blocking the road. I had no choice but to slow down. Two black SUVs.

I checked the rearview, only to do a double take. Three men on four-wheelers appeared behind me. Coming from the forest...? I mean, they'd had to. We were surrounded by it. Shit. My stomach dropped, and I had the queasiest feeling that something wasn't right. Blindly searching the passenger's seat for my phone, I watched a man step out of one of the cars in front of me, and fuck, fuck, fuck, I'd forgotten my phone.

Finnegan had an app in his car with its own contact number; I was supposed to be able to both call and text to and from it, except I didn't know how it worked. The display lit up in its night mode, and I clicked on the touch screen, opening the app—*motherfucker!* Password restricted.

I took a breath, forcing myself to stay calm. It was probably nothing.

I made sure the doors were locked.

Then I remembered my necklace. Thank God. *One* thing that didn't suck right now. Better safe than chopped up in the woods, I figured, and felt around the little padlock charm around my neck. I found the button to the panic alarm and pressed it repeatedly.

The man whose face I couldn't see clearly was about twenty feet away when the display lit up again, this time with a call from Finnegan's cell.

I pressed answer and—

"Thank fuck! You're not wrapped around a tree. What's—"

"End of the road near the compound, before the highway." The words gusted out of me as I stared at the approaching man. I didn't have much time. "Two SUVs blocked the road. I slowed down, and three ATVs came up behind me. Tell me what the fuck to do." Panic set in, and I white-knuckled the wheel. "A man's walking over."

There was a second of silence before I heard a door slam and the telltale sound of a car being unlocked. "Whatever you do, do not roll down the window. You hear me?" His voice was like the first signs of a storm, a low rumble on the horizon where the sky was black. "There's a button under the door handle. Press that, and it'll open a valve. It'll be enough to communicate. There's a gun in the glove—"

"I don't know how to use a fucking gun," I hissed.

The man was almost here. His hair was black and gleaming. Ghostly pale skin. He wore a smile and carried a cane.

Finnegan spoke again, but I was out of time. I ended the call and pressed my panic alarm a few more times. Hopefully, he'd take that to mean hurry the hell up!

Right, that other button. My hand shook, and the man rapped the end of his thin cane on the window. There, under the handle, was a button. I pushed it, and it gave off a faint mechanical whirr.

"I'm not rolling down my window," I said.

He chuckled lightly and bent down to peer into the car. Some hair fell in front of his eyes, and he brushed it away with a flick of his fingers. He looked young, around my age.

"You must be the little Emilia I've heard so much about." He had a thick Italian accent and a weirdly high-pitched voice. "Stupid you are not, but you *are* alone."

I gripped the wheel again. It was the only thing I could do to keep myself from freaking out. I held it as hard as I could and kept a foot on the gas.

"Who are you and what do you want?" I asked.

His smile widened, showing off his too-white teeth.

"My apologies, *bella*. My name is irrelevant, but I work for the

Avellino family in Napoli. I am here to ask you if you have yet met John Murray."

I didn't answer. Stalling, mind spinning, too focused on making sure I breathed.

"Will you not answer me, *ragazza*?" he crooned.

I cocked an eyebrow. "I didn't hear a question."

He let out a laugh and straightened up to say something to his friends. I didn't understand a word of it, reminding me once again that I *had* to get better. Days, if not weeks, before Sarah put on an engagement ring, she'd started a list of topics and skills she wanted to learn. Languages, to name one. They were for her own benefit, for her future, though I was more thinking I needed skill sets to cope with this new fucking life of mine.

The man bent down again. His fingers tapped along the roof of the car. "Such wit, such beauty. So I ask, have you met John Murray yet?"

Shouldn't Finnegan be here by now?

"I don't see how that's any of your business," I told him.

"On the contrary." He grinned. "You see, John Murray is family! He is my boss's beloved brother."

I blanched. This man, who was clearly Italian, claimed that John Murray was...Italian? I didn't understand. Not one bit. Yet, something stirred in my memory. What *was* it? My eyebrows knitted together. I'd read something that'd once made me think of Italy, and it was related to the O'Sheas. Or Murrays.

At the roar of an engine, there was suddenly a flurry of activity. The ATVs retreated and drove into the woods, there was someone yelling in Italian, and the man next to me looked mildly irritated.

"Until we meet again, Emilia."

I was gonna live?

I blew out a breath and watched them all drive away, and a beat later, two motorcycles pulled up. It was Shan and Kellan. My brain kind of went blank. Ian appeared as well, from a car. Grace's car. This meant I was safe, right? Where was Finnegan? I needed him.

Shan knocked on the window while Kellan rounded the car, and I saw his gun. He had a freaking gun. Like the one in the glove box? The one I hadn't known existed?

My fingers were trembling again, contradicting the utter calm that spread in my head, and I opened the door for Shan. This mobster guy who would be my father-in-law in a few weeks.

"It's safe now, hon." He squatted down and squeezed my hand. That sly fucker. He was pressing two fingers to the inside of my wrist too. Trust me, my pulse worked. "Are you okay?"

"Probably not because I'm not crying my eyes out," I said.

"You might be in shock."

It didn't feel that way.

"Where's Finnegan?" I asked.

"On his way." Shan stood up and extended a hand. "Let's get you back to the compound. I want to know what happened."

"I'm good to drive," I insisted.

"Make up your minds." Kellan came back. "It's impossible to secure the perimeters when I don't know where the fuck they went."

Well, I wasn't sticking around, that was for sure. With anxiety waking me up, I nudged Shan out of the way and closed the door.

chapter

23

Emilia Porter

How long was it going to take before my meltdown claimed me? Breaking down was just something I did. I was a stupid, naïve little girl who couldn't fucking cope, so why wasn't the anxiety bubbling over? It was very *there*. It made my fingers itch and shake, and the pressure on my chest fired flashbacks at me as I spoke. However, my emotions didn't drown me. My head was clear and level. The panic stayed back.

It was freaking me out.

I paced the lawn outside Finnegan's and Patrick's houses, and I had an audience. Shan, Kellan, and Ian listened to my story of what'd happened. Their reactions to learning the man was Italian included cursing and Shan sending a text to someone.

"You sure that's the name you heard?" Kellan asked. "Avellino."

"I'm sure. Does anyone have a cigarette?"

Kellan beat the others to it and offered me one, already lit.

"Thanks." I paced some more and inhaled from the smoke, waiting for that breakdown. "Where's Grace?"

"With the twins."

"Is it safe being out here?" I asked.

Ian looked up at the night sky. "From anything but a drone attack, I reckon."

"They have drones?" I shouted. *That* had my heart galloping.

"No! No, sweetheart." Ian cringed. "A joke in poor taste on my part."

Sweet Jesus.

Shan sighed and clapped him on the back, then approached me with concern written all over. "We think we know what's going on, so yes, we're safe. This isn't some fortress, but Finn takes security seriously. You have nothing to worry about." He touched my shoulder and tilted his head. "You're taking this remarkably well."

"I know, it's not normal." I rubbed my temples and exhaled some smoke. "Okay, so what's going on? Does this happen a lot? I don't think I can handle that."

"This is a first from the Avellino family on US soil. They don't operate here." Shan addressed Kellan next. "I need you to put together a security crew that can be here first thing in the morning —ah, Finn's here."

Finally!

"I'll make it happen, sir." Kellan stalked toward the main house.

I aimed toward the gates instead. A familiar rush of emotions pummeled through me, though it wasn't at all related to the shit-show that took place earlier. *I miss him, I need him, I think I love him.* I flicked away my cigarette on the paved road and started running when Finnegan exited what I assumed was my new car.

He didn't even shut off the engine—or park very neatly. The urgency wasn't in the way he moved as much as it was in his features. That was how he gave away what he felt. The worry, the panic, and the desperation swam in his gunmetal eyes.

He exhaled in a whoosh of relief when I jumped him and wrapped my arms and legs around him, quickly embracing me in one of his tight hugs.

"I think I just lost ten years of my life," he whispered raggedly. "Are you okay, baby?"

I nodded and buried my face in the crook of his neck where everything was safe, warm, and smelled amazing. A blanket of serenity covered me, and everything slowed down. Tears burned my eyes and trickled down my cheeks. The shivers came and went over and over. He was here, holding me, tightening his strong arms around me, whispering to me, kissing my shoulder and my hair.

"I'm gonna kill them." He didn't mean that part. I felt us moving; he was walking us over to Shan and Ian, but I felt like I was done for the day. Exhaustion hit, making it so easy to hand over the reins to Finnegan. "Seriously. The Avellinos? I thought that old fuck retired. Fill me in," he told...one of the others. "I'm guessing their roadblock was to send a message they're here?"

"Aye, it's the only thing that makes sense," Shan replied. "We've never dealt with them, and they asked Emilia about John."

"We're involved enough," Finnegan stated. "Otherwise, they would've targeted Chicago, not come all the way out here. How many were there?"

I sniffled and let all the tension roll off me. He stroked my back.

I played with the fine, soft hairs at the back of his neck.

"Emilia said she saw five or six men. Two cars, three four-wheelers."

"That's one hell of a message." Finnegan released a heavy breath and pressed his lips to my neck, lingering. "They crossed a fucking line. Our women and children are off-limits. They wanna let us know they're here, they can knock on the door or do it in skywriting. They don't cage in my fiancée and expect me to be okay with it."

I relaxed further, and the tears stopped falling.

"You've raised a man who's born to be boss, mate," Ian said. "He'd do Ronan proud, God rest his soul."

"Born to be boss... My father started grooming him when he was seven," Shan muttered. "All right. We have to talk to John and get to the bottom of why the Italians are here. Finn, thoughts on security?"

"I want our immediate family here," Finnegan answered. "It's less than four weeks till the wedding, and I don't wanna risk anything. Give them forty-eight hours' notice, and those who won't come out gotta have watchdogs on them for a while. At least until we know more."

"Sounds good," Shan agreed. "We should handle this tonight, so..."

Finnegan nodded with a dip of his chin. "Just give me a minute first."

"Of course, son."

It grew quiet, and I understood we'd been left alone.

Part of me wondered what had happened to my curiosity. Much was evidently going on, yet I was content to wait, and it was unlike me. This was the highest level of mafia talk, for chrissakes. I should be running in the opposite direction, not...literally clinging to it. To *him*.

Finnegan dug out his keys and carried me inside.

I wasn't ready to let go of him, so I wouldn't.

"What the fresh hell—did a unicorn take a shit on our walls?"

My mouth stretched into a grin against the skin of his neck, and I couldn't suppress the giggles.

"You can ask your mom about that."

"Aw, fuck. Because we painted her art studio. I should've known." For several seconds, he stood quietly in the middle of the living room. I didn't like that he wasn't holding me as tightly anymore. "You, uh... I don't know what to do now. Are you tired?"

I frowned and inched back to look him in the eye. "What?"

That was when I saw the weariness in his eyes—and the wistfulness and wariness.

"Tell me what to do, princess."

"I was on my way to you," I whispered.

A spark of hope mingled with the longing. "You were?"

I nodded and scratched a finger over his beard. I'd missed feeling it on my body. "I forgive you if you give me permission to maybe slap you upside the head sometimes. What you did really burned me, and when I think back on all that, I get pissed."

Rather than cracking a smile at my sort-of attempt at keeping it light, he closed his eyes and rested his forehead to mine. "Thank God."

"I assure you he had nothing to do with it."

He breathed a small laugh and shook his head. Then he swallowed hard and glanced over at the couch, and the glimpse I got of his eyes packed a punch. He was struggling to hold it together.

"We'll be okay." I cupped his cheeks.

He nodded once and sat down with me on his lap, and he cleared his throat. "I expected to be more relieved when I saw you'd signed the contract, but...it's not enough, Emilia. Not anymore, not with you. It can't be just a marriage on paper."

I was at a loss for words, because this meant—what did this mean? No, I knew what he was implying. That he wanted the real deal. That it meant more to him. And as my heart thumped and soared, it scared me too. All I could do was lock my arms around his neck and hug him hard.

"Do I at least stand a chance?" he whispered. "I get that you won't make any promises. I have a lot to prove—"

"Yes. I mean, yes, there's a chance." I could say that much. I could allow myself to be open to the possibility, despite that my hopes might get crushed if I ended up burned again.

He kissed me softly, with barely restrained urgency. "A chance is all I need." With a few more tentative kisses, he deepened the next one, and I responded with passion. He shuddered and hugged me the way he was supposed to. "I don't know what I would've done if anything happened to you. You sure you're okay?"

"I'm sure." For now anyway. "No more talking." If all I had were a few minutes before he...went to work, for lack of a better term, then we were going to spend them kissing and holding each other. It was a slow dance with our tongues, sweet brushes to get reacquainted, nuzzling to convey how much we'd missed one another, and a torturous buildup that promised more heat later.

I woke up the next morning to the sound of two guitars.

Faint, light strumming.

It was beautiful.

Pushing myself up into a seated position, I squinted around me, disoriented, and remembered I was on the couch. Finnegan had tucked me in last night after bringing down pillows and our duvet. He'd said he wasn't sure when he'd be back, but he was a call away. Judging by the untouched spot on the other side of the L-shaped couch, he'd either slept somewhere else, or he hadn't slept at all.

I spotted him and Alec out on the patio, with their backs to me.

"You've been practicing, cub. It sounds good."

It was a rare treat to hear Finnegan play. He'd played the piano at home a few times. This was the first time I'd heard him on the guitar, and I should've known he'd be brilliant at this too. Though, after Grace shared a recording of him playing the tin whistle at a memorial for a family member, it was the instrument I wanted to hear the most. The sound was just chillingly beautiful, not to mention unquestionably Irish.

Wanting to join them in the sun, I went upstairs and freshened up before changing into my bikini. I snatched a pair of boxer shorts from Finnegan too and folded the waistband to make them shorter. Then I redid my ponytail and went downstairs again.

Both heads turned as I stepped out onto the patio, Finnegan's eyes darkened, his gaze raking over me. I'd missed that too. Never before in my life had I felt so desired.

"I see you woke up on the indecent side of the bed," he murmured.

"Great! Now I can't wear my yellow bikini," Alec quipped.

I grinned and joined Finnegan on his lounger. "Keep playing, please."

To be a little jerk, Alec set down his guitar. "He can't now that you're here, silly Tush. It's a wedding surprise, you see."

Oh? I looked at Finnegan.

He nodded once and set down his guitar too. "You'll have to wait, I'm afraid."

If it was a surprise for the wedding, I supposed I could deal. Reluctantly. God, now I wanted to know what they had planned.

"Sleep well?" He took a sip of his coffee and patted the spot between his legs. I took the hint and scooted closer, and he returned his mug before strapping his arms across my chest. His left hand was hidden under his right arm so he could be a sneak and cup one of my boobs. I shot him a look of warning. Seriously, we had a twelve-year-old right next to us. Finnegan's eyes glittered with amusement, though what I noticed the most were the shadows underneath.

"Did you sleep at all?" I countered quietly.

He shook his head. "I'm on my seventh cup of coffee."

I scrunched my nose. "You worked all night? I'll have to tuck you in, then."

"I'll take a nap later. Lot to do today."

"Aye, I'm being shipped off again," Alec said with a sour look. "I know how kids of divorced mums and dads feel now."

That made me frown. "Why's he leaving?" I asked Finnegan.

"John's call," he replied, facing Alec. "You'll be back in a month, cub."

In the distance, we heard Grace hollering for Alec, saying it was time to get going, and he let out a string of curses no twelve-year-old should utter. There were one too many c-words.

"Oi." Finnegan gave him a wry look that held just enough of a warning. "Wash your mouth and don't skip confession next week."

I pressed my lips together to withhold my snickers, and I reached out and grabbed Alec's hand. "We'll text like pros, kiddo."

"I'll miss the stag night now, though," he grumbled.

Finnegan laughed. "Alec, you would've missed that anyway. Don't be in such a rush to grow up."

As funny as this was, he was right. Alec was much like a little adult, with the same expectations on himself as a grown man. The only difference was that he still lived to terrorize his sister, although I wasn't sure that would ever change. Just look at his family. Finnegan and his own mother pulled pranks on each other.

"Fine." Alec turned his stern gaze on me. "We gotta text a lot, Tush. We have plans to make for when yer leaving the boss for me."

Finnegan barked out a laugh, and I bumped fists with Alec.

After hugs were exchanged—and some good-natured ribbing between the boys—we said goodbye to Alec for now, and then Finnegan updated me on what they'd done all night. Namely, trying to map out the intentions of the Italians. The fact that it looked like I wasn't going to freak out about the whole ordeal last night kind of amazed me. I took it as a win. Personal growth—or possibly the disappearance of my sanity. Because I listened to Finnegan talk about retaliation and personal vendettas, and it barely fazed me.

"Can you tell me about this vendetta crap?" I sat up and turned around to face him better. "Yesterday, that man said his boss and John are family—that they're brothers. How's that true?"

He watched me pensively and lit up a smoke. "You ready for some family history?"

"Hit me with it. I took the Wikipedia crash course. I know you guys go way back for generations. The Murrays are from one place in Ireland, and you're from another. But, like, from the same province or something."

He chuckled. "All right. Yes, they're from Cork. We're from Killarney. Both are in the province of Munster." That was it. Munster. Hence the name of their syndicate. "I won't go back that far. Shit was perfect up until my grandfather appointed his best friend to be his right-hand man." He hesitated. "You're young, so I don't know how much of this you remember. My grandfather was Ronan O'Shea. He was the boss for over twenty years, until he was killed about ten years ago."

I'd read about it. The memories were too fuzzy. "His friend was killed too, right? Um...Ennis?"

He smiled and inclined his head. "That's right. Ennis Murray— Uncle John and Ma's pop." This, I'd heard. And it always gave me pause when I was reminded that Grace was a Murray originally. After reading about the in-house drama, it was a wonder they still met up for family reunions. "So the tradition we've had in our organization goes back to when everything started. When a boss retires or dies, the rank goes over to the other family's appointed new boss, usually the eldest son. It's how we've kept the peace all this time. Before my grandfather, it was a Murray who ruled. Before then, another O'Shea."

That made sense. "So then, it was John's turn, and he's the boss now."

Finnegan's smirk was a little on the dark side, and he flicked away some ash. "Not necessarily. And this is personal to me for a lot of reasons. Growing up, Pat and I always heard we were like Ronan and Ennis. It was a running joke for years. Because of my, uh, conservative ways, I guess you can say, and Patrick's looser morals. While he was chasing skirts, I was shadowing my grandfather to learn respect, loyalty, and honor. And there used to be honor in what we do." He was legit irritated by *how* they committed their crimes. "Ennis had his head stuck in the clouds. He crossed his fingers and hoped for the best, and he didn't see what he wanted to see in John. He didn't give John his vote to be the next Murray in charge."

I stayed quiet, getting sucked in.

"I used to respect Uncle John," he went on. "He was supposed to be the next boss, and my grandfather thought so too. But, since he'd chosen Ennis to be his adviser, it meant Ennis's vote mattered almost as much as Ronan's. With one vote, no one can dictate a successor, but they can veto and rule one out. John had a feeling his pop was gonna eliminate his chances of becoming boss, so he took matters into his own hands. He struck deals with foreign syndicates we don't want to have anything to do with. He dismissed sit-downs with my grandfather and got into a turf war with a gang in Chicago with trigger-happy fingers. He raised hell, in short."

"Then your grandfather and Ennis were murdered," I said.

"Yeah. And pretty much everyone with a brain knows John was behind it."

Jesus. My mind began spinning, and I pinched my lips together. If John had Ronan and Ennis assassinated, were there any limits to what he would do? He'd killed his own father in that case.

"He started sending his men to Philly next." Finnegan finished his smoke, his features clouded by what he no doubt remembered vividly. "Ronan's and Ennis's most vocal supporters dropped off the face of the earth. Pat and I were ordered to go to Europe for uni studies—our folks didn't want us in the city." So that was when Finnegan attended Trinity College in Dublin. "It didn't take long before it escalated further. As soon as the first bodies were discovered, it became a full-blown war and media circus. Patrick and I came home to help out. More men were killed—even a couple wives, and one kid died." That was *awful*. "All in all, from the moment my grandfather was murdered... It was a couple years of mayhem, and it ended for me when I was thrown in prison. A ton of us were. Most of us got set up. John had planted his people fucking everywhere, and Patrick and I trusted the wrong guy in our crew."

There were so many conflicting thoughts here. Part of me was ready to blurt out, *you knew what you signed up for*. To expect criminals to be honorable seemed...naïve at best. Another part of me knew right and wrong weren't always in step with legal and illegal, and Finnegan had grown up in the middle of this. Right and wrong were about whether or not to keep his family safe and do the work he'd been brought up to do. Even though he knew exactly what was wrong, what was he supposed to do? Let his uncle kill his family members and get away with it?

Listen to yourself.

I flinched back an inch or two, reeling from the arguments I'd built up in defense of what Finnegan did.

Why did it feel like I was about to get lost in gray areas that had once been so black-and-white?

I cleared my throat, needing to push that aside for now. "I take it your uncle dealt with the guy his dad wanted to be boss too?"

"And that brings us to the punch line in today's lesson." Finnegan rubbed his hands together. "Like Patrick, Ennis's little junior on the O'Shea side, Ennis couldn't keep his dick in his pants at the sight of a beautiful woman." *Oh, no.* "We don't even know how many bastards he fathered, but we do know one of them is older than John. Ennis wanted to include this bastard in our family, and he almost succeeded."

All the puzzle pieces connected before my very eyes, and I gasped. "I *knew* I'd read something about John and Italians! Ennis's eldest son was named Gino or something. *He's* the Avellino guy!"

"There you go. Aye—Giovanni. Ennis had an affair with an Italian girl in his neighborhood right after he got married, and his vote for the next Murray boss would've landed on Gio. My grandfather never would've let it happen, but the betrayal had already taken place. John saw his pop pick his bastard son over him."

"Holy shit." I was in a daze, shaking my head. All this drama, all this intrigue. "Your family's gotta have more drama than the telenovelas you watched this weekend."

Finnegan, my absolute *goof*, put a hand over his heart as if he'd been shot. "*Ay, dios mio, no lo creo. Se cayo!*"

I giggled up a storm and nearly fell backward. "Do you even know what you're saying?"

"No clue," he chuckled. The amusement faded kinda quickly, and he squinted at me, the sun probably bothering him. "So...how are you taking all this?"

I held out my arms in front of me, the undersides facing up. "Like there's Xanax in my veins. I don't know. Maybe my brain's short-circuited." I shrugged. "I'm okay with it."

He hummed and brought my wrists closer to kiss them. "I wanna be more transparent with you, and since we're on the topic, I have to tell you something."

Oh boy. I withdrew my hands and kept them in my lap, and my stomach tightened. "I swear, Finn..."

"So that's how it's gonna be? I'm Finn when you're ready to bite?"

"Finn can be finished too," I said. "Out with it. Tell me."

He sighed and rested his elbows on his knees, and he brought his hands together to crack his knuckles. "With everything I've told you about my uncle... And you know why Patrick and I were looking for wives..."

I nodded hesitantly, confused. They wanted to climb the ranks. Image was important to their uncle, and it just looked better if they were "traditional family men."

"Then I fucked myself over, and you became more important," he murmured. "You're more than a pretty face I want next to me when I get closer to my uncle. You're someone I've grown ridiculously protective of."

"Okay..." I answered warily. Was he feeding me sweet lines before slapping me across the face, or what?

He shifted in his seat, his Adam's apple moving with his swallow. "Up until the wedding—and most likely a while after—I can't let you go out alone. There will be two guys with you at all times, and they have the authority to restrict your outings if they deem it unsafe."

Authority. Over me.

Okay, as far as confessions went, I'd expected much worse. He surely acted as if it was worse. Annoying, *oh hell yes*, but I could survive some precautionary security measures.

Unless there was more?

"And then what?" I demanded.

He furrowed his brow. "That's it. They'll follow you wherever you go when I'm not around, and our plans have changed. No party at Mick's pub next weekend. We're staying here."

Unbidden, Shan's voice rummaged around in my head. *Adopt your own questionable methods.* I narrowed my eyes at Finnegan. Could I...? I mean, this meant I would get sucked in further. Oh, but it would be so *fun*.

I folded my arms over my chest. "Do you think I'm weak?"

He stared at me, bewildered. "The fuck? No."

"But you don't think I can defend myself," I said. "Rather than teaching me to be as able-bodied and prepared as the goons you pay, you tell two buddies to go watch your little lady. This, Finn, is the highest form of oppression of women—"

"Are you fucking—!" He smashed his lips together, so beyond frustrated that I almost burst out in laughter. "I wanna keep you safe!"

"And you take it for granted that I can't do it myself!" I argued. Then I forced in a breath and put a hand on my chest, pretending to be overwhelmed. "I'm so tired of this," I whispered and looked down. "I haven't seen you in days, and I just want to enjoy myself a little before next the next bomb drops."

"What just happened?" he muttered to himself. He scrubbed his hands over his face. "I don't wanna fight, baby. The last thing I think of you is weak—"

"I'll let it go," I interrupted. "I'll let it go if you do me a favor." I held out my hand.

Poor Finnegan, I wasn't being easy on him. He hadn't slept, who knew if he'd eaten, and he probably wanted this whole thing to be over. Maybe that was why he ignored his own evident confusion and aggravation and took my hand.

"Name it," he said.

I shook his hand to seal the deal, then stood up. "I'll name it when I figure it out, Irish boy. For now, you owe me. What's the saying...oh. I'll collect one day."

At my triumphant grin, he widened his eyes in disbelief.

"You little shit!" Oh, he fucking exploded, and I couldn't keep it in anymore.

I guffawed like a loon, only to yelp when he was out of his seat and ready to take me down. I ran away from him as fast as I could.

"Sucker!" I called over my shoulder.

He chased me around the pool, and I flew out between the two houses to escape—except, I was eating grass two seconds later.

"I'll show you who's the sucker in our bed," he growled in my ear.

Hnngh.

chapter

24

Finnegan O'Shea

P atrick folded his arms and made a face at the rain pouring
down outside. "I never thought I'd say this, but I'd rather be at
the bachelorette party right now."

I rolled my eyes, finished my pizza roll, and left the kitchen. "I
understand the concept of work is hard for you." Our break was
over, and I trailed through the ground floor of the main house to get
to Pop's study in the back.

My brother caught up with me. "You're turning into a
Michael."

I frowned, side-eying him. "What a Fredo thing to say."

"Fuck you, I'm Sonny," he chuckled.

"They both end up dead, you fucking moron."

"*Oi.*" With a firm grip on my shoulder, Patrick swiftly halted
me and pushed me against the nearest wall. His arm locked over
my chest, and his eyes showed sheer fury. "What the *fuck* have I
done to make you think so little of me? You've been treating me like
a Murray, for chrissakes. I'm your big brother—"

"Then act like it!" I growled, shoving him away from me. The
anger rose instantly, and I jabbed a finger at his temple. "I

remember when you used this more than your dick. We were supposed to go into this together, and somewhere along the way, you quit on me. You couldn't give one fuck about what happens to John, admit it."

Patrick glared at me and said nothing for several beats.

I deflated, disappointed, and took a step back.

My stag night wouldn't set any records. It was all work and no play. I was cool with it; our safety mattered more, and I was glad Emilia was distracted by her bachelorette party. She needed the fun after days of being hounded by two of my guys. The security was grating on everyone, and we hadn't made much progress in figuring out what to do, so things weren't likely to change anytime soon.

At the very least, I wanted Patrick on my side, but maybe that was too much to ask. Pop had finally woken up, for which I was thankful. With each day that passed, he grew increasingly pissed that John's shit had fallen into our lap.

"I've been trying," Patrick said quietly. He ran a hand over his head, looking tired and older. "With Sarah, I mean. After seeing you and Emilia this week... I want that with Sarah. I want *her*. I've gotten glimpses—she's hurting, I think. But she fucking refuses to let me in."

"Because you act like a dryshite most of the time." There was no heat to my voice. He just needed to realize that they wouldn't find common ground by him throwing money at everything. "Pay attention to her."

"You're saying you're no dick?" He cocked a brow.

"Not at all." I shook my head. "But I make an effort too. That's how I know to cheer up Emilia with Netflix and pizza instead of diamonds."

I'd fucked up plenty, and I had enough guilt hanging over my head because I'd yet to tell Emilia my estranged Italian uncle was married to her mother.

Heads would be rolling the day she found out, and it was a

miracle she didn't already know. Because I was willing to bet the Avellinos did.

"Do you love her?" Patrick's stunned expression was comical.

"You just figured that out now?" At this point, I was sure even Emilia knew. I couldn't hide that for shit. My work took a direct hit if I didn't get a regular dose of her, more so if we'd argued.

I'd already confessed my love for her, though I didn't think she knew that. I'd written it in Irish in one of the letters I'd sent her when I'd suffered through one of the worst moments of my life. And I'd spent five years in prison. I knew misery. Yet, that handful of days—fuck, I despised thinking back on them. I'd felt fucking broken.

"Dude, that wasn't the plan," Patrick replied.

"Neither was you getting in my way of ensuring her safety," I told him. "That's what you're doing right now. I need you on your A game."

He blew out a breath and scrubbed at his face. "You're right. I hear you. That's what's so frustrating. I keep trying with Sarah, and whenever I fail, I take it out on my job."

That was a cheap excuse. "How long have you been trying, as you call it?"

"Almost two weeks now, man."

I scratched my nose, then let out a chuckle. Two weeks. Motherfucker. "You little bitch. I've been with Emilia a couple months, and I still risk losing her. Two months is *nothing*. It's just long enough to fall in love and possibly get smashed like a bug." I shook my head and left his punk-ass behind.

I'd pick him up later, figuratively speaking. We all went through rough patches, I guess. He was a good man, and I loved him. I *missed* him. I had faith in him. But right now, giving him the kick in the balls he needed wasn't my priority.

I rejoined the men in Pop's study, a place that was now off-limits to sneaky women who knew too much about planting another type of bug.

Thomas, Aunt Viv's husband, was here. So were Pop, Ian, Kellan, and— "Where's Eric?" I asked.

Pop closed the liquor cabinet and returned to the two couches where the others were gathered for my non-stag night. "Checking out the gadgets, of course."

Yeah, I shouldn't have asked. "Speaking of. Did you consider what I asked yesterday?"

I wanted to show Emilia why we called this a compound.

"I did, and you have my permission—once you two are married." He sat down and poured them all more whiskey. "Damn girl nearly made me mushy earlier."

"What did she do?" I frowned and took my seat in the chair at the head of the coffee table.

Pop smiled a little to himself, setting down the bottle. "She asked me to walk her down the aisle at the wedding."

There was a flurry of concern that proved how fucking whipped I'd become for Emilia. Did she miss her dad? I sincerely hoped not, 'cause it would be difficult to mend that relationship now. Had Pop agreed to Emilia's request? Fuck, he better have. I couldn't imagine how vulnerable she must've felt to ask him.

"You said yes, right?" My forehead creased.

"Of-fucking-course I did. What's wrong with you?" He scowled at me. I merely relaxed. Shit was good again. "She's the daughter I never knew I wanted."

I laughed. "She has that effect."

"Viv says Emilia's warming up to her now," Thomas said. He didn't speak often and blended in easily. He was one of the few who'd managed to hide what he did for a living from his wife. Aunt Viv had no clue he was a Son.

"I wore her down the fastest," Kellan said and toasted to himself. "She didn't stand a chance."

I snorted.

"What're they doing down there?" Ian wondered. "What do women do at hen parties?"

I'd gotten four texts from Emilia so far, and it was only three in the afternoon. They were at our house, a minute's stroll down the hill. I had an inkling. "Given the number of typos in Emilia's texts to me, I'm guessing they're drinking."

I couldn't picture their party getting outta hand. Kellan had invited his annoying little sister to stay here where he could keep an eye on her, and she was the only one around Emilia and Sarah's age. The rest were...well, Ma, Aunt Viv, and her eldest daughter, Brenda.

Shortly after, Patrick reentered the study, and he pushed up the sleeves of his shirt. "What're you sitting around here for? We gonna head downstairs and work or what?"

I stared at him, and at his smirk, the relief hit me.

He's in.

"Aye, let's go." I rose from my chair and clapped him on the back.

The fucker was slow to commit, but once he did...

There were a few ways to access the best-kept secret on my parents' property. One of the entrances was in the nook next to Pop's study. The door looked like it led to a closet, except for the fact that it was locked. Once inside, there was a set of stairs that took us into an underground maze of corridors.

This was the compound.

There were living quarters with four bedrooms, a fully stocked kitchen, two living rooms, and a handful of bathrooms scattered about. There was a garage, with the exit located at the northernmost point of the property, in the small forest. We passed the room where Pop and I stored our guns. Supply closet, two empty cells, storage, Pop's vault, and then we reached the control room.

One half of it was all tech. Eric wheeled from side to side of the large desk, overseeing the dozen computer screens on the wall. The other half was where we could sit down around a big table and bitch at each other because we didn't always get along. Lastly, wholesale quantities of chips and shit in the corner 'cause snacks were good for the soul.

Eric was on my crew, a sharp guy with ginger-blond hair who'd lost his spark when his brother and sister-in-law were murdered. If I had a right-hand man, he'd be it, though Kellan was a close second.

"How're we doing?" I asked.

Eric threw me a glance over his shoulder, then nodded at a couple of the screens. "All set up, mate. Hit me with wedding security so I can move on to bigger things. No offense."

I turned to Pop. "How many have RSVP'd?"

"All two-hundred and ninety of them."

I winced. This wedding was gonna cost them a pretty penny.

"Pull up the ballroom on Four," I told Eric. If it weren't for Ma's demand that we go all out on this wedding, I would've been fine with having the reception out here. But no, she wanted glitz and glamour at one of the finest hotels downtown Philly had to offer. "Six exits..."

"Two at each door," Pop advised. "Four at the front. Possible targets?"

"Uncle John, of course," I replied. "So no guards on him."

The guys chuckled.

"Conn and Colm will be on Emilia," I said. They were also on my crew. A crazy pair of brothers from Dublin. They already liked her, and she enjoyed dicking around with them when the mood struck. "We're gonna want eyes on the kids too."

"I'm with the twins," Kellan said. "Eric, you bringing Autumn?" That would be Eric's young niece.

"No. She's with a friend." Eric filled another few screens with various areas of the hotel that would need monitoring. Next, he pulled up the church on Two and Three. "I don't see any problems here. With a few guys covering the doors, you should be set."

My phone buzzed in my pocket, so I excused myself and

stepped out into the hallway. The number didn't have a caller ID, though that wasn't too rare.

"Yeah, who's this?" I answered.

"Finnegan, my boy, that you?"

Shite. I almost dropped my phone at the sound of that voice. "Uh, yes, sir. Were you trying to reach Pop?" Because Uncle John didn't call me. Maybe once a year for family-related matters. Never work. I didn't think he suspected I knew he was the biggest traitor this family had ever seen, but he was guarded around me.

He laughed quietly. "No, you're the man I wanted to speak to. Is this a secure line?"

At a loss for what else to do in this position, I reached for whatever I could and threw it at Pop's back. My lighter. He flinched and turned around with a frown, and I mouthed that it was Uncle John.

His brows went up.

"As secure as it can be on my end, sir," I answered. "What can I do for you?"

"Well, first, I was wondering if you've got any flats in that building of yours," he said. "In these times, I'd rather not stay at a hotel."

"Of course." I should have a couple condos still available. "Consider it done."

"Good, that's good. Anne and I are flying in a few days early with the kids, and it'll be nice for them to be someplace safe."

"I understand." I *didn't* understand. This was too out of the blue, and he wasn't the type who chitchatted. If he was, he sure as shit didn't do it with me.

He cleared his throat. "The...the other reason I called is because I reckon it's time we have a sit-down."

I scrubbed a hand over my mouth and stared at the floor, my mind sprinting to work out what this meant. In the last few days, he'd spoken to Pop several times, and it never ended well. They hadn't argued, though it was clear Uncle John was holding something back, and it kept us from doing our jobs. We were flying blind, placing security where we *guessed* it would be needed.

Basically, there was a lot of guessing going on, whether it was security or...well, why the *fuck* the Italians were targeting us.

They couldn't possibly have known it would be Emilia in my car that night, so I didn't believe she was part of it—at least, not yet. Though, it didn't stop me from worrying.

"Would who be there?" I asked.

He let out a gruff laugh and took a sip of something. "Most people simply agree, Finn."

"I'm not most guys, Uncle John."

Pop cleared his throat to get my attention, and I turned away from him. I didn't need a reminder to be respectful. I *was* respectful. I was also done beating around the bush. We demanded answers.

"Actually, it would be the two of us," John responded. "You can pick the place."

I scratched my forehead, squinting. "You realize I find this strange, eh? All due respect, sir, with everything going on, I can only agree to meet with you if you can give me your word that it will clear up some of this confusion. I'm getting married in three weeks, and the thought of something happening to my fiancée is keeping me up most nights."

"Sweet Jesus, he's not my son," Pop muttered behind me.

"He knows what he's doing, Shan," Ian murmured.

I waited for John.

"Aye, I think I can clear some things up, lad. I come for your trust, and I realize it will cost me."

My head snapped up. Now we were talking. He wasn't going to get my trust, and it was interesting he knew he didn't have it. That said, I had no problems meeting with him and hearing him out.

"Dinner's on me then, sir," I said. "Looking forward to seeing you." We wrapped up the call, and I spun around to face the guys, arms wide. "What the fuck just happened?"

"I don't know, you tell us." Patrick smirked. "You having dinner with Uncle John? Seriously?"

"Seriously." I folded my arms over my chest and faced Pop. "He sounded tired. I think. And he wouldn't call me if he had other options."

Pop didn't respond, going into calculating mode.

"You know, this makes sense." It was Eric who spoke up. "Your theory, Finn. I mean, there's a shitload of bad blood between Gio and John, but it's not only restricted to them. Why ice just one when you can take 'em all out? If the Italians are coming for the whole syndicate—"

"And if they know there's a rift between the O'Sheas and Murrays," I filled in.

"They'll exploit us from every angle," he finished.

"That's a grim theory," Pop said, "but one we have to prepare for."

"It's not exactly farfetched." Patrick threw in his two cents too. "No one but old Ennis wanted Gio initiated into the Sons."

That was true, which made it even more likely that John sought out the O'Sheas to build some bridges. Because the rift was undeniable—for all of us. The syndicate had been at a standstill for years because so many of us had been—or still were—in prison. And now, as more men were being released, our members were going to demand action.

"Why a sit-down with me?" I asked. "John's got higher-ranking crew bosses in Philly who're more logical options."

Pop was one of them, and he gave only a wry smirk in response before he lit a cigarette.

"You've made enough ruckus," Thomas said quietly. "These past two years, you've gone from up-and-coming to being a threat. That gives John two options. Get you on his side to take down Avellino, or risk facing both of you in a war he wouldn't win."

I considered what he'd said, and I wasn't wholly on board with it. I was causing a ruckus, definitely, and it was starting to pay off—

in Philly. I had a good crew, I could give them all the work they wanted, my legit business was doing well, and I'd expanded. In a short period of time, I'd greased a lot of palms. However, for this to reach Chicago, I had to stand out. I wasn't accomplishing anything my father and the three top crews weren't already doing.

"You can count me out, son," Pop added. "I never had the desire to take top rank, and John knows it. Jim pisses his pants just being in the same room as you, 'cause he was there to witness my father's plans for you. That leaves Old Phil. He just lost the last strip mall north of Snyder to the Vietnamese, and I suspect you have more people on your payroll in Whitman than he does."

"God bless that old fuck. Last time we saw each other, he talked nonstop about his arthritis," I chuckled.

"Well, there you go, little brother." Patrick clapped my shoulder and gave it a squeeze. "Uncle John probably knows you'll rake in votes when that day comes."

I wasn't ready to celebrate or get my hopes up, but I took it as a partial victory—another step closer toward my goal.

A few hours later, I felt better in terms of security. We had every moment of the week of the wedding mapped out, and everything had been upgraded, from the vehicles we'd be driving in the city to the safety measures we'd take before going someplace.

Pop circled back to Uncle John to have him approve of the precautions we were taking. Despite his promises of clearing the confusion, we were still flying blind until my sit-down with him, and he reluctantly admitted everything we'd planned was necessary. Furthermore, he offered to cover our expenses, and that spoke volumes.

It was possible I ordered a few more cars for my firm because he was footing the bill.

"He's ready to kiss ass," Patrick said.

It sure seemed like it, but he would collect more points with us if he gave it to us straight rather than sugarcoating the situation in hopes of making it easier to get us to join him in taking down the Avellinos.

We weren't the wife he had to protect from the truth.

Half sitting on the edge of the desk next to where Eric was working, I eyed his scribbled notes about the week we were returning to the city. The wedding was on a Saturday, and guests would start to arrive already on Wednesday, the Murrays included. It was going to be a stressful week with dinners, sit-downs, and making sure the women weren't bothered by the security. We had to be three paces ahead of them; we had to know their every move and go there before they did.

Emilia had her final fitting with the girls on that Wednesday at one. Before then, she was having her last session with Father O'Malley. She would be out most of the day, whereas my only plan included picking up our rings.

It would be a good day to meet with John. And by then... A thought struck me, and I asked Eric to pull up the guest list on screen five. I scanned it quickly. Out of the almost three hundred guests, around sixty of them identified as Murrays and lived in Chicago.

"You're planning something." Pop was watching me.

"Everyone from John's inner circle arrives on Tuesday or Wednesday," I said, picking up the notepad. I began making notes for what I needed. "Chicago will be empty."

"Of higher-ups, not eyes and ears," Ian pointed out.

"We still have one man on our side there," I replied with a smirk.

Pat knew where my mind was at. "Liam."

I inclined my head. Our cousin loved his old man, but his loyalty had always laid with Ronan and Ennis. Like me, he was a man of protocol and tradition, and he was being released from prison in August with a big mouth and strong opinions. He was the

307

one Murray I could trust fully, partly because he felt betrayed by John for how everything went down all those years ago. I bet John knew it too. He'd dug himself a nice little hole, and he needed our help to get out of it.

I spoke up. "If we wanna be one step ahead of John—without knowing what's going on—we're gonna have to go big. We can't make any demands if we don't have a hold on him."

"But he needs our help," Pop argued. "We won't get more leverage than that. It'll secure our position."

Bullshit. This was an opportunity I wasn't going to waste. "Why stop there?" I widened my arms. "The way I see it, this is a chance to give the O'Sheas something. We can't forget we have men on our streets who count on us to make things right."

My brother was with me. "Think about it, Pop. Our low-men ain't gonna like working security at the wedding while the Murrays sit up there with us and enjoy the festivities. We gotta give them something, like Finn said."

Pop sighed tiredly and sat down at the table. "Out with it, then. What do you have in mind?"

"On Wednesday, I sit down with Uncle John," I said. "Emilia and I will take him and Aunt Anne out for a nice dinner first—we follow tradition and welcome them to our city—"

"Old-school," Thomas noted.

"In the meantime, I want a crew in Chicago," I went on. "With Liam's go-ahead, we'll have full access to Murray territory and—"

"What're you expecting to find, a nonexistent paper trail to take down your uncle?" Pop asked in disbelief.

"Can people quit interrupting me?" I barked out. "Christ. No. It's to send a fucking message. We don't sit around and wait for answers. We get the upper hand. We'll let him know we're not just ready to invade his home—we're already there." I had two years of subtle surveillance to put to use. Within the syndicate, many of the Murray properties were common knowledge. In addition to that, I knew about a handful of other operations and locations Uncle John would've rather kept private.

Ian joined my father at the table, thoughtful. He didn't look opposed to the idea. "You realize it's no longer a sit-down, lad. John will see it as an ambush."

"Funny, that's how I see what the Avellinos did to my fiancée too," I replied flatly. "I'm not putting all of that on John, but let's not pretend he's innocent here. If he knew what was good for him, he would've flown out here and delivered everything he knew on a goddamn platter."

Pop sat forward, elbows on his knees, and rested his chin on his clasped hands. Worry creased his forehead, and he couldn't let that hold us back.

"We're just sending a message," I repeated.

"Except you're not, son. You're challenging his rank. It comes with consequences."

"Then so be it," I answered. Under the circumstances, I wasn't very concerned. Uncle John was fucked one way or another. "You said it yourself, he needs our help, and we're all he's got. Who else is gonna help him with the Italians? I'm not gonna tell him to surrender all his control. I'm only gonna gain some of it."

"I agree with Finn." Kellan spoke up for the first time in a while. "We're not gonna rape his ass or nothing. Just finger him a bit."

I let out a laugh and slapped my thigh. That was a good one.

"Your sense of humor, boy—I swear." Pop shook his head at Kellan. And probably me too.

I appreciated my father's worry, but it was time to let go. We'd been doing this since we were kids, literally. It was too late to go back.

"We can do this, Pop," I said.

He waved a hand and sat back to light a smoke. "I don't doubt that. It's what happens once you succeed I'm worried about." He blew out some smoke. "You're making it clear to the entire syndicate that you're the new head of the O'Sheas."

I stared at him, waiting for anyone to speak up—to object. I was ready for this. I was prepared.

No one said a word.

chapter

25

Emilia Porter

"Time to get up, baby."

"I disagree." My voice was muffled by the pillow. "I already tried that once."

I'd woken up when Finnegan got ready for his run. With optimism in my heart, I'd stumbled out of bed and taken a shower, after which I'd collapsed on the bathroom floor. I suspected I'd still been drunk at that point. After getting up, I'd face planted in bed with my towel wrapped around me, fallen asleep once more, and that was where we were right now.

I was never drinking with the Irish again.

Finnegan shuffled around in the bedroom, probably getting dressed. Lifting my head off the pillow, I squinted at the clock on his side of the bed, only to promptly land on my pillow again. It was only ten in the morning. Fuck that noise.

"I take it your bachelorette party was a success?" There was too much amusement in Finnegan's tone.

I yelped and whined when he shifted up my towel and bit my ass.

"This ass, princess..." He grabbed two handfuls and groped me.

"Leave me alone," I complained.

He chuckled and sat down on the edge of the bed. "What did they do to you last night?"

"All of it," I whispered. If I lay perfectly still, my headache wasn't too bad.

"And how much did you drink?"

"All of it," I whispered again.

I wasn't sure who to blame. Grace, Nurse Wa—*Vivian*, and Brenda had bowed out relatively early. Before midnight, I knew that much. It'd been a day of silly games, good food, all the alcohol, gifts, and motherly advice about how to survive a marriage. Then it'd been Sarah, Luna—Kellan's little sister—and me until...four? Maybe. And we'd just kept drinking and talking and drinking. So much drinking.

I blamed them all.

"My poor baby." Finnegan stroked my butt some more. "I saw we got some cool gifts."

That was something I'd learned yesterday. The smallest gifts came in big boxes, and the biggest gifts came in envelopes. Vivian and her family had given us a fancy soft-serve ice cream maker... and a spa slash golf weekend.

Since our engagement parties had been canceled, people had sent us a bunch of things, and Grace and Vivian had brought it all over for me to open.

"Can you be lazy with me today?" I asked in a pitiful voice.

"There's nothing else to do around here," he chuckled. "I thought we could join the others at the pool behind the main house."

I was forced to lift my head again, so I could give him a weak glare. Huh, I'd half expected to see him in a suit, but he was wearing trunks and a tee. Delicious.

"That would require me leaving this bed," I mumbled.

He smiled down at me and brushed away some hair from my

face. "It does. The sooner, the better. You're too much of a temptation right now."

I wiggled my butt to sway him, and he groaned.

"Quit it, you little witch." He stood up, adjusted his cock, and held out a hand. "Let's go. We have one week to kill before we go back to the city, and I'm already struggling to remain a gentleman. Fuck—I've been struggling for months. Come on."

I giggled sleepily and let him drag me out of bed. Oops, the towel slipped off of me.

Finnegan cursed, and the heat that flashed in his eyes was so sexy.

"You'll be the death of me," he told me, stalking into our closet. "One more week, Finn, you can do it." He was too funny, muttering to himself.

We actually put the ice cream maker to great use. The weather was much better today, so it was all about pool fun and ice cream. We'd put the machine on a table on Shan and Grace's patio, and I made us two cones while Finnegan came up out of the water.

Now...Finnegan was always filthy hot and ridiculously cut. With him in black trunks and with rivulets of water coursing down his body, there was no word in the English language to describe how edible he looked. He pushed back his hair and bent down to grab a towel from the lounger we were sharing, and I almost forgot the ice cream.

"Shit." I turned off the machine. I supposed he wouldn't complain about his ice cream being massive.

Grace and Ian stepped out onto the patio with beers and pitchers of margaritas and Bloody Marys for those who were ready for that. Basically, everyone but me.

"Brunch will be served soon," Ian announced.

"Isn't this the life?" Grace was in a great mood. "If only we could stay here forever."

I snickered, sneaking a glance at Finnegan's horrified expression before he composed his face. I was learning his tells, and I knew he was growing restless. He couldn't sit still for long. Patrick and Kellan were much the same.

I walked over to our lounger and handed Finnegan his ice cream cone.

His forehead creased. "But, I want jimmies."

Oh, for fuck's sake.

"If you call it what it is," I said and licked my own cone.

"It's called jimmies," he stated. "I can do this all day."

Kellan and Patrick piped up from the pool, agreeing with Finnegan. Freaking jimmies.

"See?" Finnegan raised his brows.

"Then you get nothin'." I sat down on the foot of the lounger and—

"Fine. Sprinkles." He made a face. "Can you put sprinkles on mine?"

"Of course, Mr. I Can Do This All Day." I returned to the ice cream maker and dipped his cone in the bowl of sprinkles.

"Why do I feel like this is only the beginning?" Shan mused. I didn't know he'd been watching us from his spot. He, Grace, and Ian sat at a table under a big umbrella. "They're gonna rile each other up until something or someone breaks."

"Just my fiancé's balls," I said.

"She called me fiancé." Finnegan was all smiles. "That's how she gets away with anything."

I grinned and walked back with his ice cream.

More people emerged for a day by the pool. Conn and Colm—they were my boys—Eric, a friend of Finnegan's, Luna and Sarah—and thank fuck, they looked as hungover as I felt.

Now that the guesthouses were ready, Grace had plans to

always have people over. If there was one thing she loved, it was to play hostess to the people she called family.

Luna rubbed sleep from her eyes, then quirked a brow at me, mischief seeping through her exhaustion. "Morning."

"Good morning. No, I haven't." I laughed, answering her unspoken question.

Luna was...exciting. I felt less guilty for enjoying my new life when she was around. With Sarah, there was always that worry. If anyone took advantage of the wealth, it was her, but I wasn't certain she actually enjoyed herself. Luna, on the other hand... In the span of twenty-four hours, she'd made me feel as welcome as Finnegan's family. Like them, she'd grown up in this life.

"Well, why not?" She huffed and pulled back her raven-black hair into a short ponytail. Then she adjusted her green bikini and side-eyed Finnegan. "It'll drive him mad."

We instantly had his attention. His eyes narrowed to slits, and the suspicion rolled off him. "Kellan, control your sister. Emilia's trouble as it is."

"Bitch, please. I'm doing you a favor," Luna said.

According to Grace and Vivian, Finnegan and Luna had grown up bickering like siblings, so I was hoping to enjoy a show. They were certainly different. One was aiming toward a PhD in women's studies. The other one was Finnegan.

I didn't get my show this time, though. Finnegan dismissed Luna, and she rolled her eyes and went into the pool.

"What's she up to?" Finnegan patted the spot between his legs, and I scooted farther up the lounger. "Last time she tried to do me a favor, I ended up in a vegan restaurant."

I laughed and leaned back against his chest. "How did you survive?"

"I barely did." He bit into his ice cream. Actually *bit*.

"There are two types of people in this world," I said. "Those who chew their ice cream and normal people."

"I think we all know I'm not normal." He smirked, then nodded at me. "Don't change the subject."

I pursed my lips, thinking about it. Truth was, Finnegan would love the gift Luna had given us—or me. She said every girl needed a few, and Finnegan's gift would be to watch me enjoy them. Them, as in sex toys.

She'd given them to me right around the time Grace announced it was time for her to leave.

"Her gift," I said. "She gave me three sex toys."

Finnegan's brows went high, and the *fucker* dropped his ice cream.

I shrieked at the cold and jumped up from the lounger. "Finnegan!" Gross. It was all over my thigh.

"Shite. Sorry." He blinked and shook his head, then jumped into action. He grimaced and dumped the ice cream into his coffee mug on the side table. "Uh, here." He wiped my thigh with his towel, quickly pulling me down between his legs again. "Let's talk about this in great detail. What kinds of toys?"

I puffed out a breath and laughed. "How about I show you later instead?"

He raked his teeth across his bottom lip. "That's probably not a good idea. I want you too much."

I was sensing that, and I wasn't a fan. The last week, he'd held back a lot. Not a day passed without him ending up between my legs—with his mouth. He drove me freaking crazy with pleasure, and I was done pretending I didn't want him inside me. I wanted us to have sex; I was beyond ready. But he wouldn't go there. He didn't even let me give him blow jobs anymore, stating it was too tempting. He lost control or something.

I cuddled up against his chest and used a fresh towel as a blanket. "You and your traditions."

His smile was hesitant. "It's important to me."

I kissed his neck, not wanting him to think I didn't respect his wishes. "It's okay. I understand. It's just..."

316

"Frustrating as fuck?" He hugged me to him, and I nodded and laughed under my breath. "I'm aware. I can't wait for—fuck." He pressed a kiss to my hair and inhaled deeply. "You're it for me, Emilia."

With those hushed words, everything around me disappeared. I peered up at him and searched his eyes, and I saw it all—right there. Something I got glimpses of every day now. Something I loved to see. Foolishly, maybe. He was so serious, so open, and it filled me with stupid hope. Once more, I was at odds with myself. My heart wanted one thing, and my brain...was screaming at me.

Did he know I'd looked up the Irish words he'd written? Did he think about it?

I swallowed hard. I could see the precipice I stood on.

Falling was effortless. It was the landing that scared me. What if he didn't catch me?

"Don't you get scared?" I whispered.

"Try terrified," he whispered back. "Every morning, I wonder if that's the day I'll lose you."

Sweet Jesus, I was toast, and he was too good.

Yeah...falling was effortless, and I knew because I'd been falling for a while now. I felt it in my stomach and every time I looked at Finnegan.

He gave me another squeeze and tucked my head under his chin, and it was a good thing. He was the very definition of irresistible, and a few seconds of eye contact were all it took for me to slip further away from who I used to be.

In only a few months, he'd made me go from being thoroughly repulsed to a guilty mess because I was more or less head over heels in love with him.

For the first time in my life, I looked forward to talking to a priest.

After a day of errands in the city, Shan stepped out of the car with Father O'Malley in tow, who'd been invited out here for dinner. One of the guesthouses had been prepared for his brief stay, and Finnegan was the first to go down to the gates and greet him.

I stayed back, but only because I wasn't showing up in a bikini. Finnegan had been working...somewhere, and he'd emerged in suit pants and a nice button-down.

I made quick work of myself and changed into more appropriate clothes. Boredom had struck me too lately, and Finnegan had all but coerced me to cure it by shopping online. With only a couple days left until we were returning to Philadelphia, I had two closets full of clothes, not counting the stuff we'd had delivered to the condo back home.

Home. Huh. I supposed Philly had become my home, despite that we'd spent more time out here at the compound.

I slipped into a pair of white dress pants and hoped to all that was holy I didn't spill later. A sleeveless silk blouse in emerald green followed, and I smoothed down the ruffled front before running my fingers through my hair. It was sun-kissed, a few shades lighter after we'd spent so much time by the pool.

Lastly, I applied some mascara and lip balm, then put on a pair of flats that matched the shiny fabric of my top. This part was weirdly fun for me, and I enjoyed looking like I belonged next to Finnegan. Image mattered to him, especially around people he respected. Then it was important to me too.

I left our house and clasped a bracelet onto my wrist, and by that time, Finnegan and Father O'Malley were slowly walking toward the main house.

They both smiled when they spotted me, and the warm glow of approval in Finnegan's eyes meant more than it probably should.

"Hi, Father O'Malley."

"My dear." He gave me a hug, and I kissed his cheek. "You've been missed at the church."

Yikes. While I couldn't say I missed the silly Pre-Cana classes and his gentle prodding about my "lack of faith," he was a charming, funny man. I could see why Finnegan and others felt better after talking to him. I did too, because he knew exactly what to say when I fretted about morals and crap like that.

"I'm glad you could come," I settled for saying, and I slipped my hand into Finnegan's. "Can I get you something to drink?"

He smiled and shook his head, only to address Finnegan next. "I hope you know how blessed you are, lad."

"I know." Finnegan brought our hands to his mouth and kissed my knuckles. "She might very well be the best part of me."

My cheeks heated, and I squeezed his hand.

Dinner was going to be a semiformal affair, and the main purpose was for Father O'Malley to chat with Sarah and me before the wedding hysteria took over. Maybe she was still by the pool...? I couldn't see her. I knew most of the others had ventured out for dinner in Gettysburg, leaving us alone with two O'Shea brothers and their parents.

As a joke, Kellan had suggested they go to the diner where I used to work. I'd shaken it off quickly because I hated to think about it. Part of me knew there were matters I'd have to deal with at some point, but I had time. For now, my old life no longer existed. Dad was a distant memory I was doing a good job of suppressing. The diner and the smell of grease, the constant cloud of melancholy that hung over the town, the empty bottles, school, Franny's condescending stare—all of it belonged in the past.

Patrick opened the door as we neared the house, and he was dressed much like Finnegan. I couldn't imagine it being very comfortable for six or seven men to be crammed into Shan's study to work on whatever they did, but they'd been there most of yesterday and today.

"Long time, no see, padre." Patrick smirked and offered a hand to Father O'Malley.

"I'll say, you rascal." Father O'Malley chuckled and shook his hand. "Where's your Sarah?"

That answer came from behind me when I heard her holler my

name. I looked back toward our houses, and she gestured for me to come to her.

"I'll be right back." I excused myself and strolled down the hill again. The sun was starting to set, painting the treetops in a burning amber color.

A minute later, I reached Patrick and Sarah's house, and alarm hit me at the sight of her face. "Hon, what's wrong?"

She was damn near hyperventilating and had tears running down her cheeks, so I quickly ushered her inside and closed the door.

"I'm f-freaking out," she stuttered, grasping at my arms. "Fuck."

"Hey. Christ—breathe, sweetie. Come here." What the hell had happened? I helped her over to their couch and sat down with her. "Tell me what's wrong." The worry festered inside me. Something must've happened. She'd been laughing with Luna and me less than an hour ago.

She tried to gulp in a breath and wiped at her cheeks, smearing her freshly applied makeup.

"Breathe with me." I gripped her shoulders and made her face me, and I breathed in deeply. "Sarah, focus on my voice. Want me to get Patrick or Shan?"

That caused a reaction. She shook her head furiously and did her best to follow my lead. She closed her eyes and inhaled. I rubbed her back soothingly and felt my eyes sting with tears. She'd freaked out once like this before, years and years ago.

"You're doing great, hon," I whispered thickly. "That's it. Just breathe."

She nodded jerkily and took another breath. I pushed back her hair and brushed away her tears.

"Whatever's wrong, we'll fix it, Sarah. I swear. I'm here, okay?"

The girl needed to talk already. These past few weeks, I'd alternated between annoyed and concerned. She'd just been so...cold and shut-off, not to mention unwilling to talk about it. And her strategy wasn't freaking working. She couldn't put her life on hold completely for three years and think she could simply walk away with a bunch of money.

"I don't think I can do this," she whimpered.

"Do what?" I kept my voice soft, even as fear was shot into me.

"He's—he's changing things." She covered her face with her hands and choked on a cry. "That fucking Finnegan—it's his fault. He got through to Patrick, and now he's different. Look. Just look." She kept weeping, and she pulled out her phone from the pocket of her jeans. "He s-sent me this while I was getting ready."

The screen flashed to life, and I read the message from Patrick.

If I could go back and change things, I would. I'd ask you out for coffee and quit pretending to be someone I'm not. Half the time, I don't know what I'm doing. You make me wanna be better.

"Damn," I mouthed. Patrick was stepping up.

"Look. There's more." She scrolled up, up, up, frantic. "It's been like this for weeks now."

I caught you smiling at something Em said today. All I want right now is to be able to make you smile at me like that.

"I can't do it anymore." Sarah sniffled.

I want us to try, Sarah. I keep thinking I might regret it for the rest of my life if I don't get to know the real you.

I brushed away a tear as it fell down my cheek, and I hugged Sarah to me. "Remember when you said it's okay for us to enjoy this?"

She shook her head and put her phone on the table. "It's not the same, Em. You can't say you're merely enjoying being with Finnegan."

No, and I couldn't lie about it anymore either. "I think I'm in love with him," I confessed.

"See?" she cried. "I can't go down that road with Patrick. They'll just suck us in!"

"I *know*. I know." Ugh, I wished I were having this conversation after I'd talked to Father O'Malley. He'd helped me justify my feelings for Finnegan once before. It left me no choice; I had to parrot him. Or paraphrase. "Look, honey. I know what we used to think. Everything was black-and-white, and now it's one big mess of gray. But Father O'Malley told me we're not powerless. What if we can make a difference? What if we become the guys' consciences? Maybe that's naïve, but—"

"You think?" She wiped at her cheeks again.

I suppressed a sigh and squeezed her hand in both of mine. "I have to believe, Sarah. One day, when Finnegan chooses between hurting someone and not, I have to believe I can make a difference. No matter what, I can accomplish more by his side than...I don't know, by going back to the *nothing* we had before."

She blew out a shaky breath and sniffled. "You think I should give Patrick a chance."

"I think you should give yourself the chance to be happy, for however long it lasts."

As I said this to Sarah, I took the advice more to heart myself. I couldn't be stuck in between gray areas any longer. It was time to jump, follow the contract I'd signed, and make the best of the situation. I wasn't one of those who could keep one part of me locked up and secret. It was all or nothing, I guessed. Otherwise, I'd never stop going back and forth.

It would make me miserable in the end.

She looked at me warily, eyes bloodshot and cheeks flushed. "Are you gonna stay with Finnegan after those three years?"

I had no clue. "That's up to him." It twisted my stomach to admit it. "My limits haven't changed. If he hurts me beyond what I'm capable of forgiving, I'll walk." Of that, I had absolutely no doubt. "I'm young and dumb," I said half jokingly, "but I'm not going to be a doormat."

She accepted my answer and rested her head on my shoulder. "I fucking hate this."

"I hate that you shut me out," I countered carefully. "I might be partly to blame—"

She shook her head, but I wasn't done speaking.

"Either way, we gotta be more honest," I told her. "Seriously. I don't trust the man I've lost my heart to, so I need you with me. We have to be able to count on each other."

"I'm with you," she whispered and squeezed my hand. "I'll try. Maybe it'll make Grace like me too."

I made a noise. "What're you talking about? Grace loves you."

She chuckled and rolled her eyes, straightening up. "No way. She loves *you*. She's... I don't know. She's more careful around me."

Understandable, when seeing it from Grace's side of things.

"Probably because she doesn't know you yet," I comforted. "When you give Patrick a chance, include Grace and Shan. They'll see it."

"Maybe."

Whereas Sarah remained skeptical, I felt a lot better. More hopeful. Less in need of Father O'Malley's moral compass. Sarah was going to show everyone what a sweetheart she was underneath that tough-girl exterior, and I was going to...um, just keep hoping for the best, I supposed. In short, I could have the best life imaginable ahead of me, or the worst that would shatter me into tiny pieces.

What joy.

"Come on." I dragged Sarah to her feet. "We're gonna knock this dinner out of the park. No one's to say we can't be both ball-busters and perfect little wives. Let's show 'em, Sarah."

chapter

26

Finnegan O'Shea

For once in my life, I had no desire to talk at dinner. Instead, I sat back and watched Emilia interact with my family. Her changes had been subtle from the beginning, but something had happened recently. She was shouldering a role, and she was doing it fucking perfectly.

Something had clearly happened today too. No amount of makeup could remove the last traces of whatever had upset Sarah, and I could tell my brother was going to do his damnedest to figure it out later. Right now, though, she seemed to be doing okay. Her polite smiles were uncharacteristically tentative, yet she made more of an effort to join in on the conversations.

Ma had gone all out for dinner, and her obsession with windows hadn't waned. Not only was the dining room decked out with candles and fresh flowers, but the pool area right outside had been tidied up for the sake of our view. There were fresh flowers out there too, not to mention linen cloths on the small tables between the loungers.

Ian was the master chef as usual, and after appetizers came grilled lamb chops and at least six different side dishes. It was one of the contenders for the wedding menu. There was more wine than we normally drank in our family, and everything was served on my parents' wedding china.

The dinner wasn't *that* big of a deal. Father O'Malley just wanted to spend some time with us and to see how Emilia—and Sarah, though her wedding was a month away—fit in.

Ma treated it almost like a graduation. She wanted to know everything about Emilia's Pre-Cana classes from Father O'Malley, even though he'd bent the rules for us a bit. As far as I knew, it'd been less premarital counseling and advice and more lending an ear to Emilia and her adjustments.

I leaned in and spoke for only Emilia to hear. "Should I tell the Father that you're going against our belief with your silly birth control?"

We could joke about it now, I was pretty sure.

Although, I did hate seeing that dumb fucking pillbox in the bathroom every morning. First time I saw it, I'd thought it was a makeup thing. Then she'd opened it, and I'd seen a colorful blister pack of pills that were going to kill my swimmers.

Emilia faced me with a sugary smile. "Should I tell the Father that you're going against your own beliefs and you lie, steal, and—"

"Let's be nice," I whispered.

"Thought so," she whispered back.

I grinned and took a sip of my wine. Father O'Malley was no fool, and Emilia knew it. What my family and I were involved in was common knowledge, but sometimes we chose to close our eyes. In our priest's case, it was because it served a greater good. The O'Sheas brought in money for the community he burned passionately for, and it won out. That said, he turned a nasty shade of angry purple whenever a crime was mentioned. No one wanted to be reminded of what we turned our backs on.

"Are you kids happy to return to the city?" Father O'Malley asked as Ma refilled his wineglass. "Thank you, dear."

"Absolutely, sir," I replied. At this point, I was sick of the compound. There were only so many laps I could run around the grounds and so many hours I could spend by the pool before I yanked my hair out. In a mildly reckless moment to kill my boredom, I'd even planned a surprise for Emilia.

She'd asked me repeatedly to play for her, and we never did get to have a proper engagement party... I was rectifying that, and Mass on Sunday was gonna be brutal. I planned on being hungover as fuck.

"I asked Emilia a few weeks ago, and she wasn't sure of the answer," he went on. "Do you have any plans for where you'll settle down eventually, or are you content in your condo for now?"

Inquisitive old man. Ma was waiting eagerly for my response, and bless her, I wasn't going to give her what she wanted. There wasn't a chance in hell I'd buy property out here and build a big house next door.

I had bought a place near Villanova, which was right outside the city, as a wedding gift for Emilia. My hope was we could make loose plans for it on our honeymoon. Whether she wanted to save it for later or build a new house, I wasn't sure.

"I won't say no to a house," I said pensively, watching Emilia for her opinion on it. It wasn't anything we'd discussed so far. "I don't think either of us is interested in leaving the Philly area, though."

She shook her head, thank fuck. "No, I like the city." She shifted in her seat and put down her fork. "I, um, I would like to be part of a community somehow. I haven't quite figured out if I want to go to school yet, but I know I want to make myself useful and help out."

This broad... She made me feel ten feet tall. I had half a mind to parade her around and just say *look at her; look at how perfect she is.* She didn't even need to be groomed. Once again, I was gonna have to step up my game to deserve her. Bloody hell.

I noticed Pop was watching me, and I cleared my throat and

straightened in my seat as he smirked knowingly. That bastard could practically read my mind.

"We will find a place for you, dear girl," Father O'Malley said reassuringly. "You've clearly found a place in this family already, and it's been a joy to get to know you better, Emilia." He paused, and there was a twinkle in his eyes. "Not that our headstrong Finnegan would let anything get in his way of marrying you, but for what it's worth, you two very much have my blessing to marry. It'll be my honor to make you husband and wife next weekend."

That hit me squarely in the chest, and all I could do was hug Emilia to me and press my lips into her hair. Father O'Malley's blessing did matter to me, more than I could put into words.

Let my last week as an unmarried man begin.

And end.

"Oh my God, it feels *so* good to be home." Emilia threw herself on the couch and groaned as she kicked off her heels.

I grinned to myself and went through the mail. "You can rest for one hour. I have plans for us at eight."

She made a noise of protest. "That shows how little you know about the time it takes to get ready." What? Twenty minutes was more than enough. "Ugh. Why do you have plans? Can't we Netflix and order Chinese?"

As tempting as that was, no.

"Not tonight, princess. At eight o'clock, I want you dressed and ready to go. We're going out."

She perked up from the couch and scowled sleepily. "Where are we going?"

"That's a surprise, though technically you planned the whole thing." I'd said too much already. Grabbing our luggage and a stack of gift boxes, I carried everything upstairs. I knew exactly which box to avoid. Kellan's sister's card was still attached to it, and I wasn't going near the sex toys I was ridiculously curious about. After our wedding, I reminded myself.

It'd gotten so fucking bad that I could barely see Emilia naked without having to talk myself off a ledge.

My showers hadn't been this long since I discovered something came outta my cock if I jerked it long enough.

Emilia joined me upstairs and scrunched her nose. "If you can't tell me, I gotta know what you'll be wearing. I don't wanna show up at the movies in a formal dress."

I twisted my lips in thought and entered our closet. Tonight, I wanted to show her a good time. We had to let loose and blow off some steam—without my going too far and bending her over to bury—*fuck*. I pressed a fist to my mouth and drew in a deep breath through my nose.

There, a nice three-piece. It was bound to get warm tonight, so I removed the suit jacket from the hanger, leaving the gray pants and matching vest. A white dress shirt and a dark blue tie followed, and I placed it all on the bed for now.

Emilia tiptoed closer and peered at the outfit. "That's...smoking hot. Should I go with classy or sexy?"

"Yes," I answered.

She groaned through a giggle. "Finnegan..."

"It's a casual place, but the occasion is special." Was that more helpful?

Judging by her look, it wasn't. But she waved me off and said she'd figure something out.

Good, because I needed a shower. Again.

Was there a limit to how many showers a man could take before it was deemed unhealthy? Or fucking crazy?

Seeing Emilia in the strapless little number she'd put on was making me throw glances toward the bathroom all over again. I registered the silky fabric that hugged her body, the color that matched my tie, and...legs. Killer legs, that bitable little ass, pert tits pushed together, and fuck-me heels.

She knew what she was doing to me. Brushing her hair over her shoulder, she asked me to attach her necklace, the one with padlock charm on it. I swallowed against the desire that told me to throw her on the bed and fuck her into next week.

"Thanks." She turned around and peered up at me, her teeth sinking into her bottom lip for a quick second. "I don't think I've shown you this." She traced the necklace with her fingers, and I furrowed my brow, seeing another tiny charm next to the padlock.

I pinched it between my thumb and index finger, then cursed when I saw what it was. My name. Or the letter F, but it was *me*. Possessiveness surged in my veins, and I clenched my jaw.

"You're trying to kill me," I whispered.

I hoped she saw the warning in my eyes, 'cause it was as real as it was gonna get. She was testing my restraint.

"Just a bit." Her cheeks colored, and she dropped a kiss to my jaw. "Are you ready to go?"

Go, blow—what the fuck ever.

I nodded once, wound up, and forced myself to take a step back.

On the elevator ride down, I eyed her whenever she wasn't looking. That she had agreed to marry me was something I'd processed already. The guise of a business arrangement had made that easy enough. But this...this was more. This was heavier. The girl was fucking with my head on purpose, force-feeding me hope that she possibly *wanted* this. That maybe she felt more than the chemistry we shared. That perhaps her feelings ran as deep as mine.

In my business, you quickly learned that words meant fuck-all if they weren't proved. Emilia had told me I stood a chance—that our marriage could be more than a piece of paper—but to believe it was a whole other matter.

If only I could guarantee that I wouldn't hurt her again. The day I told her about her mother was getting closer and closer, and I wouldn't have a valid excuse as to why I'd kept it from her for so long. It was just a matter of time before she knew I was exactly the guy she'd originally feared, too. Maybe I'd never inflicted harm on women and children or gotten into the sex trade; running whore-houses was more my uncle's thing. But the O'Sheas hadn't come this far by showing mercy or giving free passes.

I had to shake that for now. The elevator reached the garage, where a car was waiting for us. Tonight was about us, and fuck if tomorrow's problems were gonna ruin that for me. Right now, she was here with me. She wore my name around her neck, one small letter she'd put there on her own.

Colm exited the car with a grin, and Emilia smiled widely.

"Oi, darlin'. I hear you've got a grand night planned." He opened the door for her.

"I wouldn't know." Emilia shot me a playful scowl that I returned with a wink. "Finnegan refuses to clue me in."

"You'll find out soon." I patted her on the ass and got in after her. Once inside, I spotted a bag on the floor, and I dug out a blind-fold for Emilia.

"Kinky," she noted. "Is that for me?"

"Of course that's your response," I muttered under my breath. She'd been reading romance novels by the pool for weeks.

Colm drove out of the garage with a smirk on his face, making me wish I were in a limo with a partition instead of a regular town car. The limos were on the way, though; they'd arrive before the wedding, and no bullets would be able to pierce them.

"Aye, it's for you." I handed her the blindfold, in no rush. It'd be a couple blocks before—never mind, she was already putting it on. "You like surprises, don't you?"

"Are you kidding me? They rock." She tied the strings behind her head before clasping her hands in her lap, visibly excited. "Unless they're bad. Then they suck. Think about that."

I chuckled and relaxed in my seat.

Colm took a minor detour, anything to throw off someone who might be trying to learn our patterns and routes. Even so, the drive lasted less than ten minutes, and he pulled up outside a familiar pub.

I'd had Mick's place ransacked, turned upside down, and under surveillance for the past two days. Tonight, the pub belonged to the O'Sheas, and other than virtually everyone invited being armed, we had security at every exit. If it weren't for the uncertainty that the Italians had brought us, I would've looked more paranoid than my uncle.

"Get ready, princess."

I ushered her out of the car where I removed the blindfold and covered her eyes with my hands instead. As I nodded at the two guys from my company outside the door, they opened up for me, and we were immediately met by blaring music.

Emilia flinched at the sudden change. Then I reckoned she knew what was going on, and her mouth stretched into a grin.

"Told you," I spoke in her ear, "you planned this."

I made sure we had a pubful's attention before I removed my hands from her eyes.

Approximately fifty of my closest friends and their girlfriends yelled out various—and creative—congratulations, from "Here's the ball and her chain" to "Almost too late to run now, Emilia." Irish flags and balloons filled the ceiling, along with a banner that read "Happy Late Engagement, Princess," which stretched from the bar in the middle of the floor to a hook in the beam above the little platform where musicians normally played on weekends.

Emilia squealed behind her hands before spinning around and throwing her arms around me. I grinned and hugged her tightly.

"It may have been my idea, but this is all you, Finnegan. Thank you so much." She gave me a big kiss before she was whisked away by Sarah and Luna.

Next thing I knew, the music was cranked up further, there was a beer in my hand, and my mates pulled me to a table.

"Why are *all* the questions about Ireland?" Emilia yelled from her table.

The princess was protesting our pub quiz.

"So that the right teams score higher!" Conn hollered from somewhere.

His brother had taken the stage to announce the questions, and if he spilled his beer over the paper one more time, I reckoned it'd be impossible to read.

It'd gotten warm in the couple of hours we'd been here, and I sat back and loosened my tie while Colm tried to juggle the quiz sheet, his beer, and the microphone.

To save time, we were all split into teams. Four or five people fit around one table, and we'd sort of naturally teamed up with men competing against women. It was a junior high dance all over again, the guys on one side of the room and the girls on the other.

"List—" Colm squinted at the paper, eliciting laughter from the crowd. "List three breweries from County Cork! Well, who wouldn't go for a Beamish right now, eh?"

"You've got to be freaking kidding me," Sarah exclaimed.

Emilia huffed and narrowed her eyes.

"He just gave you one of the answers!" Patrick widened his arms. "You gotta *listen*, sweet cheeks."

I smirked and listed three breweries. Anyone knew this, really.

"Shots, mate?" Kellan stumbled back to our table and sat down with a bottle of tequila and a stack of glasses.

"Hit me with it." I folded up my sleeves past my elbows and contemplating losing the vest, but Emilia had a thing for it. I left it on for now. "Ay, oh, top 'em up properly. What's wrong wit'chu?"

Kellan chuckled and filled the glasses to the brim. "It's good to have you back, Finn."

"Yeah, see, I never left—"

"Oi! Less chatter, ladies," Colm told us. "Question number fourteen. What's the second most popular language in Ireland?"

"Oh! You're a fuckin' sneak." I laughed and threw back my first shot, then jotted down Polish as my answer.

Colm grinned proudly. "Can't make it easy on the foreigners."

"Yeah, welcome to fucking America," Emilia retorted. "Who's the foreigner now?"

"She's talking about you, Colm," Luna said with a sniff.

Kellan and I snorted in response and went for another shot. The liquid burned my throat perfectly, heating me up even more.

It was shaping up to be a bloody fantastic night.

"How the fuck is this possible?" I tore the results from Colm's hand and read it over and over.

"I did the math twice!" He stepped off the platform and joined me. "You still did good. Fourth place—"

"I don't care about that. There are always a few nerds who gotta know everything," I said. "What I don't buy is Emilia's team's ninety-seven percent score." I looked up from the paper and narrowed my eyes at the girl in question. "Oi! Get over here, princess."

She sauntered over with an angelic smile, Sarah and one of the other girlfriends in tow. "Yes, dear?"

I held up the paper. "Mind explaining why you've got the election percentage of a dictator?"

She laughed and peered at the paper. "I guess we were better than we thought. Third place—nice job, ladies."

"Fuck that, you googled," I accused.

334

Not missing a beat or letting her smile falter, she extended her phone. "Can you prove that?"

"Oh, mate." Colm let out a booming laugh and clapped me on the back. "Good luck with that one."

"That doesn't mean anything," I told her. "You could've used someone else's phone or cleared the history."

"In other words, you can't prove anything." She was triumphant—and too fucking cute. I couldn't even pretend to be mad at that face.

I pulled her to me, the results forgotten, and kissed her hard. "Fuck, you're sexy when you play me." I spoke against her lips, hands roaming her back until I slipped them down to palm her ass. "Speaking of playing..." I moved us out of the way as Conn and Eric carried parts of a drum set through the pub. Kellan followed with the snare and a guitar case.

Emilia stayed in my arms, one hand on my chest, and gasped. "Oh my God, are you gonna play for us now? I've waited so long for this!"

"We'll do a few songs." When my brother joined with his own two cases, I bumped his fist. Everyone had been so quick to notice my changes, but this bastard... Patrick had gone through changes too, and he'd finally found his ambition again. He worked harder, he was focused, and someone who noticed was Sarah. Better late than never, the two were tentatively building something genuine.

"What does Patrick play?" Emilia asked curiously. "I assume one of those is a guitar."

I nodded. "He's brilliant on the mandolin too. Pick an instrument for me."

She scrunched her nose. "Um, how many do you actually play?"

I flashed her a grin. "All of them." Well, all of the ones present on the stage, anyway, and I had a harmonica in my back pocket that I was saving for Patrick's favorite tune. "What're the Irish without music?"

She bit her lip. "Drunks?"

I let out a loud laugh and made a mental note to tell Patrick that one later.

"Never mind, you gotta go with that tin whistle thingy," she said eagerly. "I looked it up on YouTube, and do you realize how fast their fingers work? It's like porn, Finnegan." She touched my fingers while I failed to withhold my amusement. "You already have piano player fingers. Unf, yeah, tin whistle."

I grabbed her chin and planted a smooch on her soft lips. "Whistle, it is."

As I joined the guys on the platform, more people huddled around the stage; someone thrust a Magner's cider in Emilia's hand, which was her new crack. The day I showed her Ireland, she'd learn it had another name there. Shite, there was so much I couldn't wait to show her.

"Your favorite singer has arrived," Colm announced and jumped up on the stage. "We're gonna show 'em how we do it back home." Ironically, by starting with a cover by an Irish punk band from Australia. He grabbed the mic to entertain our friends while the rest of us got ready. "There aren't many songs we all know by heart, so our set list tonight is shorter than Patrick's cock."

"What would you know about that, mate?" someone shouted.

I chuckled, listening to my brother's furious protesting, which went unheard over the crowd's hollering. Conn was behind the drums, and he handed me my case of tin whistles.

None of my friends knew how to play the accordion, so Kellan and Patrick had lured Mick up from behind the bar to play the first couple of songs with us.

Eric left the platform after setting a bottle of Tullamore and several shot glasses on one of the speakers. "To quench the thirst. Have at it, lads."

"Get ready with your fiddle for later," I told him.

"Aye."

It was hotter than Satan's asshole with the spotlights on us, so I didn't waste any time pouring a few shots.

"We're startin' with 'An Irish Pub Song' by The Rumjacks, so." Colm had left behind his recent Americanisms and returned to Dublin, where *then* became *so* and everyone who visited Temple Bar was either dumb as shite or a tourist.

Kellan tuned his guitar. Mick complained that the younger generation had forgotten the awesomeness of the accordion. Meanwhile, no one was bothered that we didn't have anyone on the bass tonight.

"Finn, we're waitin' on ye," Colm said into the mic.

"Huh?" I paused with a shot glass midair, only to remember the whistle and the mandolin started the song. That would be Pat and me. "Oh, right." I took a shot and hissed at the smooth burn. I had my whistle ready, my favorite Gen in D, a brass flute with a black mouthpiece. "Okay, gimme the count-in, big brother."

I set the mouthpiece to my lips, and he tapped his foot against the age-old wood of the floor. Then we started at the same time, the tempo cheerful and folksy, though that only lasted a few seconds. Colm's rough voice quickened the pace, and he sang of shinty balls and the craic before Conn and Kellan joined in with a bang.

I laughed as Colm fucked up the words, the tempo too quick, the drums raising the roof of the place. Throwing back another shot, I waited for my cue and removed my tie. The chase was on after that. I stood with Kellan and sped up my own playing to be a dick. He laughed, out of breath, and shook his head as his fingers slid along the strings. Conn shot me a cunty look, and what-the-fuck-ever. I had a girl to impress; he was already married.

By the third song, I got to shine and make my princess look sufficiently horny with a Cooley's Reel medley. I had help from Eric on the violin, Conn on the drums, and Kellan on the guitar, and the best way to describe the tune was to call it a battle between the whistle and the fiddle. The next part was always faster than the previous one. My fingers fucking ached. They'd be stiff and sore by tomorrow, but I couldn't very well give in.

Around us, people were clapping and stomping their feet. Every time I got a break, my brother was pouring beer down my throat. Sweat trickled down my temples, and it didn't exactly get any easier from there. Patrick still wanted us to play "Drunken Sailor," and they had to go with Barleyjuice's version. I agreed, it was the best one and a good tribute to a local Philly band that knew Irish music, but Christ, it was quick. I wasn't as skilled with the harmonica as I was with other instruments.

Conn and I took the lead in another chase, this time between the drums and the harmonica. We upped the tempo more and more until Eric came in with the fiddle, Patrick and Kellan on their guitars, and Colm on vocals.

It was my turn to fuck up, and I took a quick break to guzzle half a pint of beer. My chest heaved with each breath so I could finish the last chorus with the others. When Colm shouted hoarsely, "What should do you with the drunken sailor?" the men in the crowd yelled back, "Put 'im in bed with the captain's daughter!"

Emilia was gloriously tipsy, wearing a huge smile, eyes glassy from an unknown number of ciders she'd inhaled, and she couldn't stand still. She jumped and shimmied with Sarah and Luna, looking like she was having the time of her life.

I hoped she was.

Eric and I stepped up to the front of the platform with Colm and showed everyone how it was done. Feet tapping along with the pace of the drums, I drew from the holes and changed the pitch of the note when Eric played lower. He responded, sliding the bow perfectly over the strings, and together we let the notes fade until the song was over.

We received hoots and hollers and drinks, and we took a gracious bow and exchanged smirks.

In a brief pause in the pub's chaos, which undoubtedly

Emilia didn't foresee, everyone heard her comment. "Basically, my man is the master with his fingers and mouth. But I already knew that...um." She glanced around herself and blushed furiously.

I could not grin wider, and I ate that shit up.

"Okay, what's next?" Patrick demanded.

"Fuck you, that's what." I sucked in a breath and ran a hand through my hair, exhausted. The harmonica ended up on a speaker. "I need a break. You guys can play."

I grabbed my beer and jumped down from the platform where Emilia immediately met up with me.

"You were fantastic!" She threw her arms around my neck. "Oh, sweaty."

I chuckled and ushered her to a table in the back, wanting some privacy with her.

"Can I call you my whistler?" she asked and plopped down on my lap.

I smirked and took a kiss. If only she knew the meaning behind that nickname in our family. "Does that make you my whistleblower?"

She paused, lips pursed. "Aren't you the one blowing the whistle?"

I squinted. The alcohol had gotten to me, and I was getting confused by the innuendos. I supposed it depended on what she was insinuating. Maybe? Fuck.

"Tell you what, you can call me whatever you want, and you can blow my whistle too," I said, satisfied.

She laughed and straddled me, and that wasn't her best idea. Less so when she scooted closer and pressed her chest to mine. "Hi."

"Hey, you." I chuckled through my nose and set my beer on the table. "How drunk are you?"

The fact that she had to think about it said a lot.

I guess the other guys decided to take a break too, 'cause the live music was replaced by a rock song from the stereo system, and Mick dimmed the lights.

"I'm happy, I can tell you that much." Emilia rubbed our noses together and smiled wickedly. "I can't get over how sexy you were up there."

Fuck me, *no*. She couldn't do this to me.

"Don't tempt me," I murmured.

"When you think about it, this is your fault." She leaned in closer and grazed her teeth along my bottom lip. At the same time, she rolled her hips over me, and I closed my eyes briefly. "You knew what you were doing to me up on that stage."

I groaned inwardly and, against what I knew was smartest, I slipped my hands under her dress and cupped her ass. Not giving a flying fuck if she flashed her ass to half the pub. It was dark enough, and our friends were busy. Tables were moved back to make room for dancing, the alcohol kept flowing freely, and there wasn't a sober motherfucker in the whole place.

"What did I do to you?" I wanted to hear her say it.

My cock thickened as she dipped down and licked my neck. It elicited a shudder from me, and I clenched my jaw.

How the fuck did the atmosphere change so fast? Gone was the Irish pub feel, and now we were looking at a nightclub where everyone was getting ready to score. Even the music took on a more seductive note, the bass heavy and slow.

She nipped at my earlobe. "You made me wet."

"Fuck." Lust flared up inside me, and when she tilted her face toward mine, I was already there. I kissed her impatiently and shifted her over my cock, to which she tried to clench her thighs together. I could fucking feel her, the heat she was radiating.

"Finnegan..." She moaned breathily into the kiss and twisted her fingers into my hair. "I never wanna forget tonight. I need you."

"I need you too, princess."

An unforgettable night, she'd asked for.

chapter 27

Finnegan O'Shea

"What...what happened last night?"

"Why are you yelling?" I groaned and dug my head under my pillow.

"I'm whispering. We have to get up if we don't wanna stress before church."

"Stop screaming, baby, *please.*" My head couldn't take it. Everything hurt. Except silence. Silence was my friend. Peace and quiet were the best. *Quiet...*

"You gotta be quiet, princess." I hauled in a breath and shuddered. Every thrust between her tits brought me closer to coming, and the girl was driving me fucking crazy with her tongue. Whenever I pushed far enough, she wrapped her soft lips around the head of my cock and licked and sucked at the slit. "Shit." I bent down a bit more and planted one hand on the wall behind her.

Someone left the bathroom, and if I wasn't wrong, we were alone now.

"I want it, Finnegan..." She hummed around my cock, and I withdrew, only to fuck her tits faster. She pushed them together

341

harder, and I'd already coated the tight crease with pre-come. "Let me taste it."

I cursed and licked my lips, tasting her sweetness from a few minutes ago when our positions had been reversed. A hoarse moan left me. She'd looked so fucking sexy, one leg over my shoulder, fingers gripping my hair, gasps falling from her mouth as I fucked her pretty little pussy with my fingers and tongue.

My head snapped up, and I blinked, which fucking hurt. "Did I fuck your tits last night?" I croaked.

"Ohh...that explains why I really wanna take a shower right now." Emilia tumbled off the bed with a yelp. "Oww."

I coughed a chuckle, another thing that hurt, and shifted over to her side of the bed. Luckily for her, our bed was kinda low.

"Are you okay?" I couldn't keep both eyes open. When we arrived home last night, I'd forgotten to close the blinds. The sun was pouring in.

"No," she whimpered, pouting. She was an adorable mess on the floor. Makeup dusting under her eyes, a sleep line across her cheek, hair goddamn everywhere. She was only in a pair of skimpy black panties. "Help me up?"

"In a minute." I ogled her with one eye open first.

More memories from last night returned to me. I'd sucked on those perky breasts a lot last night, and quite fucking publicly.

"We gotta get out of here..." She tilted her head back, and I pushed her up against the wall near the kitchen behind the bar. Thank fuck her dress was strapless. I pushed it down, revealing her breasts and nipples that begged to be licked.

"Finnegan!"

"What, yeah, no, on it." I cleared my throat and dragged myself out of bed. A rugby team of leprechauns kept pounding on the inside of my skull, and I winced as I helped her off the floor. "Painkillers," I rasped. "I need all of them."

Emilia grunted and nudged me toward the bathroom.

It was as if seeing the toilet was what I needed to remember I had to take a leak, so I lifted the lid and dropped my boxer briefs, then sat down.

That earned me a cocked brow while she rummaged through the cabinet above the sink. "Really? We've reached that stage in our relationship?"

I squinted up at her. "My condition warrants it. If I stand up, you're gonna have to clean the toilet after."

She made a face and tossed me a bottle of ibuprofen. "I was more talking about privacy."

"*Ungh.*" I rubbed my temples and closed my eyes. "Can we have this conversation later?"

The horrid witch *patted me on the head* and left me, announcing she was gonna shower downstairs.

"Privacy," I muttered. "Ridiculous."

I felt marginally better after a shower, a gallon of water, brushing my teeth, and possibly one too many ibuprofen. Emilia was up to something in the kitchen, so I went there once I'd put on a pair of sweats and returned the towel on the rack where I'd been told it had to go. Otherwise, it could leave spots on the floorboards or some such shit. The girl had rules, and I tried to follow them.

I'd like to say I paused in the doorway to watch her flit around while making breakfast, and it was certainly a bonus to have her there. But the reality was I was dead on my feet. Leaning against the doorway, I yawned and got a good whiff of the coffee brewing.

"I like those." I jerked my chin at her PJs. She wore them often around the house when we were being lazy. Mostly, I loved how short the shorts where and how her nipples teased the light purple fabric.

It was a shame we had church in an hour and a half.

"Thanks. Sarah gave them to me." She smiled and reached up to grab two mugs, and it caused her little blouse to ride up, exposing her toned stomach. The running we'd been doing was paying off. "I like the buttons. Aren't they cute?"

I eyed the little pearls and felt my mouth twist. "Sure, that's what I was thinking. The buttons."

She snorted and set the mugs next to the coffeemaker. "Such a guy. Maybe I should go around shirtless and tug at my crotch all the time."

"I don't *tug*." I left the doorway to make myself useful. "I just... make sure it's still there."

She giggled, handing me a cutting board. "Dice some fruit, please."

"Yes, ma'am."

We didn't do this often enough, and it was one of my favorites. Making breakfast side by side, bantering, working together like a well-oiled machine. And...honestly, it was one of the things I looked forward to doing the most when we got married. This domestic shit, seemingly insignificant, was what took me away from the pressure at work. Pressure I thrived on but needed breaks from.

I cut up a couple bananas and divided the pieces into two bowls, and I snuck glances at her and felt I couldn't really hold it in any longer. She hummed a soft tune and put the creamer in our coffee. Four slices of bread popped up from the toaster, and a lock of hair fell down from her ponytail as she did the it's-hot-hot-hot dance while putting the toast on a plate.

"Hey." I abandoned the fruit and walked over to her. I pressed a kiss to her forehead, her eyelids, her cheeks, and her nose. She smiled sweetly. My pulse went through the roof, yet there was a strange calm in me. It was her doing. "I'm gonna tell you something,"

344

I murmured and cupped her face, "and you're gonna keep your little trap shut afterward. I know you're not there yet—and maybe you never will be—but I want you to know. I love you." I kissed her quickly, ignoring my hammering heart and her mouth popping open. "I think I fell in love with you the day you handed me my ass at the contract negotiation." Nudging her jaw up, I closed her mouth and kissed it again. "And I can't fucking wait to be your husband."

"Finn—"

"Nope." I shook my head and pinched her lips together. I prayed it wasn't a bad thing that her eyes welled up. There was a warmth in her gaze, a tenderness, and it eased my nerves enough. "Don't say anything. Just know that I love you."

"But—"

"I swear, princess," I chuckled. "Let me have this. All right?"

She pouted. "Okay," she whispered, and I released her lips.

"Okay." I dipped down and kissed her once more, softer this time, and contemplated asking her if she'd looked up the Irish words I'd written to her. Then I decided I didn't want the answer, because chances were she had and she didn't know how to respond to it. It was better to move on. "Did you nickname me Whistler last night?"

She sighed contentedly and rested her cheek on my chest. "Worst topic change ever." She hugged my midsection, and I smiled to myself. "But, yes. You were so amazing. You'll have to play more often."

"Any time you want." I kissed the top of her head, and my growling stomach settled our next course of action. I had to get some food in me.

Emilia brought a tray full of stuff to the table outside the kitchen, and I finished dicing up the fruit. Bananas, blueberries, watermelon, and a couple nectarines made it into the bowls before I joined her at the table.

"If I'm to understand this security crap correctly, I'm not

allowed to take any unscheduled outings...?" She looked at me questioningly.

I nodded and eyed the headlines in the newspaper. "Correct. I know it sucks, but we gotta be careful. If there's anything you wanna do, let the guys know a day in advance." If I had my way, she wouldn't leave the building at all until next Saturday, but then my mother would flip her lid. "All the wedding-related errands are okay. Conn and Colm will pick you up in the garage after getting Ma or whoever you're going with. They'll drop you off here after too."

"Got it." She nodded once as she spread butter on her toast. "Will you be working much?"

Unfortunately. "I have meetings all week, but I won't be home late." Next, I told her that we were taking John and Anne out for dinner on Wednesday, something neither of us was going to enjoy, but it had to be done. The good thing was we'd see Alec and Nessa again, and I could see Emilia brightened at that. "They'll be staying in our building." So would a lot of other wedding guests flying in this week. "Which reminds me—you have a decision to make."

"Oh?"

I took a sip of my coffee. "After the reception on Saturday, do you wanna stay at the hotel or come back here? I ask because we're not leaving for our honeymoon until Monday, so we'll have Sunday to ourselves. I figure between packing and leaving the bed as little as possible—stop laughing," I said, maybe laughing. "I'm serious. I might chain you to the bed."

She gigglesnorted and forked a piece of watermelon. "I might let you." Then she shook her head. "Let's stay here. We just got back, and it's been a lot of going back and forth." Certainly true. Additionally, our building was probably the safest residence in Philly right now. Pop and I had guys on watch everywhere, and as soon as Uncle John arrived, so would his own security detail. "Can you tell me where we're going on our honeymoon?"

"Not even at all." I tucked into my breakfast and smirked at her cute scowl. "I'm not sure it matters. We'll barely leave the bed there, either."

She laughed and shook her head at me. "Promises, promises."

Oh, she'd see. I deserved a fucking medal for sticking to my guns, though once we were married, all bets were off. Then I'd see about knocking her up too. Someway, somehow.

———

"I miss driving." I drummed my fingers along the armrest in the back seat and looked out at the shoppers on Market Street. I bet they could drive whenever they wanted to.

"You drove yesterday." Kellan frowned at me in the rearview and stopped at a light.

"Yeah, but now I can't," I argued. With only a few days before the wedding, we'd made the decision that no one involved on Saturday should travel alone or be in charge of their own safety. Unfortunately, Pop had told me that included me. So Kellan was now my driver, and my Aston was resting in the garage at home.

My firm's new vehicles had arrived, and the drivers sure enjoyed the armored limos.

"All right, we're here, you whiny fuck." Kellan pulled over at the valet and rolled down his window. "Oi, sir. We're just picking something up."

He got out and opened the door for me, and I headed straight inside my jeweler's shop.

"Mr. O'Shea!" Old Harry broke out his best grin upon seeing me, and I shook his hand and glanced around his sparsely decorated store. Only a handful of displays stood against the red-painted walls, each one with spotlights aimed at big rocks, one bigger than the next.

"How are you, my friend?" I asked.

"Good, good, all good. I've got your items ready in the back. Just give me one second."

I leaned against the glass counter and eyed the diamonds and sapphires and rubies. *Man*, it made my fingers itch.

Kellan joined me at my side. "Your firm does security here, right?"

"Aye." I wasn't gonna do anything here, though. Harry gave us a discount, and my mother would have my ass. "Did you hear about the gig yesterday?" I spoke under my breath. "Almost made me wanna tag along."

Work continued even in difficult times, and we always had something going on. Last night, four of my boys had installed an alarm system in the middle of a family's move to their new estate, and they'd walked away with collectibles and an ugly brooch worth a million.

If the family eventually noticed the pieces gone missing, they would do what they all did: blame the movers.

Kellan let out a low whistle after hearing the details. "Innit risky to pull that off while they're on the scene officially?"

Yeah, but we didn't do that often. Most of the time, installing security systems just meant we had the means to shut them off too, which could be done whenever. Eric loved to tamper with footage.

"They deemed it safe this time." I closed the subject as Harry returned with my order. One of the boxes was weirdly big for holding just a wedding band.

"Your lovely bride's ring." He retrieved the velvet box from its wrapping and opened it, revealing a thin platinum band that would go with Emilia's engagement ring. There were tiny diamonds all around it, and an inscription on the inside where we'd put our initials and the wedding date.

"Looks perfect. What's the story with mine?" I jerked my chin at the larger box. While it'd fit in my hand, it wouldn't look very good in my pocket.

"Ah, I trust Ms. Porter told you...?" He looked half confused, and he removed the white wrapping—then stopped. Because he literally couldn't open the actual ring box.

"Is that a code lock?" Kellan leaned closer.

I scratched my eyebrow. "What exactly was my fiancée supposed to tell me?"

I swear to God, baby.

It wasn't merely a ring box. It was a tiny-ass safe that required a four-digit code.

"She didn't want you to see the inscription in your ring," Harry explained. "She didn't tell you?"

"No." I didn't know whether to grin, send her flowers, or shake her. For a man who hated being blindsided, I had a stupid love for having her keep me on my toes. She succeeded every time, leaving me to deal with this...this bullshit. I was torn, yet falling harder every day, it seemed. "I reckon you don't have access to the code."

"I'm afraid not, sir. I'd need Ms. Porter's permission, and she would have to come in."

Great.

I dismissed it and pulled out my wallet. "I need a little something for my parents too."

"Right away, sir. Last time Mrs. O'Shea was in, she did look at these quite a bit." He carefully slid out a pair of amethyst earrings from the displays under the glass top.

"Those are good," I said. "Pair of cuff links for my pop, and I'll be set."

"Yes, sir."

Kellan clapped me on the back. "I'll get the car ready, and you know we can have that safe open in twenty minutes."

Yeah, and I also knew better. I'd let Emilia have this one. I had bigger, more pregnant fish to fry.

Half an hour later, we picked up Emilia at home, and at the sight of her excited expression, I decided not to mention the rings.

All the way to the airport, she talked animatedly about her final fitting, how much she liked her dress, and how beautiful the brides-maids would be, each one with a dress matching...something; I tuned out, but there was a mention of the colors of the bouquet.

I nodded and commented in all the right places. First of all, I wouldn't even see the bridesmaids on Saturday—hell, I barely knew who they were. Secondly, I was betting they'd served champagne at the fitting.

"You're a little flushed, princess." I pinched her cheek.

She batted me away and grinned without a care. "I had bubbly."

"You had bubbly," I repeated with a laugh. "I'll say." Draping an arm around her shoulders, I leaned down and nuzzled her neck. Her skin was so soft and bitable. "You know what I wanna talk about?"

"Uh-uh." She shook her head and put her hand on my thigh.

"Us. Getting married." I brushed my thumb over her engage-ment ring. "Did you think about what I said about our vows?"

I could admit I was doing this to save myself. On Saturday, I fully expected to be a nervous wreck, and the odds of me either having memorized my own vows or being able to hold a note with them written down—without fucking shaking—weren't in my favor. Therefore, I'd suggested we pick something to read together. It would make it slightly more interesting than doing only the tradi-tional vows, and I wouldn't look like an idiot 'cause I'd make Emilia hold the note or whatever.

"I did." She smirked, half shy, half proud, and played with my fingers. "I talked to Grace about it, and she said she's gonna send us some short prayers we can go through. Is that okay?"

"More than okay." The shorter, the better. I kissed her quickly before straightening in my seat. My hand remained in her lap, and she ghosted her fingers over the spot where I'd wear my own ring in a few days. "I have some bad news, by the way."

"Uh-oh."

Good timing. We were almost at the airport, and I'd need a hasty exit if this didn't go well.

"I gotta shave before the wedding," I stage-whispered.

Oh, the fucking horror in her eyes. I wanted to laugh.

"What? No, but you... I mean, no, you can't!" she spluttered. "What if you have a baby face?"

Whoa, lady, harsh. "What the fresh hell—I don't have a fucking baby face." I withdrew my hand and scoffed, more insulted than I should've been, maybe. *Did* I have a baby face? No, screw that. My jaw was goddamn cut. My beard, while I liked it, was a trend. "Listen, you're just gonna have to manage. For all I know, a beard will make me look like a slob in twenty years, and then what am I gonna do with our wedding pictures? Am I supposed to tell our kids I was a homeless person who photobombed your wedding and pushed out the groom?" Perhaps I ranted too heatedly, but fuck it. I pulled out my smokes from the inside of my suit jacket and lit one up.

"Oh, Finnegan." In that short little whisper of hers, I heard how close she was to laughing, and it wasn't funny, goddammit. "There's something I want to tell you, but I have to wait." See if I cared. I didn't. "How about you shave tonight or tomorrow? Then you'd have a little bit of scruff on Saturday."

I side-eyed her.

She smiled and pressed her lips to my shoulder, only because she was still struggling to hold back her giggles. I could see it in her eyes.

"Fine." I looked away from her again.

The airport might be the one place where I didn't feel the necessity to surround myself—or Emilia—with extra eyes and guns. There was always someone watching, and the place was heavily patrolled.

"We'll be back within twenty," I told Kellan, buttoning my suit.

Then I extended a hand and helped Emilia out of the car. "I reckon you can just circle around while Emilia and I go in."

"You got it," he replied and coughed. "Later, baby face."

I shot him a murderous look. *Oh, unclench, mate.* Fuck. I blew out a breath and smacked him upside the head, a little harder than intended, and gave him a smirk. "Keep it up, Ford. Keep it up."

Emilia was looking away from me, though one had to be blind not to see her shoulders trembling with laughter.

This day was going bloody well, wasn't it?

Hand in hand, Emilia and I headed inside the airport, and the Murrays' flight had already landed. I suspected the only reason John hadn't flown private was because he was trying to show he had faith in me. I'd sworn he would be safe, and not showing trust would destroy his chances of earning mine.

"Hey. I don't want you to be cranky with me, Finnegan."

"I'm not cranky." I kept watching the screens for the arrivals and did the math. My aunt and uncle weren't the types of people who got their own luggage, so they would come straight through.

"Finnegan."

"That's me."

She sighed. "*Whistler...?*"

Like that was going to work. Remembering how she'd reacted to my playing for her didn't thaw me up one bit. Not one—okay, maybe one, but sure as hell not two.

Emilia cranked it up a notch and positioned herself in front of me, and she slipped her hands up my chest and around my neck. Too bad, shortcake, I could see over her. I was marrying a gnome.

"Those twenty years...?" she said softly, "I want them too. I want us to have everything you mentioned. The kids, the wedding pictures we'll look back on."

I cared more than one bit.

"Really?" I muttered, sparing her a glance.

"Really. It's up to you, Irish boy." She lifted a finger and smoothed out the spot between my brows. "I'll honor my vows for as long as you honor yours."

Yeah, see, that wasn't very reassuring, now, was it?

I was gonna fuck up. I was gonna hurt her.

Thing was, I could sense her limits by this point. She'd learned fast that we told each other some shitty lies in my family sometimes, and she'd accepted it. She'd adjusted and made it her way too.

She had patience in spades.

What she didn't have was a biological mother, and I couldn't tell her the truth that would give her one. Not yet. And definitely not before we learned more about the Avellinos. From where I was standing, Elena Avellino wasn't on our side. She literally slept with the enemy. But to learn that Emilia *wanted* what I wanted... Fuck, this was gonna blow.

"I will never intentionally hurt you," I murmured.

Never before had I wished I could promise more.

"Tush!" And never before had Alec's timing been worse.

I suppressed a sigh, and Emilia tugged me down for a quick kiss. Then she turned around to greet the Murrays with her best smile.

"Alec!"

He flew into her, hugged her hard, and spun her around. The little Casanova was gonna be trouble one day. No one in the family could resist his dimpled grin, fedora, shorts, and suspenders.

Emilia laughed and demanded he put her down, and it was a sight that drew smiles from everyone, including this cranky fucker.

Nessa skipped over to me, stealing Alec's hat on the way, and I pulled her in for a hug.

"Welcome back, doll."

"Thanks. This feels like a second home now." She smirked up at me, and I chuckled.

Alec was next, and he hugged me tightly too. That was how he won hearts and could get away with too much. He was affectionate and cared about his family.

"Good to have you back, cub." I ruffled his hair and kissed his forehead. Hell, he was taller than Emilia now. It was difficult to reconcile. To me, he was still five.

"Good to *be* back, boss." He smiled crookedly and stole back his fedora from his sister. "Mum said we're staying in your building."

"Aye, we'll be neighbors." I cuffed him on the chin.

He grinned goofily.

"Finn, me boy!" I heard John call. Oh boy, he'd changed since the last time I saw him. He'd always been a stocky man, almost as tall as me, and now his hairline was receding while his gut was growing.

Instantly, Emilia was back at my side, her smile more forced.

I circled a hand around her waist and acknowledged the five or six men surrounding John and Anne. They were dressed casually and keeping their distance, but they weren't discreet whatsoever, and I bet they felt naked without their guns.

"Welcome to Philly, sir. It's an honor." I shook his hand firmly before stepping forward to kiss Aunt Anne's cheek. "Lovely as ever, Anne." I had a feeling her newfound youth came with injections. She'd dyed her hair blond for whatever reason.

"It's good to see you, Finn." She smiled politely.

"You too. I want you to meet my beautiful fiancée—Emilia Porter. Emilia, my uncle and aunt, John and Anne Murray."

"It's a pleasure to meet you, Mr. and Mrs. Murray." Emilia played her part like a pro, never failing to make me proud to be at her side. "I hope you'll enjoy your stay here."

"Oh, she's a treat, lad," John murmured to me. "You've done well."

Fuckin' hell, Emilia's filthy liberal ways were rubbing off on me. Before meeting her, I wouldn't have the urge to tell him I had nothing to do with her being who she was.

With the greetings out of the way, she and I were separated for a minute while John and I walked ahead toward the exit.

"Everything's been set up," I told him quietly. "Your condo's on the small side, but I figured you'd rather have three neighbors than one." Because his security would be staying there.

"I'm sure it'll be just fine, son," he said. "Business tonight, but then I wanna catch up with my family and enjoy the wedding festivities."

Patrick was right. John was ready to kiss ass. He hadn't given a flying fuck about family before.

Kellan was waiting right outside, bitching with airport security, who wanted him away from the curb.

"Christ, we're leaving." He flipped the guard off behind his back, then circled the car to pop the trunk. "Good to see you again, sir," he told John. "Finn's got something for the gentlemen. Their car is arriving in a minute."

John peered into the trunk, no doubt seeing the briefcase with handguns. "Ah, good lad. Good, good." He gestured for his men.

In the meantime, I opened the car door and let Emilia, Anne, and the kids inside.

I followed once John was in too, and we each ended up with a twelve-year-old between us.

I eyed Alec, amused.

"She'll be mine one day," he whispered.

I pulled his fedora down over his face.

chapter

28

Finnegan O'Shea

"I s it wrong I'd rather stay at home and have a movie night with Patrick, Sarah, and the twins—oh shit, I'm sorry. I didn't know you were on the phone." Emilia returned downstairs while I uncovered the receiver on my phone.

She wasn't intruding. Liam was just letting off some steam by ranting about the dumb-as-shite crews he'd dealt with in Chicago. Which evidently got more taxing when he was in prison.

"And on top of it all, I'm gonna miss yer wedding," he finished irritably.

"Are you done, dear?" I drawled.

"Fuck you!"

I laughed and threw a tie around my neck. "You'll be out in a couple months, mate." Leaving the closet, I went downstairs to seek out Emilia. "We'll throw you a big party."

I found her in the kitchen, looking gorgeous in a dark red cocktail dress. She'd mentioned the words chiffon and A-line. I was sure it meant all great things.

"I love you, Finn," Liam said, "but you can't plan a party that tops two big weddings."

I exchanged a smile with Emilia and went up to her with my tie. "Sounds like a challenge to me."

She fixed my tie for me, adjusting it just so, and smoothed down my shirt. Business meant dark colors, and I'd gone with a standard black suit and a dark blue button-down. Black tie. Emilia seemed amused by it, and she whispered that she used to wonder who'd died whenever I showed up outside her run-down house.

I smirked and touched her cheek. It was the first time I'd seen her wearing red lipstick, and it was fucking sexy.

"Are you listenin' to me, Finn?" Liam asked.

"No, sorry, I stopped a while ago," I replied. "It happens automatically when you sound like a woman on the rag."

Emilia raised a delicate brow.

"Don't start with me," I whispered. "You've infected me with your liberal germs enough for one day."

That filled her eyes with laughter, though then she merely snorted and left my ass in the kitchen.

"I gotta go, Liam." I interrupted another rant of his. "We're having dinner with your delightful parents."

He scoffed.

Ironically, one of the O'Shea strongholds in downtown Philly was a restaurant that was Italian, and that was where we took Uncle John and Aunt Anne for dinner. The dinner itself was a prelude of inane bullshit leading up to our sit-down, but it was how we'd done this for decades. Wives had the ability to lower the blood pressure where work was concerned, and their presence reminded us that once the sit-down was over, we still had to suffer through holidays and christenings together because we were family.

Uncle John was enamored of Emilia, and I was the last person who could blame him.

On the other hand, I had finally figured out *why* she found it so easy to be the perfect hostess, and that was a less pleasant reminder. She'd had eighteen years of practicing servitude before me, eighteen years of bending over backward to please her dad so he wouldn't get rid of her. She knew hard work and how to put others before her 'cause it was all she'd done.

The only difference was she did it in high-end designer clothes now.

It didn't sit well with me, and I was gonna make sure she knew our home was sacred. This role she was playing was reserved exclusively for business dinners and where she was a reflection and representation of my position.

For every other hour of the day, I needed her to break my balls. Otherwise, I wouldn't have been the type of man who fell in love with the biggest challenge of his life.

Aunt Anne guided us through chatter about kids, school districts, and the future. She planned to bring home gossip to her friends in Chicago, so she wanted to know everything about Emilia and me. Or rather, our plans.

"Your condominiums here are nice and all..." She gestured with her wineglass. "But surely it's not a place you want to raise your children."

I had to hand it to Emilia. She didn't point out the fact that John and Anne lived in a penthouse in the middle of Chicago, though I could see her sweet smile morphing into one of the fuck-you variety.

I was highly entertained.

"Actually, Finn and I were talking about it the other day." Oh, so Emilia was calling me Finn again. That meant I was on thin ice. She cut a piece of her chicken. "What was the neighborhood you mentioned, honey?"

I could play along, no problem. "Well, we discussed Glad-wyne." I wasn't sure Emilia knew of the suburb, but Anne definitely did. She grew up there in an affluent family before Uncle

John snatched her up and brought her to Chicago. "But I don't know. Maybe a bit too quaint for us."

The look on my aunt's face was fucking priceless.

Uncle John coughed around a chuckle.

"Quaint," Anne repeated with a flat expression. "You think Gladwyne is...quaint?"

"You got a problem with that?" I took a sip of my wine.

She lowered her gaze and remembered her place. "Of course not, Finn."

Good. Don't shit on my home and expect me not to take a dump on yours.

I bet it stung to be beneath one of the kids she'd watched grow up.

"Our lad's messing with you, darling." John patted her hand and snuck me a quick look. "I think."

I smiled and draped an arm along the back of Emilia's chair.

The princess picked up the conversation again by asking how Alec and Nessa had done in school last semester. Anne wasn't particularly interested in the topic, though she pretended well enough. Summer was here, and she probably banked on the kids going to Ireland soon, as they did most summers. Either they stayed in Dublin, at my house in Killarney, or their place outside of Cork. No matter where they went, they had cousins, aunts, and uncles who loved having them.

We'd see how this summer panned out. It was possible we would have to send all wives and kids on vacation while we took care of the Italian rat infestation.

After dinner, John and I walked our women to the car where Conn and Colm waited to take them back to our building. Colm gave me a subtle nod, letting me know our guy was at the bar.

I shook his hand and got close. "Call my pops and tell him to spread the word."

"Aye, sir."

It was time our local crews knew what was going on and that I was going to take care of them.

"Be careful." Emilia jumped up and kissed my cheek before she got in the car with Aunt Anne.

Be careful.

I couldn't promise her that. I'd *been* careful...for the past eight fucking years.

"Drinks are on me, Uncle." I clapped a hand on John's back and ushered him back into the restaurant.

Our table in the back had been cleared from dinner, and a waiter was there asking if we wanted anything to drink.

"A Jameson for me, cheers." I took my seat again. From my side of the table, I could see most of the restaurant. John had his back to the place, a spot he sure as fuck wasn't used to.

"I think I'll try that tiramisu," John said. "Coffee with a splash of whiskey too."

The waiter left, and I leaned back in my chair.

"So."

He sighed and fanned out his napkin under the table. "You're enjoying this too much, Finn."

"I don't think that's possible, John." I scratched my eyebrow slowly. "But how about I let you talk first? Tell me what you need from us."

The twitch in his eye and the tightness of his features told me how much he hated the position he'd found himself in. For years, he'd had everything handed to him. People came to him. He snapped his fingers, and he got waited upon.

Those days were over.

"The Avellino family isn't solely my problem," he told me. "You have to realize it's ours to deal with. If Gio wanted me dead and to

361

be done with it, he would've come to Chicago. Instead, he targeted you; he crossed a line and made himself known to your fiancée."

I didn't reply. It was better to watch him dig himself a grave.

Again, the Italians couldn't have known they were stopping Emilia. She'd been driving my car. Now, did they know about her? Abso-fucking-lutely. I believed she was a card neither of us knew how to play. With the exception of John, 'cause he didn't know her background whatsoever.

"We have to come together for this, Finn," he said. "We have to show our men—and the Italians—that the Sons of Munster are united, and we have to take the Avellinos out."

I smirked a little to myself and shifted in my seat. "Good speech." Behind him, the waiter was returning with our drinks and John's dessert. "You don't mind if I speak plainly, do you?"

He hid his impatience with a wave of his hand, and he sat back as the waiter put his tiramisu in front of him.

"Anything else I can get you, gentlemen?" he wondered.

I shook my head and waited until he was gone.

Christ, I barely knew where to begin.

As I swirled the whiskey in my glass, it caught in the glow from the candle on the table and threw amber-colored sparks across my palm. It reminded me of the flecks of bronze in Emilia's eyes.

"A few months ago," I murmured, keeping my eyes on the liquid, "we flushed out a Murray in Pat's crew. You remember Gary Lindsey, don't you?" I didn't wait for his response. "See, I had this feeling someone was watching me, either to make sure I failed and went back to prison or to just keep tabs."

"Finnegan," he said, affronted, "I'm not in the habit of spying on my own syndicate. He couldn't have been a Murray—or an O'Shea, for that matter—if he betrayed you."

"Right." I grinned and took a swig of my drink. "Just like you would never have my grandfather killed. Or your own pop."

His glare was instant.

I stared right back, no longer intimidated by him. I'd merely voiced what was on the mind of virtually every O'Shea and had been for years now.

"How dare you," he whispered furiously. "I came here in peace—"

"And I *piss* on that." Fury unleashed within me, and I returned his glare. "You took an organization our families have built up over generations, and you fucked us all. The reason the Murrays and the O'Sheas have been able to create our fortunes is because we've worked together and followed traditions. But you just couldn't do it, could you? You had to destroy everything—"

"I did no such thing." He banged his fist against the table, causing his spoon to rattle on his plate. We'd also gained the attention of a few couples nearby. "Clearly, you are too young to be reasoned with. This was a mistake. I have to speak to your father instead."

"Actually, I'm at the perfect age to handle this. Perfect age to remember how many O'Sheas dropped like flies, perfect age not to be taken for a ride by the smoke you blow up our asses." I paused to rein in my temper, and I adjusted my tie. "An idiot would sense the rift between our families, John. Why do you think it's there?"

He had absolutely no response. He gnashed his teeth together, the vein in his forehead bulging, and turned a shade or two redder.

"I'll tell you why it's there." I leaned forward and looked him dead in the eye. "It's because no one in the O'Shea family trusts the management. It's because we lost brothers, fathers, sons, grandfathers, and husbands back then. It's because not even a couple women and a four-year-old girl getting caught in the crossfire stopped you."

I sat back again and threw back half my drink.

"We know it was you, John. End of discussion."

He breathed deeply and dropped his glare to the table. I could practically see the wheels turning. Because he still needed us.

He was gonna grasp at straws next, and I was right. He shook his head and claimed, in disbelief, that he wouldn't be alive if the majority of the O'Sheas thought him a traitor. So I was polite enough to point out he'd had a lot of us locked up, but this didn't fucking matter. Unlike the Murrays, the O'Sheas stuck together. Any single person who wanted John dead could've popped him many times over by now, and then where would we be today?

John would be six feet under. We wouldn't have any dealings in Chicago. We'd be a smaller syndicate. We'd be less of a threat. Soon enough, outsiders would challenge our positions. More lives would be lost. Money would be gone. No, John and his but-what-ifs could go to hell.

"I stand by my innocence," he said.

I looked around us. "I don't see it anywhere."

Man, I frustrated him. "Finnegan, I'm sure you would've preferred Gio getting the seat back then, but—"

"I didn't say that," I interrupted. "He wouldn't have gotten the ticket either. Only your pop was gonna give him his vote. The other fourteen would've landed on you or that cousin of yours in Galway." I knew my grandfather never would've let a goddamn Italian take over from him.

"Or that cousin of mine in Galway," he repeated pointedly. "The Sons barely know him by name, but because he pulled off a few heists here in the eighties, he was praised. What if he'd gotten the seat?"

"Then he would've been boss right now." I shrugged. "Ronan had no intention of retiring before the new boss had been groomed." I pointed at him. "You took that away from him because you felt it had to be you."

"And I've kept our streets clear—"

"By screwing over half your own syndicate." I shook my head. "You would've had our help and trust—no questions asked—if you'd followed protocol. You shot yourself in the foot, uncle. Now where y'at?" I widened my arms. "You need our help to deal with the Avellinos that you supposedly kept our streets clear from—up until now. We don't even know how much they've learned about us or how long they've been here." Making eye contact with one of my boys at the bar, I jerked my chin at him.

John took another breath and pushed away his plate. Poor fuck, I'd killed his appetite.

He flinched when noticing we'd gotten company, and I accepted the tablet from my mate.

"Cheers, that'd be all." I pressed the main button and swiped past the screensaver. "This is how it's gonna be, John." I showed him the screen, where he could see half a dozen surveillance cameras inside some of his locations and operations. In front of each camera, an O'Shea or two was greeting him. Either by waving, smirking, saluting, or, uh, flipping him off. To be fair, Adam had lost both his brother and father because of John. He wasn't happy. "The O'Sheas are gonna make a move one way or another. Whether it's against you or with you is your choice."

"Is that—how did they get *in?*" John was visibly rattled and upset, and I bet he hated swallowing that anger. With his wrists touching the table, he flexed his fingers and said, "Okay, okay. Now we're here, and we have this problem. Do you suggest we deal with it separately? Do you want us to lose our numbers and split into two clans?"

That *was* going to happen sooner or later if the Murrays didn't agree to some permanent changes, but we weren't there yet.

I set the tablet facedown next to my drink. "No. I suggest you tell me what you need, and then I'll tell you what it's gonna cost you."

He chuckled humorlessly and wiped his mouth with his napkin. "Your grandfather groomed you well, boy. When did you figure out he saw you as the next O'Shea in charge?"

I didn't miss a beat. "Around the time you had him murdered." I lifted a shoulder. "Call me a slow learner."

In retrospect, I knew my folks had tried to protect me from it for as long as possible. Now, I could think back on certain things and see the plans Ronan had for me.

Pop had pointed it out a few times lately. He'd known since I was a kid.

"I didn't—" John cut himself off. Wise choice. More denial from him, and I might've offed him right here. "I'm not ready to retire."

Oh good, we were getting somewhere.

"I'm not ready to be the face of the syndicate yet either," I replied. "I am ready to call the shots about certain things, though. I'm sure we can come to an understanding."

He didn't exactly have much of a choice.

I had to admire the balls he had, however. He thought we'd force him to retire...? Fucking precious. He was lucky to be alive for a bit longer, that was all. I'd wanted this since the day I was sentenced. I wasn't gonna rush it now.

Additionally, better he was Gio's main target instead of me.

"The Avellinos need to be wiped out," he said. "My men aren't trained enough to handle it on their own."

I nodded slowly, thinking. "For that to happen, I gotta know every piece of information you have on the Avellino family. Locations, numbers, safe houses, operations, whatever you got. You also gotta send your low-men who are of age to Philly, 'cause fuck if I'm gonna put my own blood on the front line." There were casualties in every war, but the Murrays were gonna take the biggest hit. "Oh, and the Philly crews don't give you a cut of their profits anymore, and your bookies and loaners are gonna cut their vigs by five percent to anyone with O'Shea affiliation."

My uncle knew he'd been defeated. "Anything else?"

"You kidding? We're just getting started." I smirked and lifted my glass. "By the time we're done, you're gonna have to remind yourself I'm still your nephew and that you can't wait to show up at my wedding with a nice gift. I trust you've checked the registry. My princess worked hard on it."

chapter
29

Emilia Porter

"I can't get that freaking song out of my head," I mumbled, disappearing into our closet. It didn't help that I'd caught Finnegan whistling it to himself several times since Wednesday. Then tonight, at the rehearsal dinner, he and Patrick had performed it for approximately eighty of their closest family and associates.

It was one thing if it'd been a cheerful song, but this was some haunting, solemn crap that tightened a knot in my stomach. Everyone who worked with Finnegan and Patrick had stood up and bowed their heads.

It'd completely thrown me, even though the moment had lasted only two minutes, because I didn't think it'd been in celebration of the wedding. The rehearsal dinner had been over shortly after, and everyone had seemed eager to shake hands with Finnegan to exchange words.

"Did you say something, princess?" Finnegan asked from the bedroom.

"Yeah." I threw some underwear and pajamas into a bag. "The song you played on the tin whistle tonight, wouldn't it have been more fitting for a funeral?" Even Patrick had been atypically solemn on his guitar.

Finnegan chuckled quietly, and when I exited the closet, I found him lying on the bed, hands underneath his head, suit still on. Tie loosened, shirt untucked, shoes on the floor.

He'd been...a bit different since his meeting with John. More introspective, yet his spirits seemed to be at their normal high setting. Every time I asked if something had happened—if something was wrong—he shook his head and hugged me close.

"No...everything is perfect. It's exactly how it should be."

"I don't want you to go." He sat up and motioned for me to come to him. "It's a stupid fucking tradition that the bride and groom don't spend the last night together."

His feet hit the floor by the foot of the bed, and I stepped between his legs and threaded my fingers through his hair. My overnight bag landed on the bed.

He'd shaved yesterday, but he hadn't lost an ounce of his chiseled looks. I found myself touching his jaw often, feeling the shadow of his dark stubble.

"Are you nervous?" I asked softly.

He shook his head and pressed his face to my stomach. "It'll hit me tomorrow, I reckon." His hands came up my thighs and snuck under my dress. "What would I do without you, Emilia?"

"Find another butt to grope?"

I felt his smile rather than saw it, and he pinched one of my butt cheeks.

"Look at me," I murmured. He looked up, resting his chin on the belt that went around my dress. "Are you sure you're okay?"

I could *see* he was okay. Perfectly at ease and relaxed. Yet, there was that new air around him.

"My dreams are coming true. I'm fucking fantastic."

"But something did happen with John, didn't it?" I didn't know what to make of the Murrays. I freaking adored Alec and Nessa, and I knew both Finnegan and Patrick were close with Liam

Murray. Then there were John and Anne. John had been perfectly charming and polite, his accent as noticeable as his kids'. Anne was...colder. Formal. And seemed to have very little interest in the kids she called her own.

"Good things," Finnegan promised. "Well, on our end."

That was almost as ominous as the song they'd played tonight.

"Whistler." I poked his nose.

His mouth twisted up. "Did you know people called my grandfather that sometimes?"

I shook my head.

"He was the one who gave me my first tin whistle," he murmured. I remembered that part from the photo of Finnegan and Ronan in our house at the compound. "He told me whistlers were always bearers of news, and the music could convey exactly what kind of news it was."

The knot in my stomach grew heavier, and it hit me that I was worried. For Finnegan. No one could forget that John had supposedly slain his own father and Finnegan's grandpa. And now I was afraid. On the evening before my wedding to a mobster. Christ almighty.

"Did you convey any news tonight with that song?" I wondered.

He narrowed his eyes with a pinch of amusement. "Maybe." He squeezed my butt. "You don't have to worry, though. Our safety is my top priority."

I did trust him on that. If there was one thing he'd proven, it was how protective he was of me.

"Goddamn mobsters," I sighed.

That earned me another pinch. "Alleged."

I snorted a soft laugh. "I think we're well past that, hon."

"Maybe you're right. Gimme a kiss." He waited expectantly until I dipped down and kissed him silly. That drew a smile from him. "Don't stand me up tomorrow. I'll be the one in the penguin suit holding a ring box I can't open."

I laughed and pecked him a couple more times, then straightened and grabbed my bag. "I was wondering when you were going to bring that up."

I had to give him some credit for not opening it. I had no doubt he could.

"I finally saw the note underneath the safe," he mentioned, following me down the stairs. "'From your favorite thief?'"

"That's me," I sang. "Consider it your only hint."

"So basically, you're putting a new Aston key ring on my finger?"

"Ha! You wish." I gave my surroundings a glance, wondering if I'd forgotten anything. It was just one night, and Grace had my wedding dress and shoes, Sarah had my lingerie, and the stylist would have all the beauty products I could need.

We'd be back here tomorrow after the reception...no, I didn't think I had to bring anything else.

Finnegan insisted on escorting me to the garage. Apparently, the security I saw everywhere just didn't cut it.

"Have I mentioned the tradition where we spend tonight separated sucks?" he asked in the elevator.

"A few times." I smirked up at him. "But you love your traditions."

"Not this one."

I shook my head, pretending to be concerned. "Say we skip it and spend tonight together. Where does it end? Before you know it, we're smoking crack."

He let out a loud laugh and squeezed me to him. "Fuck, how I adore you."

"Can I return that sentiment, or are you gonna bitch about that too?"

He bit my nose, eyes glittering with warmth and humor. "You can return it if it's legit."

I popped a kiss to his chin. "It's so legit. I adore you."

And I'll tell you tomorrow...that I love you too.

"No, Emilia!" Vivian gasped.

I froze. With my fork in midair.

I wanted to whine because I was starving. This morning had been busy as hell, and there was no breakfast. There was, however, a big brunch set up in my suite, and right now Vivian was in the way.

"No carbs," she said, walking over to snatch the fork out of my hand. "You need better food than that if you want to make it through the day."

I sulked and said buh-bye to my delicious fries.

Instead, I was given a bowl of strawberries, a plate of scrambled eggs, another plate with vegetables and a damn steak, and lastly a smoothie and a glass of orange juice.

"I'll barf if I eat all this," I said frankly.

Sarah and Grace laughed at me.

"Eat until you're full, dear." Vivian patted me on the head.

I had curlers in my hair and looked like a dork.

"Picture time!" Nessa barged into the suite, and I could only grin. She and Alec were giving us the coolest wedding gift. They'd set up a private Instagram account where the guests could follow our big day. More than that, it connected Finnegan and me because we got glimpses of each other.

When today was over, the twins were going to put it all together in a photo book for us, including captions and some of the funnier comments from the guests.

Alec had posted most recently, and it'd been one of those funny videos that'd been sped up on a loop. It was Finnegan pacing quickly in our living room, wearing only a towel, ending with him taking a shot of what looked like whiskey. In the background, Kellan had been holding up two ties. Alec had written a short description, saying the groom was nervous and pissed because *some* people—Alec—were allowed to text the bride, while Finnegan had been banned.

"Make sure the dress isn't in the shot, please," she said. "Let's make it funny!"

Grace wheeled away the luggage cart on which the dress hung, and I was joined on the couch by Sarah and Vivian.

"Does it get funnier than PJs and curlers?" Sarah asked.

"Uh, shyeah." I snorted and stuffed my cheeks with food. "Watch and learn."

By the time Nessa took the picture, I looked like a hamster in the face, if they crossed their eyes, and I was doing the West Coast gang sign to get a laugh from Finnegan.

What a way to show off my freshly and Frenchly manicured nails.

"Now I just gotta swallow," I said around a mouthful of strawberries.

"Struggle with that a lot, do ya?" Sarah teased.

I waggled my eyebrows. "No, it's gotten so much easier."

"That's my son you're talking about." Grace stuck her fingers in her ears.

"I thought they were talking about strawberries?" Nessa looked at us, confused, only to shake her head and find an empty spot on the coffee table to sit. "Look! The first comments have come in. I swear, Finn is waiting for you to post."

"Let me see?" I was still chewing.

She showed me the post and Finnegan's comment, and I got a giggle from his response.

You're ready for the church already, and I haven't gotten dressed yet. What the fuck?

Wouldn't that be something, if I walked down the aisle in PJs.

"Breathe, honey."

"I'm fucking trying."

"Need a paper bag?"

"Give it to me." I breathed like a pregnant lady. Holy shit, the nerves had hit hard. Like a cannonball in the gut the second we'd entered the church.

Sarah left to go hunt down a paper bag, and now it was just me in the small room behind the entrance of the church. A full-length mirror was making it impossible to forget what day it was.

I mean, I'd had butterflies for days, but this...this was something else. Dinosaur birds were flying around in my stomach.

The last picture I'd seen of Finnegan was him in his three-piece suit, standing before a mirror with a look of solemn concentration. He was so beautiful and handsome and about to become my husband.

Would we get three years or a lifetime?

Everything was coming down to this. In a few months, I'd gone from hating him to falling in love and fearing he was going to crush me.

"Oh God." I caught another glimpse of my reflection, where I looked more perfect than I felt. My hair was down, teasing my chest in gorgeous waves. The bodice of my dress was like a crushing hug, and the rest was layers upon layers of silk and lace. Nothing puffy for me, although there was a top skirt that had an impressive train. Thankfully, with help, I'd have it detached before the reception.

Outside the heavy door, I could hear the guests arriving. Guests that would fill the church on both sides of the aisle, not one of them here for me. Or rather, from my side. I brought nothing to this family, and a small, wounded part of me struggled to get past that. I hadn't heard from my dad in months, and the main reason I hadn't extended an invitation was because I knew he'd throw it away.

I was stupid for thinking about it, I knew that.

Sarah reentered, raising the volume of the guests trying to get into the church.

"I didn't find a paper bag," she said, and Grace appeared next to her. "I found something better."

"My beautiful girl." Grace was already tearing up. She walked up to me and dug out a flask from her purple clutch. It matched her dress. "All you need is this, dearie."

"Alcohol," I stated.

"Mmhm." She nodded encouragingly. "Have a sip or two."

I removed the cap and took a whiff. *Oof.* "What is this? It's strong."

"Two parts vodka, one part vodka, two-thirds of a part vodka—and a splash of lemon syrup because we're not animals."

She drew the first laugh from me since I set foot in the church, and I took a tentative sip. Ugh, gross and perfect. I made a face and took another swig.

"Phew." I scrunched my face together and handed back the flask. "Is Finnegan okay?"

"He's so nervous, bless him." Grace tucked away the booze and smiled fondly. "The boys are greeting the guests, and he keeps glancing this way and forgetting to respond to people."

That made me feel better.

The door opened again, and Vivian snuck inside. "Time for last-minute preparations," she sang. Her color for the wedding was yellow, and her silky dress was so pretty. "Grace, hon, you brought the 'something old,' yes?"

"Christ, you guys," I complained. "You're gonna make me cry already, aren't you?"

"Shush, dearie." Grace smirked and opened her clutch again.

Something old. A family heirloom from the Murrays. From Grace and John's grandmother, to be exact, a lovely pearl brooch Grace attached to the satin ribbon under my chest.

Something new. A gift from Finnegan that Vivian brought me. It was a stunning necklace with a diamond-encrusted infinity symbol.

My eyes welled up. Three years didn't mean infinity.

"Don't you dare," Sarah said.

I sucked in a breath and nodded jerkily. I could weep later, but God, the bastard better not break my heart. I wanted this so much.

Something borrowed. A hairpin that Shan had given Viv after her First Communion. Little stones were embedded in the old silver, and I fastened it to my hair carefully.

Something blue. I could finally relax. This was a gift from Sarah. A bridal garter. Light blue lace. I grinned as I slid it onto my thigh, and I couldn't wait for Finnegan's expression.

"Thank—"

"Oh, we're not done, sweets." Viv produced what looked like a small coin.

"Because we're Irish," Grace said with a twinkle in her eye. "An old penny in your shoe. It's for good luck."

I laughed softly and dropped the penny into one of my heels.

We hugged it out, and I thanked them over and over for being here for me before it was time for Grace and Vivian to go take their seats. It gave me a moment alone with Sarah, my one link from the past.

"Are you ready?"

I took a trembling breath and nodded once. "I'm ready."

We could convey enough by looking at each other. In a month, it would be her. We were nervous as hell and had two uncertain futures ahead of us, and it was something we had to accept. There was nothing we could do to secure any part of the years to come.

"We're better off now," she whispered, resting her forehead to mine. "We did the right thing."

When thinking of Finnegan, my heart was in charge. I could only agree and admit the defeat of my logical mind.

"We're gonna be sisters." I smiled and did my best not to get weepy.

Sarah beamed at me, her eyes glistening. "I'm gonna need a sister to lean on when Patrick drives me crazy."

I laughed and nodded, feeling for her—a little. Patrick, it

seemed, was dead set on winning Sarah over by being as open as he could. He was essentially doing what Finnegan had done, with the exception that Patrick was trying to get all this accomplished in a few weeks. It'd led to some interesting mishaps and fights. But it was going in the right direction, and Sarah was a lot more relaxed around Patrick these days. More often than not, I'd go up to their penthouse and find them bantering and laughing.

It gave me hope.

A knock on the door made everything ten times more real. It was Shan, and he snuck in, holding my flowers. A bouquet of roses in light shades of pink, yellow, white, and purple.

Luna followed and offered a grin and a wave.

This was it.

Sarah and Luna helped me with the veil and reminded me that Finnegan would meet Shan and me before we reached the altar. It was something about the Catholics and that the bride wasn't given away but entered the marriage voluntarily and walked the last bit to the altar with her groom. I nodded and took deep breaths at each instruction. In case I forgot, the prayer Finnegan and I were reading together was tucked into the bottom of my bouquet. Father O'Malley would be there to guide us too.

"Let's not overwhelm her, girls," Shan said kindly yet pointedly. He smiled warmly and walked over to me while the ladies excused themselves to wait outside. "You look lovely, Emilia."

"Thank you." I wasn't going to hyperventilate, I wasn't going to hyperventilate. "And thank you for doing this, for walking me down the aisle."

"Are you kidding me? Greatest honor I've had in years." He was trying to make me relax, and it worked to an extent. "Are you ready to make my son the luckiest man on the planet?"

I grinned, so fucking nervous I could cry, and nodded a final time. Gripping the flowers tightly, I took his proffered arm and let him guide me out of the room. The music was starting, soft sounds of violins and piano, and the wedding coordinator had just given Alec and Nessa their cue to walk.

"Knock 'em dead, darlin." Kellan flashed me a wink before it was his turn to go, and Luna followed a couple seconds later.

Knock 'em dead.

Right. Possibly literally, if I fell on my ass.

When Sarah had gone, it was only Shan and me left.

"You'll be fine, hon." Shan patted my arm soothingly.

"I need more vodka," I whispered.

He coughed on a chuckle, and then it was time to go. I didn't look very far down the aisle because I couldn't. The low whoosh that traveled through the pews was enough to know I had everyone's attention. *Don't trip, don't trip.* I focused solely on Shan's steps. Slow, measured steps. Wow, he truly did walk slowly. Or perhaps it was me who felt the need to rush.

Halfway down the aisle, I had to look up.

Oh God, oh God, oh God.

My throat closed up at the sight of Finnegan, and he instantly became blurry for me. He was waiting for me, a tic or two letting me know he wasn't very patient. Hands clasped in front of him, feet shifting slightly because he was struggling to stand still. He swallowed hard and smiled crookedly.

I was reminded of Shan's presence when we reached Finnegan. Words were exchanged, but I couldn't for the life of me interpret them. My ears were ringing, and I wondered if a bomb was about to explode in my stomach. Then Finnegan lifted my veil, and I could see clearer. I could see he was as nervous as I was.

"You didn't stand me up," he whispered.

My smile was so wide it hurt my cheeks, and I shook my head.

"I have no words for how beautiful you are." He pressed a quick kiss to my forehead before taking my hand. Oh, clammy. We were both clammy. Shan was gone, I assumed. I only saw Finnegan, and we walked toward the altar together where Father O'Malley was waiting with bridesmaids, groomsman, maid of honor, and best man.

During the rehearsal, I'd paid more attention to the blessings, prayers, and readings from Father O'Malley. Today, I picked up a word here and there, that was it.

The women who spoke of their weddings online were right. It was a day to freaking forget. I'd been looking for tips and ideas, and I kept seeing wife after wife throwing out "LOLs" because they didn't remember the actual wedding.

May God be with you and bless you.
May you see your children's children.
May you be poor in misfortunes and rich in blessings.
May you know nothing but happiness,
from this day forward.

That was my cue to hand over the flowers to Sarah.

Father O'Malley spoke again, as both my hands found Finnegan's. "In addition to their vows, Finnegan and Emilia have chosen to recite a lovely prayer that Shannon and Grace once read at their wedding. Ages and ages ago." For a priest, he rocked. No one could withhold their chuckles at his little dig. "They bring you, The Irish Vow of Unity."

I thought I was going to forget the words, but they flowed easily, and I never once looked away from Finnegan's eyes.

"We swear by the peace and love to stand," Finnegan murmured.

"Heart to heart and hand in hand," I replied softly.

He squeezed my hands, his eyes becoming misty. "Mark, O Spirit, and hear us now."

"Confirming this, our Sacred Vow," I finished.

Father O'Malley presented a candle for us that we lit together, and then we went through the traditional vows. We got to say "I do," and that was when the first tear rolled down my cheek.

Finnegan kept me steady, my hands firmly in his, but it was his intense gaze that caused me to get emotional.

"Let us exchange rings," Father O'Malley said with a smile, "and repeat after me."

I released a pent-up breath and accepted the ring box from Patrick.

Finnegan didn't have to struggle as much to get my ring from the little box.

I had a code to remember. Oh right, okay, good, I got it. Whew.

Finnegan went first, saying the words that'd been spoken millions of times before, yet always felt personal to the one who received them. His fingers shook slightly as he slid down the elegant ring to join my engagement ring.

I flexed my fingers and stared at the sparkly stuff happening on my ring finger, and there was a good dose of disbelief. I was getting *married*. I was eighteen years old and getting married, and that disbelief echoed in my head as I was the one who repeated after Father O'Malley.

Eighteen years old—holy shit. This wasn't normal anymore—not today in this time and age—so why wasn't I running for the hills? Why did I not even want to? It wasn't a contract that held me in place. It hadn't been for a while.

Before I slipped the platinum band onto his finger, I took a nervous step closer and looked up at him. Meanwhile, he was peering down at the ring between my fingers, or more correctly, the inscription inside of it.

Tá mo chroí istigh ionat. Yours, Emilia

I'd stolen the words from him. They were the same ones he'd written in one of his letters to me, and I could think of no better declaration to steal from my mobster. The literal translation, *my heart is within you*, beat the dozen meanings the English language gave the saying. It rang the truest.

Finnegan jumped the gun, cupped my face, and kissed me hard. "I don't think I can believe it."

"I'll make you believe it," I whispered back.

He exhaled a laugh and discreetly wiped his cheek, and I finally got the ring onto his finger.

A few nervous heartbeats later, we were declared husband and wife.

chapter 30

Finnegan O'Shea

"Oh my God, we just left the guys in the dust."

"Literally," I chuckled, and I didn't give one flying fuck. The limo pulled away with the instruction to take all the detours the driver could find on the way back to downtown Philly. "Come here." This was why. The plan to have the whole wedding party in one limo had been scrapped because my girl—my *wife*—had told me her heart was mine. "I need to hear it."

She grinned into the kiss I gave her, and her cheeks turned an exquisite shade of pink. "I love you."

Motherfuck, I had no words. The tension of the day, the tension of the past few *months*, rolled off me. "I'm gonna need daily reminders if I'm ever going to believe that."

"I can make that happen." A yawn left her, and she was immediately horrified. "I'm so sorry—"

I cut her off with a soft laugh and a hard kiss, only glad we were on the same page. Getting married was fucking *exhausting*. I'd been a wreck and hadn't slept much last night, so this suited me perfectly. Tucking her close and helping her get rid of her veil, I sank down a bit in my seat and held her to me.

"Is it weird I'm glad it's over?" I touched a lock of her hair that teased her cleavage, twisting it between my fingers.

"No, there's so much pressure. I feared I was gonna trip."

I smiled and covered her mouth with mine. Her worry was cute. Meanwhile, I'd legit worried she was going to get cold feet, rethink the whole thing, and bail.

"I love you, princess."

Her smile matched mine, and it was all silly as hell. "I love you too, Whistler."

I chuckled. "So that nickname's sticking, huh?"

"I think so. Yeah." She nipped at my bottom lip and slipped a hand up my chest. "Yeah, it fits. As long as you only bring me good news."

Oh, definitely not going there on our wedding day.

An hour later, we got word from my mother who demanded we get our behinds to the hotel. Everyone had arrived and was waiting for us.

It'd been one of the best hours. Emilia and I had cuddled it up good, made out, gotten rid of her ridiculously long train, exchanged yawns, and confirmed we were both starving.

"Viv wouldn't let me have fries for brunch," she said, leaning forward to touch up her makeup. Or rather, removing her lipstick because I'd smeared it everywhere.

"Yeah, well, I threw up my breakfast." I adjusted my vest and straightened my suit jacket. "Pat kept giving me shots of whiskey to kill the nerves."

It hadn't worked.

Emilia snorted and sent me a smirk over her shoulder.

Christ, look at her. My wife.

We pulled up to the hotel, and part of me wasn't ready. I

should've skipped the reception and whisked her away on our honeymoon right away.

"Can you believe we're married?" she mused.

"Barely." But I was looking forward to letting it settle.

While I'd known her only a few months, she'd been my future wife for over two years. Now she had my name.

"Come on, Mrs. O'Shea. Dinner awaits." I kissed her hand and exited the car. Three guards were standing near the entrance, keeping watch.

I ushered her inside quickly, and we were shown to the ballroom on the top floor. The wedding coordinator, who appeared to be permanently attached to her phone and headset, was waiting for us there. She told us my pop was talking, which we could hear through the closed doors. Warming up the crowd while they waited or something.

Somehow, he was given the green light to introduce us, and Emilia squeezed my hand.

"And now, it's my honor not only to welcome Emilia into our family, but also to introduce her and Finn as husband and wife for the first time. Everyone, please stand up and raise your glasses for Mr. and Mrs. O'Shea!"

The doors were opened, and we were met by nearly three hundred people applauding and toasting for us.

Wanting Emilia closer, I put my arm around her and kissed her temple. My chest felt tight with emotion, though I managed to keep it in, thank fuck. Emilia had already made me mushy once today.

"I can't believe this is happening," she chuckled shakily.

I guided her between the countless round tables where most of the guests sat, across the dance floor in the middle, and because I was me... I spun Emilia around and earned myself a yelp from her.

"My stunning wife, everyone." I bowed like a fucking gentleman and kissed the top of her hand. "May she bust my chops for decades to come."

The men cheered louder.

I winked at her blush—and the scowl she couldn't hold—then put her out of her misery. Unlike me, she wasn't very comfortable with the attention. Of course, that made me wanna put her under a spotlight.

A long table was waiting for us in the back, and our immediate family had been seated there. There were two chairs for us in the middle, and a waiter was quick to serve us drinks. Pat had no doubt told them what beer I wanted, and someone had made sure Emilia had a soda and a vodka cranberry ready for her.

"What happened to us riding in the limo with you guys?" Alec had to raise his voice from his seat a few feet down my side of the table.

"My bad, I guess we forgot you," I replied.

He shook his fist at me, and I wiped away a fake tear.

I'd been in charge of hiring a DJ because one, weddings bands generally consisted of shitty musicians, and two, I didn't want a bunch of teen pop songs played at my wedding. Music was a language, and when my words failed, there was always a legend somewhere who could let Emilia know what was on my mind. Said DJ had set up his shit next to the stage to the right, and as the wait-staff began serving entrees, he played songs I'd approved of. On low volume 'cause my mother...she was the spokesperson for the senior citizens who wanted to eat without shouting across the table to be heard.

The stage was prepared for later. A baby grand stood there, along with a chair for Alec and his guitar case and violin case.

"Hey. You're quiet." Emilia leaned close and kissed my cheek.

"I'm perfectly content." I kissed her nose and sat back with my beer. "And hungrier than a kid in Africa."

"Finnegan!" She was already starting, and I could only laugh. "That was in poor taste."

I winked and chugged my beer.

Dinner was delicious and drawn out by speeches and toasts, and not the funny kind of toasts. I ate two servings of a fancy lamb dish and half of Emilia's seared salmon while I listened to associates and ass-kissers deliver blessings and welcome Emilia to the family.

John went on for almost seven minutes about the importance of family and how he couldn't wait for all the christenings to come.

"I'm so stuffed." Emilia clutched her stomach and blew out a breath.

"You barely ate anything, midget."

"Dude, feel how tight this bodice is."

"I would love to feel how tight your body is." I grinned.

She did her cute girl thing where I got a slap on my arm and she gigglesnorted and shook her head. *"Bodice."*

"Body." I dipped down and nuzzled her jaw, taking a playful bite.

Great time to get interrupted by the wedding photographer who not only wanted to capture the best moments but obviously break them up too.

"Can I help you, mate?" I stared at him.

He could consider himself lucky that my mother chose that moment to clink her glass.

Someone was quick to hand her the microphone.

"Can I have everyone's attention?" She turned to Emilia and me with a warm smile. "My husband and my youngest son—I'm very sorry, Patrick—were born with romance in their hearts." I smiled and clapped Patrick on the back. He scoffed. "Whether they speak through music or words, they always know what to say—and when to strike." She paused and raised her glass at my brother. "As for my sweet Patrick, I'm sure he's got something grand planned for his speech, for which his brother will want to throttle him." Chuckles traveled through the ballroom. "That's how it goes in our family. The boys are up to no good, and I keep them in line."

I smirked as the women around us applauded. Emilia snickered and hugged my bicep, her chin landing on my shoulder.

"Emilia has finally joined us to help me with that," Ma went on. "Someone have mercy on you heathens because we won't." Fuck, I loved that woman. "Keeping them in line sometimes includes telling them to go where the sun doesn't shine, but for now, my darling Finn, I'm only telling you to lead Emilia to the floor for your first dance as husband and wife."

That, I could do.

I removed my napkin from my lap and tossed it on the table, then left my seat to make Emilia blush again. I bowed and extended my hand to her.

"You're all freaking sorcerers," she whispered and took my hand. It wasn't the first time she'd told me that, and I prayed for a lifetime of having that effect on her. God knew she had it on me.

The lights dimmed in the ballroom, except for a few spotlights on the dance floor, and the first notes of the song I'd picked for this filled the air. Eric Clapton knew a thing or two about how to tell someone how wonderful they looked.

Once on the dance floor, I gave Emilia a soft spin before pulling her close to my body.

"Hey, wife." I pressed my forehead to hers and kissed her smile.

"Hi, husband."

I parted my lips to respond, only to realize there was nothing else to say. We would get one song before family cut in for an hour of dancing, and I wanted to enjoy it. The cake hadn't been wheeled in yet, and I was ready to take Emilia home.

If I'd known this beforehand, I wouldn't have made plans to crank up the party later on, 'cause I wasn't sure we'd still be here.

"What're you thinking?" she asked softly.

"That I have this whole playlist that was gonna turn this place into the third class on the Titanic, but I'm ready to steal you away."

She laughed under her breath, and I gave her another twirl.

"I hope you mean that the Irish know how to party and not so much about the iceberg that crashed said party."

"Yeah, that part kinda killed the mood," I chuckled.

She hummed and dropped her forehead to my sternum. "I'd make room for you on that door raft thing."

See? We were meant to be.

"I bet you wouldn't be stupid and drop the diamond in the ocean either," I murmured.

"Jesus Christ, no. I mean, who does that?"

I cracked a grin and pressed a kiss to the top of her head.

We danced the rest of the song in silence, and I grew more determined to sneak her out of here early. Two more hours, tops. Then she'd be mine for the next thirty-six hours.

As the song drew to a close, Pop appeared with a hand on my shoulder.

"Don't shoot." He offered a smirk.

I laughed through my nose and reluctantly let him cut in. "Holler if you need to be rescued, princess. I'll come running."

My mother was on her way over too, but before she talked my ear off during our dance, I needed a status report. Pat was the closest, so I walked over to our table in lieu of finishing my beer, and I asked him if everything was good.

"It is now," he replied with a nod. "Someone was lurking around the delivery bay, but he's gone."

"Hm." I guess I needed to drain my beer, after all.

"We've got this covered, little brother. Enjoy your wedding."

I nodded with a dip of my chin, unsatisfied, but there wasn't much I could do about it right now. "Ask your girl to dance." Walking toward the end of the table, I joined up with my mother and gave her a twirl too. They always made her smile widely.

"Sweet Finn." The woman was already getting emotional—or maybe I should say, again. "Did you pick this song?"

"Of course I did." I smiled down at her, leading her closer to the middle of the floor where Pop and Emilia were dancing. He was making her laugh at something. I refocused on my mother and the Etta James tune that was playing. "You and Pop danced to it at your wedding."

She sighed contentedly. "We did a good job with you—for the most part."

"A fantastic job."

"Let's not push it, dear. You're still as mad as a ditch and a bit of a dick." She patted my chest, and I snorted a laugh.

"My mother, everyone." I shook my head, chuckling. "Eh, you know what they say. Rather a dick like me than thick like Pat."

She smacked me upside the head, and that was how easily we had people's attention. "Don't you call your brother an idiot, boy. He's just...comfortable."

I literally had to bite down on my lip to keep from guffawing. *Comfortable.* Yeah, that was one way of putting it—although he'd been doing a hell of a lot better lately.

"Whatever, I'm your favorite."

She smirked wryly and adjusted my tie. "The trick to raising hellion sons is to make both children feel like they're their mother's favorite. In reality, the mother prays for the day they get married."

"One down then, eh?" I spun her around, causing her dress to flare out.

She tittered a breathless laugh and supported herself on me. "One down, one to go," she confirmed. "Don't forget to let her come up for air tomorrow."

Yeah, there was no way I was going to discuss my sex life with my mother, so I merely nodded.

"We'll have brunch together on Monday before your flight," she went on.

"Yes, ma'am." I wasn't gonna win this one anyway. If I had my way, we'd be leaving tonight—or tomorrow. But I supposed I could suffer through brunch with the family before the honeymoon. "Will you get some cake boxed up for us before we head out tonight?"

"Of course, sweetheart." She smiled at the other couples who'd joined us on the floor by now. "Some leftovers too?"

"Fuck, yeah." I kissed her on the forehead. "Don't come and say I'm not your favorite, Ma. Everyone knows it."

She shook her head at me, mirth swimming in her eyes. "You're certainly something, Finn."

Aye, her favorite.

Emilia and I got to cut the cake with everyone watching, and I *didn't* ruin her dress; I only smeared some frosting across her cheek. She, on the other hand, got cake on my suit jacket, so I lost it somewhere. Just as well. After dessert, there'd be more dancing, and Alec and I were playing for Emilia.

The spotlight was hot, and my twelve-year-old cub was sampling the champagne. He'd shed both his jacket and vest at this point, and his cheeks were rosy.

Before our little gig, I was shoveling cake and coffee into my mouth, and waiters left trays of pastries and liqueurs on our table that had to be tested too.

"If you eat any more than that, you won't make it to the stage, hon." Emilia was having fun watching us guys eat.

"Ye of little faith." I patted her on the head and bit into a cannoli.

"You gotta try this one." Kellan pushed another tray of something from his spot on the other side of Patrick. "The one with chocolate flakes."

He spoke my language. "Motherfuck, this is some good shit."

"Patrick, maybe you should slow down?" Sarah leaned forward, eyeing Pat as if he was gonna explode. Not an entirely wrong presumption.

"In a minute, babe." He had to try the chocolate flake pastry too. "One more, and then I'm gonna give my toast."

"I mean, she's not completely out there," I reasoned. "Sarah's the one who's gotta deal with your lactose intolerance."

"Oh my God." Emilia cracked up. "Seriously?"

"Seriously," Sarah groaned. "He always forgets to take his pills."

"Shite," my brother said. "I knew I'd forgotten something."

I slipped Sarah a couple of those small bottles of vodka. They couldn't hurt.

"Okay, I'm ready." Patrick wiped his mouth on a napkin and stood up with his glass of untouched champagne. "Someone gimme a—cheers." I'd handed him my spoon, 'cause I was a good little brother.

While he started clinking his glass, Emilia scooted closer to me, and I put my arm around her shoulders.

"Oi!" he yelled. "If I clink my glass any harder, it's gonna fuckin' break!"

I turned my head to muffle my amusement in Emilia's hair.

Someone finally came over with the microphone, and I braced myself to be roasted.

"Is this gonna hurt you?" Emilia asked. By the look in her eyes, I could tell she hoped it would.

"Probably," I chuckled. "And you're supposed to be on my side."

"Oh, I am. Technically."

Great.

The dessert chatter died down, and everyone gave my brother a platform to be a dick to me.

"As the best man and older brother of the groom, it's my honor and my *job* to make Finn suffer," he said, much to everyone's sadistic pleasure. What fucking bitches we had in our family. Where was the love? "I can go on for hours about the hell he's raised since we were kids, but since it's my turn to sit where he's sitting in a month, I'm going to keep this brief. And hopefully, he'll remember I spared his ass and limited the digs to the last few months."

I merely smirked, 'cause I was making no fucking promises.

"Who can forget," Patrick went on, "how Finnegan couldn't even score a date with Emilia on his own. He needed Kellan there to lay the groundwork by pretending to be someone else—an unbiased source, if you will." Oh, that motherfucker was going down. "So while Kellan was convincing Emilia to let Finn take her to dinner, my brother was at his house removing every trace of Kellan. Photos came down from the walls, a toothbrush vanished from the guest bath, and then he was shipped all the way to Chicago so Emilia wouldn't figure out they were all but brothers."

He wasn't sparing me for *shit*. He was, however, sparing Emilia, and for that I was grateful. She was giggling up a storm next to me, and the guests were enjoying the storytelling.

"Of course, seeing as Kellan is sitting right here..." Patrick gave Kellan's shoulder a squeeze. "Emilia eventually learned the truth, and the wrath of this chick—let me tell you, she annihilated them both."

"Yeah, she did!" my mother hollered.

I shook my head at the hate and pressed another kiss to Emilia's hair. She was having fun, way too much fun.

"I like this version of the story way better," she giggled.

I pinched her thigh.

"My boy Kellan escaped with scratches and bruised balls," Patrick said with a grin, "and Finnegan spent five days in the doghouse. Man, was he a miserable fuck without her."

Kellan leaned back, speaking behind Patrick. "Payback in a month?"

I bumped his fist. "Of fucking course, mate."

Patrick wasn't done. "He spent his days watching Spanish soap operas, binging on Twinkies, and writing love letters to Emilia." He raised his glass and soaked up the laughter all around. "And somewhere in that hole he'd dug himself, he realized he was never going to find another girl like Emilia. He'd met his match, and he did everything to win her back." He turned his smile to Emilia next. "Watching you two fall in love has been a gift, guys. I have no doubt you'll keep his ass in check, sweetheart, just like he'll drive you crazy the way I think you secretly like it. To Finnegan and Emilia, *sláinte mhaith!*"

"*Sláinte!*"

Well, fuck. Did he really have to go for the kill at the end? Amusement and annoyance mingled with the love I had for my brother, which sort of summed it up pretty well. If he wasn't cracking me up, he was pissing me off, and I wouldn't have it any other way.

I rose from my seat and hugged him. "I love you, you ugly brute."

"Love you too, kid." He clapped me on the back and left a loud smooch on my cheek. "Away wit'chu, I wanna hug my sister-in-law."

I stepped to the side, and he wrapped my wife in a bear hug. Her eyes had welled up at some point, though now he was drawing giggles from her. He had that effect.

chapter 31

Finnegan O'Shea

W ith all the speeches out of the way, I dragged Alec up on the stage, mostly to play a couple songs for my wife, and now partly to get him away from the champagne. It was cute when he snuck his first glass and thought no one was watching. Now he was hiccupping.

"Are you sure you can play, cub?" I chuckled.

"Sh't'up, 'm Irish, boss." He grinned goofily and unpacked his violin and guitar from the cases. "Only had me one glass, swear."

I gripped his chin and stared him down. "What do you swear on, son?"

He blinked. "Me mum's diet?"

I laughed and gave his cheek a playful smack. "Just don't mess up the tunes too much. I'm collecting brownie points here."

The DJ killed the music as I sat down behind the piano.

"What whistle do you want for the other song, boss?" Alec held up my case of tin whistles.

"Give me the Clarke."

"C or D?"

I snatched up the latter from him and set it atop the piano. Then I adjusted the microphone.

"Hey!" Alec loved the spotlight more than I did, and he handled the talkin'. "Finn's gonna serenade me future wife with two songs we've been pact—practising. He got into Emilia's Spotimefy—Spotify—to see what songs she liked."

I hung my head, chuckled, and pinched the bridge of my nose. That fucking kid. He wasn't supposed to tell them that last part.

"Have you been stickin' to Coke, boy?" John asked, amused.

"It's rude to interrupt, Dad!" Alec complained.

"All right, you lush." I tugged on his back pocket until he fell into his chair. "What Alec said," I spoke into my mic, "I'm going to serenade his next wife. So when I fuck up, she can look back on today and give me another shot."

"That's forward-thinking, mate!" I heard Colm holler from somewhere.

"Got into my Spotify *how*?" Well, that was Emilia, and evidently, I was already fucking up.

It had been way back when our devices had been synced. She'd had a whole playlist with just this song, so I figured it was because she liked it. It helped that it was a romantic song. More than that, it was a song I could foresee playing for her again, when I'd *really* fucked up. In the words of some British chick magnet named Calum Scott, "You Are the Reason."

Instead of answering her, I eased into the slow song, my fingers traveling across the keys. I heard Emilia's soft "oh" when she realized what song it was.

Some of the guests chose to dance, some of them watched from their tables, and some—Emilia included—gathered closer. She stood with my mother and Luna, the two whispering back and forth while the princess never looked away from me.

Right in this moment, it was easy to picture our life together. We were young and in love, I sang of shaking hands, the mountains I'd climb for her, racing minds, and how hopeless I was for her, and everything was perfect. A moment to remember. A moment to remind her of one day.

Alec, our favorite little drunk, didn't mess up even once. He'd been playing the violin since he was four and could probably do it in his sleep.

The second and last song was going to be interesting. He'd chosen it, his favorite Declan Galbraith tune, and he'd both sing and play the guitar while I would give Emilia another reason to call me her whistler.

I played the last notes before Alec finished the song, and we were met by applause and awwwing women. Those who'd been married twenty to thirty years took the opportunity to ask their men why they never did anything like that. *Score.*

"You ready, cub?" I turned away from the piano a bit, one leg on each side of the bench, and picked up my whistle.

"Yeah, I'm not nervous at all, boss." He swallowed hard and got seated with his guitar, and Patrick walked up to lower his mic for him.

"Look at it this way, champ," my brother told him. "Chances are one of the preteens here tonight is your actual next wife. You'll have them lining up for you."

"I've got me eyes on her already." Alec regained his confidence and shot Emilia a wink.

I'd give him until he hit puberty. Then those jokes would be less funny.

For now, I was happy to let him flirt with my blushing bride and turn our guests into devoted fans. 'Cause he had the voice of a fucking angel, which was fitting considering the title of the song. I remembered being praised for my own singing voice as a kid, and then I turned thirteen and everything went to shite.

Sensing that Alec was still nervous, I counted him in, my foot tapping lightly in his field of vision, and I was ready to play the intro twice in case he missed his cue.

I'd worried for nothing in the end, and it took him approximately twenty seconds to steal the show. He sang with his eyes closed to shut everyone out, and I could tell he had practiced on his guitar at home. Watching him almost made me miss my own cue to the next chorus, and I shook my head at myself and played alongside him.

He hit the wrong chord in the chorus, though I doubted anyone else noticed. It was just as his voice reached the high notes, sending an epidemic of goose bumps through the ballroom. Because it couldn't have been only me.

Once it was over, he opened his eyes and gave me the biggest grin, and I nodded for him to take a bow and collect the cheers. Then I stood up, and he closed the distance and hugged me tightly.

"I'm so proud of you, cub." I ruffled his hair and kissed the top of his head before he was off to soak up the attention.

Emilia was waiting for me as I stepped off the stage, and she snaked her arms around my middle. "Whistler...?" She was biting her lip and staring at me strangely, her cheeks flushed and eyes a shade darker.

"Princess." I lifted a brow, unsure of how to read her.

She cleared her throat. "I have a bunch of stuff going on inside me right now that I can't really describe. The playing, seeing how you are with Alec—in short, is it too soon for you to take me home?"

Ah, fucking victory. I quirked a grin and rubbed my nose to hers. "I can sneak you out in less than a minute if you want."

"If I take off my heels, I can run," she replied.

I let out a laugh and hugged her to me. "You go. I'm gonna let Pop know, and then I'll meet up with you at the elevators."

"Just like that?" Now she hesitated. "Isn't it rude—"

I cut her off with a kiss, because fuck rude. We were newlyweds. Sneaking out was practically an unwritten rule.

"Go. Now." I smacked her on the ass.

She went.

I watched her disappear between the tables and out the doors, then walked over to where Pop was expecting me. He was doing shots with Ian.

"Oh—get him one," Ian said quietly.

"You're leaving us." Pop smirked knowingly and poured a third glass. "I'm a little surprised you stayed this long."

"That makes two of us." I accepted the glass and threw it back. "Fuck," I coughed. Was this some of Ian's homemade shit? My throat was on fire. "I wanted an update—okay, that's fucking vile. The aftertaste is—"

"Not why one drinks it." Ian winked and leaned back in his chair. "You'll feel the effects of it soon."

Wonderful. I slid my gaze to Pop and cocked a brow.

"Everything's good, son. As Patrick sometimes says, calm your tits. You can go make us some grandbabies."

Aw, my father was smashed. He was a funny drunk.

"No one will bother you until Monday at ten thirty," Ian promised. "We'll be there to pick you up for brunch with the family. When's your flight?"

"At six," I replied. "All right, brunch. We'll be there."

Pop wagged a wobbly finger at me. "Does your uncle know you're grooming Alec?"

I chuckled at his drunk ass and leaned over the table to smack a smooch on his forehead. "Tell Ma I love her, and call if there's an emergency."

A couple associates wanted to talk on my way out, so I said I was just going to the bathroom, and then I sidled up to Emilia and two Dubliners by the elevators. Colm had only had a couple beers, and Conn was stone-cold sober.

I'd make it up to him soon.

"What's this?" I gestured at the wrapped gift in Emilia's hands, and I took it from her to carry it. It was heavy and solid and felt like a gigantic book.

"Luna saw me leaving and said we wouldn't wanna wait to open her gift."

"Oh, really." We stepped into the elevator, and I tore at the wrapping. "What the fresh fuck." It *was* a book.

Colm and Conn started laughing.

It was a book on sex positions.

"Oh my God," Emilia guffawed. "Baby, we have to bring that on our honeymoon."

I side-eyed her and smiled, warmth spreading in my chest. And everywhere. It was the first time she'd called me that—okay, but the warmth was more of a liquid heat, and it tingled weirdly. I cleared my throat and loosened my tie. What the *fuck* had been in that shot?

When the elevator stopped, I draped an arm around Emilia's shoulders and ushered her out and through the large lobby. A handful of our guys were spread out, all of them alert. Our car was already pulled up, and Colm and Conn took it from there. The driver that'd taken us from the church to the hotel handed over the keys and said something to them that I couldn't hear.

In the meantime, I became acutely aware of Emilia being tucked so close to me.

Colm opened the door for us, and I clapped him on the shoulder.

"Hit that mute button, mate."

He smirked and inclined his head.

On the seats by the partition—that I made sure was closed—was a stack of Styrofoam boxes. Bless my mother, there would be leftovers and cake later.

The filthy fuck book ended up next to the boxes, and I took my seat with Emilia. We were going to take this slowly; I wasn't gonna maul her and act like a teenager. Her hand came to my chest, and she pressed a soft kiss to my neck, whispering that she'd had an amazing time tonight. I agreed, though I was finding it difficult to form words. The heat kept spreading wherever she touched me, and my heart rate was already spiking.

I was gonna kill Ian.

My gaze flicked to her cleavage, to her exposed shoulders and arms, to her leg and how it was crossed sexily over the other under her wedding dress.

"Are you okay?" She nuzzled my jaw, which made it impossible to focus on the concern in her voice. Was she seducing me or just being affectionate because we'd gotten married today? I couldn't fucking tell.

I swallowed and unbuttoned the top button in my dress shirt. "Yeah, I'm fine. It's kinda hot, innit?"

"Feels fine to me. But you're in a suit," she offered. "My dress is thinner, and I'm bare up here now."

I hadn't noticed...

My brain was suddenly slammed with images of her naked body writhing underneath me. Tonight there would be nothing holding me back, and I wasn't about to remind her that she wasn't a hundred percent safe yet with her dumbass birth control. She'd said it would be up to six weeks, a milestone we hadn't crossed yet.

Those thoughts were pushing slow and steady out the window, and I cupped her cheek and kissed her deeply. The thirst for her was in-fucking-sane. I wanted my mouth and tongue on every inch of her sweet body, I wanted to lick and suck and watch the shivers run through her, I wanted to fuck her into next week.

She was taken off guard by the force of my kiss but quickly caught on and pressed herself up against me.

"I need something." Even I reacted to the urgency in my voice. "Fuck." I slid my hand up her thigh and swept my tongue into her mouth—I paused momentarily. "What's this?" There was a strap of something high up on her thigh.

Emilia flushed, her breathing unsteady. "My garter? We, um, left before we could throw it—and the bouquet."

Nothing of hers would be thrown anywhere. And fuck slow, I had to get a look. Before I knew what I was doing, my knees hit the floor of the car, and I was inching between her legs.

She cursed and white-knuckled the black leather seats.

I touched her teasingly to take in her reactions. My fingers ghosted along her calves under the dress.

"Lift your dress for me, Emilia," I ordered softly.

She swallowed hard and hiked up the layers of lace and silk, revealing soft, smooth, flawless skin. My cock grew thicker and harder in my pants, and I kneaded her thighs unhurriedly, letting the desire course through me and take over.

A light blue scrap of lace with little ribbons on it came into view, and I had to stifle a groan.

Hooking my fingers where her knees bent, I pulled her closer to the edge of the seat. I dipped down and began leaving a trail of openmouthed kisses along her thigh. Emilia gasped when I reached the bridal garter, and I was nothing if not a traditional man. I removed it slowly with my teeth until it slipped down her calf. Then I was back to kissing her thighs, my hands pushing up the dress farther until I saw the sheer thong she was wearing.

I didn't give it a second thought. Parting her legs farther, I pressed my lips to her pussy and sucked on her sweet flesh through the fabric. Emilia gasped again and exhaled around a moan.

Our time was limited, and it became my excuse to get a quick fix. Pushing aside the thong, I ate her beautiful little cunt in greedy strokes of my tongue. She whimpered and squirmed against me, her fingers finding their grip in my hair. I wrapped my lips around her clit and flicked my tongue over it, around in circles, pressing down on it.

With two fingers curling inside her, I had her crying out her orgasm moments later.

The one piece of advice that'd stuck with me from my teenage years when my parents gave me the mandatory sex talk was something Pop had mentioned offhandedly. The bedroom was the last place to be arrogant, so I wasn't gonna pretend to be an expert. I was going to get off no matter what; Emilia needed more.

It was time to break out the sex toys.

Emilia blushed, one part champagne and one part embarrassment, when she showed me the box in the drawer of her nightstand. To be honest, I'd expected some shit I'd seen in porn. These toys were nothing like it.

Were they vibrators or fucking art in a museum? I snatched up the smallest of the three vibes, one she stumbled through an explanation about being for the clit, and it reminded me of a bean or computer mouse. The white plastic surface was smooth, with one end of the toy dipped in silicone. It fit in my palm and was shaped exactly like many swimming pools.

"Are you sure this is a sex toy?" I stared at it skeptically.

She pursed her lips and pressed the button in the middle of it, and it buzzed to life. "Um, pretty sure."

"Damn." How could a guy compete with this frenetic little fucker?

I could worry about that later. So far, so good. I'd remembered to carry her over the threshold and everything. Now I had to ensure—

"Hey." Emilia stepped up to me and kissed my chin, her fingers starting to unbutton my vest. "Stop thinking you have to make everything perfect for me. The fact that we're in this together is more than enough. We'll have years to practice our own perfect."

Man, she had low standards. Or perhaps I had high ones. Either way, I could use this to my advantage. I could show her.

Turning off the toy for now, I refocused on her and kissed her. I unzipped her dress and helped her out of it, and she did the same for me. My suit landed on the floor, and we landed on the bed.

"I, um, I'm a fan of the ripping off the Band-Aid method," she mumbled against my lips.

I hummed and kissed my way down to her chest. "I haven't even gotten you out of your lingerie yet."

"I know, I'm just sayin'."

She was cute when she was nervous. All the more reason to take our time. I wanted her body ready and her mind relaxed.

I got her there eventually, by distracting her thoroughly. I barely let her come up for air between drugging kisses and the slip and slide of our bodies. We'd gotten rid of our underwear, and the second my cock was nestled against her wet pussy, the insane thirst was back. Like a beast buried under my skin, demanding more and more. Whoever that fucker was, he liked the idea of ripping off the Band-Aid.

I let out a hiss when she drew her nails down my chest and teased her tongue around my nipples. I couldn't take another ounce of excitement. It was a goddamn miracle I hadn't bent her over and taken her like an animal yet.

"Lie back down," I whispered roughly.

She was too gorgeous, her hair fanned out across my pillow.

I reached for the toy and switched it on, slipping it between us so it was trapped and pushing on her clit.

She whimpered. "Now, Finnegan. I need you."

I took a deep breath and gave my cock a few strokes, then coated it in her arousal. The smooth lips of her pussy were less soft, filled with blood and sensitive nerves. I teased her with my fingers, and each little move caused her to react. She breathed my name, let out one of her cute little whines, and shifted her hips to meet me. She wouldn't get more ready than this.

I leaned over her and covered her mouth with mine. "Say you love me."

She shuddered. "I love you."

Fuck yes.

I forced my way inside of her in one long thrust and blinded myself with the pleasure that exploded within me and pulsed around my cock. *Fuck...ing* hell. My eyes closed, and a groan escaped me. *So tight.* Underneath me, Emilia had gone stiff, her fingers digging into my biceps.

My voice came out tense. "Are you okay?" My lips brushed against hers as I spoke, and I willed my heart rate to calm the fuck down. She didn't need me to lose my shit.

"Yes." Sweet little liar. Her features were pinched in pain. She took a shaky breath and looked at me with so much vulnerability shining through. "It, um, *ow*—it hurts more than I thought it would."

"I'm sorry, baby." I shifted carefully over the vibrator so it applied more pressure on her clit.

She gasped and instinctively arched her back, and I fucking felt her. How she tightened around me. It was a goddamn chain reaction, and I accidentally pushed deeper into her and buried my face against her neck. The sensations shot through me, sharp and all-consuming.

"I'm sorry," I repeated through gnashed teeth. "But fuck, you feel so good."

"I'm glad you think so," she moaned. "Giving birth is gonna suck."

I groaned around a strained laugh and grabbed her jaw, 'cause I had to get my mouth on her. "I love you so much, you random dork."

She giggled through the pain, and her eyes glistened. "I feel better. A little. Just…"

"I'll be careful." I kissed her softly and brushed a thumb under her eye. "We're in no rush."

She evidently was. She wiggled under me and adjusted her toy, sending a violent shudder through her. A faint flush spread over her chest, and I couldn't help myself. I cupped her breast and ghosted my lips across her puckering nipple. She was warming up; she was relaxing. I heard it by her sounds too, as they became breathier and less tense.

Withdrawing from her slowly, I grazed my teeth around her nipple and teased it with my tongue before I entered her again. Her pain made a swift return, but this time, I was more prepared. I distracted her body with my mouth and fingers, kissing her until she gasped for air, sucking on her tits until she was moaning, and pushing my pelvis against the vibrator until she was begging for more.

I fucked her unhurriedly, for both our sakes, and let myself take from her. She spurred me on by snaking her feet around my calves and raking her nails across my shoulder blades.

"That toy is gonna do me in too," I grunted. "Fuck." The buzzing vibrations traveled up my shaft, heating up my entire fucking crotch until I was the one who was ready to beg. "I don't wanna come yet." I pulled out of her and planted my ass on the mattress, the vibrator buzzing in my hand. "Come here. I wanna get handsy."

She smiled, breathing heavily, and climbed on top of me. Fuck, she was glorious. Naked and flushed, she sat down carefully and took me inside her. I slipped the toy between us and circled her clit with it, and it made her forget the soreness easier.

"That's it..." I eye-fucked her as she swiveled her hips. Wrapping her hair around my fist, I gently tugged back so she arched into me. Her hands landed on my knees. Neck exposed, perky tits in my face, thighs cradling my hips, tight pussy taking my cock. "Look at you, Emilia." I stroked a hand up her stomach, between her breasts, until I got my fingers loosely around her throat.

She whimpered and tried to speed up, but I gripped her hip instead to slow her down.

"Finnegan..." she pleaded.

"I can't have you finish me off yet, baby girl." I let go of her hair so I could make sure she came again. I rubbed the toy over her clit in teasing strokes— "No, lean back like that. I wanna watch you." Her body couldn't be legal. Those smooth, wet lips were spread for my cock, and I could see every inch she took of me. I kept rubbing her clit slowly, knowing the vibrations were driving her bonkers. Her breathing changed. Impatience and need rolled off of her. "You want more?"

"Yes!"

I sucked in a breath and yanked her in for a hard kiss, and I told her to fuck herself on me. She took control of the toy and clutched at my shoulder with her free hand, and I tasted her like a starving man. The kiss became frenzied and intoxicating. I forgot myself around her. Self-restraint flew out the window. Before I knew it, my hands were on her addictive ass, and I was pushing her down on my cock.

"I'm close," she panted into the kiss. "Fuck, I hurt. Ow—I need more."

That wasn't confusing at all.

I pulled her closer, not letting her shift away from the vibrator, and she fell forward. Her lips touched my neck, her breathing unsteady. She ground against me, which shoved me closer to the edge. "Let me feel you," I said, out of breath. "Goddamn, you're gonna make me come."

I clenched my jaw as the ball of churning pleasure dropped lower.

I felt her pussy tightening around me, and she tensed up right before she came. She stopped breathing and pressed against me to the point where she started shaking, and I had to fight my orgasm.

"Finn—oh *God*..."

I lost it. With two fistfuls of her ass, I threw her down on the mattress, her head landing along the foot of the bed. Then I was hitching an arm under her knee and slamming into her. I fucked her hard, and the orgasm took over. The heat exploded. I pushed my cock deeper as ropes of come rushed up my shaft in sharp pulses.

I was thrown by the possessiveness that surged through me. For a second, I felt like a fucking savage who was claiming his prey. My body went rigid, every muscle in me protesting and aching.

Emilia trembled and squirmed, little whimpers slipping out between her gasps, and it hit me that the toy was no longer comfortable. She breathed out that she was sensitive, and I managed to turn it off before throwing it on the mattress next to us.

I swallowed dryly and shuddered. "You okay?" I wasn't sure I could get out another word. I could barely breathe, for fuck's sake. It was as if I hadn't exercised in years.

She nodded quickly. "I hurt everywhere, but it's...different. Don't move yet."

Oh, good. I wasn't sure I could.

chapter
32

Emilia O'Shea

I woke up Monday morning, one giant ache, as Finnegan shifted closer behind me and kissed my neck.

"Hold your horse peen," I croaked. "We agreed to rest today."

He laughed silently against my skin and cupped my breast. "Have I told you lately that I love you?"

Yes, about two hours ago when he'd woken me up for another round of sex. Or maybe I'd woken him; that was beside the point. That whole area between my legs was now off-limits for a day or two.

The stinging pain as he stretched me was bizarrely hot and turned me on like nothing else, but I just couldn't.

"I'm gonna let you rest." He kissed my hair, which no doubt looked like a bird's nest. "I got a message from Patrick, and I have to go to my office for a bit."

I frowned and scrubbed the sleep from my face, then twisted my body to look at him. "Everything okay?"

He nodded and pressed his lips to my forehead. "He received some weird call from Chicago—nothing to worry about. I'll meet you guys at the restaurant."

I was too tired to worry, and honestly, excited to have the shower to myself, so I kissed him back and told him to be careful.

The next time I woke up, I was alone, and I walked unsteadily into the bathroom.

Ouch.

I squinted at my reflection in the mirror. My hair was a freaking mess.

The happiness in my eyes was unmistakable, though.

Yesterday, we'd gotten everything we wanted. A whole day of nobody disturbing us. Food from the wedding, lots of cake and pastries, and even more sex. As a joke, we'd made a list of spots in the condo to christen, and we'd ticked off a few boxes.

The one thing we were supposed to do was pack, which we hadn't. I'd have to do that after brunch. Our weddings gifts were arriving today too... So much to do, so little time.

With one of two insatiable newlyweds missing, there was no cock-y surprise for me in the shower. I took my time and used all the organic products I could find that promised to be nice to my skin.

Aloe and shea butter were my friends.

When I was finished, I found myself in our closet picking out the softest clothes. Cotton panties, a bra without underwire. How the fuck had I gotten pinch marks everywh—never mind. The insides of my thighs were a scruff burn party, so I went with a pair of capri-length leggings. All the cotton. Soft, soft cotton. I borrowed one of Finnegan's button-downs and turned it into a short dress with a belt around my middle.

My hair went up in a haphazard bun.

As I did my makeup, I sent Finnegan a text.

I married an abusive Irish boy. I have marks every-where! xo

I finished applying the eyeliner and saw he'd replied.

Four guys pointed out the bite marks on my neck,

***and my back looks like a scratching post for cats.
Takes an abuser to know one, kitten shit. ;)***

I snickered to myself. "Good times."

Sarah knocked on the door shortly after, and I let her in,
surprised to see one of Finnegan's guys right outside the door.

"Um, hi. Can I help you?" I asked.

"No, ma'am. Finnegan and Patrick are just taking some precautions," he replied.

"There's one outside our door too," Sarah said. "Patrick said I
had nothing to worry about, though."

Uh-huh. I'd heard that before.

Well, we had heaps of leftovers in the fridge that were going to
go bad while we were away, so I might as well make myself useful.
We had some time before brunch, and these boys had to eat at
some point.

"So...?" Sarah stared at me expectantly and followed me to the
kitchen. "This is where you tell me everything."

I chuckled and opened the fridge. "My body is a wonderland of
scruff burns and handprints."

She waggled her eyebrows. "You guys went rough, huh?
Patrick's already told me Finnegan looks like a mess, and I *know*
what Luna gave you at the wedding."

Oh God. "Shut up." I shook my head in amusement and got out
the fixings to make a bunch of hoagies and sandwiches. For the
record, we hadn't opened that book yet. "Help me empty our fridge
instead—and tell me what you guys did yesterday."

As far as I knew, the only contact Finnegan had with the
outside world yesterday was when he arranged a quick party for
those who'd worked the wedding. All the leftover booze and snacks
had been delivered to Mick's pub. I'd suggested sending over a few
strippers too, to which I'd earned a WTF-look from my husband.

What? Boys liked strippers.

"We went to Mick's for a little while. Not much else." She

shrugged. "The so-called important people flew back to Chicago, so we had to see them off—or a few of them."

I nodded and rolled up the sleeves of my makeshift dress, then got busy filling bread with leftover lamb, gravy, vegetables, and cheese. We had some salmon and turkey too that we used up with the last of the bread.

"Excited about the honeymoon?" she asked, wrapping the hoagies. I followed her with a Sharpie, writing down what meat was in them.

"So much, and I don't even know where we're going." All I knew was to pack for the beach and the bedroom, in the words of Finnegan.

"It's like you still work at the diner, hon," she chuckled.

I capped the marker and stuck my tongue out at her.

With close to a dozen lunches, I picked one of my bigger purses and only needed one paper bag for the ones that didn't fit. Then I received a message from Grace, saying they were almost here, so it was time to go.

"Christ, look at you, Em," Sarah laughed softly. "Are you already pregnant?"

"What're you talking about?" I got my phone, keys, and wallet and left the condo. The dude was still there. "Hi again. Lamb, salmon, or turkey? Just pick a favorite."

He was understandably confused. "Uh, turkey, I guess?"

I dug out a turkey sandwich for him. "Lunch."

His mouth twitched. "Thank you, Mrs. O'Shea."

Oh...that was me now. Wow. That was going to take some getting used to.

I couldn't shake the giddiness of it all.

Sarah and I went into the elevator, and she picked up the conversation again, noting that I was "glowing" and literally mothering street thugs.

I brushed it off, because my brain couldn't handle that topic now. I didn't see them as thugs, and I knew I used to. I was *supposed* to. These days, I saw security, men with families, sons, and friends of Finnegan.

I was fucked.

I'd always liked taking care of people. The difference was, I hadn't had a choice before.

"I'm definitely not pregnant," I settled for saying.

We paused on the ground floor to hand out more lunches and to say hi to Olivier at the front desk. I left a few sandwiches with him for when other lurking Sons stepped out of the shadows to take a break or whatever.

Sarah and I became the sandwich saviors, dubbed by a guy only a year or two older than us, who looked hungover. Probably from last night.

By the time we reached the garage, there were two left.

"Mornin', darlin'." Colm opened the door for us with a charming grin, making me giggle. If I lifted his shades, I bet I'd see how hungover he was too. "How are ya?"

"Better than you, I think." I opened my bag and retrieved the last two hoagies. Conn was seated on the passenger's side, and he barely managed a two-finger wave.

"Jaysus—you're a godsend, Emilia. Cheers."

"The other one is for your brother."

"We'll see about that." He smirked tiredly.

I chuckled and slipped into the car. "Hi, brunch people." I got settled in one of the two empty seats. Sarah ended up next to me, leaving Grace and Ian across from us. "Where's Shan?"

"He'll meet us at the restaurant." Grace wore the same smile she'd donned at the wedding. It was as if she couldn't shake it. "How's married life?"

"Blissful so far," I laughed. "I hope the trouble doesn't begin until after the honeymoon."

"You never know in this family," Ian replied with a wry smile. "Has Finn spilled the beans about where you're going yet?"

I shook my head. "The man is a vault." I didn't mind the

surprise, to be honest. It was going to be a good one. "I might bribe Sarah over to help me pack."

"Because it takes two to pack a dozen bikinis and a Kama Sutra book," Sarah teased.

"You—!" I slapped her arm, mortified. "We're not bringing that!" We were totally bringing that, but there was no need to let Finnegan's *mother* know.

Grace and Ian merely laughed.

I slumped back in my seat and huffed. Outside my window, the streets of Philadelphia were relatively empty, given the hour. Tourists and some people who weren't working took their time going wherever they were off to. And I was sitting here in an armored limo. How quickly life could change.

"I asked Finnegan how long we'd be driving around in these tanks, and he said there's no expiration date on his worry."

"That sounds like Finn." Grace's eyes shone with as much amusement as fondness. "It's better we just enjoy the pampering for a while."

I guess so.

"Plus, there's nothing like disappointing the good people of Philly every time we leave the car," Sarah said. "I swear, I see someone eyeing me curiously then shrugging when they don't recognize me."

"I know!" I'd thought it was just me! "You always expect someone famous to be inside a limo. And then it's only us."

The partition behind me was lowered, and Colm spoke with his mouth full of food, causing his accent to come out thicker. "I'll drop you at the next light. Conn will escort you inside, and I'll be there after finding parking if that's all right."

"That sounds great, dearie," Grace said.

We waited in comfortable silence until the car slowed down again, just in time for the light to turn yellow. Grace was scolded by Ian for opening the door herself.

"You men, I swear." She sighed and pretended to be a good girl.

I stifled a grin, and she waited for Conn to round the car and open the door farther. "Oh, so it's okay to come out now?"

"Yes, ma'am." Mirth seeped into Conn's voice, and he helped her out of the car.

Ian scooted closer to exit next.

A weird popping sound went off, and I glanced outside. For such a low sound, it had a sharp echo that flew between the buildings. Then it sounded again—*pop, pop, pop, pop, pop*—and whatever it was, it catapulted the men into action. I grew rigid in my seat as Ian threw himself out of the car; Conn shouted for his brother, who was out of the driver's seat already. Sarah's nails dug into my arm. Someone screamed, the sound shrill and packed with agony.

"Conn, no!" The booming voice belonged to Colm.

"Oh my God," Sarah breathed.

The shock and confusion had me in a vise grip, but I managed to scramble closer to the door, and what I saw filled me with dread. They'd been fucking *shots*. Grace was on the ground with Ian on top of her, and before I knew it, there was another round of fire. This time, I heard it clearly.

Mayhem broke out. Three men ran out of the restaurant we were parked outside of.

Sarah screamed, and it shook me out of my state. Adrenaline and horror flooded me, and I tried to get out.

"Grace!" Holy fuck, holy fuck, holy fuck. I had to get to her, I had to get to her, but then Sarah was pulling me back.

"You can't go out there!" she yelled.

"Get them out of here!" someone barked out.

"Ian!"

"Conn—"

"*Fuck.*"

I didn't know where I got the strength from, but I managed to push myself out the door, away from Sarah, away from someone yelling at me. All I saw were Grace and Ian, and I crawled over to them. Frenzy set in at the sight of the pooling blood.

413

"Call 911!" I shouted. Grabbing at Ian's shoulder, I got him to roll off of Grace, and tears filled my eyes. He was alive. "You're alive, you're alive." Without thinking, I pressed a hand to where blood was quickly staining his white shirt, the spot growing larger and larger. "We need help over here! *Hey*! Someone help!"

A car skidded somewhere behind me, knocking something over —a trash can. I flinched at the crash but couldn't tear my eyes away from Ian. He was coughing up blood and mumbling incoherently about "his unit" and the "fucking desert."

"Ian, stay with me. Okay? You're here." The fright in my own voice reached my ears and caused my hands to tremble. My vision became blurry, my throat closed up.

"G-Grace," he coughed.

"She's fine, she's fine, she's fine," I rambled. "Don't speak. Help is on the way."

I didn't know the first thing about first aid. All I could do was hope I didn't make things worse. I tried to clear Ian's airway, positioning him so his back was straight, and I applied pressure to his wound.

A couple blocks away, sirens started blaring.

"Ian!" Shan! I heard him. I heard him. He was here.

Flicking a panicked glance at Grace, I felt myself moving. Because she wasn't. No, no, no, no, no. Bile rose within, and I pushed it down. There was so much blood—too much of it.

"Grace," I choked. Someone tried to pull me away, and I screamed. "Get the *fuck* away from me!" No, this couldn't be happening. "Grace, wake up! Wake up!" I cradled her head in my lap and frantically wiped away the blood from her chest and stomach. "No, no, no, no! Someone help me, goddammit!"

"No, no, no—fuck—*no*." It was Shan. He took over from me, and I fell back on the sidewalk. "No—oh God, sweetheart, no."

"They're not dead!" I heard myself yell.

So why the fuck did Shan look anguished? Fury and grief had

struck him across the face, and he tried to hold both Grace and Ian to him. He checked for their pulses, heartbeats, and their injuries.

"Emilia!"

The next thing I knew, I was airborne and thrown into another car. Pain spread along my spine, and I cried out. Then again—fuck, shit, fuck!—my ankle throbbed.

"Emilia, talk to me. Fuck, baby, where are you hurt?" Oh God, it was Finnegan. He scrambled off of me and immediately held me to his chest. We were a pile on the floor, and he wouldn't stop touching my face. "There's blood everywhere—tell me—"

"It's not mine," I managed to get out in a strangled voice. "It's not mine. Your mom—" My voice broke, and I let out a sob.

The sirens took over, the lights flooded the street, the chaos became too much, people wouldn't stop shouting, and no one would fucking let me get to Grace and Ian.

"Look at me, Emilia." Finnegan gripped my chin, his eyes searching my face. He had tears rolling down his cheeks, and it completely shattered me. "Are—fuck. Are you sure you're not hurt?"

"I'm sure. It's not my blood. But Grace...oh God—" I started weeping like a goddamn baby.

"I know." He held me tightly, and every time his body rocked with his silent cries, I thought I was going to die. Never in my life had I experienced this kind of pain. "We gotta get to the hospital," he said hoarsely. "Colm! You good to drive?"

Her eyes had been open. Flashes of the sights I'd just seen were drilled into my skull, one by one, lasting only a second. It paralyzed me, and everything else ceased to exist. My hands were sticky and covered in blood, and they wouldn't stop shaking. Grace's eyes had been open. Her eyes—I'd seen them yet refused to acknowledge them. I'd only paid attention to stopping the bleeding.

Now I couldn't stop picturing her eyes. Those green-blue eyes that'd danced with happiness a few moments ago.

"I'm gonna be sick," I choked out. A second later, I leaned away from Finnegan and emptied my stomach.

Grace and Ian were both pronounced dead at the hospital.

The paramedics had detected a weak pulse in Ian at the scene, and they had worked on him on the way, but he didn't make it. He'd been shot twice in the back, both bullets going straight through. Grace had died quickly, according to the doctors. With three bullets in her back and chest.

White-hot hatred simmered below the surface as I was forced to go through a medical examination. Other than some cuts and scrapes on my legs and a mildly twisted ankle, I was fine. Physically. My heart felt like it'd taken a bullet or two.

I looked as bad as I felt, though the blood was easily cleaned off.

Finnegan refused to leave my side, even though I knew he wanted to be with his mother.

"You sure she's okay." He asked for clarification for the tenth time.

The doctor nodded. "She might be in shock, but she'll be fine, Mr. O'Shea. Keep an eye on her, that's all. It's very possible she will need some counseling. I would recommend it, regardless. What she witnessed is never easy."

"I'm fucking fine," I whispered. "Can we go now?"

It took Finnegan another couple of minutes' worth of reassuring from the doctor, and we were finally out of there. I walked carefully on my weak foot, Finnegan's tight grip on my hand speaking volumes of what was going through his head.

We took the elevator upstairs to where we were told Grace and Ian were, and I shut Finnegan out on the way there so I could be less selfish once inside. Because as much as I wanted to fall into tears at Grace's bedside, my husband came first. It was his mom, not mine.

Taking a few deep breaths, I hugged Finnegan's bicep and took charge when he couldn't.

Conn and Colm sat outside, solemn.

I opened the door and forcefully pushed down my grief. Shan was sitting next to Grace; I couldn't see his face. He was holding one of her hands and pressing his forehead to the top of it.

Patrick and Sarah were standing in the corner, holding each other. Kellan was beside Ian's bed, silently seething.

Grace and Ian could've been asleep. I suspected they hadn't been cleaned up yet, hence the blankets covering everything except their heads. Her eyes had been open...now they weren't.

"Come, honey," I whispered. I ushered Finnegan inside the room. His eyes brimmed with tears, and he wouldn't look away from his mother. Eventually, I got him to move forward a bit more, and I guess the levees broke. He sniffled, released my hand, and closed the distance to lean over her and press his lips to her forehead.

I covered my mouth with my hand and tried—and failed—not to cry.

More memories flashed back. I flinched, remembering the shrill scream I'd heard.

I didn't want the guys to know about it, so I ducked out of the room and wiped at my cheeks.

Colm looked up from where he was sitting.

"She screamed," I croaked. I coughed slightly to clear my voice. "Grace. She screamed."

"It was quick, darlin'," he murmured.

I shook my head. That wasn't what I was getting at. "We're not gonna tell Shan and the boys about it, okay? I don't want them to know she suffered even for a second."

He understood and nodded once. "I won't say a word."

"Me either." Conn scrubbed his hands over his face and blew out a breath. "Can this day get any worse? First Grace and Ian, then I lost sight of the motherless sons'a—"

"Hey." Colm nudged his brother's shoulder. "They drove. You were on foot. Don't beat yourself up."

"You tried to run after them?" I asked, a trickle of alarm quickening my heartbeat.

"Doesn't matter. I lost them," Conn muttered.

"I'm just glad you're okay." I shook my head. I didn't want to think about losing another person.

"This is gonna blow up." Colm took out a pack of smokes and seemed to catch himself, remembering he couldn't smoke here. "Grace was like the heart of the syndicate. Everyone adored her. And now John...? Shite."

I frowned. "What about John?"

"He was kidnapped," he replied flatly. My eyes widened, and more shock tore through me. "You didn't know. Goddammit." He groaned and ran a hand over his head. "We were called into work early. Someone got word from Chicago, and we couldn't get in touch with John or his men. Pat filled us in when we got here that he'd been taken."

Holy shit. This was why Finnegan had left for the office this morning. When he texted me, joking about scratches and kittens, had they been trying to figure out what was going on?

"Really, he's been kidnapped?" I couldn't shake the disbelief.

Conn nodded. "Anne and the twins are fine, but they snagged John outside their home earlier this morning."

"Jesus Christ," I whispered. "Who do I talk to about getting the twins here?"

Despite the damage I wanted to do to John's face, he loved his kids, and he'd been lovely to me at the wedding. And at the dinner last week. It definitely didn't make him a good man, but perhaps he was a good father. Alec and Nessa must be beside themselves. Because, Anne...? Fuck that frigid woman.

"Uh..." Conn exchanged a look with his brother. "Um, probably yourself?"

"Aye, I don't see anyone else making that decision right now," Colm agreed.

Okay, that was weird, but I shook it off. "Well, then. Can you arrange for them to come back here?" Poor kids had been lugged back and forth way too much. "Put their safety first. I don't want them alone. Think like Finnegan. Like, put guards on them or whatever."

"Yes, ma'am. I'll go make some calls." Conn seemed to be the one who needed to do something the most, and he excused himself.

"Emilia?" The barest hint of panic in Finnegan's voice made it easy to ignore the pain in my ankle, and I hurried back into the room.

He exhaled in relief and hugged me to him. "Don't leave my sight. Okay?"

"I'm sorry." I hugged him back as tightly as I could and closed my eyes. I couldn't look at Grace. It hurt too much. "I'm here."

He held me impossibly tighter and breathed me in, his nose buried in my hair. "I could've lost you today."

"You didn't." I looked up at him and wiped my thumbs under his eyes. "I'm not going anywhere without you."

He nodded and pressed his forehead to mine. "I love you."

Warmth tingled inside me every time I heard those words. Today, I needed them more than ever. "I love you too."

We were gonna get through this. I had to believe that, even though I could sense my imminent breakdown creeping closer. It would have to wait until I got Finnegan home—or wherever he deemed it safe to get some rest.

Anger was brewing too. For the second time in my life, I'd been robbed of a mother figure. Grace had taken up residence in my heart fast, and now she was gone. I would never hear her laugh again. She'd have no more advice to share. I'd never get the chance to prove myself worthy of being her daughter-in-law.

I blinked back tears and sucked in a painful breath.

Patrick cleared his throat. "The cops won't wait much longer, Pop."

Shit. I should've known. Of course, they would have questions.

"Nothing will happen, right?" I asked nervously. "I mean, we haven't done anything wrong."

"Don't worry." Finnegan kissed me on the forehead. "They won't find anything."

"All right." I grew wary of the whole thing. I didn't want the police here, but I suspected there was little that could be done about it.

Finnegan glanced over at Grace and released a trembling breath.

Shan was about to fall apart, and I wanted to comfort him. Slowly easing out of Finnegan's hold, I let him know I wasn't leaving. Then I rounded the bed and carefully touched Shan's shoulder.

He wiped his eyes discreetly before facing me, albeit briefly.

"Ian tried to protect her." I went down on one knee and put a hand on his leg instead of trying to make eye contact. Maybe because it would be unwanted, maybe because I couldn't bear the heartbreak in his gaze. "He used himself as a shield, and I'm-I'm," I stammered, "I'm only saying this because I want you to know she was never alone. He didn't think twice. He just ran out for her."

Shan's hand landed on top of mine, and he gave it a squeeze. "Of course he did," he murmured thickly. "Thank you, sweetheart. I only pray they weren't in pain."

I swallowed hard and stared at his hand over mine. There was still some dried blood on his skin. "She didn't suffer," I whispered. "It was over in a second, and I didn't know. I mean, I didn't know she wasn't okay, so I guess I lied to Ian. He—he asked about her, and I blurted out she was fine."

I only dared to lift my gaze enough to see a small quirk of his lips before he scrubbed a hand over his face.

"A good lie." He patted my hand. "I'm sure that meant everything to him."

I nodded once in acknowledgment and was about to give him some privacy, but he stopped me.

"It won't be today, and it won't be tomorrow," he said quietly, "but someday soon, I'm going to give you the guilt trip of the ages for putting yourself in harm's way. But for now, thank you, sweetheart. I'm eternally grateful you were brave enough to be there for them."

A mixture of emotions raged inside me—gratitude, love, embarrassment, and perhaps a pinch of oh-shit-I-messed-up. Most of all, though, I was determined to be there for them through this.

chapter

33

Finnegan O'Shea

"Finn?"

I jolted awake, panting, my heart squeezing. I blinked and tried fruitlessly to shake the remnants of the nightmare. The same one I'd had the past two nights, where I saw Emilia's lifeless body in the street instead of my mother.

"Fuck." I swallowed dryly and pressed the heels of my palms against my eyes.

"Finn."

"Yeah." I wasn't the best host at the moment, and we had Nessa and Alec staying in our condo. "What is it, doll?" I looked my cousin over, worried she was having nightmares too.

She shuffled by the stairs and glanced toward the bathroom. "I think Emilia's upset."

Motherfucker. It was a good thing I hadn't noticed she wasn't next to me yet, 'cause I flew into a panic every time it happened. Getting out of bed, I tied the strings on my sweats and peered down over the railing. Alec was still sound asleep on the couch. The clock on my nightstand said it wasn't even five in the morning, too early to be up and get ready for the first funeral.

"Thanks for letting me know, hon." I passed Nessa with a kiss to the top of her head and aimed for the bathroom. I knocked on the door twice and listened to the shower running. She was upset, all right. And it was about time. "Princess, let me in."

I'd been waiting for this. We all had. Rather than moving around like a zombie these past two days—the way the rest of us had—Emilia had made it her goal to be there for everybody who needed something. She'd gone above and beyond. With Aunt Viv and Father O'Malley, she had made funeral arrangements for both Ma and Ian. She'd talked to the cops as well as the Feds. She'd made sure Pop and I ate. She'd taken care of Alec and Nessa.

It was a miracle she hadn't fallen apart yesterday at the Vigil. No, instead, she'd taken care of everyone else.

"I'll be right out," Emilia croaked. "Sorry, I didn't mean to wake you."

I shook my head and tested the doorknob. Locked. Yeah, well. Returning to my side of the bed, I grabbed my wallet and picked out a credit card.

"Ness, can you go upstairs to Pat and make some cocoa for Emilia? We're out." It was a lie, but I wanted privacy.

"Yeah, of course," she said, and I swiped the credit card between the door and the frame. "Or I can go to that place on the corner? It's open around the clock, and she likes their cocoa."

"No going out," I reminded her softly. "Pat's key is on the table in the entryway."

"Okay, I'll be back in a bit. Extra whipped cream, I remember."

In the second attempt, I got the latch up, and I entered the bathroom, finding my girl on the floor of the shower. She was hugging her knees to her chest, a sight that broke my fucking heart.

I grabbed a big towel and headed straight for her. I shut off the water, then squatted down in front of her. "Come here, my love." I wrapped the towel around her, and she gave up on trying to hold it together. More sobs broke free as I carried her out to the bedroom. "I've got you."

"They're not supposed to be dead," she wept.

"I know, baby." My eyes stung, and I sat down on the edge of our bed with her sideways across my lap. "It's my turn to take care of you now."

She shook her head minutely. "I'll get better, I just—"

"Quiet, you stubborn girl." I kissed her wet hair and yanked our duvet around her. "Have I told you how proud I am of you? How fucking honored I am to be your husband? You've done so much already. Now you're gonna let me be there for you."

My phone vibrated behind me, and I ignored it for now. Five a.m. sharp meant I was getting the report of how the night had been. With twenty men in and around this building alone, I trusted we were safe. Hell, we even had protection from the Feds at the moment, which was both a blessing and a curse. 'Cause they were protecting as much as they were watching.

The fine men in blue had lost their territory when an alleged crime boss named John Murray was kidnapped in Chicago. Now it was the FBI's jurisdiction, and they had more files on us.

Overnight, Philly had become the seat for the Sons of Munster. Pop and I had called in every crew from Chicago, and securing this city was our main priority. We had men working all hours of the day to fish out any of the Italians and make sure we'd never be sitting ducks again.

"I wouldn't be proud of me," Emilia whispered tearfully. "I keep having these thoughts—about the people who did this. I want them to suffer, Finnegan."

I hummed and kissed her hair again. "Kinda talking to the wrong man for that."

"I'm serious." She shivered and wiped her cheeks, and she looked at me with so much confliction. I saw the despair and the sheer hatred. "I want them dead."

I swallowed and cradled her face, dead serious. "Don't say that to me unless you mean it," I whispered.

Her bottom lip quivered. "But I do mean it," she whimpered. "I can't help it."

It was probably fucked up that I drew relief from her words. "Then I can be honest with you. I'm going to fucking kill them. Each and every one of them."

"Okay," she whispered, lowering her gaze. A fresh round of tears streamed down her cheeks. "You were planning on doing that no matter what, weren't you?"

"Yeah, sorry about that."

She smiled sadly and let me wipe my thumbs across her cheeks. "We're a bunch of liars, but we love fiercely, and we're loyal to a fault." At my curious look, she clarified. "Your mother told me that the first time we met. Which wasn't in church. She came here the day before."

I got mushy, though I managed a chuckle too. My mother... Christ. "I'm gonna miss her so fucking much, princess." I closed my eyes and rested my forehead to Emilia's.

The hurt slashed through me, and I thanked God I had Emilia with me now. There was no way I'd pull through this with my sanity intact if she weren't here.

In that moment, I knew I could go through pretty much anything as long as I had my wife.

Less than a week ago, I got married in this church. Now I was here to bury my mother.

I was supposed to be on my honeymoon.

I stayed numb throughout most of the service, focusing on Emilia next to me. She and Aunt Viv had done a beautiful job planning the whole thing, from the prayers yesterday at the Vigil to Ma's favorite flowers in the church today. Emilia had chosen a great picture of my mother that stood next to the casket too, one where she flashed a mischievous smile not everyone had been privy to. It bordered on a smirk, though it was cloaked in enough softness that no one would find it inappropriate.

Her eyes crinkled at the corners.

White and purple flowers had been put together in arrangements around the altar and where the choir stood.

Ma would've approved of everything except for everyone in the packed church wearing black.

Father O'Malley recited the last prayer, and Emilia fidgeted nervously.

"What's wrong?" I whispered.

"Aunt Viv and I picked a song for when you carry out the casket," she whispered back. "I'm afraid Shan won't like it."

I was sure it'd be the last thing on Pop's mind.

"Amen," I echoed quietly and crossed myself.

Father O'Malley paused and gestured at the front pews. "Carrying our dear Grace to her final resting place are her loving husband, three sons, brother-in-law, and nephew."

It wasn't the first time Kellan had been referred to as Ma's son; she'd kinda taken him in whether he wanted it or not when his own folks ostracized him for being into dudes.

Pop, Patrick, Uncle Thomas, his kid Max, Kellan, and I rose from our seats. I dipped down and kissed Emilia's temple, then joined the men at the casket. It wasn't my first rodeo as a pallbearer, and it wouldn't be my last; I wore suspenders under my suit. Because there was this one time...

Pat and I exchanged a grief-laden smile, probably thinking about the same memory.

Ma had been so fucking pissed. I didn't remember who'd died; I wasn't sure anyone did. On the other hand, everyone remembered the time Pat's pants fell down.

"Waist or shoulder?" Max asked nervously.

"Shoulder. We're Irish." I eyed the scrawny sixteen-year-old and positioned myself behind him instead. He'd need the help, and there was no way I would agree to Colm or Conn doing this. I needed them to stay with Emilia.

As the first notes to a painfully familiar song began, not only did I understand Emilia's trepidation, it also exhausted me emotionally. The small choir filed in, singing the opening lyrics to "The Parting Glass," and Pop clenched his jaw and looked down.

He'd played it for Ma before he was deployed way back when they'd been newlyweds and she'd been pregnant with Patrick. Since then, it'd become a departure song in our family.

As excruciating as it was, no other song would've fit better, and he knew it.

On cue, the six of us lifted the heavy casket to our shoulders, and I did everything I could not to think I was carrying my dead mom.

It was made impossible by our family and friends. We walked down the aisle in measured steps, and everyone around us was crying. Seeing Aunt Viv, Alec, and Nessa probably hurt the most.

It was the only time I didn't seek out Emilia. I was shattering enough from seeing silent tears roll down Pop's face.

Tomorrow we'd be doing it all over again for Ian.

Halfway toward the entrance, the doors opened, and I spotted six men with bagpipes a couple seconds before they began playing.

"Jesus Christ." Patrick sniffled and cleared his throat.

The hearse waited for us outside the church, and the sun shone brilliantly, almost mocking us. Then again, my mother had never liked the rain.

With a few grunts, we slid the casket into the hearse. I kissed my fingers and placed them on the casket for a second, before the funeral director interrupted to let us know our car was ready. Against my wishes, we went separately to the cemetery. It was a ten-minute drive, just long enough to get my shit together and text Colm three times.

I was gonna have to shake the nightmares where I lost Emilia.

They physically hurt, and they were turning me into an obsessing, fretting motherfucker.

"Finn." Patrick nodded out the window on his side, and I leaned closer.

We'd reached the cemetery where the presence of the FBI was less subtle. Fewer ways for them to blend in. I spotted a handful of vans, and I doubted all the guys raking leaves were part of some maintenance service.

Today, I didn't care. Every social gathering of our syndicate made us a target, so they could call in more Feds for all I cared.

The taxpayers were footing the bill.

The driver parked next to the hearse, and we stepped out into the sun. This part of the funeral was more work than...well, I wouldn't call the alternative pleasure, but it was no longer about my mother. Now was when crew bosses came to pay their respects in person, shake hands, and exchange words with no one listening nearby.

Limos arrived shortly after with our immediate family as well as the higher-ups in the syndicate.

I lit up a smoke, watching Colm escort Emilia out of a car with Sarah, Aunt Viv, and the twins. Aunt Anne hadn't even bothered trying to keep her family together, eh? It was disappointing as hell.

Patrick joined me at my side, eyeing our uncle's wife too. "Could she at least pretend she's worried about her husband?"

I guess not. The only defense I had for her was that I knew she hadn't been given loyalty by Uncle John. Even so, she'd reaped the benefits of being his wife. She had a responsibility to shoulder.

We knew too little about his disappearance, leaving the whole syndicate in disorder. On the morning he was taken, our communication had failed, and it'd taken hours before we got ahold of one of his advisers who could confirm the kidnapping. A note had been sent to his office with the word *Addio* and Gio Avellino's signature. My Italian was rusty at best, but I knew a final goodbye when I saw it, and if Gio thought he'd seen the last of us, he was sorely mistaken.

When everyone had arrived, we carried the casket to the O'Shea family plot. It was a fairly large section of graves, and the last two we'd buried here were my grandfather and a cousin of my father's.

Ma wasn't supposed to be here for another thirty or forty years.

Emilia took her spot next to me and slipped her hand into mine, and I kissed her fingers. For some confusing reason, Pop and Uncle Thomas stood to the side. I frowned at Pop; was it too much? He looked more put together now. He belonged between Pat and me.

Father O'Malley joined us. I wasn't sure many paid attention to the final prayers. My mother wasn't here anymore. The casket was slowly lowered into the ground, but everything felt empty. Her soul had departed already. She wouldn't stick around for this shit.

The twenty or so of us who remained for the graveside service participated on autopilot. Aunt Viv and Uncle Thomas's toddler was getting fussy. Even Alec and Nessa were struggling to stand still.

For the last part, Father O'Malley blessed the casket, and I reluctantly threw some dirt into the grave with the others. Pop was beyond ready to get back to his guest room at Patrick's place. Unless he was ready to face the flat Ma had decorated for the weekends they'd stay in the city, and I didn't think he was.

"Thank you for everything, Father." I stepped up and shook our priest's hand, seeing as Pop was evidently taking a back seat. "You meant a lot to her."

"And you boys were her world, son." He nodded at me, Pat, and Kellan. "I realize things are changing, but don't be strangers, ya hear?" Even he knew our next step. "We stick together around here."

"Understood, sir." Patrick shook his hand too.

I cleared my throat, side-eying Emilia hesitantly, unsure of how to tell her—

"Oh, please." She reached up and kissed my cheek and adjusted my tie. "I know this is where I go tend to the kids. I'll have Colm with me."

She just knew. I let out a chuckle in relief and hugged her to me before she trailed off with Alec and Ness.

Then it began. Only, rather than speaking to Pop, the men from Chicago paid attention to me. And it took me a minute to realize my father had positioned himself to the side on purpose. It wasn't at all related to Ma. This was him giving me his vote.

Nerves tightened my gut, though I kept my face composed. This was what I'd worked toward, albeit under very different circumstances, and the highest seat wasn't mine just yet.

"Again, very sorry for your loss, Finn." Brennan, a stocky man who'd sell his daughter if someone paid enough, was part of John's inner circle. I shook his hand and remained polite, but he'd be the first to go when the O'Sheas took over. "Your mother was an angel, then and now."

"She was." I nodded with a dip of my chin.

"I take it we're proceeding soon so we can get John home?" he questioned. "If he's still with us, God willing."

"Once Philly's cleared," I confirmed.

That satisfied him, and he moved on.

Next was Joel, a guy I'd have to pay more attention to. He dealt in heroin for the most part, and Liam vouched for him. We shook hands, and he was quick to tell me he had his crew awaiting orders. Given his connections overseas, I'd keep him closer. He would be useful.

"I appreciate that," I replied.

Another guy my cousin had vouched for was Seán, who took care of Liam's crew while he was in prison. I'd worked with Seán a couple times, and we hung out a bit when we were younger.

"I'm sorry for your loss, mate. I'll never forget when she chased Liam and me around as kids. We gave her too much hell." He seemed genuinely distraught.

431

"The way she preferred it," I answered. "No one shut it down like she did."

"Aye, that's true," he chuckled. "I, uh—mind if I ask when we're shaking the Feds?"

"A couple of weeks' time," I said. "Eric Bell will be in touch with the details, but we go underground once the city's clear and our wives and children have gone on vacation."

We were still crunching the numbers because we'd suddenly gone from making plans for a dozen smaller Philly crews to now including the entire SoM. Everyone would be involved in what would be the biggest disappearing act I'd heard of.

It was the only way we could ensure our safety while reclaiming the upper hand and eventually reappearing on Avellino soil with the element of surprise in our pocket.

I caught Emilia glancing over at me a few times, and I wondered what she saw.

I wanted her to see the man she'd married, the clown she sometimes called Irish boy, the musician she'd started calling Whistler.

Not the Sons of Munster's unofficial new boss, whose first act was a declaration of war.

Finnegan and Emilia are back in...

more from cara

If you enjoyed this book, you might like the following.

Path of Destruction (M/F) A gritty rock-star romance with sex, drugs, rock n' roll, and incarceration.

Uncomplicated Choices (M/M) A sweet, funny romance that starts with a dubious kidnapping. Well, Ellis borrows a yacht and is completely unaware that Casey is asleep below deck.

Breaking Free (M/F) Tennyson Wright, a well-known director in Hollywood, gets pushed into a fake romance in order to gain publicity for his next film. His new girlfriend? The spoiled, much younger actress Sophie Pierce.

Check out Cara's entire collection at www.caradeewrites.com, and don't forget to sign up for her newsletter so you don't miss any new releases, updates on book signings, giveaways, and much more.

about cara

I'm often awkwardly silent or, if the topic interests me, a chronic rambler. In other words, I can discuss writing forever and ever. Fiction, in particular.

The love story—while a huge draw and constantly present—is almost secondary for me, because there's so much more to writing romance fiction than just making two (or more) people fall in love and have hot sex.

There's a world to build, characters to develop, interests to create, and a topic or two to research thoroughly. Every book is a challenge for me, an opportunity to learn something new, and a puzzle to piece together. I want my characters to come to life, and the only way I know to do that is to give them substance—passions, history, goals, quirks, and strong opinions—and to let them evolve.

Additionally, I want my men and women to be relatable. That means allowing room for everyday problems and, for lack of a better word, flaws. My characters will never be perfect.

Wait...this was supposed to be about me, not my writing.

I'm a writey person who loves to write. Always wanderlusting, twitterpating, kinking, and geeking. There's time for hockey and cupcakes, too. But mostly, I just love to write.

~Cara.